PRIMAL
SHADOWS

PRIMAL SHADOWS

ALAN DEAN FOSTER

A TOM DOHERTY ASSOCIATES BOOK
NEW YORK

PRIMAL SHADOWS

This book is printed on acid-free paper.

A Forge Book
Published by Tom Doherty Associates, LLC
175 Fifth Avenue
New York, NY 10010

www.tor.com

Library of Congress Cataloging-in-Publication Data

Foster, Alan Dean.
Primal shadows / Alan Dean Foster.—1st ed.
p. cm.
"A Tom Doherty Associates book."
ISBN 0-312-87771-4
1. Papual New Guinea—Fiction. I. Title.

PS3556.O756 P7 2001
813'.54—dc21

2001023176

First Edition: July 2001

Printed in the United States of America

0 9 8 7 6 5 4 3 2 1

This book is dedicated to . . .

Tony and Sheryl Guthrie of Lae
Beverly Blackley
Captain Stuart Cooper of Air Niugini
Marie Ani of Westpac Travel
Karakiri of Sogeri
Captain Craig DeWitt of the *Golden Dawn*
Knowles
Captain David Miller of the *Tiata*
Marty-Martine
Ela and Jonathan
Kim, at Karawari
Peter, Joseph, and all the Huli people
Dik Knight at Loloata Island
Wilfred Golman
All the people of Papua New Guinea—
Highlanders, Islanders, and
the people of the coasts.

Tenks; mi hamamas tru.

PRIMAL
SHADOWS

I

They're all dead now. Except me, of course. I don't know about Stenhammer. Nothing is ever certain where Stenhammer is concerned. Not even death. He was a force of nature, the man was, raging and raving in equal measure against God, the devil, and his own inner demons. As for the others, though, I do know about them. I know that they went unexpectedly, and too soon.

Dead now. All of them.

That's what gold does. It doesn't beautify. It doesn't ornament. It kills. As some philosopher said (surely some philosopher must have said it), it is the making of some people, and the ruination of others. Nearly was both to me, and ended up being neither. What happened was, see, when Fate was dealing her cards, I got shuffled out of the deck. Ended up on the floor. Overlooked, stepped on, and out of the game. Considering everything that happened, I suppose I should count myself lucky.

Buy me a drink and I'll tell you about it. . . .

The world must be running backward, Steven Bohannon decided. Usually after you are mugged and kicked in the side of the head, you pass a certain amount of time unconscious, then wake up in a warm, dry, safe place like a hospital bed, with one or two white-clad angels of mercy gazing worriedly down at you, their kindly faces warped with honest concern.

Not him. He had originally gone to sleep in a warm, dry, ostensibly safe place only to wake up feeling like he had just been hit with a sack of loose gravel. Squinting out a couple of tears as he rolled over, trying to ignore the pain that threatened to rip off the top of his skull, his slowly clearing vision focused not on angels of mercy beaming down at him but on several silent, utterly indifferent gulls. Cold eyes like tiny black buttons sewn into layerings of angel-white feathers stared hungrily back at him. Their soulless, scavenger expressions were anything but kindly. They were silently considering whether to make a stab at his flickering eyes.

Screw you, he thought, a little giddily. *I'm not dead—I think.* Despite having been kicked in the head. To prove it to them, as well as to himself, he forced himself to sit up. What happened next was less interesting than it was educational. He fell over. This reaffirmed his aliveness but did not make his head feel any better. The watching gulls flapped their wings uneasily, but remained hopeful.

This is absurd, he told himself. *Of course I can sit up. Any damn idiot can sit up. Even a child can sit up.* The next time he tried it, he succeeded in proving the thesis. But not without an effort.

Ragged, biting shards of gravel and congealed mud fell from his hair, his shoulders, his formerly spotless, short-sleeved, knit shirt with the little green and crimson golf clubs embroidered over the left breast. Disturbed by all the movement, the butterfly that had been resting on his right foot finally took wing, a flash of iridescent blue that drifted off toward distant, high mountains.

Feeling his head, his fingers came away innocent of blood. Not kicked, then, like he'd first thought. Something else. It was all coming back to him, a slow red tide of embarrassment rushing in to shame his thoughts. As the memory did so, his mortification rose like the mercury in an old thermometer. It struck him that he was cold, which made no sense, considering how he was dressed and where he was sitting. But his mind insisted. Wrapping his arms around his chest, he hugged himself tightly and shivered in the chilly depths of his aloneness.

It was very early in the morning, dark as much as light. The sky looked like a bad day-for-night outtake from a film with insufficient funding. Somewhat surprised to find it still fastened around his left wrist, he checked his watch, having to hold one hand with the other to keep it from shaking. A cheap digital model with a rubber strap, the timepiece's flagrant mediocrity had no doubt contributed mightily to its salvation. The numbers it displayed confirmed his estimate of the time of day.

He was sitting in the dirt and gravel at the very end of the jetty that formed the western boundary of what was euphemistically called the Port Moresby Yacht Club. He knew he should have been grateful that he was not, at that moment, lying in the forty feet of tropical water that glistened greenly not more than a couple of body lengths away on three sides of him.

To his left and behind was open water, emerald-hued islands, and the even greener mainland that formed the natural and uninhabited ramparts of the city's inner harbor. Ruler-straight behind him, the thirty-foot-wide raised stone and gravel jetty terminated in a distant padlocked chain-link gate two stories high. To his right lay everything else, which comprised most of what there was worth seeing.

Slightly behind him and to his right stood a small, one-story, square gray building topped by a bright yellow plastic SHELL petroleum symbol that was much taller than himself. The single door, windowless like the rest of the building, was locked. Between the jetty on which he sat and the one that shaped the other side of the harbor, fifty or sixty boats bright atop the glassy green-black water were berthed or moored in neat, primarily white lines. Masts and communications antennae thrust out like bleached branches from cabins and flying bridges. In the entire yacht harbor was not one boat worthy of the title of "yacht."

There were power boats and sailing craft, private sport-fishing boats and smaller recreational speedsters with oversize outboards and cramped below-deck cabins. Hanging from lines suspended between the weathered masts of sloops and ketches, damp laundry awaited the full drying blast of the ascending equatorial sun. A distant radio filled the still, humid air with muffled, defiant snatches of international pop. On the biggest boat in the harbor, near-naked supplicants clad in only speedos and T-shirts checked scuba gear preparatory to setting off in search of underwater nirvanas. None noticed him sitting alone and cold and hurt on the bare gravel. Their thoughts were focused on exotic fish, colorful invertebrates, and photographs not yet taken.

Climbing shakily to his feet, he brushed grime from his gray Levis and looked past the harbor to the sleeping city beyond. A collection of overpopulated, underserved country towns in search of a metropolitan identity, only tourists referred to the rest of the urban sprawl as Port Moresby. When locals used the name, they were usually referring only to the tired and exceedingly unimpressive downtown.

Located on the narrow peninsula that defined the eastern limits of the harbor, the few important blocks that constituted the inner city squinched together in a saddle between two hills, as if all the larger buildings had slid down and crashed together in the resultant miniature vale. Hopeful homes and ramshackle apartment buildings clung like determined insects to the steep, vegetation-clad slopes, while newer but already fading high-rises made valiant, isolated attempts to insist that western civilization had indeed put down permanent roots in the rocky, inhospitable soil. He recognized the twenty-story Qantas tower and a few others, including the Travelodge, ostensibly the best hotel in town. That was where he had spent the previous evening, but it was not where he had been staying. Too expensive. The Hibiscus Motel, just across the street, had been better suited to his budget.

As the sun forced its way through the thin high clouds, the last night lights were going off in the city. Somewhere, a dog was complaining, shrill and excited about one of those things that makes dogs go slightly berserk much too early in the morning. Bohannon wanted to complain, too, but had made a habit recently of not doing so. He wondered if, like yesterday, it was going to rain again.

He did not need to feel for his wallet. The familiar weight of it was gone from his pants' pocket, along with much of his confidence and a great deal of his self-respect. He had spent two days in Papua New Guinea and had planned on spending two more. Now he resolved to leave at the first opportunity.

Recriminations first, motel next, he told himself. By putting one foot in front of the other he found he was able to manage a successful imitation of a man walking. He was careful not to lift his feet too high or take too long a stride lest the illusion, not to mention his upright posture, desert him.

Halfway down the jetty and stumbling toward the locked gate, arms still wrapped around his chest in search of elusive warmth, he heard a voice hailing someone. It took a minute for him to realize that the curt expression of concern was directed at himself.

"Yeah, I'm talkin' to you, you poor schmuck! Drag your sorry, saggin' ass over here!"

Halting, Bohannon looked to his right and saw that he was being simultaneously invited and derided by a distended beer belly of mature proportions. This impressive organic artifice (ortifice? he mused in feeble attempt at self-amusement) was framed by a deeply tanned body crowned with a bejowled face out of which glared intense brown eyes. What hair had not given up the follicular ghost was more charcoal than gray, defying the owner's age. Sixty, Bohannon surmised. Old eyes, young voice.

After a brief bout of weary self-searching during which he decided that at the expense of some effort he might after all be capable of civil communication with another human being, he responded as firmly as he dared. "Thanks, but at the moment I don't feel much like chatting."

His response appeared to amuse rather than irritate the foul-mouthed speaker, who was standing on the rear deck of a beat-up but still seaworthy forty-foot power boat. He clutched something in his right hand. A can of beer, Bohannon saw. It was not quite six in the morning.

"Do you not, now?" The belly belied those eyes, which despite the hour and the alcohol were clear and shrewd. "Lemme guess. Been rolled, have you?"

Bohannon looked away, suspecting the gesture would be insufficient to conceal the pain and self-loathing he was feeling from this unwelcomely perceptive stranger.

Without waiting for an answer, the man nodded knowingly. "A woman?"

The pain of humiliation drove deeper, down into the pit of Bohannon's gut, where it hung like a piece of undigested gristle.

"Well then," proclaimed the caller with frosty joviality, "you're twice fucked, ain't you?" He started to turn away.

Having nothing else to do, a self-pitying Bohannon glared at his tormentor. "Why should you give a damn?"

Halfway to the open hatch, the man paused and looked back. "Who says I do?" He grunted. "It's too early in the morning, you're stumbling along here all by your lonesome, you've obviously been royally screwed and reamed, and I thought you maybe could use a cup of coffee."

What a depressing species is one, Bohannon ruminated, that uses the same rude terms to refer to a mugging as it does to describe the act of procreation. It only confirmed his long-held opinion of humanity as a great squalling, squealing, sweaty mass of morons marching inexorably through useless lives toward an inevitable collective death.

Despite the coarseness of the source making the offer, however, at that moment, on that morning, he was eager to choose straight coffee over nectar and ambrosia, had it been proferred from Olympus itself.

"Look." He took a weak, hesitant step toward the boat, which was moored stern-first to the jetty. "I—I've had kind of a rough time. As you have so unpleasantly but accurately noted. And—I really would appreciate a cup of coffee."

Despite his girth the man walked and did not waddle back to the stern. When he put both hands on the gunwale, his triceps bulged like hawsers. He nodded brusquely and almost smiled. "All right, then. Come aboard. Take your shoes off first." He chuckled around a leer. "Be glad the bitch left you your shoes. Good pair of American sneakers like those would be worth a few hundred kina in town."

Advancing carefully and taking his time, Bohannon succeeded in transferring himself from jetty to boat without falling into the water or otherwise embarrassing himself. Once aboard, what little he could see of the craft surprised him. It was far from new, but the electronics on view appeared up to date, and the wood trim and paneling had been hand-buffed to the kind of rich earthy glow that on certain boats suggests that even if the timber were to rot away, a layer of polish equally thick would remain behind, the petrochemical phantom of teak lovingly treated.

The back deck contained a gimbal-mounted chair for deep-sea fishing, assorted gear lockers, and in the middle, a small teak table bolted securely to the planking. This was flanked by a pair of rattan chairs. Having vanished below, his host returned with a stainless steel pot and a mug on which a naked woman and a great white shark were cavorting in decidedly unpiscine fashion. These he set on the table, accompanied by a gesture.

"Cream, sugar?" A too-knowing grin. "Scotch?"

Bohannon eased himself into a chair. The fraying rattan was rough against his backside, but not as rough as the raw gravel of the jetty had been. "Black's fine—thanks. You're not having any?"

Ascending sunlight glinted off the explosively colorful Raggiana bird-of-paradise logo on the can of South Pacific Export lager. "One more after this. Then maybe something darker and smokier." He eased his bulk into the other empty chair. Its front feet rose up, smacked back down against the deck. "Want to tell me about it?"

Bohannon poured himself a cup from the pot. There was no visible steam, the surrounding air being hot and humid enough to compete with the issue of the coffee. A first cautious sip coated his throat and belly like paving tar. Dormant neurons snapped to attention, frayed neural connections crackled to life.

"Local beans?" he choked gratefully, trying to make conversation.

He took another swallow, bigger and longer this time, reveling in the thick, fiery sensation of it sliding down his throat. It couldn't hurt him. He couldn't be burned any worse than he had been the night before.

His host nodded approvingly. "From the Goroka co-op. Up in the Central Highlands. Good stuff. Stiffen your spine fore as well as aft. Now, talk to me."

Bohannon hesitated, squinting through the sea of white cabins and laundry-draped masts at the still slumbering city that had betrayed him. "I don't know you."

"Harlin Collins, master sergeant. Retired, thank God. Now you're one up on me, you sorry bastard."

"Bohannon. Steven Bohannon. Between jobs at present. Between careers, actually. These days, teetering on the cusp of ennui."

Collins snorted derisively. " 'Teetering on the cusp of ennui'? Christ on a crutch, I didn't know anybody actually talked like that!"

His guest sipped Goroka grind. "It's a gift. Or a curse. Depends on who I happen to be talking to at the time."

Collins sucked out the last of the Export, crumpled the can in one thick-fingered but far from flabby fist, and tossed it down the open hatch, where it clattered into oblivion. "Sounds like a lot of pretentious crap to me." When his visitor did not challenge this, he grunted approvingly. "Enough pleasantries for you? If you're not going to entertain me, then get the fuck off my boat."

Bohannon poured himself a second cup. He was waking up, and his head felt better. Within the yacht harbor, the water was as perfectly still as the early morning air, hushed not from expectancy but exhaustion. Papua New Guinea was one of those places close to the equator where nothing moved, not even a molecule of air, unless there was a good and justifiable reason for it.

"Come on, come on." The retired soldier would not let it alone. "You're not going to tell me she was the most beautiful woman you ever saw, are you? Fucking ay but I hate clichés."

It was too soon to relive it. Much too soon. But there was the coffee, and the gruff kindness it represented. "No, I'm not. But she *was* the most beautiful woman I've seen in this country."

Grinning like a satyr enjoying the last day of his vacation, Collins ballooned from his chair. "Let me get another beer. And don't leave out any of the juicy parts, you pasty-faced plebe, or I'll piss in your next pot of Goroka!"

Thus warned, Bohannon struggled to recall the events of the night before. The room at the Hibiscus Motel had been adequate for his purposes, which meant that it was cheap, reasonably clean, and he did not have to share it with too many cockroaches. He was, after all, only passing through, in transit really, from Cairns to Nandi. He thought to spend a few days exploring the capital and its immediate vicinity, only to learn subsequent to his arrival that there was very little in Port Moresby that was worth exploring.

Packed with would-be shoppers with wide eyes and empty pockets, the stores held nothing to interest the casual traveler, unless one was a collector of shirts emblazoned with the logos and insignia of Australian sports teams, or cassettes of laid-back local pop music sung in both Pidgin and English. On his first day he walked down to Steamships, which the little free guidebook they had given him at the motel insisted was the biggest and best-stocked department store in the country.

As he was strolling between counters piled high with cheap pots, pans, and kitchen utensils on one side and linen mountains of Bangladeshi-made clothing on the other, ten very short, dark-skinned men clad in an eclectic assortment of torn shorts and ragged T-shirts and armed with machetes and spears stormed into the store through the rear entrance. While customers and staff alike scattered and he crouched down behind a rack of household hardware manufactured in Taiwan, the invasion party proceeded to haul an inoffensive browser out from behind the book counter where he'd been hiding and, in full view of no less than two hundred witnesses, hack him to death. Subsequent to which brazen assault they fled at speed but without haste, trailing a good deal of blood and bits of flesh behind them.

Heart pounding, mouth agape, Bohannon found himself gaping at the body (or rather, fragments of what had recently been a body) lying on the neat department store floor between indifferently stocked displays of school texts and children's readers. It was the first time he had ever seen a human being reduced to pieces of the general size and shape normally found in the fresh meat section of a supermarket, and he was surprised both at the amount of blood and extent of the intestines.

Not long thereafter, store security deigned to show up.

"Bloody raskols!" a clipped voice growled.

Turning stiffly, a numbed Bohannon turned to see a tall, blond man in his late thirties studying the corpse. Clinging to his right hand like a commuter hanging onto a subway strap was an angelic little girl of five or six. She was eyeing the body openly, one finger in her mouth, waiting for Daddy's next move.

" 'Raskols'?" Word begat image, of fondly remembered film shorts from the thirties and forties endlessly rerun on early morning TV, of precocious child actors with names like Spanky and Alfalfa. Only, on this morning Buckwheat had been wielding a machete instead of a paintbrush, and lopping off arms instead of painting girls' names on an old wooden fence.

Gripping his daughter's fingers as firmly as the handle of any loaded shopping bag, the commentator noticed that he was being watched. From just looking at him, it was difficult to guess his profession. He might as easily have been an insurance agent as a baker—but his eyes were hard. Come to think of it, in the short time he had spent in the city Bohannon had seen only hard eyes, no matter whether they were centered in white faces or black.

"That's what they're called here. Purse snatchers or pickpockets, graffiti artists or carjackers, rapists or murderers or bank thieves, they're all raskols. Makes it sound a little better than it really is, don't you know? You're obviously a visitor, sir. You need to watch your step around here."

Bohannon could only gesture weakly at the dismembered corpse. A woman arrived, recognized the badly damaged face of the deceased, and began shrieking hysterically. Two security men dragged her away, kicking.

"But in the middle of the day, in the middle of the busiest store in town?" Bohannon was openly aghast.

The expatriate's expression did not so much as flicker. "It's called payback. Somebody from that fellow's clan or village killed someone from the clan or village of the men who stormed in swinging the bush-knives."

Bohannon had seen much of the world, had seen men do strange things as part of stranger cultures, but nothing quite so, well, blatant. He motioned toward the body. "You mean, this guy might not be the murderer?"

The expat shrugged indifferently. "Might, might not. Doesn't matter. He might not even have known about the original killing, which could have been payback for an earlier killing still. These things never end, don't you know? They go on for years, decades, generations sometimes. Unless or until compensation is paid. Pigs are best, of course. Anyone will accept pigs."

"In lieu of a human life?"

"It's their way. The gift of twenty or thirty pigs might have prevented this. And some kina shell, and a few bird-of-paradise feathers to sweeten the transaction. It will go on until one side decides there's been enough killing and comes up with sufficient compensation."

"But the police . . . so many witnesses . . ."

Now the expat did smile, pityingly. "I know it's hard for an outsider to understand, but there are no witnesses. Anyone brave or stupid enough to testify against the attackers becomes a party to the dispute, you see, and therefore subject to payback. Not necessarily against the testifier, but against his or her clan or family. So no one will say anything." He looked down and his expression transformed from one of cold indifference to that of doting father.

"Let's go, sunshine. Daddy will buy you an ice lolly."

Visions of sugar and chocolate replaced the sight of blood as the little girl gave a delighted squeal, a mouse tempted by the promise of fresh cheese, and allowed her father to lead her away from the site of murder and dismemberment.

Not unexpectedly, the images stayed with Bohannon all the rest of that day; complicating his shopping for masks vivid and bold enough to scare the bejesus out of the ordinary, everyday variety of western European demons; causing him to be severely overcharged by one of the city's rapacious and eager taxi drivers; and rendering tasteless an otherwise perfectly acceptable meal of fresh broiled coral cod with macadamia.

Seeking to shrink if not completely shunt aside the disquieting image of the disemboweled shopper, his various limbs and organs lying slick and warm in the blood-soaked aisle among fallen first-grade readers and dictionaries, Bohannon donned clean black jeans and his one pressed short-sleeved shirt and went in search of a decent glass of wine. Not in the steamy, bourgeois depths of the Hibiscus but next door. The reputed best hotel in town, he surmised, ought to have a decent lounge, where civilization might hold sway in the form of artfully distilled spirits, quiet conversation in English, and television.

The four uniformed security guards fronting the entrance to the tall ivory-colored building let him pass without a challenge. Not because he was white, necessarily, but because he was well-dressed. Passing through the small but handsome lobby he encountered few people. Like any good hotel in a third-world country, businessmen riding the waves of international commerce would constitute the bulk of registered guests. It was past nine o'clock and most of them would already be in their rooms, contemplating sleep as well as deals, calculating how many hours they could spare to rejuvenate their bodies as well as their balance sheets.

But the lounge was not entirely deserted, the gentle crescent of the queela-wood bar not wholly devoid of patronage. There was a television: an archaic nineteen diagonal inches. Bolted to the side of one of the wood-clad concrete pillars that supported the building, it was declaiming, at modest volume, the alien mysteries of Australian-rules football to the small but enthusiastic audience standing at the bar.

Off to the left and away from the boisterous punters, half a dozen empty stools beckoned. He slid onto one. At his request the bartender, a sloe-eyed native of the Milne Bay region far to the southeast, brought him a glass of fine Salitage chardonnay from southwest Australia. This brisk, apple-tinged spirit he raised to his lips as he turned slightly to his left atop the stool. Over the slightly curved, sharp-edged horizon formed by glass and wine, he saw her.

She was not the most beautiful woman he had ever seen—but she was the most beautiful woman he had encountered in the last four countries he had visited. Behind her, the wall of the hotel was glass, providing an excellent view of a nondescript office tower, a winding asphalt road, and the bushy, flower-choked hill it ascended. Loudly proclaiming its incongruous presence in a seedy tropical setting, the Century 21 Real Estate sign dwarfed the single-story converted home it advertised. Incipient night was rapidly and gratefully obliterating the scene.

Her sleeveless, low-cut dress and shoes were the color of fresh cream, her shoulder-length hair natural red, her eyes blue. Instead of a string of pearls, something more defining and intriguing hung from a gold chain around her gracile neck: the carved tooth of a full-grown saltwater crocodile. Given the distance between them he could not make out the nature of the carving, but the tooth was a good five inches long.

She had the deepest tan he had ever seen on a white person; not café au lait, not beige, but a deep pithy brown that the sun had seared into her epidermal cells with relentless insistence. Her flesh had the hue of exotic hardwoods, polished and rubbed to a glossy sheen. Small black blotches were visible where the sun had done deeper damage, but they only added to her attractiveness, like the spots on a leopard. Insofar as he could tell, she wore not a sliver of makeup. No lipstick, no blush, no eyeshadow—nothing.

She was sitting in a low padded brown chair with thick rolled arms, one leg crossed over another, holding a wineglass in her left hand and chatting with a couple of well-dressed nationals, as expats called the indigenous Papuans. Bohannon guessed her to be in her thirties, though whether mid, early, or late he could not tell. Shorter than he by several inches, she had the body of a mature gymnast, rounded by age but more muscular than normal. She was not cut, not ripped. Not a lifter—just solid.

She laughed at something one of the attentive nationals was saying, and as she laughed, she happened to look in his direction. Their eyes met.

He turned away, his backside pivoting on the bar stool.

Fiji was nice, he had been told. Friendly people, beautiful unpolluted beaches, excellent diving. He was looking forward to it, as he had looked forward to every country he had visited in the past six months. All had delivered on their various promises, but none had given him what he wanted. What Steven Bohannon needed could not be found in glossy travel brochures, on beaches that fronted water the color of turquoise, or in bars where bottles of expensive spirits glistened with false promise, like gems made of paste.

Defaulting to the television, he watched the rest of the Aussie football match, striving to try and comprehend its arcane rules and startling violence. When it was over, he listened thoughtfully to news from Brisbane, to which he could not relate. He was finishing the last of the Salitage when he felt a touch on his shoulder.

"Nobody ignores me. Especially not in this country."

Without waiting for an invitation she slipped elegantly onto the empty stool next to his. It was easy to make out the details of the pendant tooth now that she was close to him. It was of a naked woman, crudely but efficiently executed. The lines were rough and few, indicating simple knife work. The nationality of the woman thus depicted was ambiguous.

"I wasn't ignoring you. I don't flirt with strange women." Nervous, he sipped at his wine. His stomach was warm.

Her smile was full of mischief. "So you only flirt with old friends?"

"I didn't mean that. I . . ."

"You gay? Married?"

"No, and not recently."

"What do you do?"

"At the moment, very little. I'm just passing through. After hearing some of the stories about this country I wasn't even going to stop here, but I figured I can survive anywhere for a few days, and it's not much of a detour between Cairns and Nandi. So I thought I'd see what it was like."

She was watching him closely. "And what's your opinion?"

He pondered briefly before replying. "I can't say anything about the rest of the country. I've only seen a little of Port Moresby. It's crowded, not particularly dirty, ramshackle, bustling. Everywhere you look you can see contemporary western civilization clashing with the stone age. Fascinating, frightening, a bit dizzying. Too rich a brew for me. I think I'll like Fiji better."

She nodded noncommittally. "You're honest, anyway. That's a novelty. One that wouldn't do you much good here. Forget about the city. How about me? What do you think of me?" There was nothing of the coquette in her manner.

Somewhat to his own surprise, he did not hesitate. The good wine helped. "I think that looking at you, I can see contemporary western civilization clashing with the stone age. Fascinating, frightening, and a bit dizzying."

For an instant the self-confidence that she wore as casually and comfortably as the dress and the crocodile tooth fell away and he could see a hint of uncertainty and confusion beneath. Then the smile returned, mischievous as before.

"Not only honest, but clever. You're more than a novelty . . ."

"Steven." He raised his nearly empty glass. "Bohannon. I'm American."

"And I'm not. Llor Kramel and it's very nice to meet you."

"Aussie?"

"Originally. My family came to PNG when I was five. This has been my home ever since."

He nodded, because it seemed the thing to do. He had never been entirely sure of the thing to do in such situations. "And what do *you* think of this place, speaking as someone who actually lives here?"

"Frustrating, magnificent, murderous, exotic, exquisite. Wonderful people, terrible people. Dedicated civil servants and outrageously crooked politicians. Rich beyond the dreams of Croesus, poor by the standards of Ethiopia. The second largest island in the world and the damn imperialists had to go and split it down the middle, like it was a watermelon instead of a culture. I love it, and I hate it, I fear it and I wouldn't live anyplace else."

He could no longer restrain himself. The smile emerged of its own accord. "It fits you. Tell me more."

"I'd be glad to."

He could not tell if she was disappointed that he was staying at the Hibiscus instead of the Travelodge. If she was, she concealed it politely. Back in his room there was more talk, and a lot more wine. Not as good as the Salitage, but adequate for both their purposes. She made him laugh out loud, which was something he had not done in quite a while. The more he got to know her, the more he found her intriguing, and amusing, and utterly delightful.

He did not remember pulling the shades closed or turning out the lights, but he did remember much of what happened thereafter. Her body was unexpected, mature but as firm as that of an athlete, which she assured him she was not. Because of their size he expected her breasts to be somewhat pendulous. Instead, they stood up and out and were as taut as those of a schoolgirl. The rest of her was no less impressive, from the flat belly to the swelling hips to the wonderfully resilient legs.

When she eased herself down on top of him, taking her time and working slowly from side to side until there was nothing left of him to envelop, it was as if he had been surrounded by a single unbroken muscle. Despite the fog induced by the wine he matched her thrust for thrust, stroke for stroke, raising himself up to kiss and suck the only exposed parts of her sleek torso that were not brown. When they came, him first in an implosion of light and muscular collapse, her soon after like an eighteen-wheeler careening down a twenty degree grade with its brakes locked up, he felt as if he had been typhooned halfway across the South Pacific.

They refreshed and recharged themselves with the myriad contents of miniature bottles mined from the room's mini-bar, her giggling as she downed one bottle after another, him attempting without much success to appear suave and knowledgeable about alien liquors, and then they made love again.

She knew of a place, she whispered later into the glorious afterglaze of mutual orgasm, where they could watch the sun come up over the city. It was not listed in the tourist brochures, and wonderfully romantic. They could sit there adrift in each others' arms and she would point out to him the highlights of the capital as the rising sun brought it back to life. It was something he would remember all his life, a ribbon with which to wrap up and keep all the joys of this special night. He'd had no reason to doubt her.

She was right, of course. He would remember it. But for all the wrong reasons. . . .

II

"Slipped something into your last slug of schnapps, did she?" Collins was nodding knowingly to himself, a cantankerous swollen Buddha of a man who had seen much and was surprised by little. "Waited 'til you passed out in her arms and then went through your pockets. Who's the clever bitch, then?"

Bohannon put down his coffee. "I'm sorry, but I can't think of her that way."

"Oh well, excuse me, then!" the retired soldier exclaimed with exaggerated and truly mock sorrow. "Maybe you'd like to find her again so you could write her a check for what she didn't get the first time? Or was she that good in the sack?"

His guest looked elsewhere. Bohannon could find fault with his host's language, but not with his observations. There was not an ounce of subtlety or tact in the man, and at that moment Bohannon did not particularly want to be confronted with the truth of himself. Though this was a fault he shared with most human beings, he took no comfort in its commonality.

In concert with the sun, the temperature was rising. The temperature, and its oppressive companion humidity. It was enough to make one wish for the cool confines of a steam room.

"It's not that." He struggled to explain. This was not easy, because he did not understand himself what he was feeling. "I know I should be angry. Furious, even. But I'm just . . . not."

"Then you're fucking dead inside, you dumb pussy. You get screwed over and under and robbed and dumped for dead and you're not angry? Have some more coffee."

With a sigh, his guest accepted the offer of another cup. How accurate his comment was, the ex-soldier could not imagine, but Bohannon saw no reason to elaborate or explain. No matter how much time he took or how much of his personal history he related, he doubted Collins would understand, much less sympathize.

"Aren't you going to try and find her? Get some of your money back, if not some of your self-respect? How much did she get away with, anyway?"

Bohannon forced down more of the strong black brew, gazing past his host in the direction of the mountains that had produced it. "About two thousand."

"Shit! Kina, U.S., or Aussie?"

"U.S. dollars. And another couple of thousand in traveler's checks."

"Credit cards?"

For the first time, Bohannon was able to demonstrate some common sense. "When I'm traveling I always keep them separate from my wallet. They're in the safe deposit box at the motel, along with my passport and travel documents."

"Ha!" Collins smacked a beefy hand down on the thickly varnished tabletop, sending pungent droplets of hot Goroka flying. "So you're not a complete ass. Only half of one. What are you going to do now?"

"Cancel my last day here. If I can change my reservation, I'll fly on to Fiji today. If not, then tomorrow."

"What a wuss! If it was me, I'd track the bitch down, get my money back, and beat the living crap out of her."

"But you're not me, Harlin."

"No, I can sure as hell see that." Pushing back his chair, he rose abruptly. Collins seemed to do everything abruptly. "You're one sorry bastard, Bohannon. I'm downright embarrassed to have a major-league sniveler like you on my boat. It shames the roaches. How about some bacon and eggs? Real American bacon, not this greasy fried lard the Aussies and the English call bacon. Local Zenag eggs, though. Damn good stuff. Guts I can't give you, but I can do breakfast."

Bohannon eyed his host warily. "Collins, you're certifiable, you know that?"

"Yeah, but certified what? Haw! Maybe back in the States. But this is PNG, Papua New Guinea, the Heaven and Hell of the South Pacific—you ignorant prick. In case you haven't noticed, here I fit right in. In fact, I'm considered downright normal. Just a bloke with a boat." He was halfway down the hatchway stairs when he paused and glanced back.

"By the way, if while you're looking for a plane out of here and by some miracle you happen to stumble over some backbone instead, don't go looking for some broad named Llor Kramel."

Bohannon had been watching the scuba divers on the idling boat out in the channel affix gauges and regulators to their steel tanks, wishing he could go with them, wishing he too could sink his thoughts deep beneath the comforting, smothering sea.

"Why not?"

"Because she doesn't exist. Christ, are you dense! The name's an anagram." Attempting to smile, he ended up sneering as he disappeared down the gangway.

Bohannon took his host's remark to heart. Along with his coffee, he considered Llor Kramel backwards and and forwards and inside-out. "Roll the Mark" had a decidedly less exotic and more prosaic ring to it than "Llor Kramel." Perhaps if he had not been so blinded by the attentions of a beautiful woman he would have picked up on it, instead of just being picked up. In this he shared an unfortunate and debilitating condition characteristic of his gender. In such situations he tended to think with his dick.

Collins was as good as his word and Bohannon felt much better by the time they'd finished the home-cooked food. After berating and deriding his guest mercilessly for the duration of the meal, the foul-mouthed ex-soldier, unasked, advanced his guest taxi fare.

Taken aback, Bohannon assured his host that he would pay him back in full.

"Never mind that." With the flat of his hand Collins gave him a hard shove. "Go and find the bitch. Get some justice, if not your money. Recover your self-respect. Be a man, goddamn it!"

Bohannon shook his head slowly. "You think taking revenge makes somebody a man?"

"God, what an ignorant asshole you are! Be an alien, then. Be a wombat. I don't give a shit. Just don't worry about the lousy cab fare. Now get the fuck off my boat before you give the rats a bad name."

The locked gate at the landward end of the jetty was intended to keep unauthorized cars and trucks out of the harbor, not individuals. Slipping through, he walked to the curb of the main access road and began waving. A tattered Toyota pulled over and he climbed in. Ignoring the garrulous driver, Bohannon rode back to the Hibiscus in silence.

Just for the hell of it, he gave the desk clerk a description of his female companion of the previous night and inquired if he happened to know her. The clerk confessed that he did not, and was much distressed to learn of the events that had befallen the motel's guest the night before.

This helped Bohannon to obtain a cash advance on one of his credit cards. The amount was modest, but it would enable him to take another taxi to the part of the city known as Boroko. The Westpac bank there should be able to supply him with more cash as well as replacement traveler's checks.

He did not dwell on the events of the previous night. Embarrassment burned brighter than the monetary loss and the sooner he could put the entire incident out of his mind, the better he knew he would feel. Chalk it up to experience, that was what he intended to do. Not all travel memories were of sweeping vistas and bustling marketplaces. Some lessons in different cultures were more costly than others.

The funny thing was, it would not have happened to him in New York, or London, or Barcelona. There he would have been prepared, expectant, more on his guard. Collins's repeated accusations to the contrary, Bohannon was not entirely naive. But the wine had been good and he had not expected to encounter anyone like the redhead in a backwater like Port Moresby. So this once, he had allowed himself to relax, and to trust, and to go with the flow. He could not bring himself to smile at the memory, but even in the depths of his chagrin he had to confess that the mortifying episode had not been without its compensations.

It wasn't the money. Well, maybe some of it was the money. He was not a rich man. Far more than that, though, it was the knowledge that from the first words of their conversation he had been taken for a fool. He had made his share of mistakes in life, had endured failure as deeply as any man, but not because he was a fool. Unlucky, yes. Desperately unfortunate in his choice of times, and places, and certain decisions, yes. But not a fool. Nor would he admit to any of the other many names Harlin Collins had called him.

But you are a fool, he thought without rancor. She had proved it. Collins knows it. So you might as well admit it to yourself.

The funny thing was, he had undertaken his present extended journey as a way of proving otherwise. Hoping for rejuvenation, he had thus far found only disappointment. The worst possible consequence of the trip would be for him to return home less than he had been when he'd departed. Now beauty had knocked him down a notch, and sex another. He had to get on the next plane to Fiji. He had to avoid the next plane to Fiji. He did not know what to do.

Boroko district was located inland; some four miles, several degrees, ten percentage points of humidity and a couple of levels of human intensity up from downtown. The capital district of Waigani lay to the northwest and Jackson's International Airport a few miles further north. In between and all around were individual shops, unregulated industrial and commercial areas, local residences, armed encampments populated largely but not entirely by expats, tiny hole-in-the-wall Chinese restaurants serving perfectly adequate food for next to no money, Big Rooster fried chicken franchises, gas stations, and open-air markets.

There was one of the latter in Boroko, right off the main road. Surrounded by a U-shaped arc of contiguous low-rise offices, supermarkets, Chinese and Indian-run general stores, music shops, and clothing emporiums, each with its own complement of bored security guards, the open end of the "U" bumped up against a major PMV stop. Here dozens of public motor vehicles, comprised largely of overworked and undermaintained minibuses, disgorged and acquired their human cargo. They were the most economical way of getting around the sprawling city, and everyone used them.

Bohannon had the driver drop him in front of the stuccoed two-story office building that housed the bank. To his right was the open-air market where villagers from the surrounding mountains displayed for sale an astonishing variety of tomatoes, corn, squash, beans, peas, watermelon, yams, and a colorful cornucopia of other produce grown on small carefully cultivated family plots. Shade trees provided relief from the unrelenting sun, while from spigots flowed the balm of fresh if not cold water. The massed odor of hundreds of milling bodies mixed with that of sun-stroked food. Children and dogs were everywhere underfoot.

He crossed between the line of parked cars, pickup trucks, and battered Land Rovers. Their vehicles parked beneath overhanging tree limbs, taxi drivers waiting for fares passed the time discussing beer, women, and rugby. Other individuals sat forlorn and isolated in their cars or trucks, silently lamenting a fate that had condemned them to endless days of paralyzing ennui. Many were from the Highlands, having migrated to the big city in search of a piece of the rapidly expanding money economy. Very few did not look lost in space as well as time.

The wide sidewalk was crowded with seated vendors hawking more durable goods. Women in limp dresses and bare feet clutched babies and engaged in running arguments, old ladies with their heads resting on one hand stared vacantly off into space, men with massive black beards and hopeful expressions followed him with their eyes as he strode past. They leaned up against the brick and concrete walls of permanent buildings, their goods spread out on sheets or blankets in front of them.

Bohannon passed piles of wispy black cassowary feathers, sliced and polished kina shells like shards of yellow crescent moon, gleaming spotted and golden cowries, cheap tourist carvings, painted spirit masks from the Sepik river region, decorated belts and headpieces, and naked hornbill skulls intended to be worn by men as reverse necklaces, with the bare beak worn downward from the back of the neck to follow the curve of the upper spine.

A number of the men had bird-of-paradise feathers for sale. Illegal to export, they were common decorations among the Highland peoples. Iridescent blue brighter than the flashiest metal-flake paint indicated the presence of breast feathers from the male Superb bird-of-paradise, while long plumes lined at regular intervals with gray disks like faceless nickels came from the impossible twin head plumes of the King-of-Saxony. Glossy black feathers long enough to fit comfortably on a condor's wing had once decorated the tail of Stephanie's arabis, the feathers four times longer than the bird itself. *Must be something to see in flight*, he mused idly as he strode past.

Many of the women were selling bilums (literally "put-ins"). Woven from string dyed every color of the rainbow and decorated with traditional geometric patterns, the bilum was the nearest thing in PNG to a national article of clothing. Available in every imaginable size, from tiny coin purses to large sacks capable of holding gurgling two-year olds, they were incredibly strong and could expand to hold amazing volumes. Men and women alike carried them, expats included. It was common to see a woman striding along, her bilum strap knotted intricately over her forehead so as to leave her hands free, the distended bag hanging down behind her containing household goods, groceries, and a silent sleeping infant.

Offered everything, he bought nothing. In addition to the bilum vendors, feather dealers, artifact sellers, and green-grocers, the market area, sidewalks, and stores swarmed with hundreds of unemployed young men and their sad-eyed, dissolute elders. Many were recent arrivals from the Highlands or the Sepik, Milne Bay or the outer islands. They had no jobs, no prospects, no training, and no education, but most had sharp eyes and strong arms. Not a few carried machetes, known locally as bush knives. It was not recommended that visitors flash large amounts of cash on the street.

Inside the bank a winding line of people waited to reach the tellers. All the banks were like this, he'd been told. In a land of no money there were endless lines in all the banks. Eventually directed upstairs, he explained his plight to a sympathetic clerk. Most were women, he noted.

Two hours later he had cash and fresh traveler's checks. In the States the requisite transactions would have taken him fifteen minutes, but he did not complain, did not raise a ruckus. He had traveled in third-world countries before and was relieved simply to have access to a bank. The young man who sent him off with a smile and a cheery "*Apinun!*" or "afternoon" had raised ritual scars on his cheeks as big as quarters. Not surprisingly, he was unfamiliar with the woman Bohannon casually described while they both waited for his transaction to clear.

Half a block up the street was Westpac Travel, a full-service travel agency that had been recommended by the clerk at the Hibiscus. The diminutive, soft-voiced national who waited on him manipulated her computer as deftly as any agent back home. These people were all so soft-voiced, he reflected. It seemed that in PNG no one shouted unless they were attending a sporting event or a war.

The next flight to Fiji was not until late afternoon. He booked it, uncomplainingly paying the premium for the last-minute flight change. Wanting nothing more to do with the country that had betrayed him, he took a cab back to the motel, packed his one convertible backpack-duffel, checked out, and headed for the airport. There he made himself order and eat an indifferent lunch at the Airport Motel. The outdoor restaurant overlooked the runway, allowing him to slide spicy chicken satay off bamboo skewers while watching takeoffs and landings. Air traffic was modest, all of it Air Niugini or charter flights.

Three hours before his plane was due to board, he walked down the hill from the motel to the terminal. Just as in Boroko and downtown there were people everywhere, many rushing about on important errands, many more simply drifting aimlessly hoping to stumble across food, work, love, or the twenty-first century.

All flights both domestic and international departed from the single terminal building, a comparatively new one-story structure that was already showing signs of age and lack of maintenance. The air-conditioning was out and this late in the day the temperature within was daunting. Men and women hauling boxes, crates of food, bunches of yams and vegetables, bilums full of oranges and other coastal produce, rolled foam mattresses, and kids, lined up to pass through Security. With nothing on his person or in his luggage to tweak the metal detectors, he was waved through. As he passed it, he found himself wondering if the already battered security scanner actually worked.

This soon before the flight, there was only one customer ahead of him at the otherwise deserted international counter. In contrast, the domestic counter around the corner was frantic with activity. Amid much mad waving and gesticulating, one man was arguing loudly with an unfortunate agent. Apparently, the traveler had been forbidden to take a brace of live chickens on the flight to Madang and was remonstrating vociferously against this outrageous regulation, to no avail. Behind him, a trio of mining engineers towered over the much shorter nationals while griping audibly at the delay. No one paid them the least mind.

"May I help you, sir?" The international agent was fine-featured and slim. He wore dark slacks and a white shirt with the Air Niugini symbol embroidered on the breast pocket: a black silhouette of the omnipresent Raggiana bird-of-paradise. His English was excellent, his voice so muted as to be nearly inaudible.

Putting his bag down between his feet, Bohannon removed his ticket and handed it over. The agent opened it and proceeded to check it against the computer.

"Qantas flight ninety-six. You're stopping over in Fiji, then, sir, and not continuing directly on to Los Angeles?"

Bohannon smiled pleasantly. Behind him, laughing children chased each other back and forth through the open door next to Security. The guards ignored them. "That's right."

"Would you like a window seat, sir, or an aisle? The flight is quite open."

"Window." Absently he added, "I don't suppose you've seen an expat woman through here recently? Thirtyish, red hair, blue eyes, a little shorter than me. Nice figure, bright smile, really deep tan?"

The agent looked up, his own teeth shockingly white against his dark face. Too tall to be a Highlander, Bohannon decided. Probably a city native, or from somewhere down the coast, or the outer islands.

"Oh, I think the lady you describe was through here just this morning, sir. You are right. She was very pretty."

The world Bohannon had so carefully reconstructed turned upside down. Softly framed by the glow of the computer monitor, the vision of the placid beaches, clear waters, and first-class international hotels of Fiji beckoned. Unaccountably, uncharacteristically, something stirred within him. Something new and unfamiliar. Damn that fat slob Harlin Collins.

He had his ticket. He had a reservation. Shortly, he would have an assigned seat. There was nothing for him here, nothing he had not bumped up against and shied away from a dozen times in the recent past. A hundred times. This was not in his nature, not a part of the perceptibles that came together to make up the man called Him, yclept Bohannon. All he had to do was say thank you, take back his ticket, check the boarding pass, go through the security doors into the air-conditioned limbo of the international waiting lounge where he could peruse postcards, brightly packaged coffee, and overpriced souvenirs until it was time to wave a final farewell to this treacherous little country.

It was the appropriate thing to do, the easy thing to do, the right thing to do. His right hand was frozen on the counter, halfway between the ticket to Nandi and a ticket to—where? He heard himself asking, "She wasn't by any chance going to Fiji on the early flight, was she?"

"No, sir." The agent looked to his right and pointed. "She was checking in for a domestic flight. I was helping out over there this morning. There are only three international flights today. I am an Air Niugini clerk, but we all agent for Qantas as well." He smiled cheerfully, at once forestalling Bohannon's next question and damning him forever with the same helpfulness. There was an inexorable quality to his soft-voiced words that was impossible to resist.

"If you like, I will see if I can find out where she was going."

Bohannon stared at his ticket. It lay next to the agent's fingers, quiescent as a live viper. "Sure," he heard himself saying distantly, "I'd like that very much."

Demonstrating skills to match his helpfulness, the agent promptly dumped Qantas from his screen and filled it with the morning's Air Niugini schedule. "I remember her because she was so attractive," he said, making small talk as he worked the keyboard. "She seemed very happy."

"Prosperous." Bohannon corrected him as he waited attentively, wondering just what the hell it was that he was doing.

The agent did not give him a great deal of time for reflection or introspection. "Here it is. Tai Tennison, one way to Lae." He looked up encouragingly. "According to this, that was her final destination."

"Maybe not," Bohannon argued. "She might land there and buy another ticket to somewhere else."

"Why would she do that, sir? Why not just purchase a continuation ticket? It is much cheaper that way."

"Maybe she doesn't want people to know her real final destination. Could she be heading overseas from there?"

The agent looked surprised. "No, sir. All international flights must come through Jackson's. There is talk of opening the airstrip on New Britain to international flights, but that's all it is for now, only talk."

"What's in Lae?"

The agent considered. "It is the country's main port, sir. Smaller than Port Moresby, but it is the starting point for the Highlands highway, the principal road into the Highlands. Or I should say, the only road into the Highlands. You should see it, sir."

Bohannon's thoughts were churning. Silently, he was losing control. It was unsettling. He was a man who never lost control. Unless, he thought, one counted last night. Had it only been last night? He was not the sort to do crazy, impetuous things, to go off on wild, impossible quests. Especially for something as intangible and furtive as revenge. Or even, if one chose to recast it, for justice.

"Why should I see this road? Is it famous for its views?"

"No, sir." The other man laughed gently, enjoying his little joke. "For its potholes."

Of course, Bohannon thought. What else? Reason enough, he mused a little madly, for a sudden and radical change in travel plans. For a radical change in self. He took back the international ticket.

"I'll keep this, for later. Cancel my reservation for this afternoon. When's the next flight to Lae?"

The agent pursed his lips as he checked the computer. "There is a Fokker due in from Madang in thirty minutes that is scheduled to continue on to Lae, unless it has been diverted to stop at Mt. Hagen instead."

Bohannon frowned. "Doesn't the schedule say?"

The other's expression was knowing. "You are in PNG, sir. Flight schedules here are—flexible." He turned back to the computer. "There is another flight to Lae tonight, but I would not recommend it to you."

"Why not?"

"Nazdab Airport at Lae is located many miles out of town. Not a good place for a visitor to be wandering around alone after dark. I suggest we try for the earlier flight."

"I'd rather do that anyway. Is there room?"

"The flight is sold out, sir. But you are here now, and many who hold reservations are not. I can sell you a ticket. After that," he shrugged and smiled, "I suggest you get to the boarding gate early."

"I'll take my chances." He fumbled for his credit cards. Have to buy a new wallet, he reminded himself. He wondered if Ms. Roll-the-Mark was enjoying his. "Think it will be a smooth flight?"

The agent spoke while coaxing the computer. "You will be flying over the mountains, sir. But nearly all flights within PNG are over mountains. Conditions are best in the morning, but maybe you will be lucky." Beneath the counter, unseen machinery hummed. The agent produced a ticket, inserted it into a folder. "One-way to Lae. I hope you find your lady, sir."

He took the folder, wondering as he did so if he was simultaneously taking back a part of his life or giving more of it away. "I'm not sure that's what I'm looking for, but thanks anyhow." Turning, he headed for the jammed domestic waiting area, forging a path between families, expats, noisy children, and bemused Highlanders.

III

The flight over the northern reaches of the Owen Stanley Range in the twin-jet Fokker-28, known affectionately to those who flew her as the pocket rocket, was disconcerting enough. He did his best to imitate the locals, who sat stoic and uncomplaining through the worst bumps and drops. It helped that the expat seated next to him was a bundle of nervous energy, a small well-built man in his mid-forties who talked incessantly throughout the flight. Bohannon did not know whether to be grateful for the diversion or irritated at the stream of vacuous inconsequentialities that were spewed his way.

"A bit bumpy, yes, but better than the last flight I was on. That one was hijacked."

"What?" Turning away from the small window with its unreal view of towering mountains rising like green spearpoints from impenetrable rainforest, he forced himself to focus on the man seated next to him. In a stroke of good fortune unusual for domestic Air Niugini flights, the center seat between them was vacant.

"That's right. It was a local hop to the Chimbu Highlands. Enga chap hijacked it with an ax. Beautiful piece of work, it was. The ax, not the hijacking."

"Where were you hijacked to?" The thought of a hijacking taking place within PNG had not occurred to Bohannon. Hijacking a local flight seemed to make no sense at all.

As his fellow passenger explained, it did, of course, but only in local terms.

"Seems the plane was headed into the land of his tribe's traditional enemies and he didn't want it to land there. So we put down in Woenenai."

"What happened to the hijacker?" Bohannon was interested in spite of himself.

"He made a little speech in Pidgin about what irredeemable

arseholes his traditional enemies were, hopped off the plane, and vanished into the bush. Never saw him again. Fortunately, there was enough fuel on board for the pilot to take off and reach our original destination. The little chap was making a statement, you see."

"With an ax," Bohannon murmured.

"A stone ax. Don't smirk. Can crush a man's skull, they can. What are your plans after we land? You don't talk like you know the country much."

"I don't. I've only been here for a few days. I was told that the airport is quite a ways from town."

"So the new one is. The original was right downtown. Very convenient for everybody. But someone in the government wanted the land. Because of the location and the city's modest growth it's become quite valuable, you see. Of course, nothing whatsoever has been done with it. It just sits empty, a big grassy strip in the middle of town, doing nobody any good. But planes aren't allowed to land there anymore.

"Anyway, the Aussies decided to give the government one of their periodic big gifts, so they built a second airport outside of town to replace the one the big boys had co-opted. Did it up right, so it could serve as a new international destination."

"You're not Australian?"

"No. Canadian. I import and repair electronics. Mostly for businesses, but there's a growing consumer market here as well."

"I thought all international flights had to go through Port Moresby?"

"That they do. See, the government knows that if tourists could avoid Mosby and fly into Lae, nobody would bother with the capital. So they don't allow any international flights into the international airport at Lae. There's a runway ready for jumbo jets, and a nice, big terminal building. Much nicer than the one at Jackson's. All set up for a restaurant, artifact shop, customs. You'll see. It's a ghost terminal. Good for me, though. I do this run once a week, sometimes more."

"Is there a decent hotel in town?"

"Actually, there is. The Lae International. Don't laugh. It's a nice place. My truck's parked just outside the terminal. I'd be happy to run you into town." His smile faded. "You don't want to be walking around Nazdab alone, after dark."

Bohannon felt an immediate and entirely disproportionate sense of relief. "I'd appreciate that. You just fly to Moresby . . . Mosby . . . on business, and leave your vehicle parked in a lot?"

The importer chuckled knowingly. "Don't worry, I leave one of my own security people with it. He's a kukukuku."

Bohannon tried not to smile. "You're putting me on."

"You think so?" The man's grin vanished. "Don't tell him that. They're just little chaps, but nobody, and I mean nobody, messes with the kukukukus. Not even the Huli or the Enga. A Highlander will kill for money, or to avenge a perceived insult, or over a woman, or over pigs, or certainly for payback. Someone from the coast, or an Islander, will kill for stronger reasons. A kukukuku will kill just for the hell of it, for something to do. As social mavens they're about one notch above your average wolverine. Good people, though, if you treat 'em right. I make it a point to do so. All my warehouse and store guards are kukukukus." His voice, like his expression, was flat. If he was having a private laugh at Bohannon's expense, he was doing a damn good job of it. "My truck will be there."

Lae Nazdab International Airport lay at the eastern end of an astonishing geological feature. Perfectly flat, the valley of the Markham River ran right down to the sea, interrupted only by the town of Lae itself. Extensively planted in sugar and rice by the national Ramu company, it was also home to herds of cattle that grew fat on natural fodder in addition to waste from the sugar and rice crops.

The Fokker circled in and then dropped like a dive bomber to clear the sky-shearing crags of the twelve-thousand-foot-high mountains of the central ranges on one side and the Finisterre wall on the other. Following the breathtaking descent, the little jet made a smooth touchdown on the expansive, underused landing strip. Grass grew high right to the edge of the tarmac where the jungle assaulted the asphalt.

As they filed out of the plane and into the cavernous, nearly empty terminal, Bohannon's new-found friend pointed out the darkened, deserted alcoves that lined the interior.

"See? Just like I was telling you: Customs, souvenirs, restaurant—all vacant and unused. You have any baggage?"

Bohannon hefted his pack. "Just this. I like to travel light."

"Good. Parking's out back." He gestured. There were no doors on the terminal, which was as open to the elements as the front of a hangar.

Cars and pickups and Land Rovers shouldered up against one another in the dirt parking lot. Locals milled about, watching the passengers disperse. A few optimistic taxi drivers badgered arrivals in hopes of caging a fare. One or two got lucky. Bohannon noticed that everyone, white or black, carefully watched everyone else.

The small dark man who rose from the back of the importer's pickup truck was maybe five feet tall. He wore only a pair of torn shorts and on his feet, cheap rubber flipflops. His boss greeted him in Pidgin and the little man promptly resumed his seat in the truck bed, his back resting against the double cab.

"Throw your kit in back." Unlocking the doors, the importer climbed behind the wheel and shoved a key into the ignition as his passenger complied.

Bohannon glanced back through the rear window. "I didn't see a gun."

"Gun?" The importer smiled as the engine turned over. "Bara has his bow and arrows. That's enough. You ever handled a bow made from black palm? No? I can barely draw one myself, but I've seen tribesmen bury a bamboo arrow four centimeters deep into a solid wooden target at thirty-five meters."

"Someone with a gun would still have an advantage."

"Perhaps," the importer conceded, "but if they did somehow manage to get by Bara, then they'd risk incurring payback from his tribe. You see how it works."

The truck pulled out of the airport and onto a narrow, two-lane road. The importer waited to let a heavy lorry rumble past before pulling out in its dust-strewn wake. There were no shoulders, sealed or otherwise, and the road surface was broken and crumbling. Thick vegetation crowded close on both sides, bright green gnawing patiently at the slowly disintegrating pavement.

"Not much of an access road," Bohannon commented.

His host laughed. "Access road? This is the Highlands Highway, man. The country's main road. Nearly all the commerce that travels between the north coast and the center of the country goes up or comes down this road. It's the product of typical third-world thinking, you see. Plenty of money for new roads, so ministers can cut ribbons declaring them open and get their pictures in the papers and on TV, but little or nothing for maintenance. Pothole-patching doesn't make for good photo-ops. The condition of this road is a national disgrace. One of many." As if to punctuate his remarks, the front of the pickup slammed into a depression that sent Bohannon flying toward the roof. After that he hung on tightly.

Surrounded by impossibly high mountains on two sides and the Solomon Sea on a third, Lae presented a much more pleasant aspect to the eye than did Mosby. The potholes in the city roads were as rumored: enormous open craters that looked capacious enough to permanently swallow anything smaller than a compact car. Local drivers negotiated this lethal, endless slalom with skill born of long practice.

A truck and trailer rig having broken down in the middle of the road and abandoned by its driver, cars and pickups simply drove around it, making a muddy mess of the grass-covered property in front of a commercial strip mall. Unlike in Mosby, which lay in the country's only real rain shadow, the utilitarian exteriors of the local warehouses and office structures were softened by the presence of hundreds of exotic trees and flowering bushes.

The hotel turned out to be situated atop a hill that offered views of the surrounding mountains, the lush valley of the Markham, and wonderfully blue tropical waters. They passed people playing tennis and, on a larger court, two groups of women in short skirts and uniform blouses engaged in what looked like basketball but wasn't.

"Local netball teams," the importer explained. "The game's a lot like basketball but thought of as more, um, ladylike. Which is pretty funny because some of the girls who play could probably make the local rugby team. Here we are."

The hotel was more than Bohannon expected; modern, clean, and half empty.

"Hardly ever see tourists here," his friend told him. "But plenty of businessmen passing through or working in town. I'll leave you to it." Having escorted his guest to the front lobby, he turned to leave.

"Wait! Maybe you can help me with one more thing. I'm trying to locate someone. She flew in here earlier today." Using the name the Air Niugini agent at Jackson's had taken from the passenger manifest of the earlier flight to Lae, he proceeded to describe her.

The importer smiled helplessly. "I'm afraid I don't know the lady. You might ask around. This may be the second-largest city in PNG, but that's not saying much. Try the main businesses downtown. Shops and restaurants and such. And good luck."

Bohannon slept better that night than he had any right to expect, rose early for breakfast, and rented a car from the hotel desk.

Downtown Lae consisted of one street lined with clean, busy offices and stores. There was the by now familiar throng of anxious, edgy unemployed surging to and fro, up and down the street: a human wave unsure if the tide of progress was coming in or going out. But the feeling of hopeless, of oppressive poverty that predominated in Port Moresby, was noticeably absent.

As they had been in Boroko, the sidewalk vendors were present in force, hawking carvings and bilums to nonexistent tourists, but they too looked happier and healthier than their more desperate brethren in Mosby. He went into a drugstore and bought a few small personal items, noting that the majority of medicines whether familiar or alien had been manufactured in India. A bottle of brand-name pain reliever cost one-fifth of what it would have in a pharmacy back home.

In each store, at every stop, he inquired about the woman he now knew as Tai Tennison. Each inquiry drew the same polite but sorrowful response. No one had seen anyone of that description or going by that name. Either she was not well known in this part of the country, or he was asking in the wrong places.

But the expat chief teller of the local branch of the Bank of Papua New Guinea had, if not information, a suggestion.

"Have you talked to McCracken?" The teller was dressed more than casually in open shirt and shorts. Come to think of it, Bohannon realized, he had not seen a single tie since he had arrived in the country.

"McCracken who?"

"Sorley McCracken." The teller hesitated slightly. "I wouldn't suggest it except that according to what you've been telling me, you're not having much luck finding this particular lady."

"I'm not having any luck." Bohannon's gaze idly drifted over the short line of nationals waiting to be helped. "In fact, I'm strongly considering giving up, returning to Mosby, and going on with my trip." *As opposed to going on with my life*, he thought tiredly. Would he never be free of his memories? How many other men carried their own private, purpose-built prison around with them?

The teller tried his best to be encouraging. "Try McCracken. He doesn't just know Lae, he knows the country. But be careful."

"Why?" Bohannon was instantly on guard. "Is he dangerous?"

The other man considered. "Not so much dangerous. Some would say difficult. Some would say unique. Myself, I just find him a trifle odd. He banks here sometimes." The teller smiled broadly. "When he has money."

"Where do I find him? I have a car."

The man nodded, producing paper and pen. "His place is not far from the central market. Just up in the hills. I'll draw you a map."

"Thanks." When the teller had finished, Bohannon took the paper and studied it briefly. "This looks pretty straightforward. You think he'll be home? What does he do?"

"If he's not home, he's probably not in town. He does a little bit of everything, I believe. That might extend to finding people."

Bohannon turned to go. As he did so, half a dozen nationals entered through the only door. Several of them wore long shirts or coats, attire sufficiently at odds with the high temperature and humidity to attract his attention.

As he stared, jacket and shirt fronts were simultaneously pulled aside to reveal a ragbag armory of bush knives and homemade shotguns. These crude but alarming makeshift weapons were fashioned from pieces of water pipe wired to hand-hewn wooden stocks and fired with nails or leather punches activated by rubber bands. As likely to blow off the head of the owner as that of any chosen target, they were as intimidating as they were grotesque. The armed arrivals wasted no time declaring their intentions.

"*Go i go long dispela banis, olgeta man*!" shouted one of the pipe-wielders.

Stunned, Bohannon found himself rudely shoved and pushed up against the far wall, with one expat and several terrified nationals for company. While two of the armed men, none of whom was over five foot six, nervously kept an eye on the huddle of customers, two others rushed to shut the doors to the bank.

Accompanied by one companion, the leader of the band vaulted the counter to confront the chief teller. He gripped a pistol that appeared to have been hammered together out of sheet metal. As he spoke, he waved it about with reckless disregard for everyone in the vicinity, including his own men. He wore an open, thigh-length denim jacket, blue jeans holed at both knees, leather sandals that looked as if they had served as play toys for a couple of lion cubs, and a moth-eaten T-shirt advertising the 1994 PNG Pepsi-Cola charity fun run. His eyes were deep-set, his chin rounded, and his nose twice as broad as Bohannon's. A Highlander.

As if his appearance was not ferocious enough, a ten-inch long cassowary quill had been run horizontally through his nasal septum.

"Yu i op i stap safe!" he demanded in a rush of Pidgin, semaphoring with the gun.

The chief teller remained remarkably calm despite the presence of the pistol muzzle only inches from his face. "I'm sorry, but I can't do that."

Heavy brows drew together and the barrel of the homemade weapon was lowered to aim directly at the teller's forehead. *"Opim nau no yu dai pinis!"*

"Please." A slight shaking betrayed the teller's unease. "I mean I really can't open it. I don't know the combination. Only the manager does."

The leader of the raskols looked around wildly. *"Yu get menaga nau!"* He was practically screaming.

"I—I'm really sorry, but I can't. He's at lunch."

This prompted a furious exchange among the highly agitated raskols while customers and employees alike waited tensely. Finally the leader growled anew at the chief teller.

"Mipela wetim em. Yupela," and he gestured with the pistol, *"go ausait! Yu tokim mipela insait, mipela kilim i dai pinis olgeta yupela!"*

With guns and knives Bohannon found himself and his fellow customers pushed through the bank entrance and back out onto the busy street—whereupon the doors to the bank were locked securely behind them. Dazed, he stumbled off in the direction of the drugstore. Having thus locked their potential hostages *out* of the building with no more than a warning to keep quiet, and sealed themselves inside, the less than sophisticated raskols settled quietly down to await the bank manager's return from his midday meal.

Restored to freedom, one of the female customers promptly went running off down the main street as fast as her legs would carry her, screaming at the top of her lungs that a bank robbery was in progress. This brought an immediate response, since the main Lae police station was located only three blocks away.

Five minutes later Bohannon found himself diving for cover as a battered Land Rover came squealing down the main boulevard, scattering startled pedestrians and the occasional frantic dog in all directions. He caught a glimpse of one of the would-be robbers at the wheel, the leader haranguing the driver from the backseat as the other robbers attempted to return pursuing fire with their crude, homemade weapons. Blood trailed from the rear of the 4×4.

Seconds later two compact police cars came roaring around the corner in hot pursuit. Having just dusted themselves off and resumed their business, everyone on the street was forced to repeat their evasive tactics of moments earlier. Bohannon took refuge behind a porch post as the police cut loose with everything from revolvers to automatic weapons. Flying bullets struck storefronts, curbs, trees, roofs, and by some miracle, even occasionally the getaway car. Incredibly, no innocent bystanders were perforated, though a couple of stores had their front windows shattered.

As he rose slowly from behind the protective stanchion, a winded Bohannon tried to regain his composure, staring down the street in the direction the fleeing vehicles had taken.

"Wonder what that was all about?"

Turning at the sound of a new voice, he found himself confronted by a stout middle-aged black woman with plump cheeks and two highly visible gold front teeth that flashed when she smiled. "They were trying to rob the bank," he wheezed. "They locked their hostages *outside*." He shook his head in disbelief. "What kind of bank robbers lock their hostages outside?"

Shaking her head, the woman turned to go back into her dry-goods shop. "That's typical. These raskols, they come down from the mountains and all they know is that the money is in the banks. They haven't a clue how to go about getting it out."

"Do you think they'll get away?" Bohannon was still gazing down the street, where the dust was only now beginning to settle.

"Not bloody likely. In that direction there's only the one road in and out of town. You see, they can use modern devices, a lot of these Highlanders, but their thinking is still stone age. So they make sure they have a getaway car waiting, because serious bank robbers got to have a getaway car, even though it don't occur to them that they got no place to get away to."

Bohannon took a deep breath. "What will happen to them?"

"Oh, some may escape. Disappear into the bush. The rest will end up in jail with their *brata* raskols—if the *kiaps* don't beat them to death first." She disappeared back into the shop.

Gradually, normality was returning to the street. People were resuming what they had been doing before the interruption and dogs were beginning to reemerge from their hiding places. No one seemed especially animated or upset by what had just transpired. Perhaps, Bohannon thought, such occurrences were not that uncommon. Orienting himself, he headed back to where he had parked his rental car. Every now and again, he checked the street behind him. He also found himself watching his fellow pedestrians more closely than ever.

Unbeknownst to him, and entirely unaware that a significant change was taking place even as he walked, he was starting to become acclimated.

IV

Sorley McCracken's house comprised an open understory that served as a carport and storage area, with living quarters above. The open lower floor housed an impressive assortment of machine tools, battered shipping crates, empty beer cartons, cannibalized motorcycle parts, used car and truck tires, and three interlinked cages containing an equal number of live chickens. The electric gate to the walled compound McCracken's domicile shared with several others was closed when Bohannon arrived, but another vehicle entering just ahead of him left it open long enough for him to follow it through with only a scratch to the rear right bumper of the rental car.

The yellow-painted concrete-block house stood off by itself near the very top of the hill, overlooking the harbor. In order to make the steep ascent he had to put the rental car in its lowest gear. Pulling up to the storage area and setting the parking brake, he stepped out behind a white, rusting Toyota hilux that displayed the first stages of advanced automotive decomposition.

At the same time he became aware of a piercing alien wail that rose and fell in muted homage to unknown rhythms. It was coming from within the house.

Easing past the uncatalogued collection of tropical rust on one side and the hilux on the other, he found the downstairs door. There was no bell, no door knocker. Giving the handle a try, he was surprised to find that it was unlocked. When he pushed the door inward, the whine from within struck him full force, the harsh braying assaulting his ears with unalloyed exuberance. At the same time, he recognized it.

Bagpipes.

Howling through the house and shaking the undistinguished pictures on the walls, the skirling strains of "Scotland the Brave" grated on his bones as he mounted the stairs. In the course of his ascent he passed two separate lockable iron grates. Their hinges were welded to steel plates bolted deep in the body of the supporting wall. Each was strong enough to seal off the stairway against anything smaller than an armored personnel carrier.

At the top of the stairs a hallway disappeared off to the right. To the left was a small living room in which windows alternated with bookshelves. One entire wall was taken up with nothing but used hardback editions of Reader's Digest Condensed Books, another with mystery novels. Cheap framed pictures and photographs filled in the gaps. There was a simple coffee table, an entertainment center with TV, stereo, and VCR, and a couple of bamboo rockers padded with cushions.

Parading slowly and not unmajestically back and forth from one end of the room to the other was a scarecrow clad in full Scottish regalia, complete with sporran and silver buckles. Pipes tucked beneath his right arm, reed in mouth, this Ichabod Crane of the western lochs blew full blast into the chanter as if on parade at the Edinburgh Tattoo. It was no wonder he had no immediate neighbors.

Executing a neat martial pivot, he caught sight of Bohannon standing dumbstruck in the hallway, and halted. The reed slipped from his lips and, like a dying calf in a thunderstorm, the skirl of the pipes faded away.

"Who the devil are you, and what are you doing in my house?"

"My name is Bohannon. It was suggested that I . . ."

As he tried to explain, McCracken put down the pipes and reached to his left. From its brackets on the wall he drew down an enormous broadsword. Brandishing the claymore, he advanced, kilt swaying, on the intruder.

"Bugger your suggestions! Nobody breaks into my house and . . . !"

Hands held placatingly out in front of him, Bohannon started to back up. "I didn't break in. The door downstairs was unlocked. So were your stair gates."

The other man halted, looking a bit thunderstruck himself. "Unlocked, you say? Come to think of it, I *was* a bit anxious to put on the kilt and pick up the old pipes. In the rush I expect I could have overlooked a wee chore or two." To his visitor's considerable relief, he turned and placed the ancient sword back on the wall. "What did you say your name was?"

"Steven Bohannon. I wish I could say it's a pleasure to meet you."

"Hold that thought." McCracken indicated the cabinet behind the couch. "There's cold drink in there. I'll be right back." So saying, he brushed past his visitor and vanished down the hallway.

Helping himself to a soft drink from the small refrigerator built into the cabinet, Bohannon killed time studying the pictures on the wall. Some of the photographs weren't half bad. They consisted largely of landscapes and scenes of PNG village life.

I could be in Fiji, he told himself as he moved from picture to picture, *lying in a hammock looking for myself instead of dodging stone age bank robbers and transplanted madmen.*

The madman returned, clad now in khaki bush pants and shirt. Sensibly, he was barefoot. As he spoke, he fumbled at the refrigerator.

"So someone suggested you come see me, eh? About what, Mr. Steve?"

Bohannon sipped his soda. "I need to find a woman."

His host snapped the cap off a stubbie of export. "Don't we all. I'm not a pimp, mate. Nor do I recommend sampling the local wares, regardless of whether your preference extends to light meat, dark, or both. Starting to be plenty of AIDS here, and venereal disease is rampant among the country's, um, freelance businesswomen."

Bohannon tried to conceal his distaste. "I'm not after a quick lay. I'm looking for a particular woman. She arrived here by plane from Mosby this morning. Her name is Tennison."

The mouth of McCracken's bottle halted halfway to his lips. "Tai? You ran into Tai in Mosby?" This realization unleashed a gale of wild laughter from the wide mouth and long, drainage pipe of a throat. Chortling, McCracken sounded like an oboe in drag.

Bohannon restrained himself. It was something he had been forced to work at for some time, and he was very good at it. "You could say that."

The lanky piper came around the couch. He overtopped his guest only by an inch or two, but his attenuated frame gave him the appearance of someone much taller. His exposed forearms were all braided veins and arteries, like heavy twine wrapped in parchment. He wore his dirty brown hair long and tied back in a single ponytail. A gold ring flashed from his left ear while individual eyebrow hairs struck repeated blows for follicular independence, twisting and curling violently in all directions like helectites on the wall of a limestone cave. The mark of fair skin that had spent too much time in the sun, threatening dark splotches mottled his forehead, arms, and legs. In attitude, appearance, and attire, he had all the hallmarks of a first-class character.

Or, Bohannon was starting to learn, your average long-term PNG expat.

The laughter faded, much as the bagpipes had. "What is it you want with Tai?" Small, sharp eyes peered out at him from beneath those anarchic brows. Bohannon had seen eyes like that before—in zoos. They belonged to small, swift predators. Lie but once to such a man and he knew he would find himself ushered swiftly out the door.

"We had a—relationship. She borrowed some money from me and I need to have it repaid."

If possible, the cackling laughter that followed was louder than ever. "Relationship, was it? Borrowed, was it? You mean, Mr. Steve, that the bonny beauteous Tai got you drunk, or stoned, or both, fuck-ethed your brains out, and when you finally drifted off into the arms of Morpheus, relieved you of any loose change."

"Yeah, that's about it," Bohannon confessed helplessly.

Moving closer, McCracken threw a comradely arm around his guest's shoulders. Fingers like spider's legs squeezed hard.

"Don't feel too bad, mate. You're in select company, you are. I half envy you, I do. The hidden mysteries of dear sweet Tai's panties are a province of PNG I've long held a firm desire to visit. Unfortunately, she considers me a friend." Taking a step back, he eyed his visitor quizzically. "Riddle me this, if you will: is it better to be a friend to a beautiful woman and never touch her, or an enemy and well-laid?"

"What you're saying is that you won't help me find her." Bohannon had always been reasonably adept at reading between the lines, and these were about as far apart as Lae was from Mosby.

The comforting arm slithered free of his shoulders. "That is right, Mr. Steve. I will not. Chaste in my presence though she may be, dear Tai is a friend still. I will see her long after and many times subsequent to your departure from these fetid, stinking shores. So why the fuck should I lift a finger to help you?"

Bohannon thought a moment, then dug in his pocket. "I have two cards: American Express and Visa. Both gold."

"What, no platinum?" But the predator eyes flashed, alert now to the scent of natural prey.

"I promise I won't turn her in to the police. I just want my money back. It's a matter of principle."

McCracken rolled his eyes. "Oh, Gawd! Robbie Burns save us all from principle! Tell me it's the fucking money, dickhead, and maybe I'll believe you."

"Okay." Bohannon was indifferent to favored motivations. "It's the money, then."

"There now, ain't that better? Didn't that feel good? As for going to the police, all a woman like Tai has to do is arch an eyebrow or twist her hip and every kiap between here and the Fly will melt into a mindless puddle at her feet. 'Going to the police?' Where she's concerned that's less threat than none, mate." He paused—thinking, appraising, balancing. Weighing maybe-friendship against for-sure money.

"She has a little place here in town. Isn't there often, but if you're right about her flying in just this morning, maybe you'll get lucky. For another two hundred kina in addition to my regular guideabout fee I'll mediate on your behalf. See if I can keep a knife out of your guts, anyway. Anything more than talk, that's up to you." His expression darkened and his voice fell to a mutter. "Of course, you might have to deal with Stenhammer. That I won't do for you. You're bloody well on your own there."

"Fair enough." Bohannon agreed even though they had yet to settle on a full price for McCracken's services. With his search coming to an end and feeling good about himself, he found himself looking forward to the forthcoming confrontation with unexpected eagerness. Later, in Fiji and beyond, the small sense of accomplishment would grow. It was a sensation he had experienced too little of, too long ago. A small triumph that would be gratefully accepted. "Who's Stenhammer?"

McCracken looked up sharply. He seemed preoccupied. " 'Who's Stenhammer?' Who indeed? One might as well ask 'what's Stenhammer?' What's a mountain, friend? Dark and brooding in the night, difficult and hard to reach in the light of day. How mathematically do you cube son-of-a-bitch?"

Bohannon didn't flinch. "You're afraid of this guy."

"*Afraid?*" McCracken's voice rose briefly before falling, slipping, sliding, back to normal. "No, not afraid. Not afraid. Something else, maybe. Like Stenhammer, something else." Abruptly, he turned away, retreating into a space as private as if shuttered by doors that had just slammed shut.

"I'll meet you downstairs. We'll take the truck."

"That thing runs?" Tact be damned—Bohannon could not keep himself from commenting on the vehicle's condition.

McCracken did not appear injured by his visitor's comment. "Like a drunken demon, Mr. Steve. Ride in her for more than ten kilometers and she'll start to carbonate your kidneys, but she gets there."

As if to give the lie to its owner's claim, the hilux smoked and rattled outrageously when started. But it did not die in the driveway, nor on the road beyond the electric gate, nor on the pitted asphalt that wound down the hill like shavings of lava. During the twelve minutes it took to reach their destination, a concrete box of an apartment complex that overlooked the harbor, McCracken rambled on incessantly, endlessly entertaining and informative. In that time he also managed to divulge absolutely nothing of importance about himself. It was a soliloquy most significant for its omissions.

On the third floor of the nondescript building (no elevator) they walked to the end of a hallway open at both ends to allow the occasional breeze off the ocean to blow through. With the smell of salt, dead fish, and seagull shit crinkling in their nostrils, they stopped outside a white steel door. McCracken knocked. The hallway was dark and lifeless, reminding Bohannon of low-rent warrens in New York. An eye must have peered through the single peephole, because the door opened inward a couple of feet.

The woman standing in the gap did not have the rough features of a Highlander, but was even shorter than those Bohannon had seen. She was, in fact, the shortest person he had encountered since his arrival in the country. Yet she was a perfectly formed female, probably in her early thirties. Though she was only three and a half feet tall, the huge curly puff-ball of a natural added another foot to her overall height. She exhibited a pleasant, green, short-sleeved dress with a floral print, handsome black shoes, and impeccable English.

"Ah, Mr. McCracken. And a friend. What is it you want?"

McCracken replied with obvious fondness. "Hello, Rose. We've come to see Miss Tai."

"Ah, that is a pity. She was here earlier, but now she is gone."

The incipient triumph Bohannon had been savoring during the drive over evaporated like a snowcone in downtown Port Moresby. "Gone? When is she coming back?"

The elfin housekeeper looked up at him. "I don't know, sir. She did not say." Her gaze shifted to McCracken. "You remember, Sorley, that Tai never knows herself how long she will be away from home."

"Seems to me like she left in a bleedin' hurry, she did." McCracken squatted, a gesture that put him eye level with the housekeeper—if she *was* merely a housekeeper and not something else, Bohannon suddenly found himself wondering.

"This nice American gentleman has important business with Miss Tai. I would take it as a personal favor, I would, if you could give us some idea as to where she's taken herself off to. Come on now, Rose, out with it. Is she working with Heavilift again up at Hagen? Or is it another oil party she's guiding?"

Bohannon started. "Tennison is a guide?"

McCracken was clearly amused. "I thought you knew that much, at least, Mr. Steve. Tai speaks fluent Pidgin as well as some Motu and several of the Highland languages. She's always running geologists and oil company boys deep into the bush. Or did you think she made her living doing nothing but mugging easy marks like yourself?"

"I didn't—I didn't think. It's a recurrent failing, I'm afraid. Right up there with jumping to conclusions."

Rose was looking from one white man to the next. "I hope I am not understanding you gentlemen right."

"It's not a big thing, Rose. Be a good lass and tell us where she's gone off to."

The woman's mouth twisted into a half smile. "Sure I'll tell you. Why not? It won't do you any good anyway." The smile devolved into a knowing sneer. "She's gone looking for Stenhammer."

McCracken straightened, a pained expression on his face. "That's what I was wondering. I didn't think he'd come down here. Never has before." He had the look of a man angry at forces he could not control and did not understand.

Rose nodded knowingly. "I know. I told her too, to stop running after that crazy man. I've told her before. But you know Tai. The only person she'll listen to is herself, and then not all the time."

"Excuse me," put in Bohannon, "but I'm feeling a little left out here. I still don't know who this Stenhammer person is."

McCracken's pain turned to disgust. "It doesn't matter. If she's gone looking for him we'll never find her. Sorry, mate, but I did my part. If you want, I'll drive you back to your hotel, or to the airport, or anywhere else in town you'd like to be dropped off. Our business is done." He turned to leave.

Without thinking, or he might not have done it, Bohannon stepped in front of the other man. He found he did not care about the possible consequences of his action. He did not even stop to wonder why he was suddenly so upset, or angry. For one of the few times in his life he had reacted without thinking. Perversely, it did wonders for his confidence.

McCracken just stared at him, fire beginning to rise behind his little feral eyes. His tone was coolly menacing "Was there something else then, mate?" He pronounced every syllable very carefully.

Bohannon took a moment to consider what he wanted to say before replying. "As a matter of fact, there is. You're damned right there is. I'm not going to give up on this now."

"Right then," McCracken said curtly. "Good luck to you."

"No, you don't understand." Bohannon edged sideways, continuing to block the other man's path. "I *can't* give up on this now."

"Sure you can, mate." The guide smiled thinly. "Just turn around—and leave."

"No. I want—I need—to get some kind of satisfaction out of this. You don't understand. Tennison—she took more than my money. Another place, another time in my life, it wouldn't have mattered so much. But right now—I have to pursue this to a better conclusion. I have to find her. I have to find out some things about myself."

The self-possessed McCracken was a bit taken aback. "Dear me! So then maybe I was wrong, and maybe you were telling me the truth all along. It isn't just the money after all. Is it, Mr. Steve?"

Retreating a step, Bohannon looked away from him. "No, it's not. Not anymore. Not at this point in time."

"What you're asking for is crazy. But then, I've never been noted for having any great store of common sense meself." He turned back to Rose, who had been watching and listening attentively. "So Tai's gone Stenhammer-hunting. I don't suppose she happened to say where?"

"I think you are both loony white men," the maybe-housekeeper retorted. "Not as loony as the man Stenhammer, but loony enough."

"That's right," agreed McCracken readily, "and you know that the mad should always be humored, don't you? Now, where is she off to this time? Mendi? Porgera?"

Rose gave ground grudgingly, but under McCracken's practiced coaxings and flatterings eventually gave up the information they needed.

"She said something about picking up supplies in Tari. I told her not to go there. It's always bad up there. The Enga are crazy, but the Huli are crazier still. But she didn't listen to me. She hardly ever does. A pretty woman like Miss Tennison going into that country alone is asking for trouble."

McCracken looked satisfied. "Since when did that ever stop Tai from going anywhere or doing anything? Thanks, Rose. You're a luv."

"You come back in one piece, Sorley. You hear me?" Rising on tiptoe, she reached out to draw him close and planted a solid, wet kiss on his mouth. Nor did McCracken seem in the least surprised by the gesture.

Deciding that in this particular instance a little tact might really be called for, Bohannon chose not to comment as the two men left the building and walked back toward the parked, locked hilux.

"So tell me about this Stenhammer person Tai is trying to find. Is he a geologist or oil engineer like the others you mentioned?"

McCracken did not smile, or grin, or chuckle. His expression was as somber as his reply. "That's just a story to cover whatever it is she's really up to. When she doesn't want anyone to know what she's doing, she says that she's looking for Stenhammer. He doesn't actually exist, you see. He's a figment of her imagination, a convenient cover-up for activities she doesn't want anyone to know about."

"Oh." Bohannon waited for his host to unlock the hilux. "So what do I do now? Buy a ticket to Tari, I guess."

"You could do that. Lae to Mt. Hagen, Hagen to Tari." McCracken started the engine but did not pull out of the complex's parking lot. "There's three flights a week, though you'd best check first. The schedules change every month. They also fluctuate according to the pilots' moods. And then there's the weather in the Highlands. Of course, even if you make it to Tari you still won't find her. Not if she's headed out into the bush. Try following her there and you'll end up lost or dead within twenty-four hours."

"Even so, I'm going to take a shot at it."

"Then you'd best find yourself a guide who knows the area, the people, and the language. Pidgin, not one of the couple hundred locals."

Bohannon nodded sagely, taking his time before replying. "You wouldn't happen to know anyone who might fill that bill, would you?"

McCracken pursed his lips, one lean arm resting on the wheel as he stared straight ahead. "I might. If the price were right, of course."

A resigned as well as newly determined Bohannon settled back against the worn gray fabric of the seat. "Of course."

He did not want to wait another day, but McCracken absolutely refused to fly in the evening.

"Listen to me, mate. My plane, she's a tough little bitch, but these mountains hereabouts go straight up from out of the water to over twelve thousand feet. A few go higher. Morning's the best time for flying in this bastard country. The winds are lighter and the landing strips less likely to be clagged in."

"Clagged in?"

"By clouds. You ask some of the blokes who fly for Air Niugini or the Missionary Air Force and they'll tell you that New Guinea's probably the cloudiest place in the world. About once a month somebody slams into a mountain he didn't see. Then a government team has to go out and scrape his remains off some unnamed cliff-face. It's like they say—there are only two kinds of pilots here: experienced pilots, and dead pilots. It's a bad business when somebody goes down. I'm not risking my plane or myself. You want to die young, go hire somebody else. If you can find someone else."

So they waited until morning, even though it put that much more time and distance between himself and the fast-moving redhead.

Except for the local hangers-on who had nothing better to do, Lae International airport was utterly deserted at 6 A.M. Intense sunshine unadulterated by pollution streamed over towering peaks to illuminate the grass-fringed runway and empty buildings. All was not silent, however. Laughing, enthusiastic children were engaged in an energetic game of soccer inside the spacious terminal, using the professionally polished floor for a playing field. Like dark eyes, the windows of empty shopfronts watched over the youthful exertions, the dirty glass reflecting a future that in this part of the world seemed always to be one step behind every new promise.

Bohannon lowered his pack from his back and swallowed as he caught his first glimpse of McCracken's aircraft. "I thought it would be—bigger."

"What did you expect?"

"I'm not sure. A twin otter, at least. Maybe a Grumman."

His guide's gaze narrowed. "Know a little about planes, do you?"

"A little." Bohannon bent to examine the underbelly of the craft.

"When's the last time this Cessna underwent a full mechanical inspection?"

McCracken chortled delightedly as he unsnapped the cargo door in the nose and tossed his own kit in. "Probably when she left the factory back in the States. Don't you worry, she'll get us there. I always travel prepared for any emergency. Climb in." Locking down the luggage compartment, he ducked beneath the fuselage and opened the pilot's door. There was no entrance on the passenger side.

At least it's a twin-engine, Bohannon thought as he dumped his pack on the rear seat. Behind it, the narrowing fuselage was stuffed full of irregular lumps and odd shapes. Supplies, he decided. Maybe McCracken was right when he claimed to be ready for any emergency. The more he saw of his guide's plane, the more Bohannon hoped he was telling the truth.

As he settled himself into the co-pilot's seat and hunted for the catch on the safety harness, his guide bent himself like a wire and unfolded legs and arms in the pilot's seat. His head came near to scraping the ceiling.

While the left engine caught and silvery props began to spin, Bohannon studied the instrument panel. There was barely enough room for his legs between the front of the seat and the half wheel. Some of the gauges were missing their protective glass. Black holes gaped in the console where others had been removed. A wide slot had been cut to permit the installation of a CD player. He prayed nothing vital had been taken out to make room for it.

With both engines yammering like rabid lawnmowers, McCracken donned his headset and indicated to his passenger that he should do the same. The expat's voice sounded clearly over the earpieces.

"Don't worry about a thing, mate! I've flown into Tari plenty of times."

Bohannon addressed the wire mike that hung suspended in front of his mouth. "Ever have any trouble?"

"Had to abort a few times because of bad weather. According to the morning report we should be all right, but we can always lay over at Mendi, or if it's really bad, at Hagen. Don't want to play around with the winds at Tari. Collapsed the nose gear once. Downdraft shoved my face right into the runway. That's where the scrape under the front end came from. That's where I got this." He touched the side of his own nose, which had sustained worse damage than the plane's in the same accident. Bohannon was not reassured.

At least, he thought, they did not have to worry about conflicting air traffic. There was not another plane in sight.

As soon as the sturdy old Cessna cleared the end of the runway, McCracken pulled her into a breathtakingly steep climb, pulling the wheel toward him nearly as far as it would go. Bohannon stood it as long as he could before commenting.

"Isn't this a bit steep? Aren't you afraid of stalling her out?"

McCracken leaned toward him. "Not a bit of it, mate. She's used to it." He pointed. "Still want me to drop her nose?"

Directly ahead lay what could only be described as vertical jungle. The sheer rock walls shot straight up out of the valley, from sea level to heights of ten thousand feet and more. God's arrows planted in the earth. Resolving to say nothing more about the business of flying unless it proved absolutely unavoidable, Bohannon swallowed hard and pressed himself back into his seat, trying to shrink into the worn leather.

They cleared the saddle between two blade-like mountain peaks by a hundred feet. Maybe.

McCracken was grinning. "I call these flower-picking flights. That's when you can lean out the window and pick the flowers off the tops of the trees as you go by."

"Beautiful country," was all Bohannon could find to say. His throat was constricted.

"Oy, magnificent, ain't it? No place like it in the world!" Straight ahead lay mountains higher than the ones they had just left behind. Above them, thick white clouds were already beginning to build.

They did not fly over the mountains so much as through them, McCracken weaving with practiced skill between the highest peaks like a skateboarder slaloming lampposts. In lieu of a map, the guide followed the river valleys northwestward. Much time passed, during which they saw not another plane, either private or commercial.

They were less than an hour into the flight when Bohannon noticed that the needle on the fuel gauge for the right tank was sitting on Empty.

McCracken did not even bother to look at it. "She's not empty, mate. She's broken. Been meaning to get a new one, but parts' prices hereabouts are fucking extortionate."

"So how do you know when the tank's empty?"

The pilot shrugged. "Easy. The engine coughs and starts to die.

The left gauge works fine, so I know how much fuel is left there. I just mix the tank flow and divide by two. Relax, mate; she'll be right."

Bohannon leaned back and stared out the window, straining to see between the scratches. Huge rainforest trees carpeted the mountainside off to his right, many of them higher than he was. "What else doesn't work on this plane?"

McCracken's expression turned serious. "The truth now, mate: do you really want to know?"

"No. I suppose not."

As if eager to supply an answer anyway, the Cessna dipped suddenly to the left. Every muscle in Bohannon's body went taut and his right hand clutched the side of his seat in a death grip. The plane steadied, then dipped again.

"McCracken! What the hell's wrong?"

The pilot's voice betrayed little emotion, but the easygoing conviviality had vanished. That in itself, Bohannon suspected, was reason enough to be concerned.

"Main left flap is loose. Things rust fast here, you know."

"Loose?" Bohannon's eyes widened. "What do you mean, loose? Loose like in a little loose, or a lot loose?"

"I mean it's trying to fall off. If it does, we'll go into a death spin when I try to put her down."

The color drained from his passenger's face. "I don't know much about flying, but that doesn't sound real good."

"It's not." McCracken's tone bordered dangerously on grim. "We'll have to put down and fix it."

Ashen-faced, Bohannon peered through the scarred and stained glass. "Put down? Where? There's nothing out here but mountains and jungle!"

"That's where you're wrong, mate. There's grass emergency strips all over this country." Reaching below his seat, he dug out a huge map and unfolded it, blocking most of the front window. Bohannon frantically batted down the corner that interrupted his view. Directly ahead lay the highest peaks they had yet encountered.

"Jesus Christ, man, how can you see where you're going?"

"Can't," McCracken replied tersely. He was wholly involved in the map. "Don't have to. I know where I'm going." The plane lurched violently to port and he corrected it neatly, steering with his knees. "Mopingo strip should be just ahead of us. I'm going to put down there. We'll repair the bitch and be on our way." To Bohannon's immense relief he refolded the map and shoved it back beneath his seat.

"Should be just off to starboard. Have a look, mate. We're going down." Pushing in on the wheel, he dropped the plane's nose sharply.

Bohannon fought back fear and panic in equal measure. Around them, the mountains grew higher and more forbidding still as the plane plunged toward the emerald labyrinth below.

"I don't see a goddamn thing!" He felt no shame at the fear in his voice, nor did he care what McCracken thought. He was scared shitless.

"It's right there, mate! Straight on, now."

Bohannon had still been looking to his right. Shifting his gaze, he saw what appeared to be a narrow gash in the side of a mountain. It was impossibly tiny. The near end terminated in a sheer cliff while the far end . . . the far end ran up the mountainside in a rising curve. A few round huts clung to the steep slopes nearby. Astonishingly, McCracken was aiming directly for this potato patch in the rainforest.

An incredulous Bohannon turned to the pilot. "Surely that's not it? You're not going to try and land there?"

"Too right I am, mate. That's Mopingo. You might want to hang on. She can be a bit tricky."

"*A bit tricky?*" he screamed. It had no effect on the guide, who was concentrating on his flying. The engines sounded hesitant as he throttled down. At somewhere around a hundred miles an hour, the mountainside, the huts, and the great rainforest trees were coming up fast. In the middle of it all was a landing strip that was much, much too short.

"Easy now, little lady." McCracken brought the nose of the plane up slightly and pushed down on the throttle. Out his window, the loose left flap shook wildly as it was lowered, threatening to fall completely off the wing and send them into an uncontrollable leftward spin. If that happened they would come in a few feet short—and smash into the raw flank of the mountain below the landing strip.

They were too low, Bohannon thought wildly. They weren't going to make it!

The wheels touched down. At what seemed the same instant, the unyielding mountain ahead loomed directly in front of them. As soon as the wheels hit grass McCracken reversed the engines. They roared madly, complaining at what was being demanded of them.

"Oh God!" Bohannon threw up his hands and turned his head.

V

No aircraft could have slowed to a stop in so short a space and the Cessna was no exception. But Mopingo airstrip had been designed with that in mind. Reaching the end of the level runway, the plane kept going right up the manicured slope, climbing the mountain even as the increasing grade reduced its speed. Turning hard to the right, McCracken sent the plane swooping back down onto the grassy field it had just landed upon. It was not a maneuver normally taught to pilots in aviation school, but McCracken brought it off just fine.

When the little plane finally coasted to a stop, it was perhaps ten yards from the front end of the strip and the sheer drop-off into the valley far below.

Chest heaving, Bohannon slowly lowered his arms from his face as McCracken turned and taxied back toward the hillside. "Bonny bit of a rush that is, fair dinkum. Only way they could get a strip in here, you see. Have to use the upslope to reduce speed. Bit like landing on an aircraft carrier, I should imagine. Only harder."

Bohannon fought to slow his breathing. "What—what happens when it's time to take off?"

"Oh, that's much easier, mate. We just rev the shit out of the engines and let rip. Of course, you don't have enough distance to get up proper speed, so you drop like a stone when you run out of runway and off the end. The trick is to get up to climbing speed before you hit the first trees at the base of the mountain. No worries. Departure from Mopingo international is a lot less touch and go than arrival." Removing his headset, he unstrapped himself from the flight harness as the engines whirled to a halt.

"It doesn't *sound* like it's any easier." Turning to his right to check out the view through the side window, a startled Bohannon found himself inches from a face that was dark, wide-eyed, and exuberantly painted. The sight would have caused him a good deal more apprehension if not for the fact that its owner appeared to be between ten and twelve years old.

Red and black streaks coursed down her cheeks while her nose and forehead were painted bright blue. She was smiling excitedly and he could hear her giggle through the air vent at the base of the window. Behind her, children less bold but equally garishly made-up strained to see past their leader into the cockpit.

When McCracken's door refused to yield to gentle persuasion he kicked it open, his booted foot making loud banging noises against the metal until it finally swung wide. Overlapping dents in the metal suggested this was a common procedure for exiting the plane.

"Village kids. They see an average of maybe one white face a month up here. How does it feel to be the tourist attraction instead of the tourist for a change?" His arms dug deep into a duffel behind his seat. "Repairs shouldn't take but a couple of minutes, mate. Why not have a smoko?"

"I don't smoko—smoke." Bohannon was as fascinated by the faces pressing up against the glass as they were by him. "But this seat's a bit cramped. I will have a stretch."

Crawling over the seat McCracken had vacated, he followed the pilot outside. The mountain air was warm, bracing, and utterly clean, while the oxygen the surrounding rainforest exuded more than compensated for the thinness of atmosphere at altitude. While McCracken worked on the damaged flap, Bohannon strolled around to the front of the Cessna.

The landing strip and its attendant village were completely isolated from the outside world, hemmed in on all sides by sky-scraping, impassable mountain ridges and peaks. No roads penetrated this verdant tropical vastness, no telephone line, not even a trading trail. With the exception of the airstrip, these people were as isolated as they had been since the beginning of time. It was a state of affairs repeated a thousand times over throughout the length and breadth of this remarkable country. More astonishing still, anthropologists hypothesized that dozens of similar tribes remained hidden in the mountains, still awaiting their first contact with the rest of mankind.

And each, he had read in the guidebook, spoke a different language. More than seven hundred of them logged to date, and still counting. There were places where tribes on opposite sides of the same river were unable to communicate with one another because each spoke not just a different dialect, but a completely alien tongue.

Beyond the nose of the plane, the end of the runway and its attendant sheer drop seemed much too close. He would have hiked over to the edge for a better look except that he was now completely surrounded by inquisitive, giggling, bright-eyed kids, all of whom were stark naked except for their face paint and an occasional necklace or bracelet. The curious adults who had begun to arrive from the village and its gardens of sweet potato and beans wore little more. The women were topless, though a few wore skirts of grass. A couple of the men, the tallest of whom topped out at perhaps five and a half feet, had on torn hand-me-down shorts, gifts from visiting missionaries. Most wore nothing more than gourd penis shields on their genitals or in more familiar Highland style, bunches of leaves around their waists.

Making his way back around the plane, Bohannon found McCracken hard at work and inquired as to how it was going.

"She's coming along, mate, she's coming along. Won't be much longer."

Bohannon indicated the gathering men and asked about their attire.

The pilot grunted as he worked. "See that stuff around their backsides? That's arse-grass. Trade Pidgin may sound funny, but it can be a very expressive language. These poor blokes, they've had contact with civilization for less than a year. I remember when the missionary service proposed the airstrip. Everybody said it couldn't be done, but those missionaries take their guidance from God, not aeronautical engineers. First bloke what landed here gets my nod as a bloody brave pilot."

Bohannon looked toward the cliff and the encircling mountains. Dense cloud was beginning to congress around the highest peaks, thickening to the color and consistency of whipped vanilla as it slowly began to work its way downward. Though no meteorologist, he guessed that if they did not leave within the hour, they ran the risk, as McCracken had put it, of being "clagged in."

One of the older girls, innocent as a polemic by Rousseau in her beguiling nudity, stepped forward and reached into the bilum she wore slung over her back. It was fashioned entirely of natural brown fiber, devoid of the incandescent artificial dyes favored in metropolitan centers like Mosby and Lae. Bringing out carefully cupped hands, she thrust them unexpectedly upward.

Magnificence exploded in his face.

His mouth opened in an oh of awe as the butterfly, iridescent dark green with black highlights, fluttered free before his eyes. Numbed by the cold of morning, it did not yet have the energy to fly away. Instead, it settled gently onto his outstretched forearm, slowly opening and closing its wings, exercising as it gathered strength from the rising sun. Its wings would have completely covered a good-size dinner plate.

McCracken glanced over from his work. "That's a Queen Alexandra's birdwing. Biggest damn butterfly in the world."

Bohannon was utterly entranced. "It's fantastic. I've never seen anything like it."

"That's because there ain't anything else like it, mate. Just you mind they don't offer to show you any of the local spiders. Nasty buggers, they are. The bird-eaters are as big as that butterfly." He turned back to his work.

Bohannon watched the living jewel display itself until the girl gently retrieved her pet and returned it to the bilum. Seeing his interest, other children pressed close to show off their own prizes, from enormous incandescent blue butterflies to a Hercules beetle five inches long and two high that felt like it weighed half a pound when placed on the back of Bohannon's hand. When he indicated that he had finished his observation it took two of the children to pry its powerful, hooked legs free of his skin.

As the parade of amazing entomological wonders continued, he noticed that among the adults two men in the back of the crowd stood out from the rest. They were slightly taller than the others, had notably finer facial features, and carried bilums in which natural fiber mixed with dyed string. Their faces were identically painted; outlined in white, with splashes of yellow covering noses and foreheads, red circles around the eyes, and red stripes across the face. Their headdresses, consisting of woven fibrous bands into which were bound long, protruding blue, black, and green bird-of-paradise feathers and the yellow-gold half moons of trade kina shell, were exquisite.

McCracken picked them out immediately. "Those boys aren't Mopingo. Pretty tall for Highland folk. Maybe Chimbu, maybe something else. Up here, they could be anything."

"Their headgear is amazing."

McCracken let out a derisive snort. "That's nothing. Wait 'til you see some Huli."

"Think they'd mind if I took a closer look?"

The pilot considered. "Probably not, or they wouldn't have come in this close. Would've kept their distance if it were privacy they wanted. Just be ready for them to stare and pick back at you."

"That's fair enough." He moved forward, wading through the crowd.

"This is very nice, very pretty." Careful not to make any sudden gestures, he reached up and gently felt of the otherworldly feathers. "Bird-of-paradise?"

The man smiled broadly, obviously pleased at the attention. Attracting admiration, after all, was the clear purpose of such elaborate headgear. When Bohannon shook his head apologetically at the mention of a name, the man followed up with a distinctive, loud whistle that was almost a cawing sound. Children laughed delightedly while the local men nodded approvingly and murmured among themselves.

Bohannon continued in like fashion, until he had a name and sound for the former owner of each different feather. Then he started in on the second man, whose headgear differed somewhat from that of his companion. If anything, this individual entered into the spirit of the occasion with even more zest than his friend.

Finished with the headdress, a pleased Bohannon peered around the man in an attempt to see the contents of his bilum. Divining his intent, the traveler willingly swung the string bag around and pulled it wide so his new friend could get a better look at the interior. The traveling sack contained sweet potato, a dead bird with incredible orange breast feathers that Bohannon did not recognize, a long knife or digging tool fashioned from the bleached femur of a cassowary, dried tree kangaroo meat, and something else. This occupied no place of distinction nor had it been separated in any way from the rest of the baggage. Bohannon looked at it, and looked at it, as if the act of staring might transform it into something other than what it was. It was not a movie special effect, nor had it been bought at a discount card-and-gag store.

It was a cooked human arm.

Separated cleanly at the shoulder, it had been folded at the elbow, the better to fit neatly into the bilum. Burnt blacker than the rest of the limb, the fingers were frozen in half clenched position. The two smaller ones were missing.

Trail food, he thought as he backed away. Got to have something to nibble on. His heart pounded against his chest and he was sure everyone—the two travelers, the wide-eyed children, and the assembled men and women of the village—could hear it. Without realizing it or knowing how, he kept a smile frozen on his face. Nodding appreciatively, his new-found acquaintances smiled back, just as friendly as friendly could be. Bohannon's greatest horror was that their next gesture would be an offer to share their supplies with him.

When the existence of the arm was pointed out to McCracken, the pilot accepted the news with nonchalant interest.

"You don't see much of that anymore." He scrutinized the two visiting tribesmen appraisingly. "Only in the remote mountains, like this, and in the backwaters of the Sepik. Old habits die hard. So do old tastes. When we get to Tari, you'll see a fair number of old men. Remember, the whole of the Highlands had no contact with the outside world until a couple of Aussies looking for gold made it into the mountains back in the early 1930's. Cannibalism and head-hunting were widely practiced right up until the missionaries and the government kiaps embarked on an organized effort to stamp it out." He turned back to his work.

"But this, this is too bizarre! There's no such thing as cannibalism anymore. Primitive savagery, yes. Everywhere from Rwanda to Bosnia. But the victors don't eat the vanquished."

McCracken nodded in the direction of the two friendly, smiling travelers. "Evidently somebody's neglected to tell these blokes. Speaking for meself, I never understood what the big deal was. Meat's meat. Tried it myself, once."

Bohannon eyed the pilot uncertainly. "You're putting me on."

"Nope. Wouldn't do that. Now, don't look at me like that, mate. It's not as if I knew the bloke. And he was already dead. Rather like pork, he tasted. It was a bit of an honor to be asked to join in. The old boy in charge of the ceremonial feasting told me that in the days of his youth they preferred a woman to eat. Higher percentage of fat, you see, and as they didn't have much of that in their diet, it was something of a luxury." He nodded toward the pair of visitors, whose smiles were as wide and open and genuine as ever.

"If you'd like to give it a try I'm sure they'd be glad to trade with you for a tin of *ambus bulmakau*. That's corned beef, to you." He nodded toward the interior of the plane. "I think I've got some in a case near the back."

"Jesus, you're serious, aren't you?"

McCracken shrugged. "Suit yourself. Chances are you'll never get another opportunity."

"I'll pass anyway, thank you very much." Which would be tastier, he found himself wondering in spite of himself? Forearm, bicep, or fingers? With an effort, he fought down the gorge rising in his stomach. "How are you coming with that wing?"

"Almost done. There's a pair of scissors on my seat. Be a good bloke and hand 'em over to me so I don't have to let go here."

"Sure." Reaching back into the plane, Bohannon found the scissors and passed them across.

"Hold this end here." Bohannon complied as the scissors snipped. "There, that'll do 'er until we get back to Lae." McCracken climbed down off the wing.

Bohannon blinked at the repair. "Wait a minute. That's all you used? Duct tape? You fixed the wing with duct tape?" Familiar strips of steel-gray fabric now stood out starkly against the white metal.

McCracken was wiping his hands with an oily rag. "Sure did, mate. Wonderful stuff. Or did you expect me to pull a welding kit out of my hat?"

"Of course not, but—duct tape?"

The guide was already heading for his seat. "You don't like it, you fix it. Me, I'm out of here. Say good-bye to your friends." He snickered teasingly. "I'd think twice about waving. They might take a liking to your hand."

"You're a real funny asshole, Sorley, you know that? A real laugh riot."

"So I've been told mate, so I've been told." Chuckling to himself, he stood aside while his passenger crawled into the plane ahead of him. Following, he bade farewell to the assembled villagers and visitors. Those few who had picked up a couple of words of Pidgin from visiting missionaries spoke to the others, whereupon the assembly scattered, screaming and laughing, as the port engine caught and turned over.

"Remember now, mate," McCracken reminded Bohannon as both men donned their green plastic headsets, "there's likely to be a bit of a drop when we go over the edge." Bohannon chewed on his lower lip and did not reply.

The pilot revved the engines until the Cessna shook, spitting RPM's and straining for release. The tail was right up against the curving back of the runway. With a cry that was halfway between a war whoop and a drunken holler, McCracken let the props have their release.

Accompanied by cheering, waving villagers and children who

raced it the length of the landing strip, the plane roared down the grass. When it reached the end of the runway, it shot out into clear, humid air and, exactly as McCracken had predicted, dropped like a stone. Bohannon closed his eyes and held his breath.

They fell for what seemed like an eternity but was only seconds, not enough time for even a small part of his life to flash before him. Then they leveled off and began to rise, climbing slowly but steadily, as the landing gear threatened to clip the tops of the tallest trees. Something black, feathered, and wondrous burst from the top of a towering klinkii pine and soared toward a companion tree off in the distance. The bird's head was a runaway dream, a hallucinogenic avian phantasm.

"*Kokomo!* That's hornbill to you, mate." As he rolled back the half wheel, McCracken banked sharply to the left. Bohannon held his breath, but except for a few frayed ends that snapped vigorously in the air flow, the duct tape held fast. Circling out of the gorge, the Cessna scrambled to gain altitude.

At seven thousand six hundred feet, a satisfied McCracken leveled off and resumed their original heading.

"Not bad for a ten-minute wing job, wouldn't you say, mate? Calls for a bit of a celebration." He thrust a thumb over his right shoulder. "There's a cooler full of stubbies under the sleeping bag. Be a right bloke and pinch us a couple, will you?"

Bohannon nodded, resumed breathing more or less normally, and slipped out of his harness. Moving about in the confined space was not easy, but he managed. Shoving the sleeping bag aside, he reached for the cooler's handle.

The handle twitched.

"Holy shit!" Jerking sharply backward, his butt slammed into the co-pilot's wheel. With a complaisant roar, the plane dove sharply downward.

"Christ Almighty, man, watch your ass! Sit down!"

Bohannon complied, panting hard. McCracken fought for and quickly regained control of the plane. Any semblance of humor had fled from his face.

"Don't do that again, mate. Next time I may not have room to pull 'er out. Now, what the bloody hell happened?"

"The handle on the cooler cover. It's alive."

"Handle? There ain't no bloody handle. Here, take the stick."

Bohannon gaped at him. "Say what?"

"I said take the stick! Just hold her steady and level. Any idiot can do that. Even you."

In no mood to argue, his passenger settled himself back down in the co-pilot's seat. Putting both hands on the half wheel, he felt it tremble slightly as McCracken relinquished control.

"That's it, mate. That's fine. Just hold her steady like that."

Bohannon replied without moving and without taking his eyes from the ragged, mountainous, cloud-clogged panorama dead ahead. "What happens if we start to bounce?"

"Bounce with her, ya daft lump of useless lung!" As his upper half disappeared in back, Bohannon heard him fumbling about.

"What is it?" Bohannon wanted to turn to see what was going on but did not dare. As it turned out, he did not have to. Settling himself back into the pilot's seat, McCracken held something in his hands.

"I have to admit, mate, she's a beaut. Haven't seen one this big in a long time."

Realizing that he was not going to see much of anything if he didn't turn his head, Bohannon looked slowly to his left.

Resting on the pilot's arm was the creature he had mistaken for the handle of the beer cooler and nearly grabbed. The woody brown body was a good two inches in diameter and no less than two and a half feet long from back feet to questing antenna. It rocked slowly back and forth as it considered its new perch.

"Must've crawled in while we were working outside. Or else one of the kids snuck it for a gag." With his free hand McCracken gently stroked the incredible back. "Consider yourself lucky, Mr. Steve. This morning you saw the world's biggest butterfly. Now you've met the world's longest insect."

Bohannon was still wary. Where he came from, insects were something to be squashed on sight, sprayed, swatted, or otherwise disposed of, preferably with as little personal physical contact as possible. They were not to be coddled or petted. But then, he had never seen one big enough to walk on a dog leash before, either.

"So it's harmless?"

"As harmless as your senile old grandmother, mate. This here is *Hemachus*, a stick insect. I told you, they grow their bugs big here." He toyed with the inoffensive creature for a few moments longer before returning it to the rear of the plane. "We'll give it a lift and put it out at Tari. It'll do just fine up there—if one of the locals doesn't catch it and eat it."

Bohannon repressed the urge to keep checking over his shoulder to see if the somnolent monster was lumbering slowly in the direction of his neck. "Nice to hear that something around here is harmless. By the way, I'd be real happy if you'd take back the controls."

"What? Oh, right. You were doin' such a good job I nearly forgot about it, mate." The vibration of the wheel stilled beneath his fingers as Bohannon felt his companion resume control of the plane.

By the time they reached the central Highlands the clouds had joined together overhead to blot out the sky with a single continuous layer of sooty white. This had been descending steadily, as if a giant hand was pressing it down into the valleys. To maintain visual contact with the ground, McCracken was forced to fly lower and lower.

"That's the town of Mt. Hagen." His voice crackled on the headset. "Just off to your right. Biggest burg in the central part of the country."

Bohannon pressed his face against the window. "Where?"

"Coming up." McCracken grinned. "I said it was the biggest town in the Highlands. I didn't say it was big."

Two thousand feet above the lush, narrow valley below, the Cessna roared past a ramshackle sprawl of buildings and a single airstrip considerably smaller than the ones at Lae and Mosby. As was true everywhere in the central part of the country, unscaled peaks soared to dizzying heights on all sides.

Leaning forward, Bohannon looked out and up at the impenetrable cloud layer. McCracken tried to put his passenger at ease. "Don't worry, mate." Despite the rigors of the long flight, the pilot appeared relaxed. "We'll make Tari. She's not far ahead, there's enough fuel, and the tape's holding fine."

Bohannon had forgotten about the repaired wing. Given a choice, he would have preferred not to have been reminded. Peering past the pilot he saw shreds of gray fluttering in the airflow, and was not reassured.

The heavy cloud cover had dropped to the point where McCracken was forced to mountain hop, hugging one valley after another for as long as possible before ducking into the clouds only long enough to clear the next peak. Surprisingly, the plane performed these passages with nary a bounce.

"Lucky today." A jovial McCracken cleared a cluster of four huts by less than fifty feet, sending half a dozen locals scrambling for cover.

"On the usual Hagen to Tari run you get kicked all over the fucking sky."

Bohannon watched the huge canopy trees and impenetrable montane rainforest whip past his window no more than a hundred feet or so away, and tried to imagine what it would be like to fly through such country in turbulent instead of calm conditions. Such speculation helped to pass the time—albeit not pleasantly.

VI

Much to his own amazement, he found that he had dozed off. So it was later than he hoped but sooner than he thought when McCracken was nudging him awake with a sharp elbow and nodding to his left. "There she is. Tari."

Pushing down on the sides of the seat to raise himself up, Bohannon looked past the pilot. The paved runway visible through McCracken's window did not look much bigger than some of the jungle airstrips they had overflown on the way up from Lae. A couple dozen buildings were visible nearby. This was the town, which was completely surrounded by dense forest and, where the ground was reasonably level, small subsistence gardens.

"This is Huli country," McCracken informed him. "Home to about forty thousand of the toughest blokes on the planet. You'll see Duna and Enga in town, too, but not out in the countryside."

"Why not?"

McCracken made a face. "Too many old feuds. A lone Huli wouldn't go wandering into Enga country, either."

Looking out and down, Bohannon studied the approach to the narrow airstrip. He was too tired to be nervous. "We're going past the runway. Why are we going past?"

"Settle down and take it easy, mate. See these mountains? We'll circle around and lose some altitude. I've got to make a flyover first anyway."

Bohannon did not understand, and said so even as McCracken put the Cessna into a steep, spiraling dive.

In the midst of making preparations for landing, his guide tried to explain. "There's a ten-foot high chain-link fence topped with razor wire around the runway, but even that doesn't always keep people off. Like I told you, this was the last part of PNG to be discovered by the outside world. Took three months to get here from the nearest outpost, and three men died hacking their way in. My point being that some of these people still don't know what modern technology can do or how to deal with it. If they were allowed to wander freely back and forth across the runway, some of them would just stand there, stupid-like, and watch while an incoming flight headed straight for 'em. That wouldn't do them or the plane much good.

"Then there's the pigs. They'll root under the fence to get at the fresh grass that grows around the tarmac."

Bohannon now understood the reason for the flyover. "I get it. Hitting a big pig might damage the landing gear."

"Bugger that! Run into a half-ton hog and you'll bloody well 'damage' a hell of a lot more than a wheel or two. But that ain't the worst thing that can happen. Kill a Huli pig and you'll have ten warriors on you faster than flies on a fresh turd. And every one of 'em demanding compensation. A good, healthy pig's worth three to six hundred kina. The fence is there to protect the pigs from the aircraft, not the aircraft from the pigs." He peered out the window. "Looks clear. Make sure your belt's secure."

Bohannon checked his harness as the Cessna pivoted like a ballerina over the far end of the runway. Bringing her around so close to the nearest hillside that the twin propwash startled a flurry of yellow-faced birds and rainbow lorikeets from the trees, McCracken leveled off and throttled down. A few strips of duct tape went flying as the flaps lowered sharply, further slowing their speed and reducing altitude, but if anything else fell off the plane it was not significant enough to inhibit their descent.

The asphalt runway was full of cracks and potholes, but a relieved Bohannon felt as if he had just touched down at O'Hare. As McCracken brought the plane around they taxied past half a dozen helicopters of varying size and manufacture. One was in the process of lifting off, blades fanning the back part of the tarmac. The Cessna was the only plane out on the runway.

They passed a single story structure clad in peeling white and yellow stucco. As airport terminals went, it was definitely last year's model. The whole building wasn't much larger than a standard two-car garage back home, and not as well maintained.

"Welcome to Tari International." McCracken slipped off his headset and hung it on a hook that protruded from the underside of the console. Finding an identical hook on his own side, Bohannon did likewise.

"That's it?" Methodically, he raised and lowered his legs, trying to loosen cramped muscles.

Cursing under his breath, McCracken was forced to kick the door open again. "What did you expect, Mr. Steve? A control tower? Gift shop and restaurant? There are only two or three commercial flights in here a week. No jets, nothing bigger than a Dash-Eight. Everything else is charter, just like us." He stepped out onto the wing and hopped down to the tarmac.

Bohannon followed. Once back on the ground, he inhaled deeply. Tari was a mile up and the air was crisp, clear, and fragrant with woodsmoke from dozens of unseen cooking fires. Somber faces stared through the fence at them, hands hooked in the chain link. Beyond, a few tormented pickup trucks and Land Rovers bumped along muddy tracks. The bed of every truck was filled to overflowing, either with goods or people or both.

Bohannon indicated the silent crowd. "What's with the audience?"

"Nothing else to do here, mate. Watching planes and choppers take off and land is the number one form of entertainment at these backwater airports. Plus, it's free."

"I don't get all the helicopters." Bohannon watched as the one that had been warming up rose noisily into the lowing sky. "Tourists?"

McCracken let out a hoot. "Not bloody likely! There's one lodge here and nothing else for hundreds of miles in any direction except Hagen. Mostly, the choppers shuttle geologists around. Ever since the Kutubu field was brought in the big international oil companies have been over this country like transvestites at a lingerie sale. New Guinea exports the stuff, you know. Chevron, Mobil, and British Petroleum are the big players, but everybody wants a piece of the pie. Now there's gas, too. Trillions of cubic feet of the stuff. Can you imagine what it takes to drill in this country? Everything from rig sections to pipe has to be brought in by chopper. There's more big Russian heavilift copters in PNG than anywhere in the world outside Russia itself.

"Some of these charter pilots have weekend homes in Cairns and Brisbane and drive BMW's and Mercedes. The ones that live long enough to cash their checks, that is." He started toward the terminal.

Bohannon followed hesitantly, pausing to look back at the battered Cessna. "What about our gear?"

"Leave it," McCracken told him. "It's safer here inside the plane than outside the gate on your back."

The interior of the terminal boasted a single small wooden counter topped by a protective metal grate, presumably to prevent irate and unsophisticated Highlanders from venting their anger over canceled reservations or misdelivered packages on handy if innocent clerks. A large blackboard displayed chalked messages in arcane techno-speak, informing persons unknown of bundles due to arrive, or missed, or forthcoming. A couple of more-or-less recent Air Niugini schedules were posted on a wall, stapled over several large, colorful posters advertising hopeful resorts with minimal facilities and unspoiled islands with unpronounceable names. Boxes and crates were piled high against the rear wall.

Through a door Bohannon could see a back room. Like a vacant meeting hall in a small West Texas town, it was empty of everything save a long fold-up table and a handful of chairs. Off to the right, a half-open door led to a restroom whose miasmatic comforts and dank tropical depths he was not sure he was ready to explore. Behind the blackboard was a worktable and a stark metal desk. A metal file tray occupied one corner of the desk, a few papers the other, and looking as out of place as a gun control advocate at a meeting of the Michigan militia, a computer rested in the center. He could tell that the computer was functional because of the generic screen-saver that was cycling silently across the screen.

Leaning way back in a reclining wooden office chair, the airport staff was sleeping soundly, both feet propped up on the table, head lolling slightly to the left, hands clasped together atop a broad chest beneath a beard the color and consistency of blackened steel wool. The agent/clerk/supercargo wore a yellow knit shirt, beige slacks, and the ubiquitous sneakers. In a corner behind him were three boxes wrapped in brown paper and heavy cord, and an enormous bound bunch of sweet potatoes with the leaves and stems still attached.

Walking around the desk, McCracken leaned over the man and yelled sharply. "*Paia, paia!*"

Sleepy eyes snapped open, the feet came off the desk, and the man looked around wildly. Only when he caught sight of the grinning pilot did the attendant's expression change from panicky to amused. A broad smile broke through the thick expanse of facial hair as its owner punched McCracken hard on the shoulder.

"Sorley, you sumvabitch! Fire, eh? Some day somebody'll stick a flare up your arse. Then we'll have us a fire, for sure!"

"*Apinun* to you too, Joseph. How's the family?"

The attendant nodded once. "*Orait.* And you? How you doing?"

"Same old same old." McCracken introduced his quiet companion. "This is my friend, Mr. Steve. We're looking for someone. A white lady. Steve, you want to do the honors?"

Bohannon provided a detailed description of Tai Tennison, to which the terminal attendant listened closely.

"Sorry, my friends," he said when the American had finished. "I am not here all day yesterday or the day before or even today, except for the regular flights from Mosby and Hagen. Maybe she come by charter."

"It's starting to look like it," McCracken agreed. "Rose didn't say how she was traveling. Might not have known anyway."

"So what do we do now?" Through the single open window Bohannon saw a gray Land Rover jounce past. It was filled with young men in dark green uniforms. They wore blue berets and carried automatic weapons.

McCracken noticed the direction of his gaze. "Rapid reaction force. An elite branch of the national police. They're pretty much unbribable. The government sends them in wherever things get too tough for the local cops to handle." His smile was grim. "These boys are on permanent station here."

To the attendant he said, "We could use a car while we're visiting, Joseph. Just for a little while."

The shorter man clapped the pilot on the arm. "You can use my truck. I don't think you will have any trouble, but if you are going out of town, be careful."

"Thank you," Bohannon responded gratefully. "But if we take your truck, how will you get home?"

Joseph smiled and pointed out the window. "That's my house over there. You don't need a car in Tari, but the kids like to drive around in it. Every couple months I take the family over the gap to Mendi, just for a change." Sliding open a drawer in the metal desk, he produced a keyring from which hung exactly one key. It clicked against a white plastic rectangle featuring the usual Raggiana bird-of-paradise that was the symbol of the locally brewed South Pacific Export.

"*Tenks*, Joseph." McCracken took the key. "We'll take good care of it for you."

"You betta, or I send my woman after you." Returning to the

chair, the attendant put his feet back up on the desk and gestured with a thumb. "Right front wheel is a little low. Tank is half full."

"That's plenty. Keep an eye on my plane, will you?"

"For sure, Sorley. No worries." So saying, he put back his head and closed his eyes, resuming the posture he had been enjoying when they had first entered.

The instant they stepped outside the building, half a hundred eyes shifted in their direction. Bohannon tried his best not to stare back. Most of the men were considerably shorter than either the pilot or himself, but a couple topped six feet. They were clothed in the most eclectic, riotous miscellany of attire he had yet seen, from feathered headdresses and arse-grass to ragged jeans and boxer shorts. One old man traipsed along the fence line in sandals made from used tires, arse-grass around his waist, a severely faded black T-shirt with the Batman movie logo emblazoned across the chest, and an old Akubra hat that had been artistically recovered in possum fur. The hatband was fashioned from the feathers of parrots and lorikeets. And it was by no means the most outrageous ensemble to be seen.

"Papuan peoples like color," McCracken explained by way of masterly understatement. "Especially the men." He led the way toward a yellow Mitsubishi pickup.

At least, the upper half was yellow. The rest was caked with a layer of fossilized brown mud that obscured not only the paint, but the wheels, door handles, and front grill. The truck was not locked and the windows were down.

"Not much point in stealing a car here," McCracken told Bohannon when queried about the evident lack of security. "There's only one road in or out: this end of the Highland Highway. A car thief's got nowhere to go. Besides, anyone who stole it would put themselves in a payback situation with Joseph's tribe."

The engine turned over immediately, the pickup's appearance belying its mechanical condition. Except for the gas gauge, nothing else on the console worked. As they pulled away from the terminal, the speedometer remained resolutely on zero. But the fancy radio-cassette player looked brand-new. Bohannon found himself speculating on the condition of brakes and other non-inconsequential automotive accessories.

They passed a couple of tree-shaded, dirt-fronted buildings. Dozens of people strode purposefully back and forth along the dirt road.

The parade was comprised primarily of women, children, and old men. Every woman carried a large, colorful bilum and often, an infant. Older children ran or followed alongside. To a man, the stooped, bewhiskered oldsters seemed to have emerged fully formed straight from a foundry, their bodies cast in solid bronze. Come to think of it, Bohannon reflected, he had not seen an ounce of fat on any Highlander, including the ones he had encountered in Lae and Mosby. He remarked on this to his guide.

"You're right, mate. And it ain't just looks, either. These guys are all muscle, every one of 'em. You tap one of these old farts on the back or chest and your hand just bounces off. That's from a lifetime of hard work and harder fighting. To give you an example, just you try drawing one of those black palm bows. Most of 'em have a forty-pound pull, or more. Partly it's diet, and partly sport."

"Sport?" Bohannon blinked.

McCracken chuckled at some private joke. "Highlands football. All of 'em play it as soon as they're old enough."

Bohannon was intrigued. "You think we might have time to see a game?"

His host nodded thoughtfully. "I'd be surprised if we didn't."

The road narrowed slightly but once beyond the town limits quickly spread out. Considering the remoteness of the location and what he'd already seen of local roads, Bohannon thought it was in remarkably good condition, level and dry.

"Not much traffic up here," McCracken explained. "The locals use it, so they keep it in shape. Of course, this ain't the rainy season. She's a bit rougher then."

Bohannon studied the clouded sky. "Looks like it could rain any time."

"Guess I'm not making meself clear, mate. Except for Mosby, which is in a rain shadow, the rest of the country has only two seasons: the dry wet season, and the wet wet season. This is the dry wet season, which means it only rains most of the time instead of all the time."

True to his description, a steady downpour commenced not long thereafter. It slowed but did not halt their progress, and did not have the force of the tropical deluges Bohannon had experienced elsewhere. Twenty minutes after it had begun, it stopped.

McCracken leaned out his open window and scrutinized the

clouds. "Be dark soon. Don't want to be driving around here after dark."

"That's what Joseph said." Leaning his right arm on the window sill, Bohannon marked the passage of lush forest. "Must be hard to find your way around without any lights."

"Naw, it ain't that, mate. You can't get lost, because there's only the one road." The guide glanced at his passenger and drew a finger sharply across his throat. "The problem is nocturnal life-forms—if you get me drift. Not the wallabies, tree kangaroos, cuscuses, or bats. It's the local raskols."

Bohannon barely heard him, having been distracted by movement up ahead. "Speaking of raskols, there's some kind of commotion going on in front of us."

Straining to see, McCracken eased off on the accelerator. "Sure is. You're starting to wake up, Mr. Steve. That's good. Useful survival trait in this part of the world."

"Well, what is it?" Bohannon asked as the truck slowed. "Whatever it is, it seems to be coming toward us."

"I think it's moving both ways," McCracken corrected him. "Sort of swirling back and forth. That's normal, it is." Stern-faced, he eyed his passenger. "You might want to bring that arm inside, mate. You wanted to see Highlands football." He nodded forward. "That's a match in progress right in front of us."

Holding their speed down but taking care not to come to a complete stop, McCracken plastered a wide smile on his face and advised Bohannon to do the same. As they approached the playing field, the road widened slightly. Off to their right a clearing backed up to a small but fast-moving river. Its watery drone was completely drowned out by the blood-chilling war cries that emanated from the embattled mob the truck was approaching.

Bohannon stiffened in his seat. There was no need for McCracken to explain the rules of Highland football because they were immediately obvious to even the most unsophisticated observer. Each participant singled out an opponent and then did his damnedest to kill him.

Highlands football, it seemed, was war by another name.

Though it was impossible to guess with any accuracy, given the number of men involved, the undisciplined surging back and forth, and the amount of dust kicked up, Bohannon estimated that between one and two thousand gaudily painted, heavily armed warriors were doing their best to beat one another's brains out in the middle of the idyllic clearing, the road, the river shallows, and the surrounding forest.

The majority of the combatants were armed with five-foot tall bows. Wickedly barbed featherless bamboo and palm arrows were notched and fired from scraped-bamboo bowstrings. A warrior would carry four or more of these fearsome missiles in one hand, an arrow gripped between each pair of fingers. Bohannon watched as several of the men fired off five arrows in twice as many seconds.

At close quarters, eighteen-inch long cassowary-bone knives and heavy stone axes were brought into play. Occasional flashes of metal amid the chaos hinted at the presence of a smattering of store-bought steel knives and axes. Fortunately, neither the sight nor sound of firearms was in evidence. Modern weapons would have replaced the traditional, drawn-out fight with an instant massacre.

Many of the men wore huge, crescent-shaped wigs of human hair. This was their own hair, McCracken explained, allowed to grow out for future shearing specifically for the purpose of wig-making. In shape resembling a slice from an orange and worn crosswise on the head, each wig was fronted with the brilliant azure breast feathers of the Superb bird-of-paradise, set off by exquisite inch-long, orange, red, and blue lorikeet feathers, and topped off with the flaming rust-orange fan tails of the Raggiana. Additional individualistic decoration was provided by the yard-long black tail plumes of Stephanie's arabis or the magnificent blue-black sicklebill.

Those men not wearing wigs went into battle with purple and yellow daisies in their hair, or woven garlands of green ferns, or in one ferocious fighter's case, gleaming metal strips cut from beer cans.

Headgear aside, the combatants' battle dress reflected the inescapable collision of civilizations ancient and modern. Bohannon saw everything from blue jeans to dress slacks to bathing shorts, from arse-grass to heavy metal T-shirts to denim and leather jackets. Nearly every face was completely obscured by broad swathes of red and yellow ocher. Bare chests and legs were barbarically stained with red stripes and entire bodies glistened wetly, having been coated from head to foot with black oil from the tigaso tree. Kina shell, cowries, palm nut and bead necklaces, hornbill and cuscus skulls bounced against muscular necks and chests. One man wore an elaborate breastplate fashioned from nothing but pull-tabs scavenged from empty soft-drink cans.

The truck rolled past one pair of combatants who were kneeling by the side of the road. They were bending over a fallen comrade and preparing to extract the three-foot long arrow that pierced his left shoulder clean through. Further on, two men rolled about on the ground flailing at one another with black stone axes heavy and sharp enough to cut through the trunks of rainforest trees. The air was filled with almost as many arrows as screams.

So utterly absorbed was Bohannon in the fantastic sight, so enthralled by the anarchic episode that seemed lifted intact and unforced and brought forward from ten thousand B.C. to be set down in the present day, that he momentarily overlooked his own potentially awkward position within it.

"I don't mean to question your knowledge of local habits, Sorley, but shouldn't we be turning around and getting the hell out of here?"

McCracken pointed to where the swift-running river curled around the back of the clearing. "See that bridge? That's the only way across. That's where we've got to go."

"Yes, I guessed as much, but . . ."

Before he could finish, a boldly dyed face thrust itself through his open window. White teeth flashed and he flinched reflexively. The ones in the front had been filed to sharp points.

A second face jostled for position alongside the first, then another, and another, the curious, gathering warriors effortlessly keeping pace with the slow-moving truck. More faces appeared on the opposite side of the pickup to stare unblinkingly at the driver. A stiffly smiling McCracken kept both hands on the wheel and eyes straight ahead.

Too late to do anything now, Bohannon thought nervously. The pickup was completely surrounded. Just as he was on the verge of screaming at McCracken to gun the engine and get them the hell out of there, a loud *bang* sounded from beneath the truck. He half ducked, but there was nothing to indicate the presence of a rifle or shotgun. McCracken's irritation confirmed that it was something even worse.

"*Shit!*" He slammed both palms down on the upper curve of the wheel. "What a time for a fucking blowout."

Bohannon gripped the dashboard. "Keep going! Maybe we can make the bridge. All the fighting seems to be on this side!"

They were not given the chance.

Except for the stoic moans of the wounded, all screaming and shouting suddenly ceased. Dust began to settle as more and more of the combatants packed around the truck, sealing off the road in both directions and blocking any exit.

"Steady now, mate." As he turned off the engine, McCracken kept nodding and smiling at the dense mob of combatants. "Keep calm, keep smiling. Let's see what the bloodthirsty little buggers want."

A hand thrust through the window on Bohannon's side. He jerked back, but the dirty, sweaty-damp fingers held no weapon.

Not knowing what else to do with the questing hand, he shook it.

"Apinun, apinun! Gude, yu stap gut?" warrior after warrior inquired. Every face was illuminated with paint and a wide, open smile.

"What do I do?" Bohannon mumbled uncertainly to McCracken.

"They're saying 'afternoon' and asking if you're doing all right. Say *'mi stap gut.'"*

Bohannon complied, only to see the smiles grow wider still. The heavy pounding of many feet immediately behind him made him turn. Through the rear window of the cab he could see a dozen or so warriors fumbling about in the truck bed. They seemed to be looking for something.

One of them let out a delighted, as opposed to bloodcurdling, yell. At the same time, the front end of the truck was lifted bodily off the ground. Chanting rhythmically and with evident enthusiasm, the several dozen men who had raised the vehicle with their hands had their song taken up by a thousand or so additional throats as the rest of the onlookers urged them on to greater efforts. Muscles strained and veins bulged beneath taut blood- and sweat-streaked skin. Feathers splendid beyond imagining bobbed in time to the chant.

The men who had climbed into the back of the truck had departed, taking something with them. Forced back into his seat by the angle at which the vehicle was being held, Bohannon struggled to see what was happening. McCracken had already figured it out. Hands behind his head, he was leaning back and relaxing.

"Settle down, mate. Everything's right. They're changing the bloody tire for us."

Bohannon's eyebrows rose. "You mean they stopped the war just to help us?"

"I mean exactly that. See, you and me, we ain't a party to this dispute. It's strictly local. We don't belong to either of the conflicting clans, so there's no reason to involve us. But that's this country for you. Meet any half dozen of these blokes in the same place in the middle of the night and they're as likely to cut you from ear to ear as give you directions. Depends on the day, the mood, and how many stubbies of *bia* they've downed.

"But right now they've got other business to attend to, and we ain't a part of it. So the right and proper thing to do is see us politely on our way."

Moments later, with a concerted shout, the front end of the pickup was lowered back down to the road, gently and with care. Mindful of McCracken's words and taking a chance, Bohannon leaned out the window to have a look. Sure enough, the newly emplaced tire sat on its rim as neatly as if it had been installed by a professional mechanic back home. As he watched, several men obligingly put the blown tire in the back of the truck and tied it down so it wouldn't bounce out.

"*Gutbai! Lukim yu, lukim yu!*" Cheerful smiles and waves launched them on their way as McCracken restarted the truck and eased forward. Bows, axes, and knives at the ready, the mass of warriors parted like a feathered sea of red and yellow to let them through.

The bridge loomed just ahead, one-way but wide enough to accommodate a good-size bus. A haphazard jumble of steel beams, pipes, and heavy wooden planks, it could not have presented a more attractive appearance to Bohannon had it been fashioned of mother-of-pearl set in a finding of pink enamel.

Horrific shouts and heartrending screams filled the air behind them. Leaning out the window and looking back down the road, Bohannon saw that the battle had resumed in all its barbaric fury. Once again, arrows filled the air and axes flew. It was as if the smiles, greetings, and helpful hands had been only a dream. Having halted in mid-Armageddon to cooperate in fixing the strangers' vehicle, the two sides had resumed their dispute with renewed vigor.

Within moments, the sights and sounds of battle as it must have been millennia ago faded from view, and the pickup was once again bouncing along through rainforest primeval.

"How long is that likely to last?" Emotionally if not physically drained, Bohannon rubbed dust and sweat from his eyes as the truck rattled down the winding dirt road. He could not help but notice that it was lined in places with eight-foot high mud walls topped with sharpened stakes and fronted by twelve-foot deep ditches. From time to time tiny, narrow entrances barred with wooden gates broke the red-earth monotony of the primitive but efficient fortifications. In addition to the stakes, trees had deliberately been planted atop the walls, adding their bulk to the already formidable barriers.

"What, the fighting?" McCracken looked thoughtful. "If it's the same dispute I'm thinking of, and I expect that it is, then the folks hereabouts have been contesting this particular disagreement for going on three years now."

In spite of everything he had seen thus far and come to expect from this astounding country, Bohannon discovered he was still capable of being shocked. "You mean they've been killing each other over the same thing for three years?"

McCracken nodded. "Off and on."

"Will it ever end?" Off to his right, something unutterably beautiful, with a bright orange breast and tail feathers like loops of guitar wire, went squawking off through the treetops.

"Only when the offended side is offered enough pigs by way of compensation."

"Pigs?" Bohannon shook his head in disbelief. "This is all about pigs? Men were dying back there!"

His passenger's passion left McCracken unmoved. "I tried to tell you earlier. A lot of what goes on in the Highlands is about pigs. Pork has been the principal unit of currency here since time began—or anyway, since people first settled here. Everything is accounted in pigs. Personal wealth, payback compensation, brides." He glanced over at his companion. "You want a bride? Cost you fifteen to twenty pigs, plus extras. If she's real pretty, maybe as many as twenty-five."

Bohannon sat back, brooding. "Death shouldn't be accounted in pigs."

"Know a lot about death, do you, Mr. Steve?"

His passenger whirled sharply on him and for the briefest of instants a different person stared out from behind the eyes of Steven Bohannon. It was someone McCracken had not met before. An individual who lingered momentarily behind tormented eyes and replied cuttingly, "You would be surprised how much I know about death, Sorley." Then it was gone.

The other Bohannon, the one McCracken had come to know, turned away to stare contemplatively out his open window as evening began to steal over the twittering, motionless rainforest. "I thought this country was supposed to be emerging into the modern world."

"The key word there would be 'emerging,' Mr. Steve. So it is. Only, parts of it ain't emerging as fast as some of the others."

"Where are we heading, anyway?"

McCracken gestured up the road as the pickup slammed through a deep rut. "Friend of mine lives up here. He'll put us up for the night. There ain't much that happens in this part of the country that he doesn't know about. If Tai's been through here recently, and unless Rose lied to us we know she at least transited through Tari, Andersvoot will know about it." He grinned expectantly. "Don't let Jan put you off. He's a bit—different."

Like everyone and everything else in this crazy country, Bohannon reflected. Unable in good conscience to add, "present company excepted," he kept the thought to himself.

VII

From the time they had left Tari in the battered ute (as McCracken referred to the pickup) they had not passed a single branching or side road. There was the dirt track of the Highland Highway, and that was all. His guide pointed out a series of blackened ruins off to their right.

"Local health clinic. Office and outbuildings. The clan from the other side of the river burned it down. See how they cut down as many trees as possible and dug up all the flower beds and vegetable gardens?"

Bohannon stared at the wooden shells of former structures, scorched two-by-fours sticking up out of the ground like used matches. "And I suppose this side immediately retaliated?"

"What else?" McCracken swerved to avoid a couple of dogs in the road. Lost in the avalanche of other surprises was the fact that Bohannon had not seen a starving dog anywhere in the country. He was assured by his guide that dog was one animal the locals did not eat.

"The people here burned down the school on the other side of the river." He smiled humorlessly. "Last I heard it, the clans were arguing over whether one health clinic equaled one school, or if either side was entitled to additional compensation because of a disparity."

Bohannon inhaled deeply. "So everybody continues to suffer. Especially the children."

"Oh, it don't bother the kids. They're raised up to understand that this is the way the world works. If you believe what the anthropologist blokes say, intertribal and internal warfare and the payback system has been a way of life up here since the Highlands were first settled thirty thousand years ago. It's the local brand of population control. The Highlanders understand that, and accept it. Accept it, hell—they thrive on it!"

With a sweep on his arm, his passenger took in the surrounding devastation. "How does something like this get started?"

"Lemme think. I don't get up here all that often, you know. Want to make sure I get the details straight. Oh right, now I remember.

"Seems a bloke from this side of the river found himself taken with a young lass from the other side. He made a formal offer to her family that he claims was duly discussed and accepted. When he showed up to claim his bride—number four I think it was—the family claimed they hadn't agreed to shit and told him, in so many words, to come up with another half dozen pigs or get stuffed. As you might imagine, this left the would-be groom feeling shamed before his friends and family." As they headed up a moderate slope, McCracken shifted down.

"So, one night he snuck into the family compound and stole the girl away. Dad promptly rounded up some friends and relatives and they crossed the river with the intention of getting her back. Turns out Mr. Bridegroom and his buddies were waiting for them, but it didn't do them any good. In the ensuing fight, a couple of the groom's friends got offed. By now, mate, you ought to be able to figure out for yourself what happens next."

"Payback." Bohannon found himself scanning the shadowed forest for signs of movement.

McCracken spat out the window. "Too bloody right. The offended groom gets together a big raiding party and goes looking to even things up. Expecting him, the bride's family has organized a defense. They've also brought in a local magistrate to try and mediate the mess. But the groom and his mates are all dressed up and painted real fine and spoiling for a fight, and before anyone gets the chance to explain things, arrows start flying. One of 'em hits the magistrate in the neck, cuts his jugular vein, and he bleeds to death in the middle of all the confusion.

"Now this magistrate, he apparently was a well-liked bloke in this part of the world. A number of clans who before this weren't a party to the bride dispute and didn't give a damn about it are suddenly involved. And they're fucking furious, see? A couple hundred warriors get together, screaming and howling, cross the river, and burn a bunch of houses and sweet potato fields, only a couple of which belong to the immediate friends of the groom. That stirs up other previously disinterested folks on this side of the river." The road leveled off and he shifted accordingly.

"That was three years ago. They've been fighting and slaughtering one another over it ever since."

"And there's no way to settle it peacefully, no way to bring it to an end?"

McCracken grunted. "Sure there is, but there's a new problem, you see. The dispute's grown so big and so many offended folks are involved that there aren't enough pigs in the whole area to pay proper compensation all around. So while the local big men argue over how to moderate payment, the fighting goes on. I only see one thing stopping it."

A surprised Bohannon turned back to his companion. "Based on what you've told me so far, I don't see how anything could."

"You're forgetting that there's a third party with an interest in all this. The government. National police from outside the area aren't a party to the dispute, so they can bash in heads on both sides without becoming directly involved. The Highlanders are gradually learning that you don't do payback against the cops. They're now treated as neutral combatants because it's recognized that they abuse all sides equally. The cops do their best: try to arrest war leaders, confiscate bush knives—that sort of thing. But it ain't easy, mate. You stop the fighting here and it'll break on the other side of the valley. It's hard to change thirty-thousand-year-old habits in less than a decade." Slowing, he pulled the ute off into a small clearing on the left side of the road. "We're here."

Leaning forward slightly, Bohannon peered past him. "I don't see anything."

For a change, McCracken had a door he did not have to kick open. "That's the idea, mate. Come on."

A little ways up from the clearing a narrow footbridge fashioned of four-inch wide logs spanned a sheer-sided moat that was no less than fifteen feet deep. A sloping wall of dried red-brown mud rose from the bottom of the muddy ditch to a height of eight or nine feet. Like similar fortifications they had passed along the road, the narrow crest was lined with sharpened poles and vine-tangled bushes.

At the sturdy wooden door that constituted the only opening in the wall, McCracken conversed in soft Pidgin with someone on the other side. Following a cheerful response, the door was unbolted and opened outward by an elderly Highlander wearing a red construction hard hat decorated with cassowary feathers, tattered black dress shorts, and a necklace of pandanus palm nuts and iridescent forest green beetle carpaces. From his aged, wizened face shone forth enough character to satisfy a master woodcarver. Standing five foot four, he was armed with bow, arrows, and two impressive store-bought steel kitchen knives. He was maybe sixty years old; a grinning senior-citizen assassin. Bohannon would not have wanted to meet him in a dark alley.

Stepping aside to let them pass, the elderly guard carefully shut and bolted the gate behind them. Ahead, a claustrophobic winding path followed the bottom of a ten-foot deep ditch gouged from the surrounding forest. The gap between the walls was barely a yard wide. A natural water magnet, the muddy floor was filled with rocks and logs. Flashing a wide smile, the gnomic guard led them down the ominous path, hopping lithely from rock to log while McCracken and Bohannon slid and slipped awkwardly along behind him.

The expat gestured at the top of the enclosing walls. "The Highlands are honeycombed with these fortifications. Many of the homes hereabouts are set up like this. These deep, narrow paths are the only way in and out of individual properties. Any enemy trying to reach the houses and gardens either has to fight his way through thick jungle or come down these paths. Meanwhile the defenders, who know the ground, can ambush them at will from overhead. Even the Rapid Reaction Force boys won't try forcing their way into these compounds—not even with AK-47's and M-16's."

In the early stages of advancing evening, Bohannon felt as if they were stumbling down a tunnel that led back in time. "I wouldn't either."

After an intimidating but brief trek, the sloping ditch finally opened onto a clearing that had been meticulously cultivated and planted. The compound was completely surrounded by impenetrable rainforest. Banana trees shaded four-foot high earthen mounds in whose nurturing depths the staple sweet potato matured in damp silence. Off to their left, a couple of women mixing ash into the dirt of a fresh mound looked up from their work long enough to wave. Smoke rose from a nearby round building with a peaked thatch roof.

"Woman's house." McCracken was careful to step between and not on the well-tended mounds. "The men in this country are deeply suspicious of women. Any woman. Anytime something bad or inexplicable happens, it's usually thought to be the fault of some woman. Touching a menstruating woman is considered a harbinger of horrible bad luck."

"And the women stand for it?"

McCracken shrugged it off. "It's their culture. Oh, the lassies will fight back. Make no mistake, it's not all deference and submission. The men do all the heavy work like building the houses, maintaining the fortifications, and clearing the fields. Not to mention dealing with payback. The women do the planting and take care of the pigs. In fact, they sleep with the pigs, in the women's house. Inheritance is through the matrilineal line, not the man's.

"But there's no denying it can be a hard life. Women who don't get out of the way fast enough get killed in fights all the time. For that matter, so do kids." He pointed to another thatched structure. "That's the men's house over there. Women aren't allowed inside. They're too dangerous to sleep with, you see."

"Then how do they, um, you know?"

"Screw?" said McCracken with his usual subtlety. "They do it in the fields or out in the forest, mostly. It gets done. There sure as hell's no scarcity of kids around here." He gestured past their escort. "That'll be Andersvoot's place up ahead."

Set among exquisite flowering bushes and more banana trees was a real house. With a raised floor set on sturdy pilings, milled siding, and glass windows glinting from wooden frames, it looked as out of place among the traditional thatched huts and sweet potato mounds as a fast-food emporium on the Champs d'Elysses. Deceptively expansive, it boasted a wraparound porch reached by a wide set of wooden steps fashioned from split logs. From a nearby thatched shack came the muffled sputtering of a generator, explaining the lights that lit the windows from within.

"Doesn't look like much," McCracken commented, "but it's solid rosewood and queela. White ants won't touch it."

"How did it get here?" As soon as the words left his mouth, Bohannon corrected himself. "I mean, why here?"

The expat grinned at him. "Jan's taken a couple of local wives, so he's entitled to a bit of land. Likes his privacy, the man does."

Their escort stepped aside and gestured for them to enter. Bohannon followed McCracken up the broad, smooth wooden steps and onto the porch. From within, a voice could be overheard angrily declaiming. Every so often a sharp *crack* would punctuate the rambling discourse.

Poetry, Bohannon realized. Someone inside was reciting poetry.

Screaming it, really. The source of the periodic cracks that were almost but not quite gunshots mystified him.

A young woman opened the door and stepped shyly aside to allow them entry. A very young woman, Bohannon noted. Barely five feet tall, she wore only a colorful print wraparound about her waist. Her skin was unscarred, her delicate face unpainted, her breasts high and full. Framed by a clutch of feathery, fairy-like branches from some exotic tree fern, a magnificent red and yellow orchid was entwined in her hair.

McCracken chucked her affectionately under the chin. The resultant smile would have melted iron. "*Apinun*, lassie. No, don't bother your pretty self. I know the way." Straightening, he leered at Bohannon. "Unlike the local blokes, Jan don't mind sleeping with women, you see. They think he's crazy. They're sure his wives are going to slice him up one night and sacrifice him to Ne, or one of the other local gods."

They walked down a hall filled with nightmarish masks and sculptures. In the deepening dark the grotesque faces and posturing bodies with their grossly exaggerated genitals and bulging eyes evinced entirely too much animation for the increasingly uneasy Bohannon. Noticing the look on his companion's face, McCracken chuckled.

"This stuff is all brought up from the Sepik. Pretty powerful, ain't it? A drunk wouldn't last five minutes in here before he either balled himself up in a fetal position or ran screaming into the woods." He singled out one especially large and repulsive figure whose flattened backside protruded to form a seat. "That intimidating little beauty is an orator's chair. Take some guts to argue with somebody sitting on that."

Ahead, the thunder of raging poetry was growing louder while the explosive accompanying cracks increased in frequency.

The hall opened onto a large living area filled with rattan furniture. Padded couches and chairs surrounded a low round table cut from the trunk of a single rainforest giant. The wood was a deep, rich red streaked with black. Dramatically lit by the few overhead lights, masks even more bizarre and frightening than those in the hall lined the walls along with a cluster of framed photographs. An overflowing, hand-hewn bookcase leaned against the far wall.

To the right of the portal an astonishing and completely unexpected mass of state-of-the-art electronics took up no less than a fifth of the floor space. With no less than three keyboards, half a dozen speakers, amps, and monster cables linking everything to a pair of computers and a monitor in the center, it was a setup any contemporary composer would have been proud to have in his studio. The twenty-inch monitor was active, showing a series of half-filled musical staves.

Striding back and forth behind the couch and waving his arms while reciting from memory at the top of his lungs was the master of this bemasked and bemusicked domicile. Living somewhere in the vicinity of fifty, Jan Andersvoot was puffy-faced, with a severe blond crewcut, perpetually sunburnt pink cheeks, and deep-set blue eyes that darted about in all directions as he bellowed verse after verse of Poe, Whitman, Robinson Jeffers, Keats, Milton, Virgil, Aristophanes, and several poets Bohannon did not recognize. The master of the house was six feet tall, weighed close to three hundred pounds, and along with a substantial beer gut had a beer-barrel chest to go with it.

He looked like a giant Dutch troll.

The source of the gunshot-like cracking was the heavy whip the master of the house gripped powerfully in his left hand. At unpredictable moments during the recitation this would be flung out to explode against empty air. It made a bullwhip look like a child's toy. Bohannon shuddered to think what it could do to human flesh.

Blue eyes suddenly and suspiciously aware of their presence, Andersvoot challenged them with a pair of lines from Eliot. Almost as soon as he'd finished delivering them, he recognized McCracken. Abruptly, the agony which had been writ large on that round face vanished as the whip-cracking troll metamorphosed into a passable imitation of a beardless Santa Claus.

"Sorley, you whoreson!" Immense arms enveloped the slim form of Bohannon's guide. "Py damn, what brings you up here?"

Fighting for air, McCracken fought to extricate himself from the suffocating embrace. "This bloke here, Mr. Jan."

Bohannon forced himself to stand his ground as the troll turned to him. His extended hand vanished in the other man's grip, which was firm without being overpowering. He could see those incongruously tiny blue eyes, half hidden in the deceptively cherub-like face, sizing him up.

"Ameerican?"

"Yes, I . . ."

"Ha! I never miss." The huge body turned to McCracken. "Tell him, Sorley."

"He never misses, mate," McCracken obediently confirmed.

Striving for instant conviviality, Bohannon indicated the heavy whip. "Interesting way you have of punctuating your sentences, Mr. Andersvoot."

"Jan, please. Punctuating my seentences—ha! That's very goot. This one, he has some education." Their host snickered at McCracken. It was an astonishing sound, like something one might hear at night in a secret place deep within the rainforest. He held out the whip.

"This is a sjambok, my friend. Made from the hide of the Cape buffalo."

"I didn't know there were Cape buffalo in PNG."

"There ain't," McCracken informed him. "Jan's from South Africa. He was a cop there."

Like a pint of ice water, a cold chill trickled down Bohannon's back. Unable to stop himself, he studied the whip closely. So this was the dreaded sjambok, the bane of South Africa's blacks and coloreds for a hundred years. He'd read about it, seen it used in old newsreels. One stroke could take the skin off a man's back. A dozen could kill. Unreasoning hatred started to well up in him—and was as quickly extinguished.

If Andersvoot was one of those unrepentant Afrikaaner supporters of apartheid who, unable to stand the new multiracial South Africa, had chosen to emigrate, what was he doing in a place like Papua New Guinea? It hardly seemed the ideal retirement haven for a racist ex-cop.

But then, racist ex-cops did not usually recite poetry and compose music. The troll, it seemed, was complex.

"I see it in your face, my friend. You wonder what I am doing here, ja? I tell you, I did not hate the kaffirs, but I was involved in some—happenings. Not what you are thinking. There was money involved, and some bad doings, and wealthy, powerful people. Important people, white *and* black. I was just a poor policeman who got in too deep. It was better for me to leave, and so I did. This country," and he made as if to embrace it all with both huge arms, "is a goot place for a man to lose himself. So I come here. Nobody ask too many queestions. Those who do are always willing to take a fistful of kina for an answer." He winked.

"Since Mandeela, the rand has become much stronger. That is goot news for a poor retired cop like myself." Turning, he laid the vicious serpentine length of the sjambok across the high, curving back of an elaborately woven cane chair and settled himself in. The rattan squealed beneath his weight.

"You don't miss Africa?" Bohannon and McCracken ended up on the couch opposite the big chair, on the other side of the radiant table. Light seemed to emanate from within the wood itself.

For an instant the beaming, rotund face darkened. "Anyone who has lived in Africa misses it. All of it, even the bad things. You go for a long drive, a safari, and you look out your window and all you see is MMBA." The grin returned. "An early British expression. It means, 'miles and miles of bloody Africa.' Of course I miss it. But I am happy here. I make my music and commune with my poets and nobody bother me." He nodded at the sjambok, lying like a sleeping mamba near his head.

"Do not ask me to explain any of this to you, because I cannot. Now then: how can I help you?"

A jangle of long legs and nervous arms, McCracken scrunched his scrawny backside into the couch. "We flew in a little while ago, Mr. Jan. I was hoping you could put Mr. Steve here and me up for the night."

"Done." A massive hand slapped an equally impressive bare knee. "You would insult me if you tried to leave. So. Tell me why you have come to this end of the earth?"

McCracken looked to Bohannon, who explained. "I was robbed by a woman named Tennison. Tai Tennison. We're pretty sure she flew into Tari recently. Possibly on a commercial flight, possibly via charter."

Andersvoot's thick lower lip curled up over his mouth. "I do not know the lady. Can you deescribe her?" Once again McCracken sniggered.

Bohannon ignored him. "She's almost my height. Somewhere in her early thirties. Red hair, blue eyes, nice figure. . . ."

"Great figure," McCracken interrupted, correcting him. "An ass like molded rubber, tits like . . ."

"Jan gets the idea." Bohannon glared at the guide and McCracken substituted an amused leer in lieu of further description. "She's very deeply tanned, almost as dark as some of the nationals I saw in Mosby.

Very self-possessed, very knowledgeable. Sorley says she speaks fluent Pidgin as well as some of the local languages." He thought a moment, added, "She may be traveling with a man named Stenhammer."

Andersvoot's heavy brows furrowed and he glanced at McCracken. "True, this?" Lips tight, the other expat nodded. Bohannon could not miss the silent byplay that passed between the two men.

"I'll ask it again: who is this Stenhammer guy, anyway?"

Staring out into the night, Andersvoot shrugged. "A nobody. No one of any importance. Rumor or man, what difference does it make?" Bohannon knew instantly that the big ex-cop was lying. Lying, and something else. Something more.

He was afraid.

He hid it well, ramping up a big, wide smile. "This sounds like a special lady, yes. How much did she geet from you?"

"Enough."

Heavy brows rose eloquently. "Oh ho, so it is peersonal, this. Now I see. Darani!"

A tall young Huli appeared from out of nowhere. He wore denim shorts, sneakers (no socks), a soiled but recognizable Chicago Bulls baseball cap, and a prized leather flight jacket worn open at the chest. The haft of a store-bought knife protruded from one frayed pocket. His face was unpainted. He barely glanced in the couch's direction. While McCracken and Bohannon waited, Andersvoot spoke to him in Huli.

When he finished, the youth nodded, flashed a cursory smile at his employer's guests, and vanished back the way he'd come. Andersvoot returned his attention to his visitors.

"Tomorrow we will know something. If your lady friend is in the Tari basin Darani will find out where. If she has been here and left, he will try to find out where she has gone." Pushing off on both arms of the chair, Andersvoot levered himself erect. "Tell me, American Steve, do you like conteemporary classical music?"

It was not a question Bohannon was prepared for. "A little, I guess. I'm not really familiar with it."

Their host lumbered over to the wall of electronics and settled himself into the chair before the computer monitor. Huge hands hovered over the midi keyboard. "Tell me what you think of this. Myself, I think maybe too much peercussion, but I have always had a weakness for loud noises." Fingers flipped switches and settled on the keyboard. Above the forest hoots of the little brown owl *Ninox theomacha* and the rustling of insects the size of birds, high-powered Japanese speakers brayed, pushing back the night.

VIII

In place of the cot he had expected, Bohannon had a bed, with a mattress and real sheets. Instead of the anticipated outside drop loo there was a bathroom, with a sink and flush toilet. In the stall shower he found lavender-scented soap and glorious cascades of hot water. All these wonders he encountered after trying and eventually failing to keep up with McCracken and Andersvoot's drinking.

When he finally awoke, dressed, and joined their host in the living room after seven hours of the soundest sleep he had ever enjoyed in his life, Bohannon found himself lauded for his noble attempt to keep pace.

"You did well, my friend Steve." Andersvoot clapped him on the back with a massive hand, a blow sufficient to rouse anything internal that still lingered in slumber. "I am, as you can see, bottomless, and Sorley has a hollow leg through which he pours that which he cannot piss. Your share was honestly downed. Now come and eat."

They were taken outside, to where the very young woman who had greeted them at the door the night before and another equally as attractive but slightly older had set an unblemished cloth of ivory muslin over a round rattan table. On this had been placed a glass carafe of freshly squeezed mango juice and another of pineapple.

Bohannon pulled out a chair and sat down. As soon as the men were seated the women brought hot toast, pastries, scrambled eggs, bacon, ham, and as a concession to origins, thick boerwore sausages.

It was early. As they ate, birds-of-paradise, arapis, manucodes, hornbills, and lorikeets fussed in the trees, picking off insects left numbed by the lingering chill of morning. One by one, McCracken gave names to a Mad Hatter's assortment of moths clinging to the posts and rails of the porch. Drawn to the house by the previous night's electric lights, they had remained, waiting for the sun to warm their wings.

There were green moths and black moths, moths impossible to tell from dead leaves and moths with horns. There were red moths with yellow stripes and blue patches, pure white moths like the ghosts of departed souls, moths with antennae longer than the average moth back home.

Andersvoot pointed out one giant hanging from the porch rafters. Light brown with prominent wing spots, it was nearly a foot in length from antennae to tail.

"That's an Atlas, my friend. Or a Heercules. I forget which. One of them is . . ."

With his mouth full of egg, Bohannon interrupted him. "Let me guess. It wouldn't by any chance be the biggest moth in the world, would it?"

His host nodded approvingly. "Yes, it would." He grinned across the table. "Sorley has been teaching you."

"It's not hard." Bohannon swallowed, sawing at the half-inch thick slab of ham that threatened to overwhelm his plate. "Bug-wise, everything here seems to be the biggest."

"Not everything. Not all is so pretty, either." Andersvoot chugged down half a glass of pineapple juice. "You watch out for the mossies. Not so many up here, but it's different on the islands and teerrible down on the Seepik or the Fly. Most of theem are not so bad. Just irritating. But the big black ones can give you ceerebral malaria." The ex-cop waved a fork in his guest's direction. "No joke, that. First it drive you mad, then it kill you."

A subdued Bohannon watched as the gigantic moth began to exercise its enormous brown wings. Almost directly overhead, they reminded him of hands clapping. "I'll remember that."

His meal half-finished, Andersvoot pushed back from the table. "You two eat up. I'll be back in a minute."

"Where are you going?" Bohannon did not receive a reply. It was left to McCracken, whose chair faced outward, to explain.

"Look behind you. His boy is back."

Bohannon turned in his seat. Past the flowers and decorative bushes, out where the landscaping bumped up against the sweet potato mounds, their host was conversing animatedly with a new arrival. Bohannon recognized Darani, the young man from the night before.

"Think there'll be any news of Tennison?"

McCracken held his gaze a moment longer, then dove back into his meal with renewed gusto. "Can't tell, mate. I ain't much of a lip reader and it don't matter because I can't speak any of the Huli variants anyway."

Bohannon stared hard. "I thought you told me you could speak the language up here?"

Half-masticated toast garbled the other man's words. "Pidgin, mate. I can speak Pidgin. That's the *lingua franca* of this country. Getting started on fifty or so local languages, that's not for me. Here, he's coming back."

Andersvoot rejoined them and resumed his seat. "Darani's a good boy."

Bohannon discovered that he was suffused with an odd mix of excitement, anticipation, and uncertainty. "Then he found her?"

Their host dove back into the ruins of his breakfast. "Well no, my friend Steve. Not exactly. He found somebody who knew where she has been."

"Damn. Probably someone who saw her getting off a plane at the airport." To have come all this way, he thought disappointedly, only to find the trail dead-ended, was more than a little discouraging. It bordered on the devastating. And yet, he still did not know why he should feel so strongly about it. So he'd missed the woman. So what. He'd tried. That was enough, wasn't it? Wasn't it? To try?

If only he had tried harder, before . . .

Before he could decide how to respond, Andersvoot was consoling him. "Do not look so discouraged. He also found someone who had heard from someone who had overheard her talking with a heelicopter pilot about taking her upcountry to Mt. Yogonda."

McCracken paused over a piece of heavily Vegemited ten-grain toast. "Upcountry? Bugger that, man, right here is as upcountry as anyone in their right mind should want to get!"

"Yes, that's so." Andersvoot agreed readily. "But that's what Darani was told."

At first Bohannon thought McCracken was angry, but closer inspection revealed that he was downcast. In fact, his tone and attitude were reflective of a man grown suddenly despondent. It made no sense. Disappointment Bohannon would have understood, or irritation, but despondency was a reaction he would not have anticipated.

"All that sweet succulent loveliness gone to waste, over a madman. You're right, Jan. Nobody in their right mind goes upcountry from uncountry. But Stenhammer's not in his right mind. It's all very well for the mad son-of-a-bitch to go bashing and banging all over the mountains. He'll kill himself soon enough, if he ain't already. Any day now I'll hear no more about him, and good riddance it'll be. Fall over a cliff or step on a Death adder or insult some tribal big man and get himself pin-cushioned with arrows, he will. But for him to drag Tai down to hell with him, that's bloody unfair!"

"So she *is* with Steenhammer, eh?" Andersvoot nodded slowly and solemnly, like a corpulent priest receiving confession. He looked sharply at Bohannon. "Better you go home, my friend Steve. Or at least back to Lae. Forgeet about your money. It's gone, py damn. If this woman has gone to Mt. Yogonda, then your money is gone. If she is using it to look for Ragnarok Stenhammer then you will not find her, either." He belched massively. "Maybe nobody find her, ever."

Bohannon looked from one solemn face to the other. "First Sorley, and now you, Jan. Will somebody please explain to me what kind of hold this Stenhammer character has on Tennison?"

"'Character.'" A small sly smile crept over Andersvoot's plump face. "He is more than a 'character,' your Steenhammer. Sorley is right. Sure he's crazy. But he knows the back country. He's smart crazy, Steenhammer is. Sure he's going to die, but every time somebody says his body has been found, or spotted from the air, he turns up someplace. Alive. Every time someplace different. Yogo, or Porgera, or Mt. Kare, or Mendi, or Hagen. A couple of times right here, in Tari, but I don't see him for myself. I only hear about it. He stocks up on supplies and then he disappears."

Bohannon blinked. "Disappears? Where?"

Andersvoot turned in his chair and brought his huge right arm up and around in a sweeping, all-inclusive arc. "Out there, my friend Steve. In the mountains. In the Central Range, and the Müllers, and the Schrader and the Victor Emmanuel. Out there where there are no more roads, out past the last surveeyed trails. Out in places where even the Huli and the Enga and the Duna are afraid to go." He dropped his arm and regarded his guest, a flinty hardness in his little blue eyes that bespoke long, difficult years as a cop operating under intolerable conditions in a country torn apart by strife and revolution.

"If your lady has gone after him in such places you will never find her. You don't want to try and find her. Probably nobody else will, either. There is a fair chance she will not come back." He was apologetic but unyielding. "Mt. Yogonda is nowheere, and beyond it lies nothing."

"So why does she go with a guy who can only be found in such dangerous places?"

McCracken looked up, his tone surprisingly bitter. "How the fuck should I know, mate? You'd have to ask Tai that one."

"Fine." Bohannon rose. "Then let's go and ask her."

Both men gaped at him. "Did you not hear what I just told you, my friend Steve?" The genuine disbelief in Andersvoot's voice counterpointed McCracken's despondency.

"I heard you. I'm not ready to give up." He smiled ruefully, sadly. "I'm not going to try and explain, and I wouldn't expect either of you to understand, anyway, but at this point, I can't give up. I'm not sure I understand completely myself. Maybe I'll be able to explain better, later." He turned expectantly to his guide. "How about it, Sorley? You quitting?"

"Jesus Mary, mate," the other man muttered, "it ain't a matter of 'quitting.' This ain't no bleeding football match we're talking about here. You think the country we flew over from Lae was untouched? You're talking about going someplace nobody goes. Not even local people. It's bloody murderous back in there! Mountains straight up and down, they are. Leech-filled jungle at the bottom and snake-thick rainforest all the way up the slopes to the top. Valleys seven, eight thousand feet deep, with uncrossable rivers at the bottom of every one of 'em. And it rains all the time. Up there, it's the Big Wet all year 'round.

"You get in trouble in there, nobody will ever find you. A hundred planes couldn't spot you under the canopy. That's if they could see the bloody canopy, which they can't because of the permanent cloud cover. You talk like this is some bleeding Sunday stroll in Regent's Park. It's fine for the likes of Stenhammer, because the man's mad. If Tai wants to throw in after him, that's her business. Bleedin' stupid, I calls it. But I ain't stupid, mate, and I rather like myself just the way I am—alive."

Bohannon's voice conveyed acceptance of the other man's position—along with something else. Something more that neither of the other men could quite place. "Then I'll find somebody else to take me."

"Goddamn it!" McCracken shoved back from the table violently enough to spill juice and send silverware flying. "You're not listening to me, mate! You want to commit hari-kari, there's simpler, neater, cleaner ways. Cheaper, too!"

"I have no intention of killing myself." The expat's outburst left Bohannon unmoved.

McCracken glared at him a moment longer, then sat down heavily in his chair. "Oh now, you have no intention of killing yourself, is it?" His tone had turned mocking. "Well then, that's bloody all right then, ain't it?" His head snapped around to confront Andersvoot. "Ain't that too right, Jan? A stupid twit chasing a stupid twat. *You* try and talk some sense into him."

Drifting in and out of thought and remembrance, Andersvoot studied his other guest. "For many years I tried to talk sense into people. People who had their houses burned down, their limbs broken, their wives and children killed before their eyes. They did not listen to me, many of them, because each of them was holding onto something they believed in. Believed in so strongly that nothing else mattered to them. This man Steve, I think he believes in finding this lady."

Bohannon smiled his thanks at the other's understanding. "That's right. Right now, that's what I believe in."

The ex-cop nodded knowingly. "You are wasting your time trying to turn him, Sorley. He is going. I can see it in his face as clearly as I have seen it in the faces of others. Sometimes reason works on the minds of men, other times it does not. I cannot talk him from it, and neither can you."

"Bloody fool," McCracken muttered angrily. For a long moment no one said anything. Then he looked up and snarled "SHIT!" loud enough to bring the women running. Andersvoot dismissed them with a glance.

"I refuse to accept that as your final word on the subject." Bohannon waited patiently.

McCracken's face was a study in resigned disbelief. "Christ, but sometimes I hate the way you talk, Mr. Steve." He gestured in the direction of the standing man's pockets. "How long a line of credit you carry on those cards?"

"Bigger than you suppose, smaller than I'd like. Why? We need to buy fuel for the plane?"

The guide's broken cackle contained a little madness of its own. "Plane?" He shook his head slowly, his expression pitying. "You can't take a plane where you're talking about going, mate. There's no runway at Mt. Yogonda, not even a little arse-grass strip like the one at Mopingo. The Cessna stays in Tari."

"Then how do we get up there?" Bohannon inquired impatiently. "We're losing daylight."

Leaning back in his chair and deliberately taking his time, McCracken presented a picture of false thoughtfulness. "Well now, I suppose you could trek it. It's only about fifty miles as the kokomo flies, or a bit over twice that on the one trail. Through rainforest, and mud, and warring clans, and rain, and bands of murdering raskols. Yes, you could trek it mate—but without me."

Bohannon was not fazed. "You didn't ask me about my credit line so we could buy granola for a trail hike."

"That's right, mate. I didn't." The expat straightened in his chair. "Even if I were so inclined, which I ain't, we haven't got the time to hoof it. The only sensible way in to Mt. Yogonda is by chopper. That's how Tai would've gone. That's how we'll have to go." He glanced at their host. "What's the going rate these days, Mr. Jan?"

With the aid of sausage-like fingers, Andersvoot performed a quick calculation. "Six or seven hundreed kina for each. That's if you can find somebody to take you. Since the strike three months ago, it's hard to find a chopper for hire anywhere in the Highlands. Those that the newcomers aren't hiring, the oil and mining companies are keeping on retainer. But you might get lucky."

"Strike?" Bohannon returned his attention to their host. "Who's on strike?"

Andersvoot hesitated until he realized that his guest was not making a joke. "You really don't know, do you?" He turned to McCracken. "He really doesn't know?"

For Bohannon, their host's comments compounded his confusion instead of clarifying matters. "Know what?"

McCracken's expression twisted. "Nobody's 'on strike,' mate. They're 'on' the strike. I guess you never heard of Mt. Kare?"

Bohannon resumed his seat. "What's Mt. Kare?"

"A place southeast of Mt. Yogonda." Andersvoot shifted his oversize butt in the overstressed chair. "From 1988 to 1991 it was the site of the biggest gold-rush in the South Pacific since Joburg."

"That's funny. I keep up on world news pretty good and I don't remember ever reading anything about it."

Andersvoot was philosophical. "Maybe that's because it was here. No reporters come here. Also, it was all local. No outsiders were allowed in. Before all the easy stuff was gone and the big companies moved in to do the hard rock mining, the Highland people took gold worth three hundred million U.S. dollars out of Pinuni and Lewa creeks and the Upper Gewa River. All with nothing fancier than picks, pans, and their bare hands.

"I myself saw them coming through Tari. Men with few clothes and little else carrying screw-top jars and Neestle coffee cans they had filled up with their diggings. Each can held U.S. one hundred thousand dollars worth of dust, flakes, and nuggeets. They paid for their chopper flights with nuggeets and flakes and crystalline gold.

"All that in three years. North of Mt. Kare is Porgera, which is today one of the biggest gold mines in the world. Southwest, where the Fly River starts down to the Torres Strait, is Ok Tedi. That is larger still and makes silver and copper besides. To the west of it in the Indonesia half of the island, West Papua, is the Freeport-McMoRan mountain of metal that is even more impressive. Just north of the big PNG province of Neew Britain is an island called Lihir where there's a mine that's expeected to be bigger still. The engineers, they say the recoverable gold reeserves at Lihir are forty-two million ounces. Forty-two million. And Lihir, she is a little island.

"This whole country, my friend Steve, was thrown up by volcanoes, and the volcanoes, they vomit up the gold from deep inside the earth. Tons and tons and tons of it. Each week, each month, in a different part of the country, somebody announces that they've found the biggest gold mine in the world. And you know what?" He gestured with a butter knife. "This is the only place in the world where nobody laughs at people when they say things like that. Because it's the only place in the world where they just might be telling the truth.

"You have been in Lae. Just north of there, in the thirties, there was a big gold rush where the towns of Wau and Bulolo are today. Now they have found gold at Mt. Yogonda, to the north and west of here. Colluvial gold, like at Kare. The kind of gold that is just lying around waiting for somebody to trip over it. Children pick nuggeets out of the grass and the women sluice out flakes from the soapy water they have used for their washing. The strike is neew and rich but it is not as big a thing as Mt. Kare was—so far."

Bohannon mulled this new complication. "I'm surprised you're not up there yourself, doing some prospecting."

Andersvoot's deep-throated laugh boomed over the table and across the porch. McCracken too was chuckling.

"Not me, py damn! Like Mt. Kare, Mt. Yogonda lies on land claimed by both the Huli and the Enga. I like my head where it is, on my shoulders. Didn't you hear what I said? The local people, they fight among themselves, but when it comes to outsiders, they are of one mind. A homicidal one.

"Oh sure, sometimes a few tough guys try to step in and set up a claim of their own. Coastal people, Islanders, white fellas from Oz and Kiwiland and even the States. They are found facedown in the mud, cut to pieces by bush knives or with their faces blown off by homemade shotguns. Pretty quick the word gets around. Mountain gold is for mountain peoples."

"And the police don't do anything?"

The rolling laugh boomed a second time. "The police in the Highlands have enough to do taking care of themselves. There were hardly any police at Mt. Kare. There are none at Yogonda. No cop is going to let himself be stationed someplace like that, with no electric, no running water, no heat, no roads in or out, Huli and Enga at each others' throats and the police in the middle. He'll quit first. The governmeent knows better than to try and force anyone to take that kind of duty."

McCracken flashed a sour grin. "It's the bloody Wild West, mate, only this time it's the Indians who are calling the shots."

Bohannon nodded thoughtfully. "So, how do we go about hiring a copter?"

For a second time McCracken rose abruptly from his seat. "What's with you, Mr. Steve? You listen, but you don't hear." He touched the side of his head, his finger tapping away like a berserk woodpecker. "Outsiders ain't allowed in!"

"Contrary to what you might think, *Mr.* Sorley, I do listen. If I'm hearing what Jan is saying correctly, outsiders aren't allowed in to mine for gold. That doesn't mean their presence is forbidden." He glanced at Andersvoot for confirmation. "How about it, Jan? Have I got it right?"

Their host nodded sagely. "Sure enough you do, my friend. If you steer clear of the diggings, with any luck the Huli and the Enga won't find a reason to cut your throat."

Satisfied, a determined Bohannon turned back to McCracken. "Helicopter."

"Oh, too right, mate, too right!" Waving his hands aimlessly and out of arguments, the expat started down the porch toward the stairs. "Helicopter it is. One chopper to Hell, if you please, and don't spare the napalm!"

As an angry and frustrated McCracken stomped off through the kaukau patches in the direction of the ditch-path that led to the road, a pensive Bohannon followed. Halfway between house and forest, he paused for a last look back. Andersvoot was standing on the porch of his mislaid castle, massive hands resting on the top rail, watching his visitors depart.

"Thank you for your hospitality, Jan Andersvoot!"

The big man waved. "Good luck to you, Mr. Steve. If you find your lady, I hope she is worth it!"

Returning the smile, Bohannon nodded once by way of farewell and lengthened his stride to try and catch up to McCracken. How could he explain to a man like Andersvoot that this was not about any particular woman, or about the money she had taken from him? How could he explain that when he did not fully understand it himself? He knew only that if he quit now, he would be leaving more than his money behind. Something that was much more valuable, and not at all tangible. The longer the pursuit continued, the more deeply drawn he was to finishing it.

No, Andersvoot would not understand any better than McCracken.

His guide spoke little during the drive back to Tari. Along the way they passed newly burned-out buildings and ruined earthworks, the legacy of the previous day's battle. Using simple digging sticks and stone axes, half-naked men were already busily engaged in making repairs. Women and children who had been little in evidence yesterday were everywhere now, clustered alongside the road selling fruits and taro and sweet potato and freshly gathered pandanus nuts. Others strode along beneath buckets or baskets, brightly colored bilums hanging down their backs, simply walking up and down the highway. There were no cars, no scooters, no motorcycles, and no trucks. All the way back to Tari, the ute encountered not one other vehicle.

When McCracken leaned on the horn to warn people, or dogs, or chickens, or pigs out of the road, the men and young women on either side invariably responded with affable smiles and friendly waves. Yesterday they had gleefully butchered their neighbors, tomorrow they might do the same. But right now, all was bucolic and benign. Birds sang in the treetops while giggling, squealing children shadowed by barking dogs cavorted in water-filled puddles.

Today Eden, tomorrow Hades, he thought. If the anthropologists were to be believed, it had been thus in these mountain valleys for thirty thousand years. His presence had not changed that, nor had that of men like McCracken and Andersvoot, or that of the national government. In time, it might. But today was not next week, and in this astounding, forgotten corner of the world, yesterday was still tomorrow.

Past the police station, with its stained white exterior and mud-caked Land Rovers parked out front, past the few shabby buildings that comprised the commercial district, past the high fence that enclosed the runway and the dilapidated airport terminal building, there stood a single large steel hangar. Four helicopters that varied in size from a tiny glass bubble suspended beneath twin rotors to a huge twin-engined Sikorsky were parked out on the tarmac. The reliable old Cessna waited motionless nearby, like the molted skin of a dragonfly. Within the hangar a number of tiny offices clustered together against the left-hand wall, as if for warmth.

McCracken brought the ute to a halt outside. "Let me do the talking, mate. You just listen and stand by to make ready with the money." Out of habit, he kicked his door open.

A couple of small, single-engine planes huddled together against the rear of the hangar. From wings to tail to fuselage, they looked too flimsy to make it over the nearest pass, much less as far as Mendi or Hagen.

Stopping outside the first office, McCracken rapped on the glass insert set in the door. The thick viewport was reinforced with wire mesh. A buzzer sounded, granting admittance, and he turned the knob and pushed.

Inside, the single small room was overflowing with books, operations manuals, undelivered crates and boxes, a pair of metal desks, gray metal filing cabinets, a massive radio, water cooler, cables, and two men, one black and one white, who were at once overworked and bored to tears. The national did not look up from the IBM Thinkpad he was massaging, but his expat colleague put aside a sheaf of papers to favor his visitors with a jaundiced eye.

"Morning, gents. Something I can do for you?"

McCracken helped himself to water from the cooler. "Got a charter for you." He used the cone-shaped paper cup to gesture at the silent Bohannon. "Mt. Yogonda."

The office manager grunted and his associate glanced up from his laptop long enough to grin. An Islander, his skin was fairer and his body twice the size of the average Highland male.

"Sorry, mate. Can't help you. I've got two charters out right now and a big group coming in from Mosby on Friday."

McCracken nodded understandingly. "Placer Dome? Broken Hill Proprietary?"

The man shook his head. "Both new outfits I haven't heard of before. The big group is from Singapore and Malaysia. Tunku Leong Ltd." His expression was one of disgust. "Looking for logging concessions."

McCracken downed his water and flipped the cup into a half-full metal wastebasket. "Brownnosers looking for brown gold." He looked over at Bohannon. "Smiley little bastards have cut the tops off their own countries and a lot of the rest of Southeast Asia. New Guinea's one of the few places they haven't butchered yet. But don't worry; they're working on it."

Mindful of this admonition, Bohannon merely nodded acknowledgment and turned away while the guide pumped the chopper company rep for more information. While he did so, Bohannon took time to study the office walls. These were papered over with a madcap crazy-quilt of girlie calendars, large adverts for everything from Coca-Cola to Port Moresby machinery repair companies to Zenag chickens, splashy color shots courtesy of the PNG Tourist Promotions Board and private travel agencies, and maps. All kinds of maps, large and small, relief and resource, geopolitical and aeronautical.

One of the largest caught his eye because of its exceptional detail and the strange lines and compass headings printed on it. In a corner he read, *CAUTION! Air information current through 23 July 1990. Before using this chart, consult the current DMA Aeronautical Chart Updating Manual CHUM/CHUM Supplement or the RAAF Chart Amendment Document, and the latest Flight Information Publications (FLIPS) and Notices to Airmen (NOTAMS) for vital updating information.*

The map was divided into finely delineated squares, the maximum altitude for each square given in bold numbers and purple ink in the center of each square. In addition to showing every town, radar site, beacon, and artificial structure in the region described, there were also sections marked "Unsurveyed" or "Survey Data Incomplete." Somehow he was not surprised that there were many of these.

A hand grabbed his shoulder and he turned. "No freeways, eh mate? Not bloody many roads of any kind. Let's go. We'll try the next one over."

They were nearly out the door when the expat behind the desk remembered something. "You chaps aren't by any chance heading up Wengu Camp way?"

"Wengu? That's east of Porgera, ain't it?" McCracken asked him. When the man nodded, the guide explained, "No worries then. We're off in the opposite direction."

"Good." The manager looked relieved. "Four engineers from Chevron got hit up there just two days ago. Robbed and raped, but nobody killed, thank God. Bloody raskols!"

A disbelieving Bohannon could not withhold his anger. "What kind of thoughtless company would send four female engineers out into that kind of backcountry?"

The manager's clarification was dry as road dust, his voice emotionless. "Who said anything about them all being female, mate?"

IX

The chopper agent's words left Bohannon with something extra to ponder as they tried the next office, where they had no more luck than they had at its predecessor. The news was the same at Pan Air, Pacific Helicopters, Goldenair, and Nationair.

Never one famed for an excess of compassion, McCracken was nonetheless moved to offer consolation to his companion as they walked slowly from the hangar.

"Look at it this way, mate. Fate never intended for you to get your money back. Or satisfaction, either."

"I've come this far." Bohannon lifted his eyes to the other side of the runway, past the razor-wire-rimmed fence that marked the limits of the recently mown grass, to the green-cloaked and cloud-crested mountains beyond. "I'm not giving up."

Since it had never been very large, McCracken had quickly exhausted his store of patience. "Suit yourself. Lots o' luck."

"Wait a minute." Bohannon grabbed the other man by the hem of a short sleeve. McCracken's gaze dropped slowly, significantly, and the American released his grip. "You're positive the Cessna can't land at Yogonda?"

"Oh, she can land, all right. She'll just never take off again. Terrain-wise, Yogonda's a lot like Mt. Kare in that . . ."

He was interrupted by a loud *whup-whup* as a chopper plunged precipitously toward the tarmac from above and behind the hangar. So sudden and unexpected was its approach that both men started to duck before realizing that it was going to miss them by plenty.

It almost did not miss the Sikorsky, nearly clipping the rear rotors before smacking into the runway and bouncing once. McCracken winced. As it hit, two large brown suitcases and one small red-faced Chinese came tumbling out of the passenger-side door. All three rolled over several times, the suitcases disgorging their contents slightly before the Chinese. It was a toss-up as to which made the more extensive mess.

After the initial bounce the copter settled to a stop. As the blades slowed, a second Oriental clad in slacks and tropical cotton shirt hopped out of the cockpit and ran to assist his badly unsettled friend. The latter was sitting up and holding his right arm which, Bohannon reflected, was better than holding his head.

"Not a very good landing."

McCracken had already started forward. "Remember what I told you, mate: any landing you can walk away from is a good landing."

"He's not walking," Bohannon pointed out.

"So it was a semi-good landing. So shoot me. Let's see if we can help."

By the time they reached the site the chopper's blades had stopped spinning and the two passengers were struggling to reassemble their baggage. In response to McCracken's smiling offer of assistance the one who had taken the bad fall unleashed a farrago of lightning-fast Cantonese the details of which escaped both Caucasians—which under the circumstances was probably just as well. Helped by his companion and mustering as much dignity as could remain in a man who had just had the bottom torn out of his pants, he marched off in the direction of the tiny terminal, stumbling only occasionally. Clothing and personal effects trickled from both damaged suitcases.

"Some fellas just can't handle the idea of help." McCracken turned to go.

"Hold up a second." A sudden notion impelled Bohannon to walk back to the copter and around to the other side, where he could see the pilot through the transparent door of the cockpit. Smiling ingratiatingly, he waved at the seated figure. Taking notice of the supplicant, the man responded with an equally amiable smile and the upthrust middle finger of his right hand. Bohannon was delighted.

He had the certain feeling they had just found themselves a chopper.

When several moments passed with no further response from within, he walked over, reached up, and rapped hard on the transparency. The pilot continued to ignore him for another minute before finally swinging the door wide.

"What is it, bud? Can't y'all see that ah'm busy?" Grabbing the door handle, he started to pull it shut.

Unable to interpose himself, Bohannon had to settle for hurried words. "My friend and I want to charter your copter. Well, I want to charter it. Assuming it is for charter, of course."

"Sorry, bud. Ah'm all booked up." A two-day growth of stubble darkened the pilot's face, his eyes were bloodshot, and oil stained his cheeks and hands. Maybe twenty-five or six, he wore blue jeans held up by a leather belt with a huge silver buckle and a red-print flannel shirt whose sleeves were rolled up to the elbows. The trashed, grease-stained hat on his head was not Akubra but pure Americana, right down to the snakeskin hatband. A glance at his feet confirmed what Bohannon had suspected from the moment the man had opened his mouth. They were boots. Not gumboots, or steel-toed workboots, but oilfield western. Noconos, or maybe Larry Mahan's.

"You're no Aussie."

At this the pilot looked up and grinned into the distance, tugging on the brim of his hat. "Ah'm an Abilene boy, mister. That's as in Abilene, Texas, not Abilene, Kansas." Young-old eyes squinted down at him. "Y'all are no swinging son of Oz yourself."

"San Diego." Bohannon stretched, extending a hand upward. "I'm Steve. That's my friend, Sorley."

The young man took the proffered hand. "Tom Oxley. Well, it's nice to meet a fellow 'Merican an' all, but that don't make *Black Lightning* and me here any more available."

"That's an interesting name for a chopper, mate." McCracken had walked around the front of the machine and was listening to the conversation.

"Named her after a riding bull on the national rodeo circuit. Famous, he was. Crippled so many riders, those that drew his number started refusin' to get on him." He patted the dash affectionately. "Mine's a mite less ornery, but she still kicks plenty."

Bohannon jerked a thumb in the direction of the terminal. "We saw."

Oxley pushed his hat back off his forehead and sighed deeply. "Ain't no first class seating in this part of the world. Ah tried to tell 'em that."

"That's God's truth, mate." McCracken turned and pointed. "That's my Cessna over there."

The copter pilot squinted in the direction of the twin-engine. "She's nice."

"Are you sure you can't help us?" Bohannon was not shy about pleading openly. If it should prove necessary, he was willing to grovel. "We've got to get to Mt. Yogonda as quickly as possible."

Oxley chuckled softly. "What're you gonna tell me, mister? That it's a matter of life an' death?"

McCracken beat his companion to the reply. "It's a woman."

"Well shee-it, why didn't y'all *say* it was really important? Mt. Yogonda, huh?"

"You've been there?" Bohannon hardly dared hope.

"Yeah, ah been up there. Nasty place. Get in an' get out, that's the way ah like it. Ah fly you boys up there, after that you're on your own. Ah ain't leavin' Black Lightning on the pad. Not on *that* pad."

"Then you'll take us?"

The young Texan made placating gestures. "Now hold on just a minute. Don't get your ass in an uproar. Lemme think." This took a minute, more or less. "Ah've got a delivery for Porgera, but ah can put that off 'til Sunday. They can wait another day for their beer and cigs. Ah can fill the back of the chopper with a half-load of dry goods and sell 'em to the dealers at Yogonda." His eyes flicked back and forth between the two men. "How soon can you lucky dogs be ready to leave?"

Bohannon glanced over at McCracken and replied without waiting for comment. "Immediately!"

"Not so fast, mate." The guide's thoughts were racing, trying to keep ahead of his companion. "I've got most of the gear we'll need in the Cessna, but if we're going to spend more than a day up there we're going to need a few other minor items. Like tinned food, for example."

Oxley looked past him, toward the town. "This time o' the month the grocery on Main Street should be up on stock. If it's fresh eats y'all want, there's always the Central Market."

"I know." McCracken's expression turned thoughtful. "Can you give us a couple of hours?"

Bohannon did not allow himself to relax until the Texan finally nodded. "Got to refuel, check the engine, get a load on board. We're lookin' at a thirty-minute flight. Yeah, I can work it. But no longer, or the weather'll have us for supper."

Bohannon was satisfied. "You can take a full load if you want. It won't affect us since we won't be bringing much."

Liberating a pack of fragrant Indonesian cigarettes from a shirt pocket, Oxley stuck one between his lips and lit it with one of those cheap plastic pinup lighters that when tipped, slides the bathing suit off the girl imprinted on the side. A scent of cloves filled the air as the cigarette flared to life.

"Got nothing to do with whether it affects you or not, bud. With the two of you comin', ah can only contract for half a load. Yogonda's above the nine thousand foot level. That high here, a chopper can only carry half the load it can at sea level. Be pushin' it as it is, but ah like to push it. That's how you make money in this business." Removing the cigarette with two fingers, he exhaled aromatic smoke. "Beats what ah was doin' this time last year."

"What was that?" McCracken wondered.

"Flying spotter for a Taiwanese tuna boat. Got to the point where it was either leave or punch the captain out. Watched 'em take too many dolphins." He took another drag on the cigarette. "Besides, ah was gettin' sick of noodles, rice, and bad kung-fu movies."

"Christ, I just thought of something." McCracken put a sympathetic hand on his companion's shoulder. "We can't do this, mate."

Bohannon stared at him. "Why not?"

"You've got nothing to pay him with."

"Oh shit, that's right." Bohannon turned back to the pilot. "The woman we're chasing took all my cash and traveler's checks. I was able to replace the checks, but only a little of the cash." He fumbled in his pants' pocket. "In Lae I was able to get an additional advance on my Amex, but I had to use most of it to pay my friend for flying me up here. I don't know if I have enough left over to pay you, and I bet I can't get an advance here in Tari. Certainly not within the next couple of hours. I know an independent operator like yourself doesn't take credit cards. Not out here, in wild country like this."

For a long moment Oxley said nothing. Then he dug beneath his seat. White stuffing hung out the side, escaping through a rip in the upholstery. In rapid succession Bohannon watched him pull out an eighteen-inch spanner, a socket wrench set housed in a banged-up green metal box, a flight log, three dog-eared Louis L'Amour novels and the book version of the Clint Eastwood movie *Pale Rider*, an empty stubbie, the half of a Superb riflebird that goes over the fence last, and finally, a manual credit card processor, one with an imprinted metal plate set in the top and a push-pull grip for processing a charge slip by hand.

Settling the machine in his lap, where it looked very out of place, he peered back down at Bohannon. "Visa, Mastercard, Barclay's, Sumitomo, Bank of China, Discover, or American Express. 'Course, ah got no way of gettin' an electronic authorization number on y'all, but that's all right. You cheat me, ah'll find you and kill you." The friendly grin returned to his face. "If that meets with y'all's approval, California, then you got yourself a charter."

Bohannon turned to McCracken. "We're wasting time. Where's this grocery?"

Shaking his head, the lanky expat turned and headed back toward the hangar. "We could walk it, but we'll do better with the ute. Come on."

Climbing down from the cockpit, the clove cigarette dangling from his lips like the fleshy lure of a bottom-feeding anglerfish, Oxley called out to them as they strode across the tarmac. "Y'all don't be late, now, y'hear?"

In addition to a number of small decrepit wooden shacks that sold cigarettes, beer, ratty T-shirts, and other staples of Highland life, there was one real honest-to-God store. A single large two-story rectangle, it boasted a raised wooden walkway with steps at either end and in front, no windows anywhere, and a covered porch beneath which a horde of non-customers surged aimlessly up and down as if the sheer weight of their presence might bring forth a flood of goods from within. Most of the structure, including the roof, was painted bright blue. Probably, Bohannon surmised, because the last time the building was due for a paint job, blue happened to be the cheapest color available in sufficient quantity.

The end of the edifice facing the airport housed a snack and food take-out shop. Next to it was a pharmacy whose front was painted white, and next to it, occupying three-quarters of the building, was the grocery. A fence of weathered wooden slats ran from the far end of the structure to the wooden palisade that encircled the town marketplace. Through a single entrance, defended by a trio of grim-faced armed guards, vendors and sellers and browsers entered and exited the noisy enclosure.

Parking across the wide dirt street and avoiding the worst of the mud, McCracken led his companion up the wooden stairs and onto the porch. Off to their right, against the fence line, women sat tending naked children and pigs. Most of the crowd on the porch were men, all of whom glanced at least once in the direction of the new arrivals.

A few stared openly. They constituted a fashion spectacle the likes of which for sheer outrageousness not even the Sydney Gay Pride parade could match.

It would have been easy for those Highlanders with a taste of sophistication or visitors from the cities to criticize the primitive attire of their Highland cousins. No one did so because all knew better. Laugh because a man wore arse-grass instead of pants and your casual critique might cost you your tongue.

The heavy steel door that barred the only entrance to the grocery was dragged aside. Bohannon found himself in a narrow, claustrophobic, two-story high, one-way, single-file hallway, hemmed in by featureless concrete walls on both sides. Fifteen feet long, the restrictive security passage finally opened up into a single large room perhaps seventy feet square. After emerging from the tunnel, they had to pass through a tall chain-link gate and slow turnstyle guarded by one of the biggest Highlanders Bohannon had yet seen. Over six feet tall, with an impenetrable bush of a beard and an equally ferocious head of hair, the guard was well dressed in khaki pants, black surplus army boots, long-sleeved white shirt, and cap. In place of a gun he carried two canisters of pepper spray.

Male or female, adult or child, he stopped and hand-checked every national before letting them through. The two white men he let pass without a word.

"What's he doing?" Bohannon could not see clearly because he was being swept into the market by an irresistible tide of shoppers and browsers.

McCracken did not have to look. "Checking for weapons. They're not allowed in the grocery. People here who get to arguing over who first picked up a choice piece of pork or head of lettuce are liable to resort to blows to sort it all out. It's less messy if they can't pull bush knives on one another."

Nodding his understanding, Bohannon studied the shelves and coolers. "This is better than I expected. I mean, more than I expected."

Locating a couple of battered baskets, McCracken handed him one. There were no carts. "This place can afford to carry decent stock because a lot of the field teams for the oil and mining companies do their shopping here. It's a long haul back to Mt. Hagen. Don't look at the prices and you'll be all right." A lopsided grin split his unshaven face. "Actually, the local stuff's not too bad. It's the imports that'll bust your pocketbook."

McCracken did all the shopping, methodically filling their baskets with rice, sugar, beans, coffee, and other staples. "No fancy trail foods out here, mate. No dehydrated chicken à la king. The field packs I've got in the Cessna will hold about ten days' worth for the two of us, on top of sleeping bags, tent, medical supplies and cooking gear. After that, if you want to eat sago grubs and pandanus nuts you can go looking for Tai on your own."

Bohannon did not comment. He could not, because he had no idea what his reaction would be if faced with such a decision. He took comfort in the knowledge that if he had to make one, it was at least ten days off.

All four checkout lines were open. Complimentary paper or plastic sacks being unheard of in this part of the world, McCracken picked up a couple of cheap, monochromatic bilums with which to haul their supplies. The well-groomed, efficient young woman who checked them out manipulated her computerized register as deftly as any cashier in suburban Los Angeles.

Where there had been only one security guard scrutinizing new arrivals, four shared the task of inspecting those who were leaving. Bags and parcels were opened and their contents compared against register receipts. Any visitor departing without having made a purchase was treated as a potential shoplifter and required to submit to a thorough, no-nonsense search of attire and person. These examinations were usually restricted to the more youthful and well-dressed browsers, since their elders did not wear much in which to conceal stolen goods. It would be difficult, Bohannon reflected, to shoplift a canned Danish ham wearing nothing but arse-grass.

The exit was little wider than the entrance, another narrow tunnel crammed to capacity with a heavy flow of stinking humanity. Bohannon found himself shuffling along side-by-side with an old man no more than five feet tall. His battered, torn hat was decorated with possum fur and a single enormous, backward arcing feather. Bright orange with black chevron striping, it brushed several times across Bohannon's face when the oldster turned away from him.

The old man's features were blunt, wide, and rugged, his eyes dancing and alive, his smile wonderfully open and friendly if one ignored the dark red stains on his teeth caused by a lifetime of chewing betel nut. The ugly, unhygienic red splotches that stained streets and sidewalks throughout the country were the result of endless spitting by the adherents of that ancient addiction. In the Highlands especially it was difficult to tell betel juice stains from those caused by blood.

McCracken kept checking his watch. "We've been here about an hour. We'll make it back to the airport in plenty of time."

A couple of hopeful Highland mutts followed them halfway across the rutted, unpaved street before deciding to try their luck elsewhere. Bohannon imitated his guide and slung his grocery-filled bilum in the back of the ute. Heading for the passenger side, he found himself confronted by a pair of locals. Neither was smiling.

Perhaps he was expected to go first. Raising a hand in greeting, he put on his cheeriest expression and said brightly, "Moning!"

By way of reply the nearest man reached inside his jacket and brought out an ugly-looking knife with a six-inch blade. The handle was of carved bone, but the blade was store-bought. His grim-visaged companion kept his own right hand inside his dirty jacket and looked around anxiously.

Bohannon found himself backed up against McCracken. Two other raskols had come around the other end of the truck to similarly confront them. Dozens, hundreds of shoppers and strollers crowded the entrance to the central market, the grocery and pharmacy, the street. None looked in their direction. In his haste, the usually cautious McCracken had parked a little too far off the main drag.

The tip of a meter-long bush knife tickled the guide's throat. Its owner's voice was harsh, guttural, and impatient.

"Mipela laik you mani." The ragged blade of the deeply scarred machete thrust threateningly upward. *"Nau!"*

"Sure. Whatever you boys want." McCracken kept his voice low and reassuring. *"Yupela be isi. Mi no laik trabel."* Reaching into a pocket, he pulled out his wallet and handed it over. Bohannon was not given the chance to dither. Strong fingers searched through his pockets. His credit cards were tossed in the mud, but the bandits found the little wad of kina and traveler's checks. One of them roughly removed his cheap watch from its owner's wrist.

The bush knife was slowly withdrawn from McCracken's neck. *"Mipela go nau,"* the leader of the group told them curtly. *"Yupela stap liklik hia."* To emphasize the order the knife-wielder drew the blunt side of his blade across his throat. Then he and his companions turned to go.

Bohannon let out the breath he had been holding and bent to retrieve his credit cards from the mud. McCracken also knelt, but not to help. Reaching under the cuff of his right pants' leg, he drew from an ankle holster a small gray pistol with a custom abbreviated clip. Before his startled companion could express concern, shout, drop to the ground or do anything else, the guide had taken aim and emptied the weapon. Bohannon thought he heard five shots.

Three struck the unsuspecting leader of the raskol pack in the back, the other two one of his companions as the man started to flee. He went down looking back over his shoulder. As bystanders first flinched and then surged forward, the two survivors vanished, swallowed up by the crowd.

Rising slowly from his firing crouch, the compact pistol dangling from his fingers, McCracken walked purposefully over to the two bodies. Considering the small caliber of the gun, there was a surprising amount of blood, largely but not entirely due to the fact that in falling, the head raskol had collapsed onto his concealed bush knife. Sharper than it looked, it protruded through the man's left side, having slid between a couple of ribs.

In contrast, his equally unfortunate companion looked like he had merely fainted, if one discounted the small, neat hole in the back of his skull. Though still twitching spasmodically, he was just as dead. With one foot, McCracken pushed him over onto his back. Then he knelt and searched through the leader's pockets until he found his wallet.

"Well?" Bending over the body, he looked quizzically up at his companion, then nodded at the other corpse. "Don't you want your watch and your money back?"

"I . . ." Bohannon's speech was as paralyzed as his movements.

"Christ! Now I'm a fucking nursemaid." McCracken moved to the other body and began to check its pockets. "Worse than having a kitten to look after."

Looking around, a nervous Bohannon saw that they were now hemmed in by the curious. In most cases, the locals' expressions were impossible to read. He chose to think of them as neutral.

A husky, uniformed figure pushed its way through the pack, which parted with obvious reluctance to make way for him. The cop had no hat and no gun, but the club hanging from his belt looked formidable enough.

"Trouble here?" His accent was strong and he spoke in English instead of Pidgin.

McCracken straightened, indicated the bodies. "Four of the buggers jumped me mate and I over by our ute. Took me wallet and his watch and money but missed me gun. When they turned to take off, I popped 'em. Got these two." He prodded the nearest corpse with his foot.

The cop turned to the crowd. "*Lukim man o meri dispela?*"

In response to the call for witnesses, an old woman stepped forward and replied in Pidgin. She was followed by two young men, one of whom wore a denim coat that had been made into a vest, the other the remains of what had once been an exquisite silk dinner jacket. Instead of arse-grass they wore ragged shorts beneath their coats, but neither had any shoes. Considering that while it was going down the altercation appeared to have been roundly ignored by every passer-by, there was suddenly no dearth of volunteers to attest to what they had seen.

The Pidgin flew too fast for a novice like Bohannon to follow, but McCracken looked, if anything, like a man vindicated. After conversing with a dozen or so eager, voluble observers, the cop turned away from those still anxious to contribute their version of events and back to the much taller expat. He indicated the weapon McCracken still held in plain view.

"Private ownership of handguns is illegal in PNG."

"So the government says." McCracken kept a straight face.

"Private ownership of handguns could be very dangerous to the body politic." The policeman was watching him closely.

"Especially to certain parts of it." The guide glanced significantly down at the two bodies.

Nodding agreeably, the cop nudged the nearest corpse in the ribs. "Bad doings, these raskols. Bad enough on the roads, but when they come into town it is I and my colleagues who have to deal with them."

"Except for these two." McCracken managed the thinnest possible intimation of a smile. "You won't have to deal with them anymore."

"I was told that two got away."

The expat turned apologetic. "Sorry. This is a small gun, a tiny gun, really, and it only holds five bullets."

"You could have killed an innocent person." The cop eyed him reprovingly.

"But I didn't, did I? See, when you carry a gun that only holds five rounds, you have to practice your shooting. I was very careful."

The policeman agreed solemnly. "If two got away, they will be telling their friends. And the friends of the dead men, and their relatives. You know what that means."

McCracken nodded as he bent to slip the pistol back into its ankle holster. The cop observed the procedure with interest. "I know. Payback."

"It would be foolish of you to remain in Tari. You would not even be safe in the jail."

"There's a helicopter waiting for us at the airport." Bohannon smiled helpfully.

The cop seemed to see him for the first time. "You are an American?" Bohannon nodded. "I have heard that America is a very violent country. That there is fighting in the streets all the time."

"That's right, but most of the time we don't use guns, we use lawyers."

"Lawyers." The policeman considered this. "I have met one or two lawyers. Myself, I think I would rather settle matters with a bush knife. But this country is still poor and uncivilized. Not like yours." He smiled hopefully. "Perhaps someday we will be as civilized as America and have lots of lawyers." He turned back to McCracken. "If the friends and relatives of the dead men find you, there will be more killing. Killing means paperwork. Since I cannot guarantee your safety here, it would be wrong of me to restrain you. Therefore, in my official capacity as a constable, I order you to leave Tari immediately."

"You're a hard man." McCracken kept his expression carefully neutral. "Come on, mate." Putting a hand on Bohannon's shoulder, he turned his companion back toward the waiting truck.

Behind them, the excitement over, the crowd began to disperse, leaving the policeman to deal with the bodies. Despite having been left completely unguarded, the highly visible and valuable groceries were still where the two visitors had left them, untouched in the bed of the pickup.

"That's this country for you." McCracken pulled his door shut and started the engine. "For every bloke, or family, or clan that invites you in for tea and puts you up gratis for the night, there's a neighbor just down the road who'll gladly tear out your gizzard for the pair of used sneakers on your feet and the couple of kina in your pocket." Pulling out into the street, the ute scattered dogs and kids as it headed back toward the airport.

A brooding Bohannon could not shake his memories of the encounter. "You killed two people."

"My apologies, mate. Next time I'll just let the buggers kill you."

"That's not what I mean. You were justified in defending your property—I suppose. But not only didn't the officer arrest you, he didn't so much as issue you a citation."

"You heard what he said about paperwork. Citations are another form of paperwork. That's about the only thing the local cops hate more than raskols and drunks. Most of 'em can barely read and write. As for me gun, the government doesn't allot the local cops enough money to buy bullets, let alone weapons. Only the Rapid Reaction Force is properly armed. To his way of thinking, I was just helping him out. There are no judges up here, mate, and no juries. So the local cops have to do it all on their own. Every time they enforce the law by making an arrest, issuing a warning, or knocking some belligerent knife-waving wife-beater in the head, they run the risk of incurring payback. Oh, a swell job, it is!" He turned a corner. "When I come back in the next life, I surely want to do it as a Highlands cop."

Bohannon thought about it, and the more he thought about it, the happier he was when they left the town behind them and he could stop thinking about it.

X

No one challenged them on the short drive back to the airport. Once through the gate in the heavy fence Bohannon felt reasonably safe again. While Oxley ran a final check on *Black Lightning*, his two passengers stacked packs, gear, and food on top of the crates of beer, sacks of rice, and bunches of fresh vegetables their pilot was hauling to Mt. Yogonda for quick sale.

When all was at last in readiness, Oxley climbed in and beckoned for them to join him. "Move y'all's butts, boys. Visibility up top will be down to yards in less than an hour. I don't much like flyin' through mountains by havin' to reach out the door and feel my way through 'em."

McCracken started to climb in, then hesitated and looked back. "You want the window seat, mate?"

Behind him, Bohannon shook his head. "I'll sit in back, thanks."

The expat nodded and climbed into the seat next to Oxley. As soon as both passengers were strapped in, the pilot kicked over the engine. The rising whine of heavy rotors soon drowned the cramped cockpit in a mechanized roar. Mindful of the landing they had witnessed earlier, Bohannon hung on to a dangling strap with one hand and the seat in front of him with the other as the pilot let out a resonant "Yee-hah!" and *Black Lightning* lifted. This time it did not bounce. At twenty feet, Oxley inclined her nose forward and they accelerated, clearing the airport fence by plenty, the surrounding trees by rather less.

Behind them, twenty howling, gesticulating, wild-eyed friends of the men McCracken had killed burst through the unlocked gate and out onto the tarmac, intent on extracting payback for their dead comrades. Along with their battle cries, their arrows and spears fell laughably short of the chopper shrinking rapidly into the distance.

But that did not stop them from trying.

As the copter continued to gain altitude and the bumps and jolts kept to a minimum, Bohannon gradually released his death grip on the strap and seat back. Below, steep hills and serrated ridges separated individual valleys, each with its quota of neatly dispersed huts and gardens. A few dirt tracks, all leading in the direction of Tari, were the only marks man had made on the landscape. In less than five minutes these too had disappeared.

As the chopper banked slightly to the right, the door promptly flew open, admitting a blast of cold, incredibly moist air. McCracken's arms flailed madly for a moment but his harness held him inside. Their pilot's reaction was nonchalant.

"One o' these days I'm gonna have to get that latch fixed. Grab that rope there and hang onto it, will y'all?"

Stabilizing himself, McCracken threw the younger man a look that promised sudden death and dismemberment. Then he located the end of the indicated rope and pulled the door shut. For the remainder of the flight he kept a firm grip on the length of knotted hemp.

Occasional huts and kaukau patches interrupted the greensward below for a while longer. Then they were in the wild mountains again, tree-clad ramparts rising to heights of twelve thousand feet and more on all sides. Whistling to himself, Oxley followed one river canyon after another as he tracked northward.

Here, where bountiful tropical moisture gave rise to towering cloud masses and thunderheads too imposing even for commercial jets to rise above, the trick was to stay below the clouds, not to try and get above them. While he sometimes dropped low enough above roaring streams choked with downed logs and broken boulders to put out a fishing line, there were times when Oxley had no choice but to push on through ground-hugging clouds the color of dirty cotton.

At such moments a supernal peace enveloped the chopper. Instead of bouncing, the ride became utterly calm and flat. Even the pounding *whup-whup* of the rotor blades was muted. It was as though they were no longer flying from point to point but from time to time, traveling not northward in kilometers but back in centuries. When they emerged from the last cloud they would be not thirty minutes but a thousand years from Tari.

It was a time for contemplation. Forced to rely on imperfect machinery and a suspect pilot, Bohannon reflected that he was a long way from Southern California. In point of fact, he was a long way from anywhere; about as far from anywhere as it was possible to get in a world of cellular phones and fax machines and broadband Internet connections. Out here, a man's connection to other men extended only as far as his voice could carry.

Death could steal up on a man quick and personal, removing him from the global equation without ceremony or witness. Decades ago, the Sepik had claimed the daring but reckless oil heir Michael Rockefeller without a trace. All the Rockefeller billions had not been able to find a trace of the vanished scion of that legendary family. This land would make no exceptions for a Steven Bohannon.

"There she is!" Oxley was shouting as he pointed. "Mt. Yogonda, dead ahead!" The grin that spread across his boyish face was pure country, and infectious. "Can I navigate crud or what?"

Like the velvet curtains of some early twentieth-century picture palace, the heavy cumulus parted to reveal the slopes before them. The chopper had been climbing steadily ever since leaving Tari, and at this altitude large trees survived only in isolated clumps. Where the ground was rolling instead of precipitous, it was covered with grass and pockets of shrub. Giant tree ferns and similar primitive growths clung to the steeper ridges.

From the cloud-swathed crest of the brooding, dark massif off to their right, a handful of waterfalls tumbled, only to lose themselves in impenetrable vegetation at their bases. Every cascade was slim and ribbonesque. None was less than a thousand feet high.

Oxley glanced over his right shoulder as he negotiated *Black Lightning* past an intervening hillock. "You boys plan on doing much hikin' in this country, y'all better watch your step. A lot of what looks like solid ground, ain't. It's just decayed vegetable matter. You can be walkin' along on what seems to be good old terra firma and *wham*, you're up to your belt buckle in green-brown muck. Or over your head. This country swallows people whole."

McCracken nodded knowingly and pointed through the transparent bubble. "That'd be the Yogonda Puga down there." As the pilot confirmed this with a nod, the expat turned to face Bohannon. "Puga's a local word. Means a large, marshy place."

Leaning forward, Bohannon strained for a better look as the copter began to descend.

Off to their left a rickety aggregation of makeshift shelters spilled down a hillside like toys from a child's storage locker, following the course of a single stream. Less than a handful could qualify as permanent structures. Below the last building the streambed had been turned into a battlefield in which men fought the earth with shovels and digging sticks. The fragile alpine vegetation had been stripped away to reveal the bare, gray, clay-like soil beneath. This blasted heath was pockmarked with dozens, hundreds of small holes. A spadeful at a time, the once virgin streambed was being turned upside down and inside out.

"Hang on." For the first time since they had cleared Tari, Oxley concentrated intently on his flying. Bohannon took this as a warning to be ready for anything.

A glance out the window as they banked left showed nothing but mud, moss, and grassy hillside. "Where's the landing pad?"

"Just ahead and beneath us." Oxley did not look up from his instruments.

Bohannon caught a glimpse of an impossibly tiny platform. It seemed to be built up of rough-cut logs, the largest not more than six inches in diameter. A pile of rusty 44-gallon fuel drums sat off to one side. The whole landing site was maybe twenty feet square. "We're going to land on that?"

"Hopefully, bud." It was all Oxley had to say on the subject. Bohannon sat back in his seat and closed his eyes. He opened them almost immediately. It would be foolish, he thought, to die in self-imposed darkness.

The underside of the copter rewarded him with a swift kick in the butt, jarring his teeth and compressing his coccyx. Engine whine began to fade. They were down. Shaken and rattled, but intact.

For a change, McCracken had a door that opened itself. All he had to do was let go of the rope he had been holding onto all the way from Tari and the door swung open of its own accord. As pilot and passengers piled out onto the crude log landing platform, a thin, cold rain began to fall: mist become misery. Bohannon pulled his shirt collar up behind his neck and wished for the hat he did not have.

One was handed to him. An Akubra in the last stages of decomposition, it had been patched with several plastic bags. Bohannon accepted it gratefully, not even bothering to check and see if it was inhabited.

The man who had given it to him smiled and nodded before stepping past to greet their pilot. Tall and hefty for a Chinese, he wore only a white T-shirt, gray shorts, and rubber sandals. The light, intermittent rain did not seem to bother him.

"Thank you for coming, Tom. I was running low on a number of things and I did not expect you until next week."

Oxley nodded and somehow managed to light another cigarette, indifferent to both the rain and his proximity to the leaking, oil-streaked chopper. "No sweat, Tiny." He indicated his passengers. "These boys needed a lift, so that made it worthwhile for me and the old gal to make the hop up a little ahead of schedule." He rewarded the shell of the chopper with an affectionate pat. "Gentlemen, meet Tiny Hong; entrepreneur extraordinaire, noodle and electronics expert, and all-around good guy."

The Chinese shook hands with both of them, then turned to spew a stream of Pidgin at the four Highlanders who had been waiting silent as statues nearby. Clad in the usual outrageous assortment of second-hand clothing, they moved forward and organized a line leading from the chopper to the edge of the landing platform. McCracken and Oxley watched carefully as the cargo was unloaded.

"I have a store here." There was no mistaking the pride in Hong's voice as he watched his employees stack cases and cartons and bound bunches of vegetables and fruit.

Bohannon peered into the mist. It appeared to be falling in slow-motion, rain reluctant in time. "Looks like a hard place to do business," he commented conversationally.

"Yes it is." The merchant's smooth brown belly protruded between the bottom hem of his T-shirt and the low-slung beltline of his shorts. His arms were large but not muscular. "But I go where the money is. You are here to look for gold, yes?"

Unsure how much he should reveal to a complete stranger, Bohannon turned away as if he had not heard. He was learning to let McCracken deal with the leading questions. The expat preferred it that way, and the arrangement was growing on Bohannon.

When the last sack of trade goods had been dragged from the back of the copter's cabin, Hong beckoned for them to follow him downhill. Oxley demurred. Bohannon saw that the pilot was conversing with a brace of newcomers: a man and two women. The women wore new, long-sleeved blouses and skirts; the man dark slacks, an incongruously fancy white shirt, new hat, and shiny waterproof gum boots. All three were between five and five and a half feet tall.

The man was gesturing elaborately with one hand while the other held an open can. The logo and design were familiar: Planter's Peanuts. Something inside caught the minimal sunlight, held it, and cast it back out redoubled. Edging closer for a better look, Bohannon saw that it was three-quarters full of washed gold flakes. Most were the size of fingernail clippings but a few, ragged and rippling, would have smothered a quarter.

Oxley saw him staring and grinned. "Sorry I can't stay and have supper with you boys, but I think I've got a fare to Hagen. Y'all be careful out here, y'hear?" Enveloped in the cloud of clove smoke rising from his cigarette, he returned to his negotiations.

The backpack McCracken handed Bohannon was heavy, crammed full of supplies, and had a tightly rolled sleeping bag tied to the bottom. Slipping his arms through the shoulder straps, Bohannon let it settle against his shoulders without complaint. They were here at his behest, after all, and the expat was carrying the tent. The least he could do was carry his share.

They followed the merchant and his line of heavily laden employees away from the landing pad. Each of the four short, stumpy Highlanders bent low beneath a load that would have taxed Andersvoot. None of them uttered a word of protest.

The trail consisted of primitive duckboards; short sticks nailed to lengths of log that formed a path about a foot wide. Rendered perpetually damp by the mountain mist, they provided slippery and uncertain footing that nonetheless was a vast improvement over the bare ground beneath and off to either side. McCracken glanced back to check on his companion's progress.

"Don't step off here, mate."

Wiping water from his forehead, Bohannon studied the peaty black soil. "It doesn't look that deep."

"Appearances can be deceptive. Anyway, it ain't the depth here, it's the consistency. This muck is like a hundred-dollar whore. It'll suck the shoes right off your feet." He returned his attention to the winding path ahead.

As they descended further they began to pass some of the ramshackle structures they had seen from the air. Frames fashioned of crudely logged poles laboriously hauled from nearby forest were covered with waterproof plastic tarps. Bright blue, red, yellow, and white, the unexpected colors added a falsely festive tone to the undisciplined community while creating an unintentional and unexpectedly effective approach pattern for arriving copter pilots. Hopes of future affluence fluttered in the light breeze in the form of waterproof polypropylene.

The edges of thinner plastic sheets could be seen peeking out from beneath walls that were abstract collages of cardboard, canvas, and scrap metal. When not ripped or damaged, these interior, hanging sheets formed relatively watertight walls and, when laid flat, floors. Everything from logs to flat rocks to empty metal containers had been placed on the fragile roofs to keep them from being blown away. Each structure was encircled by a deep trench designed to carry rainwater away from living quarters and down the hillside.

In the middle of the makeshift town, a handful of semi-permanent structures stood apart. The most substantial of these utilized the same pole and plastic sheet construction for the walls, but the roof was of corrugated iron and the floor featured raised logs wrapped in metal to keep out vermin. As a smiling Hong beckoned for them to enter, Bohannon noticed there was no sign over the door. With only two stores in town, advertising of any kind would have been superfluous.

Behind a counter built up out of strips of surplus metal paneling and supported by empty oil drums were neatly nailed-together shelves stocked with a surprising selection of goods. Dividing the shelving, another door led to a back room. It was into this dark grotto that the heavily-laden Highlanders vanished with their burdens.

Off to the left, a wood fire burned invitingly in a handmade stove fashioned from another old oil drum. Set on flat black rocks to raise it safely above the floor, it disgorged its smoke through a long water pipe thrust through the ceiling. Two comparatively well-dressed Highlanders sat in handmade chairs on either side, warm and cozy and out of the rain.

Standing silently just inside the main entrance were two other locals. One wore shorts that had been reduced to strips of denim fringe, and an old army jacket. His thickly bearded companion was slightly better dressed in long pants badly holed at the knees and a Megadeath sweatshirt from which the left sleeve had gone missing.

Each held tight to the most prized possession a man could have in the mountains; the holy grail, the Excalibur, the royal scepter of repressed male Highland desire—a shotgun. Not crude, homemade, wire-wrapped, nail-fired single-shots these, but double-barreled twenty-gauge weapons of refined North American manufacture. They were old and battered, and one had half its stock broken off and missing, but they looked serviceable enough. Taking the measure of their muscular, grim-faced owners, Bohannon did not imagine that the store had much of a problem with thievery.

Labels familiar and foreign stared back at him from the rough-hewn shelving. Australian canned and packaged goods, hardware, medicines, priceless cigarettes, gold washing pans, kerosene, batteries, and other supplies competed for space with multiple boxes of Kellogg's Corn Flakes and Heinz Ketchup. No doubt the bulk of Hong's inventory was kept in back, along with some sort of impenetrable safe. In place of a cash register, a calculator and two sets of gold scales sat atop the counter.

While restocking proceeded, the rain intensified. It drummed insistently on the corrugated iron roof, as if to remind visitors that this was a country and a place within that country that would not be ignored. Only after it relented, having delivered its daily message, did customers begin to arrive, filtering in and out of the establishment. Some paid for their purchases with gold flakes and tiny nuggets doled reluctantly from small jars and coffee cans, others with fistfuls of newly printed kina banknotes.

A very few were nattily attired in work pants or jeans, shirts with all their threads and seams intact, wide-brimmed hats, and expensive Dryzabone overcoats. In contrast, most of Hong's customers wore only the minimum required by propriety. A pair of shorts or ragged work pants for the men, simple wraparound skirts and blouses for the women. Several of the older men and a couple of the younger wore traditional headdresses and arse-grass. Few members of either sex bothered with shoes. Footwear was expensive and reserved for use in mining or on special occasions. Besides which, the puga tended to swallow them.

One burly middle-aged man, a cord of solid muscle barely five feet tall, wore an old lumber jacket over a once-fine sweater of New Zealand wool, a blue construction site hard hat, and a strip of bark around his waist from which had been hung suspended for modesty's sake strips of bright yellow plastic tarp. The gum boots on his feet were old, the two King-of-Saxony bird-of-paradise feathers trailing from his hard hat a more recent acquisition.

Carefully dispensing gold flakes and granules from an old aspirin bottle, he filled his red and green bilum with two small bags of rice, a bunch of precious bananas, tinned fish and corned beef, a large plastic bag of saucer-sized wopa biscuits from the Morobe bakery in Lae, one small bottle each of catsup and mustard, small shakers of sugar and salt, and a six-pack of PNG export lager. The six-pack alone, McCracken estimated, probably set him back the kina equivalent of forty or fifty U.S. dollars.

"They'd get twice as much for their gold in Hagen," the worldly McCracken pointed out, "and they know it, but this ain't Hagen, or even Tari. And our mate Hong here has, um, expenses to meet. Even with the guards and the guns I expect somebody tries to rip this place off at least once a week."

"He seems to be doing all right," Bohannon countered.

McCracken made a rude noise and moved a little closer to the radiant stove. From the moment they had put their packs down in a corner he had not taken his eyes off them.

"Everybody here saw our chopper come in. They'll all be hoping it might have been carrying something special. Those bananas, for instance. That's special, up here. But it's still daylight out, and the light hereabouts ain't for shopping. It's for digging gold, and for washing it. Eating, shopping, screwing—everything else can wait 'til after dark. So you're right, mate. Mr. Tiny should be doing just fine."

Among the last customers Hong dealt with personally before turning the counter over to an assistant were two young women. As diminutive proportionately as the Highland men, these two were slightly fairer of skin. Both wore their hair cut short, for the sake of hygiene and for convenience.

While her companion did the shopping, the one closest to the new arrivals unleashed on Bohannon a smile as radiant as the stove. Ignorant of what constituted a polite but proper reaction, he smiled back in what he hoped was a noncommittal manner. Her grin only grew wider as she mischievously ran a delicate finger along perfect white teeth. A jaunty red-and-green silk scarf flared from her neck above a maroon jacket proclaiming the fighting kangaroo mascot of some major Australian rugby team. Behind the open jacket was a loose sweater embroidered with butterflies. Below the waist she wore a pleated European-style skirt printed with a tropical flower motif that reached to her ankles. The Reeboks on her feet looked expensive and new. Between them and her skin she wore one of the few pair of socks he had seen in the Highlands. Despite his exhaustion, spatial disorientation, and the lateness of the hour, he felt an unmistakable stirring.

Finalizing their purchases, the two visitors from Café au Lay shoveled their respective goods into handbag-sized bilums and turned to leave. As she skirted the already steamy Province of the Stove, the one who had smiled at Bohannon bent over to flick a fragment of plant matter from the top of one sneaker. In the course of her sylph-idean dip, her sweater gaped not quite as wide as the top of one of the ubiquitous fuel drums, revealing a shadowed pair of incredibly firm coffee-hued mammaries. An Oscar-winning cinematographer equipped with lights and scrims could not have framed a more enticing picture. Each was the size and shape of a slightly distended ripe cantaloupe. The dark nipples were thick and erect.

As she straightened, her gaze met his as boldly as that of any foraging buccaneer. The memory of those dark, penetrating eyes and lightly jouncing, barely constrained breasts remained with him long after she and her companion had sashayed boldly out the open door.

McCracken nudged him from behind, making him jump slightly. "Fancy a go, mate?" Before Bohannon could respond, the guide was jabbing a warning finger repeatedly into his ribs. "That were one right meri for this part of the world, but you'd best put it out of your mind right now. AIDS ain't too bad in this area. Not yet, anyways. But good ol' syphilis and gonorrhea and their prick-rotting relations are—what's the word I want?"

"Omnipresent?" Bohannon suggested.

"No, that ain't it—but she'll do. You can check with Hong, but this being a typical diggings, my guess is that the infection rate among the local whores is right around one hundred percent." His expression twisted into an unlovely sneer. "Besides which, I don't expect they take American Express."

Purely out of academic curiosity, and because an unsuspected and unfamiliar part of him was reluctant to abandon the subject if not the girl herself, he asked matter-of-factly, "How much?"

McCracken took the question seriously. "Most times I'd say fifty to seventy kina. But a meri that pretty, up here in a god- and woman-forsaken place like this, might run a hundred. That's for one dip o' the wick, not the whole bloody candle." His gaze narrowed. "Didn't you hear what I said, mate? You ain't seriously considering . . . ?"

"No, no." Bohannon hastened to reassure his companion. "Academic interest only."

Hong had observed the byplay. Bohannon suspected there was not much that escaped the merchant's notice. "You want woman? I get you special discount."

"Actually, mate," responded McCracken with a smile, "we could do with a place to crash. It's bloody cold out there and I don't fancy wrestling with the tent right now." He indicated the two-man pop-up strapped to his backpack.

"Certainly!" Their host gestured expansively at the two men seated next to the stove. "*Yupela lusim nau, lusim!*" Compliantly and without a word, the men rose and moved to the opposite side of the room.

"Here." Hong gently stamped one foot on the metal floor close to the stove. "Any friend of Texas Tom is friend of mine. You sleep here tonight. Sorry I got no beds for you." He chuckled merrily. "Four Seasons Yogonda not open 'til next week. But you be warm here, and dry." Leaning close, he winked conspiratorially. "I got some Gold Cup in the back. Later, after I close, we have a drink, yes?"

"You bet, mate." Seeing the blank expression on his companion's face, McCracken elaborated. "Gold Cup is sort of the local firewater. There's them that says it was first brewed in Mosby, others who claim the miners at Mt. Kare invented it. It ain't Dewar's Black Label, that's for damn sure, and it ain't quite Everclear, either, but chugged in improvident quantities it'll kill you quick enough. Makes a good mixer, it does. I've also seen blokes use it to remove paint and de-grease engines."

"Straight up or on the rocks?"

"Don't matter. You're a dead cobber either way." He slapped his flat stomach. "Fair dinkum stuff!"

"Don't you mean, 'fair drinkum'?"

For half a second McCracken looked confused. Then he broke out in a grin that was almost heartfelt. "That's the spirit, mate! Stick with it and this little walkabout will make a man of you—if it don't kill us both first."

When the last customers had departed, clutching their bilums full of precious goods, and all but the two armed guards had been dismissed for the night, Hong vanished behind a curtain with a lockbox full of loose gold and rubberband-bound banknotes. Returning shortly thereafter with a bottle and three glasses, he pulled a chair up next to the stove and ceremonially poured drinks for all of them.

"Sip it," McCracken advised Bohannon. The expat's tone was reverent. His words were not a suggestion: they constituted a warning.

Bohannon complied cautiously. Actually, the pale liquid did not even burn going down. Like a package of gelignite attached to a timing fuse, it went off in his gut about fifteen seconds after hitting bottom.

"Shit on a stick!" he gasped. At the risk of adding oxygen to the conflagration but unable to restrain himself, he inhaled sharply.

McCracken nodded approvingly. "Two glasses of Gold Cup'll get a naked man through the night up here. With two bottles you could walk across Greenland." He raised his glass to their host. "Bottoms up, mate, and me on top." To Bohannon's astonishment (and not a little apprehension) he threw down the rest of the tumbler's contents in one long, continuous swallow. Contrary to his traveling companion's expectations, the guide did not die, pass out, or show any immediate visible signs of internal hemorrhaging.

"So." Tiny Hong sipped decorously at his own glass after refilling McCracken's. "Sorley told me up at the pad that you two are not here to look for gold. That's good. I don't like to drink with people I might have to bury next week." Perhaps it was the deep-sea glow of the single overhead bulb that prevented the merchant from camouflaging his eagerness. Or maybe he just didn't care. "What then? You hear something about the sapphires, maybe?"

Bohannon blinked. "Sapphires?"

Leaning back in the artless but sturdy chair, McCracken kicked off his sneakers and held his feet up to the fire, his long legs hanging suspended above the floor like a tarantula's forelimbs.

"Been rumored for years that people have been picking up gem-quality sapphires between Hagen and here. Meself, I've yet to see one."

"If you not here for sapphires, then what?" Hong was not to be denied. "Diamonds, maybe? You looking for diamonds?"

"God knows there's plenty of 'em to the southwest of here, mate, in Northwest Australia, but to my knowledge the only argyles you'll find in PNG are in the men's department at Steamships. No, we're looking for something just as flashy and just as flawed. A woman. If you can believe it."

The merchant sat back and rested both hands on his bare knees. Very slowly he looked from one man to the other. "This is a joke, yes?" he exclaimed finally.

Eyes closed, McCracken moved his head slowly from side to side as he rested his neck on the back of the chair. "Oh, she's a joke, all right, Tiny-me-mate. Only, the joke's on Mr. Steve here, and on me for agreeing to help him."

"I see that you are serious." Shrewd eyes focused on Bohannon. "Since you could do much better in Mosby or Lae or even Madang, I am thinking there is more to this woman than what one might assume."

When McCracken offered no objection, Bohannon felt free to elucidate. "She stole some money from me. If you factor in the traveler's checks, quite a bit of money."

"Oh so?" His lower lip pushed out, Hong nodded understandingly. "And you think she come up here? This would be a white woman?" Bohannon nodded.

McCracken's seeming indifference vanished. He dropped his legs and sat up straight. "You've seen her." It was not a question.

"Sure I seen her, Sorley. I've been Yogonda almost a year now in this place and in that time I see maybe three white women up here." He turned back to a suddenly attentive Bohannon and held his left hand out in front of him, palm flat and facing the floor. "About this tall, red hair, real good looker lady?"

Bohannon nodded once. "That's the one. Her name is Tai Tenison."

"I not hear a name, but yeah right everything else."

McCracken leaned forward eagerly. "Is she still in camp?"

Making a face, Hong shook his head no. "She leave day before yesterday with another white guy. I was out of the store and Menam, my number one, he waited on them. Sold them a lot of stuff. Hundreds of kina worth."

The two visitors exchanged a glance. "Did he happen to also describe the man?" McCracken asked slowly.

"Sure you bet. Said he was big." Hong eyed the guide appraisingly. "Real big. Bigger than you, Sorley." The merchant slapped his chest. "Bigger every place, I think. Long hair, older too." His brows drew together as he strove to recall his assistant's words. "Menam say something else about him."

"What's that?" Bohannon prompted their host.

Hong turned to him. "Menam said the woman did most of the picking and paying, but one time he got a good look at this guy's face. Look straight into his eyes." He paused. "Menam say guy was crazy. Said guy didn't look at him—he look through him."

McCracken took a deep breath and swung around in the chair, putting his feet back to the fire and wiggling his toes. "Stenhammer."

"You're sure?" Bohannon pressed him.

The expat sipped Gold Cup. "Not many candidates fit that description, mate. I'd be just as sure if we were in Mosby. Or Sydney, for that matter. Good ol' Tai. She went looking for him, she found him, and now they've gone off together somewhere into the Devil's own backyard in search of his Flamin' Highness's only knows what."

"If I remember right," Hong went on, "Menam told me they had a lot of equipment with them. Strange equipment, that he had never seen before. And ropes. Many ropes."

"Swell." McCracken raised his glass in a toast. "Here's to mountaineering, may they fall off a wall and she land on top of him." He slurped a melodramatic sip. "That's it, mate. We've no alpine gear and no way of getting any."

"Maybe the equipment's not for rock climbing." Bohannon was deep in thought.

"Say what? What then?"

The other man shrugged. "Maybe they plan to erect a platform in the canopy, to collect bugs or study medicinal plants. Maybe there's a place where they'll need to bridge a river that's too wide or too deep to throw a log across. Rope could be for lots of things."

"Like maybe they need to hang some folks," McCracken growled. "You never give up, do you, mate?"

Bohannon's reply was quiet but firm. "On the contrary, Sorley, I usually give up. But not this time. Not anymore. Maybe it's because I've come this far already, maybe it's this country—hell, I don't know. Ask me an easy one."

"I would, if I thought I might get a sensible answer. If I wasn't a guest in another bloke's place, I'd puke." He sighed. "All right—tomorrow we'll see if we can figure which way they've gone and have a quick look for 'em."

Hong turned to him. "They are one or two days ahead of you. This country leaves no tracks to follow. Not for outsiders, anyway. You need a guide."

"Christ on a crutch," McCracken muttered. "More money thrown away!"

"Why should you give a shit? I'm paying." Bohannon eyed their genial host expectantly. "How much?"

Hong considered. "You want to come back alive?"

"Oy, that would be nice, that would." McCracken had closed his eyes again and was pretending to luxuriate in the glow of the fire.

"Just kidding. I think I know somebody. Actually, I know several somebodies, but this is the only one you might be able to talk away from diggings. There are a few people who know some of this country, but not many. Not even local people go beyond the mountain. Back there is too high, too cold, too wet. The Huli and the Enga like places where the soil is good and they can grow things."

"I'm with them," admitted McCracken. "This guide you have in mind, is he Huli?"

"Part. He must have relations in this corner of Highlands or he would not be allowed by the others to dig here. The Huli and the Enga fight each other all the time, but when outsiders try to come and look for gold, they will unite against them. Then they go back to fighting again." He smiled at Bohannon. "It has always been this way in the Highlands."

"And always will be," McCracken added for good measure. "What's this bloke's name?"

"Alfred. His diggings are on the north edge of strike. Perhaps he is having not so very much good luck. If so, maybe he will take you into the mountains. More importantly, maybe he will bring you back out."

"We'll make sure and put that in the bloody contract, we will." McCracken pulled his hat down over his face.

Hong rose. "I will leave you now. I am up at four but will try to let you sleep. Good rest, gentlemen."

"What about the fire?" Bohannon indicated the oil-drum stove.

"The boys will tend to it." He indicated the two silent guards still standing station on either side of the store entrance, which was now barred with a heavy metal grate. "It should last until morning. Don't worry about it." He smiled amiably. "There is one good thing about steel floor. It's not very soft, or very warm, but it will not catch fire beneath your bed and burn your balls, either."

XI

Hong's hospitality extended to providing a breakfast of hot coffee, toast, jam and marmalade, ham, and bully beef. Such largess from a merchant operating under strenuous and difficult conditions struck Bohannon as unexpected, if not unprecedented. As usual it was left to McCracken, when they had a moment to themselves, to draw his companion aside and explain.

"The first thing anyone interested in gold does is insist that it's the last thing they're interested in. Mr. Tiny here, he thinks your story about coming all this way to find a woman who stole some money from you is, in a word, a crock. The story ain't made much sense to anybody else you've told it to, including me, so why should he think any different? He figures that by kowtowing to us now, we'll look to him for help and supplies after we've made our big strike."

Bohannon listened carefully. "But we're not carrying any mining gear with us. Not so much as a pan. He can see that."

McCracken chuckled softly. "That makes him even more suspicious. To his way of thinking, we're either devilishly clever or incredibly stupid. He can't convince himself to buy into the second, so he's sticking with the first."

Their smiling host emerged from the back room. "If you ready, we should go and try to find Alfred."

"Sure, I'm just itchin' to get out into those mountains. How about you, mate?"

Anything resembling a napkin being an unimaginable luxury in a place like the Yogonda Puga, Bohannon wiped his mouth with the back of his sleeve and pushed away from the folding table. Sometimes it was difficult to tell when McCracken was being sarcastic. This was not one of those times.

The early morning cloud cover was receding, creeping up the sheer mountain slopes like heavy snow falling backward. Dense fog carpeted the narrow river valley below. Everything was moist and clammy from the previous night's rain and the morning dew. Water droplets clung to plastic walls, roof tarps, piles of scrap wood and metal, and the shaky but much appreciated duckboards.

Shading his eyes against the intensifying glare, Bohannon indicated the barren downstream they were heading for. "Looks like steam rising. Cooking fires?"

Hong looked back at him. "People working. Hundreds of people. As the temperature rises, their sweat will become invisible. But not their smell."

It did not take long to leave the transitory town behind and enter the diggings. There the duckboard path forked. One branch swerved downslope to the left. The other curled off to the right, hugging the comparatively dry, stable ground on the far side of the narrow creek.

Dozens of small coffer dams thrown together out of rock, clay, and brush shattered the stream that fell from the heights of Mt. Yogonda into innumerable tiny rivulets, each a vital component in the search for gold. For without access to a share of the dirty, freezing water, a miner could not wash his dirt.

Between the low, scrub-lined banks of the creek, the streambed was being systematically destroyed.

Nothing grew in the ravaged puga. Isolated plumes of smoke rose from small drum-fires used for cooking or warming chilled, arthritic hands and fingers. Mounds of excavated earth and clay gave the streambed the look of a prairie dog town designed by Dr. Caligari. Music by indigenous groups like Barike blasted from cheap boom boxes, a melodious miscegenation of Pidgin and English underscored by instruments both traditional and contemporary. The tunes were pleasant, the lyrics reflective of hard times and true love—Papuan easy listening.

Flanking each mound were from one to three holes. The better excavations were six to ten feet across, with squared sides. Most were no wider than the shoulders of the man or boy who stood entombed within. Varying in depth from five to ten feet, these chilly pits suggested vertical graves. Not one had reinforced walls. On the puga, wood and metal were too valuable to waste on shoring.

Crouching at the bottom of each pit, the miner would scrape with crowbar, digging stick, shovel, or bare fingers at the muck in which he stood, often in water up to his ankles. This paydirt would then be passed by hand or by makeshift pail to a colleague up above, usually an older man, brother, or wife. The dirt would then be kneaded like dough until it had been broken down sufficiently to be washed, both jobs often being done by women and children. Mixed with water, the resultant slurry of gray clay and gravel would be swirled in pans, any gold carefully picked out and put aside, and the scoured dirt added to the growing mound of detritus nearby.

"Very hard work." Hong led the way along the duckboard path that followed the north bank of the creek. "Very uncomfortable."

To Bohannon the feverish scene resembled a landscape by Bosch. Hundreds of holes were being worked simultaneously, dirt rising magically from below the earth to be passed to waiting, eager hands.

"How many people have died in cave-ins?"

"None. A minor miracle, everyone thinks. They believe the god Ne is watching over them. Or Jesus, or in a very few instances, Allah. Perhaps the deities are all working together to protect these people. I like to think so. It's a very inefficient way to look for gold, but at least it is cheap. You can't tell them different, anyways." He pointed to where four men were furiously quarrying four large holes and piling their debris in a single huge communal mound between them. No four ants could have worked with more single-minded determination and intensity.

"Look at that. There is probably as much gold beneath that mound of dirt they have thrown up as in the holes they are digging, but they can't get at it because they've built a small mountain on top."

One hole was quite close to the duckboard walkway. Bohannon took the opportunity to peer over and down. At the bottom of the seven-foot deep pit, a Highlander naked save for a pair of shorts happened to choose that instant to look up. Their eyes met. The local was caked in gray clay and mud from head to foot, so that only his eyes showed through. His eyes, and his teeth, which became visible when despite his miserable circumstances he grinned cheerfully.

"I know these people can't afford expensive machinery, but surely they could do better than this? Picks instead of crowbars, for instance."

"There are very few homemade sluice-boxes and rockers." Hong stepped over a gap in the path where the wooden cross-members had gone missing, probably pressed into service as digging tools. "The trouble with such devices is that in order to work properly they need lots of water. I've seen people killed and maimed over water allocations. As for picks, I won't sell them. Look how close together many of these holes are. A man with a pick would kill two people with every backswing." He pointed. "That's Alfred and David's claim over there."

Bohannon was grateful that their destination lay close to the walkway. Hong leaned out and called toward the nearest pit. Two women and a young girl glanced briefly in his direction before returning to their dirt washing.

A man emerged from the hole, then another. The first was much taller than the average Highland male, about five eight or nine, and built like a linebacker. His companion was pure Huli, short and muscular. Both wore their curly hair cut short, a sensible choice in a place where a bushy natural would only become caked with mud. Like every other miner, each was covered in a cracked coating of thick gray clay.

The bigger man waved curtly. "*Moning*, Tiny." Turning, he murmured something to his companion, who nodded and dropped back into the hole as neatly as a weasel into its burrow. The speaker slogged through the muck to greet his visitors. Out of courtesy, he did not offer to shake hands.

"How is digging this morning, Alfred?" Hong asked him.

The other man put one hand on his hip and wiped at the caked clay coating his face, a comparatively futile gesture. Fully expecting a reply in Pidgin, McCracken and Bohannon were pleasantly surprised.

"Not so good. My cousin's daughter is sick and won't stop coughing."

The merchant was sympathetic. Sympathetic, but not altruistic. "Come up to store and I give you something she can take."

A subdued, almost shy grin appeared amid the clay. "We have no cash money this week, Tiny. All we are getting now is galena and pyrites. Maybe a little dust, but we have to buy food. Everyone is hungry."

Hong nodded understandingly. "Your credit is good with me, Alfred."

The miner gestured back toward his hole. "You'd better talk to David about that. I don't like to take credit." He eyed the merchant's silent companions appraisingly. "Credit is an invention of the Europeans. Their replacement for slavery."

Hong chuckled. "Then it is everybody's substitute for slavery,

Alfred. Africans, Orientals, Hindus—don't go singling out the white folks. If you won't take credit maybe these guys advance you some wages—if you interested in their proposal."

A flicker of curiosity gleamed through the clay and came to rest on McCracken. "So you got a proposal for me? Well, let's hear it." He jerked a thumb in the direction of the unproductive pit. "My cousin, he's for sure there's a layer of 'ice' just another meter down. Always just another meter." He sighed tiredly.

"We need a guide." McCracken took over. "A guide and a tracker. At least, as much as it's possible to track anything in this infernal country."

Alfred frowned. "You are looking for something? Or someone?"

"Two people. A man and a woman, both white. They bought supplies from Tiny a couple of days ago and took off into the bush. The woman stole money from my friend here."

"Ah! And he wants payback!" The Highlander nodded vigorously. "You want my help to find them and kill them." This was spoken in the same tone of voice Bohannon would have employed to order a club sandwich on toast.

"No, no! I just want to find them and get my money back. What's left of it, anyway. It's—a point of personal pride." Was that what it had become? he thought to himself. Well, it would do until he sorted it out more thoroughly for himself. If he ever did.

"Of course it is. I did not mean to misunderstand." The miner shrugged indifferently. "I can kill them if you want, but I will do what you pay me for."

"Then you'll take the job?" McCracken was watching the Highlander carefully, trying to analyze what lay beneath the clay and behind the words. There was something there, something unspoken. When he couldn't quite put his finger on it, he forgot it.

"Sure, why not? Tiny says you might give me some kina in advance. Will you do that?" Everyone could see that the miner was struggling with himself not to beg. "It would help pay for medicine for the girl."

Bohannon looked at McCracken, who nodded reluctantly. "Two days pay now, the rest when we get back. A bonus if we find the people." He smiled thinly. "Nothing if we die."

"That is fair." Alfred's gaze shifted back to the merchant. "Send the medicine down."

"Consider it done."

"*Shay-shay.*" It was the only Mandarin the miner knew. He turned to face his new employers. "You say these people you want to find were here, at Yogonda?" Bohannon nodded. "I did not see them, but others besides those at Tiny's store would have. Some might have seen which way they went." The tall Highlander considered. "There is one old trading trail that goes from here to several small outlying villages. If they started out on it, they could have gone west to Piauwa or east toward Yogo. When can you gentlemen be ready to leave?"

McCracken squinted at the sky. "The sooner we get started the better. If we're going to catch them we'll have to do some walking in the rain."

"Our gear is up at Tiny's," Bohannon added helpfully.

Alfred nodded. "I will need to get a few things together and ask some questions. As soon as I have any news I will meet you at the store." He extended a hand. Bohannon hesitated, then gripped the grimy fingers. McCracken looked on approvingly. The clay was gritty, not smooth at all. It must be hell to work with, Bohannon thought. The Highlander's grip was powerful but restrained.

Returning to the store, they found themselves waiting impatiently in the comfort of Tiny Hong's front room, watching as a stream of browsers and buyers surged in and out. Wide-eyed children hungrily eyed the few shiny packets of candy stacked on a back shelf. The sweets stayed where they were.

Notwithstanding the ersatz potbellied stove, Hong's was no corner drugstore in small-town mid-America. While its amiable proprietor tolerated the unrelenting silent stares, there were no free handouts. There must be little that children in such a place, Bohannon reflected, did not learn at an early age. The vision of dark voluptuousness he had locked eyes with the night before did not put in an appearance, an omission that found him emotionally as well as physically conflicted.

He did, however, see more gold in an hour than he had in his entire previous life. One young man, still half caked with mud and clay from the diggings, bought a brand new steel shovel and paid for it with a dirty, unpolished nugget the size of his thumb.

McCracken's impatience was turning to irritation that was only assuaged when their erstwhile tracker finally arrived. The lanky guide's distress quickly evaporated in the light of good news.

"Two people saw the ones you spoke of leave on the trail going north."

McCracken eyed the other man intently. "I thought you told us the only trail goes to villages that lie to the west and east?"

"It does," Alfred admitted, "but to reach Yogo you must first walk north a little ways before turning east." He smiled proudly. "So that is where they are going. To Yogo."

"Or in that direction." McCracken was reluctant to concede the point. "They may just be making use of the trail as a starting point. Their real destination may lie elsewhere."

Now it was the tracker's turn to appear uncertain. "But where else could they be going? There is nothing else in that direction. Nothing, not even little villages. Beyond the trail the mountains climb to the top of the Central Ranges. Too cold and too wet to farm, too steep for hunting. Many difficult rivers to cross."

Seeing that McCracken was ready, even eager, to escalate the argument, Bohannon interposed himself verbally. "Look, you've found out what direction they've taken. That's good enough for now. Let's get after them. With luck we'll catch up before they've gone very far." He hesitated. "If they're after rare birds or butterflies or God knows what, they may set up a permanent camp just over the next ridge. If that's the case then we may stumble onto them as early as this evening."

McCracken was willing to concede at least the possibility. "Maybe you're right, mate. Just maybe you're right. I'd like to think so." He turned to Hong. "What about it, Tiny?"

The merchant was not one to waste time overanalyzing. "If I were going for walk in this country I would not want to stray far from the nearest source of help. That would be right here. Your friend may be right. With luck I will see you again in day or two."

Especially if we've been lying to you all along, as you think, and we're just going over the hill to scout the next couple of creeks for possible paydirt, Bohannon told himself. He said nothing. If that particular mendacious scenario satisfied their host, why should he not enjoy his delusion? Mt. Yogonda offered little enough in the way of intellectual diversion.

"I am ready," Alfred declared simply.

"Then as me mate says, let's get on with it." Tugging his hat down tight on his head, McCracken bent to pick up his fully-loaded pack. Bohannon did likewise.

Alfred was waiting for them outside. His kit consisted of a simple bedroll and a small bilum slung over one shoulder. He wore no hat and had traded in his gum boots for rubber sandals. Bohannon was not surprised at the absence of leather. In this climate it would rot quickly. An old black jacket with white stripes on the sleeves and wrists complemented his walking shorts. Like his better-equipped companions, he carried a small plastic water bottle. Canteens would not be necessary. They might run short of many things, but water would not be one of them. Any problems would stem from a surplus of that particular item, not a shortage.

Almost anywhere else, an emergency flare or two would have been a welcome addition to their kit. Here such devices would only constitute unnecessary extra weight. Only the rare charter plane flew anywhere near where they were going, and McCracken had assured him that even if a flare could somehow be seen in the narrow cloud-filled gorges, no one would be able to respond to the distress call. Not even a small chopper could set down to search for them. Not where they were going. For the same reason, a cell phone would draw nothing but static, and even an Inmarsat phone would fail to make contact unless a contracted satellite happened to be directly overhead at the moment of calling.

The trading trail was less than a foot wide, an infrequently trod rut in the earth. In places it was hidden by tussocks and moss or literally vanished beneath swampy pits of liquefied vegetable matter. At such times Alfred quickly located the place where it re-emerged. Skirting bogs and water-filled depressions, they soon found themselves climbing the north ridge that overlooked the Yogonda Puga. Above nine thousand feet the going was slow and difficult. It would remain so until they grew more acclimated.

Such a climb would be tough on Tennison as well, he reminded himself, no matter how well-conditioned she was. If this Stenhammer had been up here for long, he was probably used to it. But Tai should slow him down.

Ascending the ridge was hard, but at least they were out of bog country. As the inevitable, depressing daily drizzle began to wrap them in its damp embrace, he looked back. Thanks to all the garish plastic tarps, the provisional community of Mt. Yogonda remained a highly visible Pollockian splash of color in the crotch of the narrow valley below. Downstream from the town, the creek bed was a bombed-out swath of exposed clay and degraded soil. From a distance it was difficult to see any people and impossible to see any gold.

Aware he was already falling behind, he turned his attention back to the trail ahead, blinking away rain as he focused on the backs of

McCracken's long legs. They were thin, the knees knobby and almost comical in their protrusion, but the wiry muscles that flexed beneath the fabric of the sodden pants were like corded steel.

When it quickly became evident that Bohannon was the slowest member of the trio, no one said a word. But McCracken slowed down and let him pass, and thereafter he and Alfred kept the American sandwiched between them. No one asked if he needed to stop and rest, no one offered him a drink. When McCracken was the first to propose a short break, Bohannon cheered silently at the small triumph.

Feeling a hand on his shoulder, he turned to see Alfred's broad-featured face smiling back at him. "It will get better, Mr. Bohannon, sir. You are not used to this country, but in a few days your body, if not your mind, will feel much more at home."

"If we're still searching in a few days," he reminded the tracker hopefully.

XII

It was a surprise but not a shock when, on the second morning out, Alfred called a halt and pointed not to the east but straight ahead.

They were standing on the crest of a ridge surrounded on all sides by mountains that soared another two thousand feet higher than their present position. Active as a legion of ghosts, cloud poured in wispy streams over the top of the ridge, smiting them with dew. Sheer limestone pinnacles like the jagged teeth of some prehistoric deep-sea monster thrust ominously upward from the steep slope below, their flanks deeply grooved. The dirty white rock fingers were heavily eroded, pitted, and crowned with jungle vegetation.

" 'Broken bottle country' one of the early pilots called this." Pushing his hat back on his head, McCracken scrutinized the rough terrain below. "Karst topography. Constant rain dissolves the limestone away and you get caves, hidden crevasses, brush-covered pits, and sinkholes, as well as these crumbly, unclimbable stone towers. 'Tis loverly country for a stroll." He turned to their tracker and pointed to his right.

"Why are we stopping? Yogo village is that way."

"Yes. The trail to Yogo does turn here, but your people did not." Again Alfred gestured. "They went down this way."

"How can you tell?" Hefting his pack higher on his back, Bohannon drew near.

The tracker knelt and indicated specific places on the ground. "It has rained here, of course, but in clay like this footprints will stay for awhile. See here." He pointed.

"That might be the remains of a footprint," McCracken conceded, "or it might just be an oval depression in the dirt."

"It is a footprint." Rising, the Highlander gestured downslope. "There are more."

McCracken moved to the edge, grass parting beneath his boots. "I don't see anything."

"I will show you on the way." Alfred started down the steep grade, watching where he placed his feet as he left the trail.

McCracken was reluctant to abandon the distinctive footpath that was their only remaining contact with civilization. Bohannon moved to stand next to him.

"Either he's the tracker Hong says he is or else we've been wasting our time since we started. We hired him to lead, so let's let him lead. If you're still unhappy with the way things are going by tonight, we'll discuss alternatives."

McCracken inhaled deeply, then nodded. "That's fair enough, mate. If he's right, I'll apologize for having doubted him. If I'm right, then we've only lost another day. This ain't life or death decision time. Yet." With a last longing look at the trail, he started down in the tracker's wake. Bohannon hung close, picking his way carefully down the slippery grade.

Halfway to the bottom of the ridge, at the base of the third limestone pinnacle, the Highlander provided all the confirmation even a congenital skeptic like McCracken required. Bohannon had missed it completely, as had his companion, so it was left for Alfred to point out his discovery to both of them.

There was no arguing with the crumpled ball of cellophane wrapping. The Nabisco logo and the partial words "Chee . . ." and "acker . . ." were clearly visible.

McCracken was as good as his word. "Sorry, mate. I won't question your skills again."

The Highlander shrugged it off. "I am the tracker on this trip, not you. This is my country, not yours." He turned to Bohannon. "In America I would need you to show me how to find my way around on the freeways."

Near the bottom of the gorge he found another footprint. Situated at the base of a large tree and somewhat protected from the rain, even Bohannon could see that the oval depression had been made by a boot. It had also been made by a foot larger than any of theirs.

"Stenhammer." McCracken rose from examining the imprint to eye the narrow but fast-flowing river just ahead. "They must have crossed here."

"I'd like to find one of Tennison's footprints." Bohannon started down the last few yards of slope, toward the water.

"She doesn't weigh near as much as him," the expat explained. "So she's not as likely to leave prints."

Of course, Bohannon told himself. He ought to have realized that. He was still chiding himself when he reached out to grab a low-hanging vine to steady his descent—and the vine contracted violently against his fingers. Jerking his head around to look up, he found himself staring into a pair of bright yellow eyes. Slitted pupils regarded him icily as the reactive mind behind them sought to place him in one of three simple, straightforward categories: prey, threat, or neutral-of-no-consequence. As he released his grip he let out a startled shout and fell over backward.

His companions came running, Alfred with his bush knife drawn and ready. When they saw that he was unhurt, both men slowed and turned their attention to the inhabitant of the tree.

"Green python." McCracken spat to one side. "The juveniles, like this one, are bright yellow."

"Yes. They are harmless, except to birds and small animals." Bending, the tracker gave his fallen companion a welcome hand up. "Are you all right, sir?"

"I didn't know." Bohannon was as embarrassed as he was uncomfortable. "You don't see many snakes in metropolitan San Diego. I thought it was a vine."

"You're lucky you didn't get bit, mate." McCracken tracked the python as it abandoned the exposed branch in search of better concealment. Unhurried coils disappeared slowly into the greenery. "True, they ain't poisonous, but a snake that size can give you a nasty nip." As his gaze fell, his expression changed. "Here now, what's this?"

Looking down, Bohannon saw that in falling he'd scraped a hole in his pants leg and a nickel-sized piece of skin off the front of his left shin. "It's just a scratch. Forget it."

"Not a good idea, mate. Not a good idea at all. You don't 'forget' scratches here. Nothing heals in this bloody country." Swinging his pack off his back, he unfastened the rain fly and felt around inside until he found the medical kit. As Alfred looked on with interest, the expat removed a small clear plastic bottle and unscrewed the cap. The label on the side informed the interested reader that the contents had been manufactured in Calcutta.

"Have a seat."

"Are you sure about this? It doesn't even hurt." As he spoke,

Bohannon sat down on an exposed root of the snake tree and presented his barely injured leg.

McCracken removed a white and red capsule from the container and carefully screwed the top of the bottle back on. Bohannon expected the other man to offer the capsule to him with a swig of water, but after replacing the container in his pack, the expat did something entirely unexpected.

Holding the capsule vertically, McCracken shook it several times. Then he slowly removed the top portion of the digestible gelatin container to expose the lower red section. This was filled with white powder.

After dumping perhaps a quarter of the contents on the open wound, he replaced the top half of the capsule and handed it to Bohannon.

"Amoxicillin. Hang onto that. Apply the same dose every morning."

"Directly onto the wound?"

McCracken nodded. "That's the idea. Works a lot faster than taking it internally. You don't know what you banged your leg on. Bark, root, ground, rock. You're in microbe heaven, mate. Untreated, that little scrape would become infected in less than twenty-four hours. Then it'd start to ulcerate, then turn necrotic. Right on the shin like that, the infection would go straight into the bone." Unsmiling, he straightened and extended a hand. "Inside a week we'd have to take a hard look at taking your leg off."

Bohannon accepted the hand up, brushed at the grime and fragments of grass on his legs. "You're very convincing, Sorley. Unpleasant, but convincing. I'll try not to fall down anymore."

"Too right, mate. From now on, watch what you grab. If it doesn't bite back, there's a good chance it'll stick you, cut you, or give you a rash you won't forget." He started forward. "Let's see if we can figure out how the fuck they got across this river."

Closer inspection revealed footprints near the edge of the fast-moving torrent. The swift current was dangerous, the water ice-cold, the streambed slippery with rocks and moss. No one place looked any safer or easier than the next.

Not unexpectedly, it was Alfred who found the marks on the tree.

"Look at this." He pointed to where a large branch that overhung the raging creek protruded from the moss-covered trunk. At their feet, the river rumbled and growled through the narrow canyon, the noise of its passage echoing off the limestone walls. Masked by mist and dense vegetation, unseen birds announced themselves to one another in alien tones, the only indication of their presence an occasional, brief glimpse of impossibly bright plumage flitting between the trees.

A deep groove cut through the bark of the branch. After studying it for a moment, McCracken turned and gestured toward the opposite side of the creek. “Right. So now we know one use for the ropes they took, but just stringing a rope across wouldn’t be enough. I don’t know about Stenhammer, but tough as she is, I don’t think Tai could make it all the way across hand-over-hand. They must’ve rigged a flying fox.”

Bohannon eyed him querulously. “I thought a flying fox was some kind of giant fruit bat.”

“So it is. We’ll see them as well, but what I’m talking about is a kind of seat and cable arrangement. Like a bo’sun’s chair—but you probably don’t know what that is, either.”

Bohannon stiffened slightly, then relaxed. He could hardly get mad when the other man was right. “I get the idea.”

The tall expat studied the frothing watercourse. “Well, we ain’t got ropes or rigging for a chair, so we’ll just have to bash our way across. That’s how people usually make progress in this country anyhow.”

They searched upstream. It was rough going, with broken rock underfoot and every plant in the vicinity fighting for its piece of sunlight. After half an hour of hacking and tearing their way through bushes and vines, Alfred’s sharp eyes picked out a place where the water ran shallow except for a narrow gap between two boulders. This deep, sluice-like cataract, he and McCracken decided, could be bridged by a single small log.

They found one, waterlogged and heavy but the right length, wedged against another tree slightly farther upstream. With Alfred in the lead, they carefully edged their way out into the swift current, manhandling the log between them. Flowing over the tops of sneakers and boots alike, the water was shockingly cold.

Come to the tropics and die of hypothermia, Bohannon mused. A couple of hours submerged in one of the innumerable mountain rivers and a man would freeze to death as readily if not as rapidly as in the Arctic. Less than a hundred kilometers by air due north of their present position lay the vast basin of the Sepik River, a festering humid hellhole where the danger was from overheating. It was no wonder the island of New Guinea contained some of the last unexplored localities on earth. As far as humans were concerned, the place was remorselessly inhospitable.

Thinking too much instead of paying full attention to his footing, he slipped and nearly fell, the precious backpack full of supplies complicating his balance. Regaining his stability, he nodded reassuringly to his companions, who resumed their measured advance. The footing was slick and treacherous, but downstream the water would have been deep as well. Here they were only chilled up to the knees.

Reaching the two large boulders in the middle of the stream, they struggled to jam one end of the log into a crevice on the other side of the thundering, six-foot high cascade. When it was affixed as tight as possible, Alfred took the lead without having to be asked. His companions watched attentively and in silence as the tracker maneuvered himself onto the log and started across. If he fell, and didn't crack his skull on the rocks beneath, he would be swept inexorably downstream.

Sodden but tested, the tough rainforest hardwood held firm. Moments later the tall Highlander was standing on the other side, grinning and waving for them to follow. Bohannon went next, taking his time and gingerly picking his way along. The waterfall thundering through the stony gap beneath him was not high, the river not deep, the length of the makeshift bridge measurable in feet, but the minutes he spent crossing were among the longest of his life. He experienced a feeling of accomplishment entirely out of proportion to the achievement when he extended one arm to grab Alfred's outstretched hand, made the last stride, and stood standing alongside him.

McCracken crossed in less than a minute, his legs dangling down on either side of the log, hunching across in the least risky fashion. Wading the last few yards on the other side of the second boulder, they soon stood together on the opposite bank.

Forcing their way back downstream was easier than coming up. Now that they knew what they were looking for, it took Alfred only moments to locate worn bark on the branch of a tree opposite the one that had been similarly defaced on the other bank. Broken branches and disturbed soil showed where Stenhammer and Tennison had forged a path up the steep mountainside.

"We're behind them," McCracken pointed out, "but in this country it's the ones in front who have to make the road. The thicker the vegetation, the easier it'll be to follow them. They'll have done all the cutting for us."

"What are we waiting for?" Bohannon started past him, heading upslope. The successful river crossing and the cold water had invigorated him.

McCracken put out a hand to hold him back. "Just a minute, mate. You don't go smashing through this kind of brush in this kind of country without picking up a few hitchhikers." By way of explanation he bent and rolled up the hem of his pants legs, then pushed down the lip of the heavy sock on his left foot. Between pants and sock he wore an uneven black bracelet.

Leeches.

The internal imbalance Bohannon had experienced when he'd grabbed the python returned—with a vengeance. He felt as if he had just chug-a-lugged a quart of sour milk. While he watched, the expat sat down on a comparatively dry log and removed his boots and socks. Thanks to the heavy woolies, only a couple of the parasites had succeeded in working their way as far south as his ankles.

Fighting down rising gorge, Bohannon joined his companions in similarly divesting himself of his footwear. His high-top sneakers and skintight socks had saved his feet, but above the top of his socks beneath his jeans' legs and below the knees, he counted no less than twenty of the disgusting, inch-long, jet-black bloodsuckers.

"About time to put on repellent, boys." McCracken did not seem particularly upset at the discovery. Seeing the expression on Bohannon's face, the expat was clearly amused. "Better get used to it, mate. From here on we'll do this two or three times a day."

"I can imagine what happens if you don't." The image of little black blobs finding their way to considerably more sensitive and private parts of his body was one he fully intended to keep restricted to the realm of imagination. Not completely ignorant, he knew enough not to try and pull them off.

"They'll leave a little round scar if you do," McCracken told him as he treated himself. "If you have to pick 'em up, do it like this." Demonstrating, he rolled one between thumb and forefinger before flicking it off into the river. "Rolling 'em in your fingers reduces the stickiness and makes it hard for them to hang on."

As soon as he had finished, he moved to help Bohannon. "First we get rid of your passengers, then we treat exposed skin with two kinds of repellent."

"Why two?"

"The one with permethrin in it goes on your clothes and shoes. Clings to the material and for a week or two will kill or repel any bug that comes in contact with it. Depends on how wet we get. It's pretty water-resistant stuff, but eventually the rain will dilute it. The other is a timed-release diethyl-m-toluamide formulation. It goes on your skin and has to be reapplied every time it washes off. I like it because the time-release means you can use a one-third to one-quarter concentration. The undiluted stuff is effective but nasty, especially if you're doing repeated reapplications.

"One geologist I was cozying around used a one hundred percent formula. At the end of the day he found that the DEET on his hands had left impressions of his fingerprints on the housing of his camera. Permanently." He started working on Bohannon's leech-infested legs.

"Then why fool with the stuff at all? Why not use something else?"

"Because DEET works really good on leeches. Kills 'em outright. Salt's safer, or vinegar, but the salt we're carrying is more useful inside us and I didn't happen to bring any aged, gourmet wine vinegar with me. Not that there ain't plenty of salad makings around."

Sure enough, as the repellent was applied, the nauseating black parasites lost their grip, the barbed mouthparts peeling away from Bohannon's skin as their owners tumbled to the ground. Each time McCracken smashed one of the more resistant ones beneath the heel of his boot, blood spurted in all directions. *My blood*, realized Bohannon queasily.

"Just one more. Stay there." Reaching back, McCracken fumbled in his pack.

Bohannon checked his legs, then took a moment to look warily inside his jeans. "Where? I think you got them all, Sorley."

"Not quite, mate. That's why the little bastards are so dangerous. You never ever feel 'em." Turning back to his companion, he held up a small waterproof flashlight and flicked it alight.

Bohannon frowned. "What's that for?"

"You can't see this one, mate, because it's on your eye. Just above the right one, to be precise."

Bohannon's hand instinctively jerked upward. The expat knocked it aside. "Don't touch!" He brought the beam of the light close to the other man's face. "You don't want a bloody scar up there." He chuckled. " 'Bloody'—that's funny."

"Yeah. Look at me, I'm laughing myself silly." Bohannon sat rock still, trying not to move a muscle in his face.

"I can't use DEET this close to your eye, mate. Wouldn't be good if any got in it, not even in the diluted formulation. Salt wouldn't be any picnic, either. But put up a light, y'see, and the little buggers'll move toward it. Ah, there he goes."

Bohannon felt something small and wet moving across his right eyebrow. It took every ounce of willpower he possessed not to reach up and rip it away. What if McCracken was wrong and didn't know what he was doing? What if the horrid little bloodsucker crawled down instead of up and fastened its barbed mouth onto the exposed cornea? Would it suck blood out of his skull right through the retina?

"Hurry up!"

"It's moving, mate. What's the rush?"

"I—I'm afraid I'm going to be sick."

"I guarantee you'll be a damn sight sicker if you upchuck on me. Just keep it down another second or two—there!" Lowering the flashlight, he picked up the can of repellent. "Close your eyes." Shielding them with one hand held edge-on against the bridge of Bohannon's nose, the guide applied a minuscule burst of aerosol. A tiny but perceptible weight vanished from his companion's forehead.

Bohannon did not even want to look at the gruesome, squirmy blob. Rising abruptly, he turned to concentrate on the shadow path their predecessors had cut through the bush. "Let's get out of here."

Chuckling, McCracken pocketed the spray can. "Better get used to it, mate. The little buggers are everywhere. One of the joys of trekking through this country. No matter how careful you are, no matter what kind of repellent you use, you can travel sure in the knowledge that you'll always have company." Moving to stand alongside the squeamish American, he clapped a hand on his shoulder.

"Couple of blokes I know once spent two weeks in country a lot worse than this. Looking for signs of oil, they were. Their pick rate for leeches averaged a hundred per man per day. Made it into a kind of competition, they did. The winner got three hundred and ten off him in one day. So you ain't entitled to bitch. Not yet." He started past Bohannon and up the slope. "Thank Tai and her friend for being ahead of us instead of behind us. Them cutting away a lot of the vines and lianas and loose vegetable crap means less for us to brush up against. Maybe it won't be so bad."

It wasn't, but it was bad enough for Bohannon. Leech removal became a daily ritual, once after breakfast, again at midday, and last and most importantly, at night. At least once they had de-leeched themselves they could sleep in reasonable, if damp, comfort. According to McCracken, the revolting bloodsuckers were strictly diurnal. Along with their warm-blooded quarry, they too rested at night.

The mountainous rainforest was full of far more dangerous creatures, from highly poisonous spiders to some of the world's most deadly snakes. But there was something about small invertebrates that fed on man that made Bohannon's skin crawl. A taipan or death adder, even a spider, was something you could see and deal with. Whether through size or movement or weight, they made themselves known to their quarry. Leeches were silent, their bites undetectable thanks to the natural anesthetic they exuded with their saliva. Under their tiny, soulless, individual ministrations a man could be bled to death without ever feeling a moment's pain. It was unnatural.

He was wrong, of course. It was perfectly natural. It was his home environment that was no longer a part of the natural world. There were leeches there, too, only they had internal skeletons and walked upright on two legs. He knew this for a fact, having done business with a number of them.

Trying to switch his train of thought to a more pleasant track, he remembered the night he had spent in the company of Tennison. For a few hours, he had been bewitched. Beautiful, she'd been. Not stunning, not ravishing, but comely in a genuine and (though it pained him to think of the word in connection with her) sincere way. It was difficult to envision her plodding and crashing through this horrendous terrain, coping with leeches and biting flies, voracious mosquitoes and stinging ants. Impossible to imagine the sophisticated, forthright beauty he had shared drinks with in the bar of the best hotel in Port Moresby opting to come to a place like this voluntarily.

And for what? For the company of a man who might be certifiably insane? For a rare butterfly? It made no sense. But then, he was here as well, and that made no sense to him either. From the depths of the cold, wet, unwalked, parasite-infested rainforest, laid-back, tourist-oriented, civilized Fiji seemed as far away as Manhattan. From a practical standpoint, it was.

At least he had been fortunate in his choice of companions. Alfred led the way uncomplainingly, forging a route up the slippery mountainside, occasionally looking back to warn them of a protruding root or suspicious hole. McCracken followed, scenting their path with a steady litany of complaints much as Perseus left a trail behind him while exploring the Labyrinth in search of the Minotaur.

And everywhere there were bugs: some small and innocuous, others gigantic chitinous apparitions sprung full-grown from the fevered depths of some demented science-fiction writer's imagination. But these horned and barbed monsters were real; butterflies with foot-wide wingspans, jagged-legged stick insects longer than a man's forearm, horned beetles as big as baseballs. Six-inch-long cicadas vibrated in the branches and bizarre mantids snatched dragonflies with iridescent purple wings out of the sky—one predator preying ruthlessly upon another.

A flush of bright wings accompanied by alien hoots and squawks marked the passage of a barely glimpsed bird-of-paradise. McCracken identified one, glimpsed as it flew between trees, as a possible new species. After all, he reasoned, thirty-eight of the world's forty-three known species of bird-of-paradise existed nowhere else but in PNG, so why shouldn't they be the ones to discover number forty-four? Anything was possible in such a country. Anything.

Including marching forever toward an unreachable goal.

XIII

They were five days out from Mt. Yogonda, having crossed ridges and rivers that ran together in a continuous, exhausting stream in Bohannon's mind. He saw the island of New Guinea as covered from one end to the other in enormous bright green pleats, each of which had to be crossed slowly and on foot. Beyond each craggy pleat lay another, and another, and still another. Up and over and down, up and over and down, until the soles of the feet were worn raw and the muscles of one's lower body began to scream for mercy in fear and anticipation of the day's trekking yet to come.

Seated beneath a low-spreading tree ablaze with brilliant red blossoms, they consumed without enthusiasm a lunch of dried fruit bars, water, and chocolate, supplemented by a handful of pandanus nuts Alfred had gathered earlier that morning.

McCracken chewed reflexively on the last of a nut, spat out the indigestible residue, and said matter-of-factly, "That's it, mate."

Bohannon looked up sharply. Tired, filthy, and unshaven, his jeans and shirt matted with grime and sweat, the sorry excuse for an Akubra that Tiny Hong had given him still perched precariously on his head, he hardly resembled the confident, neatly-groomed world traveler who had arrived in Lae not so very long ago. He felt as if he had not had a bath since the beginning of time. Somewhere in the vicinity of a simple hatband fashioned from bark, sweat and rain and the essence of Papua New Guinea met and mingled.

" 'That's it, mate?' What's 'it'?" Guessing where the expat was leading, his tone was subdued.

McCracken proved himself nothing if not predictable. "Look here now, mate; be reasonable. We've been five days on this wild pussy chase. We've gone through half our supplies, maybe a little more. That means we've enough to last us the five days it'll take to get back to Yogonda." His eyes met the other man's unswervingly.

"There's a time to challenge Fate, mate, and a time to acknowledge her supremacy."

"But we can't give up," Bohannon protested. "Not yet. With them making the trail we have to be catching up to them. You said as much yourself." He sought support from the tracker. "Isn't that right, Alfred?"

The Highlander looked up from his food. "For sure we are closer to them, Mr. Bohannon, sir. The question must remain—how much closer? A day, two days? The rain on the earth makes it impossible to tell. Closer? Surely. How much closer? No one can say. Certainly I cannot."

Bohannon turned back to McCracken. There was a desperation in his voice that he could not explain. "Surely we can go on for another couple of days? Everyone's become trail-hardened, even me. We're making better time now on lower rations than we were when we started out, we're not slipping and sliding all over the place, and we have the trail they're making to follow."

McCracken looked away. "Mate, in this country you learn not to push the limits. Understand? People die out here all the time. They don't know what they're getting themselves into and they don't know what they're about." His gaze snapped back. "Are you hearing this, Mr. Steven Bohannon? *This country kills people.*

"Sure, we could keep going. We could keep going, never find them, stagger back, and collapse and die a hundred meters short of the copter pad at Yogonda."

"*They're* still going." Bohannon made it sound like a challenge. "And one of them's a woman."

His forearms resting on his exposed, dirt-encrusted knees, McCracken leaned back and laughed. "Which proves what, mate? That a woman can be as big a fool as a man? That stupidity can kill her just as quickly? I'm neither a fool nor stupid—though looking around right now, at where I am and whom I'm with and why I'm here, I ain't so sure I'd take bets on it." He spat to one side.

It started to rain. Hard.

They clustered together beneath the tree, the thick red blossoms and multitude of healthy green leaves providing a small amount of shelter.

Bohannon was not ready to give up. "I'm paying. Alfred and I will go on without you."

"Will you, now?" McCracken became contemplative as he studied the phlegmatic, silent tracker. "How long before Alfred decides that you're crazier than this Stenhammer? You think *he* wants to die out here? Or do you think that because he's a Highlander, a native, that he can live off the land and make it all the way back by himself? When he's had enough and it suits him, you'll wake up one morning and find him gone. Ain't that right, Alfred me mate?"

The tracker did not reply; simply sat and chewed the last of his fruit bar. His silence was eloquence enough.

"And without him or me, Mr. Steven Bohannon, you'll die out here. You think maybe you can find your way back to Yogonda along the 'trail' Stenhammer and Tai have made?" He gestured back the way they'd come. "By now the rainforest has filled in the gap where we started. Growth here runs about two days behind a man." In the cloud-dampened, subdued light and steady drip-drip from the leaves overhead his eyes blazed.

"One wrong turning, mate. That's all she takes. You make one wrong turn on the way back and you're a dead man. No one will find your body. In a week there'll be nothing left but bones. The forest will strip out your blood and brains and body like a spider draining a fly. In two weeks the vegetation will have covered what's left. You'll die alone, with no one to mourn you, outside a grave and without a marker. Pieces of you will nourish maggots, and no one will know."

"Then you have to stay with me, or it'll be on your head."

McCracken regarded him sadly. "If me moral sense is what you're relying on, mate, then you're as good as dead already."

For the second time, Bohannon turned to Alfred. "You've been supplementing our stores ever since we left Yogonda. Couldn't we do more of that?"

The tracker considered. "Got no bow, no arrows. But if you will eat what I can find . . ."

"I'll eat anything," Bohannon assured him. "Whatever's necessary to keep us going."

McCracken grunted derisively. The Highlander ignored him. "There are always pandanus nuts. In the rivers are fish, and crawlers. I have hooks with me. I always carry certain things when going up-country. There are wild fruits, other kinds of edible nuts." He studied Bohannon unblinkingly. "At the lower elevations, sago grubs." His lips smacked expectantly.

In light of what he had already said, McCracken's reaction was predictable. "You bloody well don't know what you're asking, mate."

As suddenly as it had begun, the downpour ceased. He rose to point. "Over this ridge is another river. Beyond that is the crest of the Central Range. The roof of this part of PNG. If you think the country we've come through already is empty and hard, wait 'til you see what's ahead."

"I'm ready." Where was this determination coming from, Bohannon found himself wondering. From whence the drive? And would he be able to summon up the energy to match it? "What is on the other side?"

"What do you think? More ridges and more rivers. More up and down, more bugs, more leeches, more of everything we've already been through, only worse. Because the farther north we go from there, the closer it gets to the Sepik. You know what that means?" He was shouting now, furious at the position Bohannon was putting him in, angry at himself for having allowed himself to be put in that position. "*If* we can reach the crest, when we start down the other side we'll still have mountains and rivers and rainforest to deal with, only the montane rainforest will give way to lowland growth. Real jungle. So in addition to the climbing there'll be heat and humidity. And mossies; the big, black, ugly ones that can bite right through your clothes. Then there'll be the flies, and the no-see-ums, and pretty soon you'll find yourself wishing for the courteous, considerate company of leeches. Here the bugs are bad, but down in the Sepik there are places where they're thick enough to drive a man crazy. Worse snakes, too. Worse everything."

Bohannon let the expat ramble on. When he was finished, or out of breath, the American spoke softly into the vacuum.

"Alfred says he can supplement our supplies. With careful rationing of essentials like salt and sugar I don't see why we can't press on for another week or so."

McCracken wouldn't look at him. "Another week or so," he snorted in disbelief.

Bohannon held out a carrot. "All right. One week, then. If we haven't caught up to them by that time, we'll turn back, and no more complaints or objections from me."

For a long time the guide did not reply. Then he looked up and squinted at the sky. "Clouds are coming down, but they're light. Might mean a couple hours' dry hiking." He rose.

Bohannon stood next to him, too tired to beam but gratified nonetheless. "Then you agree? We'll go on?"

McCracken glared back at him. "Give me one good reason why I should?"

"I'll do better than that. I'll give you two. Another week out here means another week's pay for you."

McCracken nodded slowly. "What's the second reason?"

"If you go back without me and I die out here, not only will you not get paid for the extra week, you won't get paid the balance of what I owe you already."

"I see," the other man murmured softly. "Of course, I could break your arms and legs, tie you in a bundle, and then Alfred and I could haul you back and make you pay—but that would probably be more difficult than just wandering about in these mountains for another few days."

"Yeah, right," admitted Bohannon. "You could do that."

McCracken did not smile. He seemed to be debating the available options. "I want a fifty percent bonus."

Bohannon swallowed hard, did some mental calculating of his own. By now money seemed to mean a good deal less than it once had—but it still meant something. "That'll just about tap out my cash advance line of credit."

"Life is tough." The expat was unyielding, his voice brutally indifferent. "You can work your way back to the States for all I care. That's me offer."

"Twenty percent."

"Forty."

"Thirty. No, I'll make it one-third. That's a lot of money, Sorley."

While the two men bargained, the Highlander stood off to one side, seemingly oblivious to the conversation. His gaze, if not his attention, was fixed on the ridge line that marked the apex of the Central Range.

"One more week." McCracken's concession was heavy with reluctance. "If Alfred can find enough food." Having made the decision he pushed past Bohannon, bumping him hard. "After that," he declared, looking coldly back over his shoulder, "if you want to keep on, you're on your own. At that point you can come back with me or die out here. I don't give a shit."

"That's fair." Bohannon's shoulder throbbed where the other man had struck him.

McCracken whirled angrily. "Fair? Fair? It's bloody fucking generous, is what it is! You ought to get down on your fucking knees and kiss my feet in gratitude, except you'd probably pick up a couple of leeches on your lips." A humorless smile creased his grime-soaked face. "If you ain't already, you'd best get used to them now. They're going to be your closest friends for the next seven days." Turning sharply, he started down the slope, heading north. "Let's get the fuck off this stinking ridge-top. And don't you talk to me, mate, don't you say a word, until it's time for our miserable, lousy supper that I wouldn't give to an honorable dog to eat!"

There were times when a quick joke, an offhand remark, were in order. Sensing that this was not one of them, Bohannon held his tongue as he picked up his pack and followed the expat over the edge, his now entirely mud-encrusted sneakers sliding as much as striding through the muck. Silent and stoic, the ever-competent Alfred continued to lead the way.

Evening brought exhaustion. Sliding his pack off his shoulders and sitting down heavily, Bohannon leaned back against the damp trunk of the tree they had chosen to shelter them for the night. He was completely worn out. At that moment, for all he cared, the tree might be home to a million biting insects and a dozen poisonous snakes. He had to rest.

Even McCracken was beginning to show the strain. He removed his own pack slowly and placed it on a fallen log, trying to keep it as clean and dry as possible. This was an almost impossible task in the montane rainforest. If the rain did not drench everything from the head down, then wading across freezing streams and through bogs that sometimes reached waist-high soaked a traveler from the feet up.

A familiar rumbling reverberated in Bohannon's ears. It was not the cry of some mysterious forest creature, or the echo of a distant, unseen aircraft, or the grinding of river stones against one another as current pushed them downstream. It was his stomach.

Having long since reduced their rations to the minimum, their bodies were running dangerously short of proteins and carbohydrates. Vitamin and mineral supplements helped, but did not provide proper nutrition.

It was then that the prodigal tracker, who had disappeared into the forest earlier, returned. Spotting something in the bush and admonishing them to silence, Alfred had rushed on ahead, leaving them to collapse in his wake. He had been gone nearly an hour.

"What'd you find, Alfred me mate?" McCracken had his hat pulled down over his eyes.

Bohannon had a better view. "He's carrying something on his back."

Tired but triumphant, the grinning Highlander dumped his burden on the ground in front of them. Despite his fatigue, Bohannon was intrigued. About thc size of a small turkey, the dead bird was a sleek gun-metal gray with a russet breast and white underwings. An eye-catching crest composed of five-inch-long feathers formed a magnificent arc along the top of the skull. Each feather looked like a miniature Japanese fan. The lifeless eyes were blood red. Except for its size and outlandish topknot, it looked exactly like the king of all urban birds.

"Bugger me." McCracken pushed back his hat and sat up straight. "A crowned pigeon." He looked at Bohannon. "Largest pigeon in the world, mate. As if you couldn't guess. How'd you get him, Alfred?"

The tracker's grin widened. "With this."

For several days the Highlander had been whittling with his bush knife at long pieces of wood. As these were too long for arrows, too short for a bow, Bohannon thought he was just passing the time on the trail, or perhaps fashioning stakes to hold down their tent more securely in the winds that occasionally whistled through the mountain passes.

Now he saw that he had been right about Alfred's intentions if not his methods. One stick, larger and more solid than the others, had a long, narrow groove carved into it. The deepest part of the groove abutted the solid back end of the stick. The other lengths of wood had been sharpened to fine points. Too small for spears, they fit neatly into the groove in the largest piece.

"Throwing stick." McCracken admired the tracker's ingenuity. "A lowland weapon. This is what happens when cultures start to cross-pollinate."

"It doesn't look very accurate." But the dead crowned pigeon at Bohannon's feet suggested otherwise.

Taking a couple of steps to one side, Alfred demonstrated the handmade weapon. Pointing to another tree a good ten yards off, he placed one of the sharpened stakes in the throwing slot and brought his right arm back behind him, like a javelin thrower. Taking a step forward and bringing his arm down sharply, the stake shot forward to bury itself in the center of the trunk opposite.

McCracken applauded. "Where'd you learn how to use a throwing stick, Alfred?"

Taking a seat next to them, the tracker began to pluck feathers from the dead bird. "I am only part Huli, Mr. McCracken, sir. The rest of my family is from Wewak."

The guide nodded knowingly. "Biggest town on the north coast," he explained for Bohannon's benefit. "Hell, it's the only town on the north coast. Pretty much everything that travels in and out of the Sepik goes through there." Sliding off the log on which he was sitting, he began helping the tracker denude the bird. "Good eating, this, if we can get a fire going."

Bohannon did not offer to help. His sole experience in preparing birds for dinner consisted of making sure the plastic wrap around the frozen chickens at the supermarket had not been violated. Besides, despite the size of the pigeon there was room for only two pair of hands to get a decent grip.

There was no such thing in the Highlands as dry wood. Knowing this, McCracken had come prepared with special fire-starters. A red, putty-like material, it caught instantly, burned hot, and with careful preparation could dry out enough kindling to get a real blaze going. Bohannon would have made a mess of it, but both guide and tracker knew just what they were doing.

An hour later he was gnawing voraciously on a drumstick. It was gamey and undercooked and it tasted like the head chef at the Commander's Palace had worked on it for hours. It was quite possibly the most delicious meal he had ever had in his life. With every bite his spirits, in tandem with his energy level, soared.

"I've had this before."

"Crowned pigeon?" Lips glistening with grease, McCracken clutched a piece of breast in oily fingers and eyed his companion dubiously. In front of him, the tiny camp billy steamed merrily. Alfred ate nearby, indifferent to the conversation. Having already finished two substantial pieces of meat, he was now snacking on the dead bird's lightly seared feet.

Bohannon looked up from his food. "No, just ordinary everyday garden-variety pigeon. At a place called the Five Crowns, in Amsterdam. Real gourmet nouvelle cuisine." He chuckled at the memory.

"What's so funny?"

The American gestured with the remains of the drumstick. "It was twice as raw as this."

For the first time in days, McCracken smiled. Turning without rising, his butt making a circular depression in the damp soil, he pointed to a cloud-swathed massif off to their right. "See that mountain? That's Yakopi Malenk. Highest peak in this part of the Central Range." He sought a figure, found one. "A shade under twelve thousand feet, if I remember correctly. Never thought to see it from this close." His teeth clamped back down on the still-warm meat, ripping at the pungent flesh.

Bohannon considered the distant summit. Despite his physical fatigue he was feeling very satisfied with himself—a dangerous conceit in such a place. "It almost looks like it's behind us."

"Almost my arse. It is behind us, mate. We've crossed the central crest. From here, everything flows north, toward the Sepik. Quite a river, the Sepik. Drains more water than most rivers on the planet. You ain't seen flooding 'til you've seen the Sepik at high water. The whole basin turns into one big lake." He waved the remnants of his meal. "That's when you'll see mossies. Black clouds thick enough to choke a plane's intakes. Suck a man dry, they will, but he won't know it. Go mad, first." He looked back at the Highlander.

"Alfred, me mate. We still on the right track?"

Looking up from his meal, the other man raised his left arm and pointed, the edge of his palm facing the ground like a knife blade.

"Plenty of signs. Footprints, broken branches."

"Yeah, I seen 'em. Just wanted to make sure I wasn't dreaming 'em." McCracken turned back to Bohannon and to his food. "I would've thought we'd have caught up with them by now, what with them having to cut a trail and all that. Damn but they've been moving fast."

"We'll catch them." With his belly full for the first time in days, Bohannon was feeling expansive.

Flinging the stripped bones into the brush, he rose and headed for the nearby stream. Since leaving Mt. Yogonda, which at the moment seemed as far away as Paris (and might as well have been), they had been tired, hungry, frustrated, and hurt, but never thirsty. Away from human habitation, uncontaminated by human fecal coliform bacteria or runoff from pig wallows, the water in the mountain streams was perfectly safe to drink.

Keeping a watchful eye out for snakes, he decided to follow the stream a short distance downhill. No obstacle this, it gurgled and bubbled merrily through moss-covered black rocks and lumps of half-dissolved white limestone, the creek bed a checkerboard of perambulating geology sluiced down from the heights above. Subalpine and montane flowers sprouted where soil had accumulated in gentle backwaters and eddies, flourishes of blue and red and pink and lavender against the green background.

Only during such moments of isolated tranquillity did he have time to appreciate the real beauty of the place, the pristine magnificence of a wilderness untouched not only by civilization but by man. For all he knew, every flower whose intricate design he committed to memory, every butterfly that dipped and bobbed its way across the stream, every bird that chortled querulously in the treetops, might easily be a species new to science.

He sighed inwardly. He was not here to collect, or to observe. He carried no camera to document unexpected discoveries. Fame and fortune awaited those trained in the proper techniques of field observation, scientists and researchers who would eventually follow in his footsteps to document this place. Unable and unequipped to collect specimens, he could carry only beauty away with him. Reluctantly, he pivoted on his heel and turned back to rejoin his companions.

Something stopped him.

It was soft, without thorns or stickers but not without menace. Making simultaneous contact with his entire body from head to foot, it stuck instantly and held fast. Reaching up instinctively, he soon had both hands entangled in the cottony mass. It would only take seconds to rip free, but quickly recognizing what he had blundered into, he decided that an excess of violent movement might not be a good idea. Instead, he tried to stand absolutely motionless while calling for his companions.

They came running, bashing through the brush a moment later. "Oy, mate," McCracken called to him, "what the Devil is . . . ?" Initially full of irritation, the expat's voice dropped like a stone cast into a deep well the instant he caught sight of his companion's situation. "Oh good Christ!"

"Do not move, Mr. Bohannon, sir." That was Alfred, though Bohannon did not turn his head to see him. "Stay as still as you can."

"What do you think I'm trying to do?" Deceptively innocuous soft strands of silk clung to his face, his neck, his body and limbs. "I thought it might be dangerous. I take it from both your reactions that I was right."

"Could be, mate." The hard edge that was always present in

McCracken's voice was gone. In its place was a tenseness marked by a wholly uncharacteristic concern. "Just stay like that and we'll have you out of there in a flash."

Since they had moved around behind him, Bohannon could not see either man approach. But he could hear the metallic whisper of bush knives as they were drawn from their long leather scabbards.

There was movement out of the corner of his left eye. Two small spiders were advancing across the web strands toward him. The biggest was no more than an inch across. He relaxed a little. Even if they were poisonous, how much toxin could they carry? To draw their attention away from his face, he moved his left arm slightly. Sure enough, they turned immediately. Neither had fangs long enough to penetrate the tropical weave of his cotton shirt.

Abruptly, they scattered, their tiny black legs scrabbling rapidly as they raced off down the web. Probably they recognized that his arm was a lot larger and more dangerous than a fly or moth, he told himself. He heard McCracken mutter a muffled curse—and then he froze.

Something else was coming down the web, emerging from concealment behind a clutch of fat green leaves. Something big.

Yellow and black, the spider's body was only an inch across but a full half-foot in length. With rear legs extending five inches behind her and long front legs reaching out another ten, she was nearly two feet long. Eyes like black diamonds glistened in an arc across the front of the blunt head, while paddle-like palps fluttered up and down in slow-motion. Unlike with her predecessors, he had no difficulty making out the curved, downward-hanging fangs. Lightly tinged with red, slightly curved like miniature scimitars, they looked long enough, and sharp enough, to penetrate not only his shirt but the much heavier material of his jeans.

As his heart commenced a slow metaphorical crawl up into his throat, he heard McCracken alongside him. "Just hold it there a moment longer, mate. Don't move your arm—there!"

Descending in a carefully measured arc, the bush knife sliced cleanly through the web to strike the spider in mid-abdomen. As legs and guts and severed body went flying, Bohannon wrenched himself backward, tearing free of the sticky, clinging strands. Stumbling, arms flailing, he went down on his backside. Leaping to his aid, Alfred caught him under one arm and helped mitigate the fall.

McCracken stood next to the torn web, staring at the ground. As Bohannon rose shakily to his feet, ripping lengths of web from his arm and torso as he stood, the expat brought his bush knife up and down a second time. Only then did he turn away, satisfied, to confront the others.

"I was watching the ground for snakes and I turned without looking up," Bohannon explained lamely. "Stepped right into it." He prepared himself for a stream of insults, curses, and snide comments pointing out once again his unsuitability for the country in which he presently found himself. McCracken surprised him.

"That's all right, mate. You can't watch for everything at once. Not here, where there's just too bloody much to watch out for." He turned. "Come and have a look."

Even in death, the spider was impressive. Its web, Bohannon now saw, would have been difficult to avoid in any case. Stretching across the only open area paralleling the creek, it was no less than ten feet across.

"I saw some other spiders first," he mumbled. "Little guys. I thought it was their web."

"Argyrodes, probably." McCracken nudged the upper half of the black and yellow arachnid corpse with the toe of his boot. "It's a lot easier to share a big web like this than weave one of your own. Catches a damn sight more prey, too. But if big mama here finds you in her house and you're not paying rent, she'll suck you up and spit you out. So the argyrodes have to watch their step." He indicated the still twitching halves of the black and yellow body.

"Say hello to *Nephilia maculata*. The giant wood spider. Not that poisonous, mate, but she's so damn big she carries enough venom to make herself a real threat. You're lucky she decided to take a look at you first before biting."

"I am told that is the longest spider in the world," Alfred added unnecessarily.

Bohannon knew he would be scratching for hours, maybe days, as strands of ghost silk tickled his flesh. Like most people he had no love for spiders, but on returning home he doubted any would ever disturb him again. Not after having his face frozen inches from one with a leg span greater than his keyboard. Looking down at its remains he tried not to shudder, and failed.

Neither McCracken nor Alfred took the opportunity to make a

single joke at his expense. Both men had a rough sense of humor, and were not shy about employing it, but some things simply are not funny, not even in the high mountain rainforest.

Among those subjects considered unamusing were spiders with two-foot leg spans.

XIV

They made camp the following night in the welcome shelter of one of the many small caves water and wind had worn into the base of a limestone pinnacle. Near the back of the comparatively dry cavity, revealed in the beam of his flashlight, McCracken found a couple of small stalactites.

"This whole country is honeycombed with caves," the expat explained, "but very few have been explored. The really big ones are too dark and deep for the local people to enter with only torches for illumination, and the rest are too inaccessible. I've heard that a few geologists with an interest in speleology have done some poking around in the Southern Highlands, but as far as I know nobody's done any caving anywhere else. Too fucking expensive, and the government has no money for it."

"A nice cave makes a good tourist attraction." Bohannon was laying out his sleeping bag on the wonderfully dry, sandy floor. All of them were looking forward to spending the night on something besides damp dirt for a change.

McCracken had to laugh. "This country's nothing but one tourist attraction after another, mate, and they still can't get people to come here. It's too fucking far away from anywhere else, too primitive, too rugged, and too dangerous. As soon as the word gets around about how drop-dead marvelous the place is, some bunch of raskols knocks off a hotel somewhere. As far as the professional travel people are concerned, that kills any interest for another six months to a year. That's what me friends in the business tell me, anyways." He looked to his left. "Ain't that right, Alfred?"

"I would not know about its effects on the travel industry, Mr. McCracken, sir, but the raskol problem is a bad one, for sure. A man never knows when he is going to run into some of those people. They respect no laws, they have no tribe, and they are their own clan. It is a very bad business. You need to watch out for such people. One never knows when and where they will turn up."Carefully, he spread his kit out to dry atop the opened bedroll.

The sun was dropping steadily into the west, setting behind mountains that were, for a change, lower than the ones behind them. Somewhere out there, beneath the mists that cloaked the northern horizon, lay the basin of the great Sepik River. If McCracken was to be believed, except for a few sleepy, small towns near the coast, the vast swampland and savanna had changed little in thousands of years. It was in similar country that oil-heir and would-be anthropologist Michael Rockefeller had vanished on an exploratory expedition in the early 1960's.

"Some say his boat overturned and he drowned." McCracken was telling the story as he began setting out their meager supper. "Others claim that a croc got him. There's giant saltwater crocs all the way up and down these rivers. Saw a photo of one some professional hunters up from Darwin got. Must've been a good twenty feet long, couple of tons, and sixty or seventy years old." Removing a rusty opener, he set to work on a can of bully beef.

"Or a snake might've done him in, or starvation. Me and most of the long-timers here, we think river people killed him so they could eat his brains. Makes a man smarter, you see, to eat an enemy's brains. Want a white man's knowledge? Eat his brains. Beats four years of university." He gestured toward the horizon.

"Those people down there have been hunting heads since the first dugout picked its way upriver twenty or thirty thousand years ago. The national government supposedly has put a stop to such captivating forms of indigenous recreational activity, but just like up in these mountains there are villages tucked back in among thousands of tributaries that have never seen outsiders. Old habits die harder, right Alfred?"

The tracker looked up and, seeing that he was being teased, mustered a smile. "Personally, I prefer a good steak or a nice piece of broiled fish." Looking past the guide, he met Bohannon's gaze. "But Mr. McCracken is right. There are no vegetarians in the Highlands, and I do not think you would find any in the Sepik."

For once, the paucity of food available for supper occasioned a minimum of sarcasm, thanks to their munificent meal of the day before. Having packed up all the pigeon they had not been able to eat yesterday, they finished the remainder over a fire more easily called into being than its predecessor, thanks to scraps of wood that had been washed into the cave and subsequently allowed to dry out.

As McCracken and Alfred were settling in, low hoots and murmurings echoed through the surrounding forest. It was that magical transitory time of day after the sun has set but before darkness has secured its grip on the world. Luxuriating in surroundings shielded from the nightly rain and for once not having to concern himself about stepping into ankle-deep mud, Bohannon rose from his sleeping bag to gaze at the deepening silhouettes of rock and tree outside.

Something went running up his bare right leg, just above his sock. He jumped a foot, slapping violently at his skin. McCracken's sharp laughter rose above the soft forest noises outside.

"You son of a bitch!" Bohannon snarled at the cackling expat. Behind them, Alfred struggled to repress a grin.

McCracken waved all five fingers at the American. The same fingers that had just gone crawling lightly up his leg. "My, but we're jumpy tonight. Better make sure your sleeping bag's zipped up tight. The bedbugs around here are as big as golf balls." Still chuckling to himself, he settled back down into his own swag.

"You're full of shit!" Slowly regaining control of himself, Bohannon turned to the tracker. "Bedbugs the size of golf balls! He's full of shit, isn't he, Alfred?"

Leaning to one side to look around the American, the Highlander stole a glance at McCracken. Satisfied, he smiled reassuringly at his employer. "Certainly he is, Mr. Bohannon, sir." Holding up both hands with the palms facing one another, he widened the gap between them until they were two feet apart. "But the centipedes here are this long, they love dark places, and they come out at night. Their bite does not kill. It just makes you wish that you were dead." Having divested himself of this reassuring information, he slid down onto his bedroll and wrapped the ancient blanket securely around his legs and torso.

Not knowing quite which part of the cave floor to scan first, Bohannon picked up the flashlight, flicked it to life, and headed out into the gathering darkness. Following his progress, McCracken called after him.

"Where the hell d'you think you're going, mate? Possum hunting? Looking to cuddle a cuscus?"

An angry Bohannon replied without looking back. "I have to take a dump, if that's all right with you."

"Well in that case, take as long a hike as you want. Just watch your arse—so to speak." He settled back down into his swag.

After his encounter with the monster web and its equally monstrous mistress, Bohannon had no intention of stomping madly off into the rainforest. Keeping the comparatively sterile (and therefore unthreatening) limestone pinnacle on his immediate left, he worked his way down to its base and started around the other side. That way he could have something solid and safe behind him while he was doing his business.

Turning a corner, he played the flashlight over broken, crumbling rock until he found a suitable spot. Enough fragmentary daylight still stained the sky to make the flashlight unnecessary, but he wanted it for the short walk back. As he slipped it into a pocket, something like a warm steel cable wrapped itself around his neck. Gasping, he reached up but could not budge it even with both hands.

Snake! he thought wildly as he tried to call out to his companions, *and a big one.* It was tight enough around his throat to prevent him from shouting. McCracken and Alfred had both mentioned repeatedly that the country they were going through was likely to be thick with pythons. But as he stood there struggling desperately he began to have second thoughts.

For one thing snakes, even the exotic varieties that infested PNG, were not known for interrogating their quarry.

"*Who the fuck are you, what are you doing here, and what do you want?*" The voice was primal, powerful, commanding, and it paralyzed Bohannon as effectively as the razor-sharp blade that had come to rest just below his Adam's apple and above the major tendons that secured his head to his shoulder blades. He did not look around. He did not have to.

He had just made the acquaintance of Ragnarok Stenhammer.

"Jesus, take it easy, will you!" Struggling futilely against the unyielding bear-hug, Bohannon felt himself being lifted slowly and effortlessly off the ground. His feet kicked at empty air. Would McCracken and Alfred overhear and come running? And if they did, what could they do?

"Put him down, Rags," requested a new voice. A voice Bohannon recognized.

As he was lowered slowly back to the ground, the knife was removed from his throat. He rubbed reflexively at his neck as Tai Tenison emerged from the deepening shadows.

She was wearing khaki jungle culottes, a matching short-sleeved blouse, high beige-colored socks, and lightweight hiking boots. The hatband encircling the by-now standard battered Akubra was lined with small crocodile teeth, the points facing upwards. Crocodile Dun Tai, he thought. Though very different from what she had been wearing when he had first encountered her in the lounge of the Port Moresby Travelodge, the outfit was, in its own utilitarian backcountry way, equally fetching.

The onset of evening masked the presence of dirt and sweat on her face and hands, but while her current condition could be considered less than glamorous, she looked as lovely as ever. As before, she wore no makeup. Deep, tight cleavage punctuated the sharp open V of her blouse, a narrow canyon rife with the dark perfume of recent memories. Beneath the blouse he could see the cartographic lines of a plain white jogging bra, an infinitely more practical piece of attire in the humid climate that its more sedate and stultifying cotton cousins.

She also wore a belt holster. The butt of a compact pistol was visible beneath the black leather overstrap.

While the booming, reverberant voice in his ear fell to a comparative whisper, an underlying tension remained, as if before being uttered, each word was first nicked with the glottal equivalent of the knife that had been held at Bohannon's throat. Stenhammer scraped words the way a fisherman would scale a cod.

"You know this outlander?"

"Goddamn right she knows me." He took a step toward the woman who had cost him so much time, effort, and most burdensome of all, decision. "She stole several thousand dollars from me."

Tennison did not turn away or otherwise try to hide her face. The same directness that had been so great a part of her personal appeal when he had first met her had not been doffed along with dress and jewelry.

"I needed money. You had it. I fully intended to pay you back."

His sardonic laugh filled the ensuing silence. "Oh right, sure you did! And how did you plan to do that? You didn't even ask for my address."

"Didn't have to. It's in your wallet. 13229 Conquistador Drive, La Jolla, California. You'll have to excuse me but I don't recall the zip code. I've been busy."

He hesitated, taken aback by her coolness, her calm, and the forthrightness with which she had recited his address. Why memorize it if she had no intention of contacting him in the future?

Without employing beckoning lips, exotic perfume, or honeyed words, she was already managing once again to weave a spell over him, a web less deadly but in its way no less effective than that of the giant wood spider. With the ire and outrage that he had kept bottled up for so long his only means of defense, he fought against being entrapped a second time.

"Yeah, you'll pay me back. When you win the national lottery, or break the bank at Townsville Casino. That's why you're out here tramping around in the middle of the bush—so you can pay me back. Or did you plan to reimburse me in pandanus nuts?"

"If Tai says she is going to pay you back, she is going to pay you back."

Even when moderated, a voice so full of anger and angst barely held in check could not be ignored. Fully intending to pursue the argument, Bohannon turned. Granted his first sight of Stenhammer, disagreement about money died aborning on his lips.

He knew the man would be tall. Descriptions of him to this point had mentioned that. The wild, shoulder-length tangle of slightly curving blond strands was unexpected. But height and hair color are insufficient means by which to convey the measure of a man. In the gathering darkness Bohannon could see that he was solidly built; heavily muscled, broad at the shoulders, and tapered elsewhere. A rugged, rough-hewn slab of man who might have been sculpted by Rodin—or at least by one of his disciples.

But it was the face that derailed conversation and made Bohannon rethink everything he had heard. A house built of unsupported preconceptions, the image he had constructed in his mind fell apart the first time he found himself face to face with the actuality of the man's tormented visage.

Stenhammer had the body of an athlete in his thirties and the face of a ravaged seventy-year old. Splitting the difference, Bohannon guessed him to be in his mid-to-late fifties—not at all the age of the individual he would have expected a woman like Tai Tennison to run off with. Long and lined, with eyes sunk deeply into the skull, it was a European rendering of one of the nightmarish, mythical masks he had seen on display throughout the country. Not unhandsome, perversely magnetic, it at once attracted and repelled the onlooker.

His eyes were the palest blue Bohannon had ever seen, so pallid in hue that in the dim light the corneas were almost transparent, as if only the whites were showing. The effect was spectral, giving those penetrating orbs an eerie depth one wanted to avoid but could not. One was drawn in simply out of a desire to find something human with which to make contact. They were haunted eyes in a harrowing setting.

It was the face of a man, Bohannon concluded, who had been slapped by God.

All of this he absorbed in an instant; the gripping, stentorian voice as well as the striking young-old face atop the imposing body. In his mind questions began to replace anger, curiosity to overtake outrage. As was usual for him when confronted by such a situation, he responded with an inanity.

"How and with what is she going to pay me back?"

"With my share," she told him.

"Tai!" Stenhammer's exclamation reverberated off the limestone.

She did not back down from the big man. "It's all right. Haven't we been trying to think of a way to bring in extra help for the final push without giving away any secrets?" She indicated Bohannon. "This guy and his mates already know we're here, they're better suited for the work than nationals, and it means not having to share what we know with a bunch of villagers and maybe half the Highlands."

For days lost in space, Bohannon now found himself rapidly losing touch with the conversation. "What are you two babbling about?"

"You will find out. Maybe." With singular deliberation, Stenhammer sheathed the knife. The blade, Bohannon noted academically, was more than an inch wide, a veritable short sword. "I agree they would be better suited to keeping the secret, and you have made the acquaintance of this man and have a debt to discharge to him, but I know nothing about the others."

"Then we'd better go and find out as much as we can, hadn't we?" She smiled, illuminating their immediate surroundings with the warmth of it. "I'm afraid we're going to have to wake your friends, Steve."

With questions multiplying inside his head, Bohannon turned to lead the way. It never occurred to him to try and keep the camp's location a secret because he was pretty sure that these two already knew where it was.

"They're around the other side, in a cave."

"We know." Stenhammer's curt response confirmed Bohannon's supposition.

Turning the corner that marked the base of the limestone spire, they started up the slope on the other side. Bohannon knew what McCracken's reaction would be if he was startled out of a sound sleep.

"I'd better warn them that we're coming."

"No need." Stenhammer pointed, not ahead, but upward. "One is already in the rocks above us, waiting with a loaded throwing stick and tracking our approach. Better tell him we are friends. The other is moving about in the shelter you have chosen."

Bohannon's gaze immediately shot upward. In the darkness he could see nothing. Nor could he hear anything, either from above or from the vicinity of the cave they were approaching. A little awed by Stenhammer's perceptive abilities, he looked back in the big man's direction. He made no noise as he walked, absolutely none, and was as oblivious to Bohannon's stare as the gravel underfoot seemed to be to his presence. It was as if one of the nearby limestone spires had suddenly pulled itself free of the earth and decided to go for a contemplative evening stroll.

A hand brushed his arm and he jerked around sharply. "Hey, take it easy." Tennison's eyes flashed in the evaporating light. "I don't remember you being this jumpy."

"That was before I made the acquaintance of leeches and pythons and giant wood spiders and a few other of the fascinating local denizens that all move with a light touch."

"Don't let a few bad experiences blind you to the good. This is magnificent country." There was no mistaking the enthusiasm, however misplaced he thought it might be, in her voice. "Not everything here bites. There's plenty that's warm and cuddly."

"You cuddle it," he responded tersely.

Something chittered deep within the forest. "Hear that?" She pointed. "There's a spotted cuscus back in those trees somewhere. Judging by the tone, I'd say she's probably talking to a baby."

He did not strain to listen, having during the past days heard more than his fill of nocturnal rainforest noises. "If you're trying to make me forget why I came here, it won't work."

She blinked at him. "You came all this way, out here, into these mountains, just because of a little money?"

"Several thousand dollars is not 'a little.' But there's more to it than that." He looked away. "It's hard for me to explain. Maybe before this is over I'll try. You might say I was driven to this."

She studied him silently for a moment. "Then you and Rags should get along. He's more than a little driven himself."

"You said you were going to pay me back out of 'your share.' Your share of what? You said something about a 'strike'?"

"I'd like to tell you all about it but it's not for me to say." She nodded at the massive figure striding along just ahead and to one side of him. "The decision is Rags's." She jabbed a thumb upward. "Better talk to your friend before somebody gets hurt."

Bohannon tilted his head back. Frustrated, he still couldn't see anything. "Alfred, are you up there?"

A man-shape made itself known amid the limestone. Now that the Highlander had emerged from concealment, Bohannon could see not only the tracker's outline, but the dark splinter that was the throwing stick.

"Mr. Bohannon, sir, are you all right?"

"I'm fine," he called back. "These are the people we came looking for. We've found them."

Tennison laughed gently. "Did you? I thought we found you?"

"Okay, so we found each other," he conceded.

Her tone turned unexpectedly playful: one more example of the long list of contradictions that went to make up the woman he knew as Tai Tennison. Despite the intimacy they had shared, he realized he was a long way from knowing anything significant about her.

"How romantic. I remember you as being more than a little romantic, Steve."

"And I remember you as being honest," he muttered. "Funny how the mind plays tricks on you."

She punched him lightly in the bicep. "Don't be like that. I'm sorry for what I did, I really am, but I had no choice. Rags is a good friend, but to get in on this I had to pay my way." She looked past him, staring at the rising and falling back of the big man. "When it comes to working or otherwise paying your way, he's something of a fanatic."

"Plenty of people seem to think he's crazy." Bohannon hesitated. "Is he?"

She turned serious. "No. At least, I don't think so. Obsessed, yes. Burdened, yes. But then, anybody who willingly spends any more time in this part of the country than they have to is considered certifiable. What else can I say?" The coy grin returned, threatening to slide over into a smirk. "Now you're here as well. What would others think of that? Welcome to the madhouse, Steve Bohannon."

McCracken was waiting for them, his upper body illuminated by the flickering fire as he sat on the edge of his swag with his bush knife laid out across his knees. When he saw that Bohannon and Alfred were safe and unharmed, he relaxed. But he did not set the heavy machete aside.

"So you finally found your lady." A reluctant smile split his fire-lit features. "Hello, Tai."

"Hello, Sorley." She took a seat on Bohannon's sleeping bag. "Never expected to see you up here."

"Wouldn't expect to see anyone up here," he countered. "You right?"

"Too right," she replied. "Leave it to an outrageous American like Steve, here, to hire the best. How'd you find me?"

"Rose started us in the right direction. From there it was all a matter of asking the right questions of the right people."

She nodded knowingly. "Rose always did have a soft spot for you, Sorley. I won't say which one."

Bohannon sat down next to her. They were very close, and he had yet to decide if he found the proximity enjoyable, but the floor of the cave was hard and gravey, and it was *his* sleeping bag. Easing himself down onto his bedroll, Alfred wordlessly set his throwing stick aside. The small spear remained in its groove and within easy reach.

"Right then, mate." McCracken eyed his employer. "You've found 'er. I've fulfilled me end of the contract. You two settle your personal financial arrangements and then we'll start back."

"I'm afraid it's not that simple." Tennison shifted her admirable derriere against the padding. "For one thing, I've spent all his money."

Bohannon gaped at her. "All of it? Already? On what?"

"On supplies. And on buying in."

McCracken's expression twisted. "Buying in? Buying in on what? Coffee? Tea? Possum fur coats?"

Stenhammer spoke up. In doing so he instantly and effortlessly dominated the discussion. "There was a time when I needed money. Tai and I had become—friends. When I explained to her what it was that I planned to do, she agreed to help me in return for a share in the final result." He favored her with a steady, unreadable expression. "She has done so for years. While I have stayed here, in the mountains, and worked, she has traveled for me. To gather advice and buy necessary things. Across the length and breadth of PNG, sometimes to Australia.

"Now that we are ready to proceed to the next step, I find that I cannot do so without additional help. This because after many years of work there may be only one brief opportunity to benefit from it all, and I find that the one thing I cannot buy is time. Not without sacrificing the secret, and with it my privacy. These are things I wish to try and retain." He regarded each of them in turn. When his gaze fell upon Bohannon, the American felt as if his soul had momentarily been touched by the Void. The chill passed quickly.

"We had discussed, Tai and I, hiring several Highlanders to help us make the final push. But Highlanders love to talk, and have relatives who love to talk. Restricting information to only a few would be difficult. Faced with this dilemma, I confess to not knowing what to do. I am still not sure, and this troubles me because I am always sure. Tai suggests taking you into our confidence. I am not sure about that, either. But the time for talk and contemplation is over. Now it is time for decision-making."

McCracken's gaze had fixated on the pistol the big man wore holstered on his belt. Far larger than Tennison's, it was in fact the biggest handgun he had ever seen; in person, print, or on television. Even resting against that oversize thigh, it looked like a small cannon.

"And have you reached a decision about us?" His fingers rested on the steel bush knife as lightly as a pianist's on the familiar white keys of a Steinway.

Stenhammer looked away. "No. I need help, and I hate asking for help. It too often proves itself inadequate, unworthy, and deceptive." So much naked pain revealed itself in this observation that McCracken's fingers withdrew from the vicinity of the machete.

The big man walked to the edge of the cave and stood in the opening gazing out at the dark forest. A towering but unfathomable figure, his intentions were as indistinct as his silhouette. "Tai says that she knows you, a little, Mr. Bohannon, and that she knows your companion Mr. McCracken rather better." Turning abruptly, he addressed himself to the hitherto silent tracker in a language that was neither English nor Pidgin. A surprised Alfred found himself responding in kind.

"One of the Highland Huli dialects." McCracken whispered the observation. "The old boy's pretty fluent."

Bohannon kept his own voice down. "You think he's mentally unbalanced, like we've been hearing all along?"

The expat's response was sober, considered, and in no way flippant. "Don't know. Haven't decided yet. He sure as hell has a lot on his mind. Any fool can see that. But preoccupation don't make a man mad. Depends on what it is and how much of the real world he ignores while staggering about in pursuit of it."

"He seems to know what he's talking about. His speech is clear enough."

McCracken grunted. "Intelligibility ain't no proof of sanity either, mate. Me, I'm reserving judgment."

Stenhammer must have found the tracker's responses to his liking, or at least adequate. "I cannot make a decision on matters of importance based on a discussion held in a dark cave in the middle of the night. Pick up your belongings and follow me."

McCracken's response was cordial but noncommittal. "Hang on a minute there, mate. Why should we follow you anywhere?"

Tennison stepped forward. "You can follow me if you prefer, Sorley. Or you can stay the night here." She regarded her brooding companion. "Rags and I just think you might be more comfortable at the house."

"House?" McCracken was intrigued, but wary. "There are no houses out here."

Stenhammer was almost amused. "There are a great many things in this part of the country, Mr. McCracken, that people do not believe exist here. Among them is my house." Drawing a flashlight from his belt, he turned to go. "Of course you may remain in your cave, along with any snakes, spiders, scorpions, and other local creatures who find dry shelter and warm sleeping bags especially appealing."

Bohannon was already rolling up his kit. "Give me thirty seconds, Mr. Stenhammer, and I'll be right with you." Behind him, Alfred was gathering up his bedroll and gear. After a moment's pause, a recalcitrant McCracken gave in and joined them.

With four flashlights between them, they had no difficulty picking their way down the slope. Stenhammer led, and every five minutes

Tennison had to remind him to slow his pace lest he lose the others. It was remarkable to see the big man slip gracefully between trees and step effortlessly over rocks and fallen logs. Where Bohannon and his companions were forced to struggle, Stenhammer seemed to float along regardless of the terrain.

XV

An hour passed: an hour of clumsy slip-sliding down an increasingly steep and difficult slope. They were a long way from the cave and had descended nearly two thousand feet. Bohannon was tired, sore, and beginning to have trouble focusing. With the drop in altitude the temperature had risen significantly, so there was no danger of anyone freezing. But the more the muscles in his legs throbbed, the more the cave, many-legged intruders and all, began to seem increasingly attractive.

The character of the forest, too, had changed. The open grassy meadows with their islands of bushes and ferns that characterized the upper Highlands had long since fallen behind them. The trees had grown taller, more numerous, and more diverse. Vines and creepers had reappeared together with denser undergrowth and a multitude of broad-leafed plants. Night-sounds intensified, and insects piped their presence with an assurance that came from dwelling among warmer temperatures and higher humidity.

Stenhammer halted so abruptly that Bohannon nearly ran into him. "Welcome to my home, gentlemen. You are the first to see it besides Tai, and with any luck, you will be the last."

"Gregarious sort o' bloke, ain't he?" murmured McCracken as he stared dubiously at the sturdy but tiny structure fashioned of cut poles and thatch. A single narrow portal marked the entrance. He raised his voice. "Hardly looks big enough for one person to unroll his swag in."

Tai burst out laughing. "That's not the house, you silly twit! That's the latrine. Of course, you can sleep there if you want."

Tired and grumpy, McCracken was not amused. "I don't see any bloody house."

"That is the idea. The world is full of accomplished architects, Mr. McCracken. They put up wonderful buildings in New York and Paris and Hong Kong. But one man working alone must utilize the techniques of those whose knowledge of design and construction arises from intimate familiarity with their immediate surroundings, and with the less flashy but no less utilitarian construction materials available to them.

"I required a domicile that would keep me safe from marauding snakes and most arthropods. I also wished to be able to enjoy the occasional breeze, for it is much hotter here during the day than where I found you. Even though we are still standing on a slope, periodic downpours frequently churn the ground beneath us to mud. I wished to be free of that annoyance as well.

"So I determined to employ the techniques of a people not of the Highlands, but who have dwelt for thousands of years in the southern mountains. Have you heard of the Koiari, Mr. McCracken?"

The guide frowned in thought. "The name's vaguely familiar."

"I made myself a Koiari house. It was not easy to build, but it is comfortable to live in, and it more than suits my needs. You might call it my Pei in the sky." Stenhammer walked over to the base of a huge tree. Reaching up into a clump of leaves, he unfastened a vine from where it had been secured and let the slack length slip through his powerful fingers.

Heretofore hidden in the dense branches, a handmade ladder of branches and vines dropped down from above. The bottom rung made contact with the ground as the last foot of liana slid through their host's hands.

Tilting his head back, Bohannon saw that the ladder was attached to a small platform located in the crotch of two massive branches.

"Not much of a house," McCracken observed disparagingly.

"That's not the house." Tennison stood at the base of the ladder as Stenhammer, agile as an ape, started up. Then it was her turn. Alfred followed while his companions debated who would go next.

There was barely enough room on the log platform for everyone to stand. Never fond of heights, Bohannon tried to crowd the middle, pushing up against McCracken and Tai. He was grateful for the darkness: it hid the ground.

Stenhammer unfastened another vine and a second ladder dropped from above. Further up, the branches parted to reveal a very respectable structure situated firmly among the leaves. Walls and roof were of palm and pandanus thatch. There were at least two windows in addition to the unbarred entrance.

Once safely inside, Bohannon found himself standing on a floor that creaked with every step. He tried not to think about what would happen if the thick, woven mats and crudely-sawn cross-members beneath his feet gave way and he fell through. If they could support Stenhammer's weight, he told himself, then he ought to have nothing to worry about.

The big man was fussing with a kerosene lamp suspended by a cord from the center of the roof. "The Koiari built these as watchtowers and places to perform magic. My needs were similar."

The treehouse was surprisingly spacious, but with five inhabitants instead of two it was crowded. While their host coaxed the lantern alight, Tennison was putting thatch screens up over the windows and door.

"The light will draw insects," she explained to Bohannon. "This part of the world is home to insects whose attention it's better to avoid." As she finished with the last screen, something solid smacked into the one she had fastened to the opposite wall. It sounded like a football.

Taking stock of his surroundings, Bohannon recognized two bedrolls unfurled on foam mattresses, a homemade table with camp stove and cooking utensils, pole shelving stocked with foodstuffs, medicines, and other supplies, a drum that reeked of kerosene, and much else he was unable at first glance to identify.

"Dump your gear anyplace you like," Stenhammer told them magnanimously. "On the way here I came to a decision about what to do with you."

McCracken's voice was tight. "Not to throw any water on your revelation, Stenhammer, but me mates and I might have a thing or two to say about that."

"I am sure you will, but I have no doubt that you will see things my way."

Bohannon checked the reply that was forming on his lips. Better to wait and see what the big man had to say. When properly directed, that booming voice could be persuasive instead of intimidating. He decided to listen to Stenhammer but watch Tai. Her reactions would be a truer indication of their host's intentions than his words.

As they were unburdening themselves of their packs and arranging their sleeping bags, Alfred let out a high-pitched yelp and leaped backward from his bedroll.

Stenhammer was there in an instant; muscles tensed, eyes alert, knife drawn. "*Wanim samting?*" he inquired sharply in Pidgin.

A wary Alfred held his ground and pointed. *"Stilman!"*

Stationing himself between Tai and the doorway, Bohannon strove for a better look. "Stilman? What's that, some kind of snake?"

Tai shook her head impatiently. Like everyone else, her eyes were fixed on the dark corner beyond the tracker's bedroll. "Stilman means 'thief' in Pidgin."

"It's a quoll, mate." McCracken stood poised to move fast. "A bleedin' quoll."

Bohannon frowned. "A quoll? What the fuck is a quoll?" As he confessed his ignorance, the creature in question suddenly stepped out into the light.

Expecting to be repelled, or at least intimidated by the sight, Bohannon instead found himself charmed. About the size of a small domestic house cat, the creature looked like a cross between a miniature possum and a large mouse. Covered in dark brown fur with prominent white spots on its back, it had small rounded ears, alert black eyes, a fleshy-pink nose and long furry tail. It looked about as threatening as an underfed tabby.

"Here, kitty kitty!" Before anyone could stop him, he took a step toward it.

Baring a mouthful of hypodermic-like teeth and hissing homicidally, the diminutive intruder leaped straight for his throat.

Tai screamed a warning while McCracken let out a startled oath. Arms pinwheeling madly, Bohannon stumbled backward. Striking his attacker in mid-leap, a can of corned beef knocked it sideways. Rearming himself with a tin of sardines, Alfred stood poised to throw again while with a single giant stride, Stenhammer interposed himself between Bohannon and the spitting, yowling invader.

Rolling over where he'd fallen, Bohannon found himself staring between Stenhammer's pillar-like legs at a display of fang and claw sufficiently ferocious to do justice to an apoplectic badger. The small scale of the organic weaponry confronting him did nothing to lessen the threat it presented. Slowly rising to hands and knees, he began to back away, keeping his gaze fixed on the crazed features of the tiny berserker before him. Incredibly, as he retreated it went for Stenhammer.

Displaying reflexes honed sharp by years of living in the rainforest, the big man brought his right foot up and out to block the attack. Teeth and claws dug into the thick leather and hung on. Stenhammer promptly brought his foot down, stomping hard on the brown fury that had attached itself to his boot. It let go and scurried toward the doorway. There it paused, slightly dazed but still full of fight, apparently debating whether to have another go at the whole room. After a moment sunk deep in predatory murderous contemplation, it turned and darted out, vanishing into the darkness. A slight rustling of leaves and branches, and it was gone.

Something clutched at Bohannon's right shoulder and he jumped, only to look up and see McCracken grinning sagely down at him.

"And now, mate o' mine, you know what a quoll is, and why it ain't wise to fuck with one." He helped the unsettled American to his feet while Stenhammer secured the door.

Tai had moved to the table and was setting a billy on the camp stove. As she worked, she looked back over her shoulder. "A quoll is a marsupial, Steve. Just like the possums and the cuscuses and the kangaroos. Only it doesn't eat bugs and leaves. It's a predator. It also happens to be the toughest critter in all of Papua New Guinea."

"No." Stenhammer rejoined them. "On the planet." His unblinking stare as he confronted Bohannon was half accusatory, half empathetic. "In the future, Mr. Bohannon, you would do well not to say 'here, kitty kitty' to anything ambulatory until you are safely back in the States. The subject of your invitation might accept."

Bohannon wiped sweat from his forehead and neck. "I'll keep that in mind, Mr. Stenhammer."

"See that you do." The big man looked toward the door. "That is only the second one I've seen up here. They climb very well but prefer to hunt on the ground." He moved to assist Tai. A pair of dull *thunks* sounded as two more baseball-sized bugs slammed into the screen covering the nearest window.

Strong, steaming tea was passed out in cheap ceramic mugs. Bohannon's cup featured a picture of a smiling koala on its side. Its benign features were in sharp contrast to those of the psychotic marsupial that had gone for his jugular. Of course, there was nothing inherently benign about a koala, with its sharp, powerful claws, smelly musk glands, and irritable disposition, but he knew as much about them as he did the rest of the Australasian family of pouched mammals. As with the quoll, appearances could often be deceiving.

Everyone sat except Stenhammer. Bohannon wondered if the man ever relaxed, or if like the elephant and giraffe, he slept standing up. Taking an indifferent swig of his tea, he stared toward the shuttered window, toward the east.

McCracken stood the silence for about a minute. "Right then: what's all this about needing help?" His gaze narrowed. "And a 'strike'?"

Their host's gaze returned from a far distant place to focus on the guide. His evident preoccupation served to moderate the normal brusqueness of his tone.

"This place, this section of rainforest, this empty corner of nowhere, has been my home for many years now. My home, and my work."

"Yeah, it's a bloody charming little house in the country you've got here, mate, but what does that have to do with us?" The impatient guide was more than a little irritated and clearly less than impressed.

For the first time, Stenhammer seemed genuinely unsure of himself. He glanced at Tai, who could only smile encouragingly. Then the momentary hesitation vanished.

"My efforts have reached a point where I must move to the next logical step. Everything is in readiness, but I have not been able to figure out a way for Tai and me to proceed by ourselves without minimizing the results of our exertions to come." He studied each of his guests in turn. "Once committed to the chosen course of action, our window of opportunity will be severely limited. Just as importantly, with attendant geologic consequences being unpredictable, arrangements may not be repeatable. In other words, we may get one shot at this. The participation of additional hands would go a long ways toward improving the operation's safety factor."

"What operation? What 'geologic consequences'?" Distaste tinged McCracken's voice. "If you're trying to persuade us of your sanity, mate, you're tuned to the wrong channel."

"I am not trying to persuade you of anything—*mate*," Stenhammer replied coldly. "I am doing my best to explain.

"A number of years ago my life—changed. For a long time, nothing mattered to me. Not money, not friends, not life itself. Then it occurred to me that if not for the lack of something artificial and immaterial to true happiness, my life might not have been altered. I resolved to free myself from any future dependency on this particular commodity and at the same time do it in such a way that I would not have to rely on anyone else for help ever again." He sipped at his tea.

"As it turned out, my ambitions exceeded my capabilities. I first was required to take Tai into my confidence and now, it would appear, possibly also the three of you. If you will forgive an oft ill-used metaphor, the tree that does not bend in a storm, breaks. I can bend if I have to, so long as my goal is not compromised.

"There was as much anger in my heart as determination. When I was told not to come to this part of the country, I came. When I was told no one could live here without perishing or going mad, I made a life for myself. As you can see, I am still here. As to my possible madness, that is a matter you will have to decide for yourselves. As we all must ultimately judge our own sanity."

"Very noble," McCracken quipped snidely.

Stenhammer took no offense. It must be hard for someone who is mad all the time, Bohannon mused, to take offense.

"No. Not noble. Ignoble, if anything. And probably irrational as well. But I had only myself to satisfy, without the opinions of others to concern me. That much I have done, or nearly so. Tomorrow there will be satisfaction, of the sort I have sought for so many years. And you, if you so decide, can be a part of it. I will share my satisfaction with you."

"Me, I'd be satisfied to get a chopper ride back to Yogonda." McCracken gulped the last of his tea.

Stenhammer focused that piercing, unblinking stare of his on the irreverent expat, and Bohannon could see that even the usually imperturbable McCracken was unnerved. "I think that you are not a man of vision, Mr. McCracken."

"That's right, mate: I bloody ain't. I'm content just to get along. A stubby of beer and a bit of tucker and I'm a happy man." He eyed the other belligerently. "That's enough for me."

"Is it now?" Stenhammer's query was gentle, perhaps even slightly amused. Turning, he walked to the back of the room and began rummaging through the pile of supplies. Opening an old plastic tool chest, he removed something from within, turned, and casually cast it in McCracken's direction. Bohannon had a glimpse of something round and bright soaring through the air.

As it described a smooth arc toward the expat, a startled McCracken dropped his cup and reached up to catch the flung object. It struck his cupped hands—and slipped right through them, landing on the thatched floor with a muffled *thump*. The expat yelped, shaking the bruised fingers of both hands, and started to say something unpleasant. But his intentions were diverted by the sight of what he had dropped. Wide-eyed and struck dumb, he picked it up and turned it over in his fingers. As he held it up to the buttery glow of the kerosene lantern, Bohannon got his first good look. So did Alfred, who sucked in his breath.

The irregular-shaped lump was the size of a softball. Waterworn and flattened, full of smooth humps and depressions, it looked like specimens of lava Bohannon had seen in Hawaii. Except for the color.

With an effort, McCracken picked it up in one hand. Bohannon recalled the ease with which Stenhammer had flung it. "This ain't real. It can't be."

"It can and it is." There was no arrogance, no hint of triumph or vindication in the big man's claim. "That is one nugget, Mr. McCracken. There are others. Not as large, but just as pure. If you know anything about gold you will notice that this is remarkably clean. There are no pyrites or galena clinging to it. It is entirely waterworn and not adulterated in any fashion."

"But this . . ." the guide was all but at a loss for words, "this must be worth . . ."

"Using for comparison purposes a straightforward benchmark of four hundred American dollars an ounce and taking into account possible included but unseen impurities, I would guess between ten and twenty thousand." Still he did not smile. "What do you think of your 'stubby of beer and bit of tucker' now, Mr. McCracken?"

The expat looked up. His whole attitude had been transformed. His voice was flat, calculating. "Where did you get this?"

Half expecting the big man to demur, Bohannon was surprised when Stenhammer did not. Instead, he turned and waved toward the forest. "Out there. In the curve of a streambed, not far from where you are sitting."

It is an intangible but undeniable property of gold that it frequently makes men forget themselves. McCracken did just that when he declared sharply, "You're lying."

Bohannon tensed, Alfred looked uneasy, and even Tai glanced anxiously at the master of the tree house. But once again, Stenhammer betrayed no distress. His response was calm and measured.

"You do not know me, Mr. McCracken. We have only just met. If you knew me better you would know that I am guilty of many things. To those I freely admit. But telling untruths is not among them." He nodded at the remarkable nugget. "I removed that from a small stream less than a thousand yards from where you are sitting. If you do not believe me, I will take you there and show you more of the same. The specimens will be considerably smaller, of course. Flakes and fragments and dust-sized grains, but gold nonetheless."

Oblivious to the hazardous insult he had just thrown, a stunned McCracken could only stare dumbly at the dreamlike lump of gold in his cupped hands. "But this—this is impossible. Everyone knows there's no gold on this side of the Central Range."

"How many have looked?" Once again Stenhammer's gaze turned eastward, half his thoughts focused elsewhere, the rest of him left to deal with his guests. "And how many who looked have lived to tell of their looking?" This time when the big man's eyes fell from whatever distant locus they had been fixated upon, Bohannon thought he detected the trace of a tear. Or it might have been only perspiration.

"I came here searching for gold because everyone insisted there was no gold here. I could have gone to Kare, or Porgera, or Yogonda, yes, I could. That is where everyone else went. I did not want to go where everyone else was going. I determined to make my own coup, or die."

Alfred spoke up. "No white men are allowed to dig at Kare or Yogonda, and Porgera is mostly hard-rock mining now. Big companies."

"Nevertheless, I could have done it. Instead, I came here. And I found my diggings." He raised a hand and pointed. "Out there, gentlemen, is a system, a network, of dozens of creeks and streams." His hand panned sideways: from west to south, south to east. "There, there, and there. Three mountains, ancient volcanoes all, covered with impenetrable rainforest, and full of gold. Three mountains that form a single watershed drained by those many streams. Streams that flow into one river. Each cataract runs bright with gold, and the river they form is richer than any watercourse to be found at Kare or Yogonda."

"Then you've been panning the main stream," McCracken surmised.

Stenhammer turned to face him. "At first, yes. One stream, then another, then the one over the next ridge. But I was not satisfied. Not like you, Mr. McCracken. I kept following them downward, and the lower I went, the richer the diggings became."

"That makes sense," the expat agreed. "Over the millennia rain would leech the gold out of the soil and wash it down the slopes. It's the same at Kare and Porgera, was the same at Wau and Bulolo years ago."

"Yes," admitted Stenhammer, "but it is different here. At Bulolo and Kare and Porgera the richest diggings were where the main stream spread out over a flat plain, dropping most of the gold there as the streams slowed. Here the geology and hydrology are otherwise. It is true that a man could take a fortune out of each of the tributary creeks alone. That does not interest me."

"Well Christ, man, it interests me!" McCracken sputtered.

"As I told you," Stenhammer replied quietly, "you lack vision. Therefore, you will have to share mine. That is all right. I have vision enough for many."

"Look here," Bohannon broke in, "if there's gold for the picking all over this place, why did you need Tai's money? I mean, the money she stole from me?"

"Borrowed," Tennison corrected him. "I was going to pay you back out of my share, remember?" Blue eyes flashing, she stared at him evenly, hands on hips, her legs crossed in front of her.

"Yeah, right. At least now I understand that you might have a share of something."

Stenhammer looked at him. "I needed paper money, kina, to purchase supplies. She has provided it on more than one occasion. Can you imagine what would have happened if someone like myself had gone into Tiny Hong's store at Yogonda and paid for rice and tea and sugar with a jar full of flakes and small nuggets? As your tracker points out, white people are not allowed to participate in the diggings at those places. Even if Hong, or any other merchant, were inclined to keep the news quiet, it is impossible to do so. Not where gold is concerned. Sooner or later, I would have been followed. The same thing would have happened to Tai if she had taken gold out with her. She would have been trailed all the way to Lae, or Port Moresby."

McCracken's interest had turned professional. "What about carrying it out of the country? I've heard that in Hong Kong you can buy and sell gold right on the street."

"So you can. I have done that myself on several occasions. But I dislike the company of my fellow humans because so few of them are. Sometimes such travel was a necessary evil, but it is much easier, simpler, and far less time-consuming for Tai to return with supplies paid for with kina."

Sudden realization blasted through Bohannon's mind, demolishing the few remaining illusions he retained of his encounter with Tennison. "I'm not the first, am I? All those compliments, all those sweet words. You've used them before, on other poor schmucks like me." All the more intense for being unexpected, a red-hot rage boiled up inside him. He jumped to his feet, glaring at her. "You're nothing but a goddamn traveling whore!"

It did not occur to him that Stenhammer might take offense. If it had, despite his feelings of betrayal and distress he might have moderated his reaction. As it was, he was lucky. The big man simply stood and watched, taking little interest and no part in the confrontation.

Tennison's mouth tightened but for the most part she held any hurt inside. "I've done what was necessary. No, you weren't the only one, Steve. But you were the nicest."

"Is that supposed to make me feel better? I'll bet you say that to all the johns you roll." He turned away, beside himself. "I tried to make myself believe that you desperately needed some money just then. It didn't occur to me that you walked the streets on a regular basis."

"I don't. Believe it or not, Steve, I don't."

He whirled to face her. "Only when you need the bucks, right? For 'supplies.' So you can buy your share. You fuck for money, Tai. In my book, that makes you a whore."

She shrugged and looked away, not meeting his eyes. "I'm sorry that's the way you think of me, Steve. I'd rather it were otherwise, but if I can't change your mind, well then, fuck you."

"You already did that," he muttered disconsolately. "Twice. Once when you were in bed and once when you were out of it."

McCracken eyed his companion, took a deep breath, and turned back to their host. "If you can find nuggets like this, what do you need our help for?"

"To find something like nothing else that has ever been found, Mr. McCracken. To make a discovery so great, so overwhelming, that it can never be surpassed. To achieve maximum results from this, I need more hands. Strong, willing hands. In return, I will let you keep half of what you can carry out on your backs."

"Half of what we can carry." McCracken studied him shrewdly. "Even if this strike of yours is substantial, that's a pretty damn generous reward just for the loan of some helping hands."

Stenhammer waved indifferently. "It is the achievement that calls to me, the vindication of my efforts. Not vulgar pecuniary totals. There is plenty for all."

"Suits me, mate. I'm real big on vulgar pecuniary totals. What do we have to do?"

"Tomorrow." Suddenly Stenhammer sounded tired. For a moment or two he looked like a very old man. This passed, and then he carefully scrutinized each of them in turn, nodding as he did so. "I will show you tomorrow. For now, get some sleep. When we begin, you will need it." So saying, he reached up to turn out the lantern, then turned and walked to the oversize sleeping bag that lay atop the foam mattress near the rear wall. McCracken made an effort to inquire further, but the big man would not say another word.

The expat gave it up, his mood greatly improved by the direction the conversation had taken. Not to mention the reality of the enormous nugget that the big man had yet to ask him to return. Stretching out on his swag, he turned onto his side and pulled the nugget close to his face, staring at it, the golden mass only inches from his eyes. In that manner he drifted off into a sound and nearly instant sleep.

Alfred climbed silently into his bedroll and turned away from the others. That left Bohannon awake, if not exactly alone, with Tai Tennison.

As time passed he thought she must have gone to sleep like the others, but he was wrong. After a pause of some minutes during which the silence and the night had begun to slip over him like a blanket, words of whispered conciliation wafted through the darkness toward him like tiny moths on silent wings.

"For what it's worth, I'll say one more time that I'm sorry." When he did not respond she added, "Look, a whore is someone who offers sex in exchange for money. I didn't do that."

"No." He did not meet her gaze, preferring (at least for the moment) to concentrate on the dark outline of the nugget lying like a scavenged chunk of solar shrapnel alongside the somnolent McCracken. "You just seduced me so you could drug and rob me. Pardon me if I'm a little weak on the fine points."

"I needed a lot of kina fast. Men traveling alone are usually very well off. The middle class travel in guided groups, and the poor choose to backpack."

"Well, you were wrong where I was concerned." Except for their whispering, it was dead quiet in the room. None of the others appeared to be paying the slightest attention to the nocturnal conversation. "I'm not a rich man. Independence doesn't always mean wealth. Sometimes it just means independence."

"I said I was sorry, and you are going to get your money back. With interest and then some."

"Is that a fact?" He finally rolled over to face her in the darkness. Sitting cross-legged on the sleeping bag, her deeply tanned legs exposed beneath the legs of the bush shorts, back straight and eyes front, she reminded him of the jade sculptures of seated goddesses he had seen in innumerable Hong Kong shops. "Tell me—how much do you think the hurt is worth? How many dollars for my pain and bewilderment? What's the going rate on making someone feel like a complete fool?"

"Oh, don't be so melodramatic! You enjoyed every minute of the time we spent together."

"Sure I did. Because I was laboring under the wild delusion that someone like yourself might actually like me for me." His laugh was hollow. "I suppose I should give you credit for telling me the truth."

"Whether you believe it or not, Steve, the money aside, I did like you for you."

"But not enough to modify your business modus operandi."

"No," she admitted softly. "Obviously not."

"That's okay." He nodded vigorously. "I'll take my share of the gold—if there *is* any more gold and the nugget's not just a come-on of some kind."

"The gold is there, Steve. It's as real as I am."

"If that's supposed to reassure me, you sure as hell picked the wrong analogy."

He'd finally gotten to her, he saw. Her face twitched as she turned away, but she kept any deeper emotions to herself. Instead of opening up, she sucked it all in. As she doubtless had done on previous occasions, he told himself.

"Fine. Think of me however you will."

"Oh, I've already made my decision about you." He nodded in the direction of the large figure lost in slumber at the back of the room. "It's him I'm still not sure about. You say the gold is for real. What about him? Is he that clever, or is he really crazy, or is he just lucky? Or is it some combination of all of the above?"

Her gaze shifted to Stenhammer's reclining form. His back was to them, his rib cage rising and falling rhythmically with his breathing. "I've never thought he was crazy, but then I've always believed that sanity was a gray area with plenty of room for discussion. Men who are driven to extremes by something deep inside themselves sometimes strike the rest of us as—unbalanced."

"Now there's a convenient euphemism. So he's driven, is he? Driven by what?"

Her reply was shaded with wonderment and resignation. "You know, I've never asked him. I've just accepted him as he is." In the darkness she peered challengingly at Bohannon. "Why don't you ask him sometime? Maybe he'll tell you."

"If there's anything to tell."

"He wasn't kidding when he said that you'll need your sleep." Straightening her legs, she pulled off first her boots, then her socks. Rising, she removed something from her shorts before sliding them down her legs and laying them out neatly at the foot of her mattress. Then she slipped free of the khaki shirt. In jogging bra and straightforward cotton panties, she slipped into the warm embrace of the light sleeping bag. As she turned toward him one more time, he saw her pat the thatched floor next to her. Her tone was teasing but noncommittal, the words simultaneously bitter and sweet.

"You can sleep over here if you want. Maybe we could talk. Maybe I could make you understand."

Within him, newborn passion and old anger clashed. Memories swirled, ran into one another, and shattered, making it hard for him to sort out how he was feeling. The result was frustration. Removing his sneakers and socks but keeping his clothes on, he climbed into his own sleeping bag.

"Thanks but no thanks. I made the mistake of getting too close to you once. Try McCracken. Maybe you'll have better luck there."

She peered past him. "Sorley? Sorley's an old dear, but he's not my type."

"Broke, huh?"

"Oh, go fuck yourself, Steve Bohannon!" With that she threw something at him, then turned over smartly inside the sleeping bag to face the other direction. He thought he heard something. It might have been a whimper, it might have been a sob.

For a moment he considered replying, considered saying something less harsh, less accusing. His lips tightened. She was damn clever. Knowing that was enough to protect him. He was convinced there was a lot she wasn't telling him; not only about herself, but about Stenhammer, this place, and the gold—if there was any gold besides the extraordinary nugget.

Stenhammer insisted they would find out tomorrow. Well, he could wait. Having waited this long to get his money back, he could damn well wait another few hours. If Tai Tennison had anything else to say to him, she could do it in the cold light of morning, in front of witnesses.

Meanwhile he intended to get some rest. Not because he needed to ignore her, not because Stenhammer had advised it, but because he was utterly worn out. As he started to turn over, he remembered the object she had thrown at him. It lay nearby, on the floor, not readily identifiable in the darkness. Reaching out, he picked it up.

It was his wallet, intact except for the missing money. He thought about saying something, then decided against it. Shoving the eel-skin folder into his pants, he put his head down on the integrated pillow and closed his eyes, wondering as he did so if despite the tension and anger flowing through him he would be able to fall asle . . .

In the middle of the night, at the height of the dead time, when the body is completely relaxed and the mind has shifted wholly into neutral, he was awakened by a moaning the likes of which he had never heard before. It sounded like chords from a soundtrack to a particularly unpleasant horror film, vibrant with torment and hopeless dismay.

In the darkness he saw Tai rise silently from her sleeping bag, a voluptuous wraith in the shadowed confines of the tree house, and tiptoe to the back of the room. There he watched her kneel alongside a larger sleeping bag and its agitated, disturbed occupant.

"Hush, Rags!" Her whisper was urgent, soothing, verbal balm. "It's all right. It's me, Tai."

The thrashing slowed, stopped. She remained bent over him for another minute or two before returning quietly and wordlessly to her own sleeping bag. Bohannon raised himself up slightly on one elbow and looked around the room. If either McCracken or Alfred had observed the brief nighttime drama, they gave no sign of it. Slowly, he let his head fall back onto the pillow.

He had not caught any words and therefore was not privy to the exact nature of the other man's nightmare. With that hideous, smothered moan still echoing faintly in his ears, he was not sure that he wanted to be. In his tormented sleep Stenhammer seemed to have been calling out to someone. Not to Tai—of that Bohannon was reasonably sure. Just as he was sure that she had carried out such nightly ministrations before, very possibly on a regular basis.

Nightmares were indicative of a disturbed mind, but not necessarily an unstable one. As he lay there listening, a few noisy sniffs and gurglings came from the direction of their host, like a pig snuffling in its slop. He watched for a while, but the unsettling scenario was not repeated.

Eventually, his own exhaustion overwhelmed his curiosity, and he fell back into the relaxing sleep from which he had been so unexpectedly and temporarily roused.

XVI

It was the chortling that woke him; an avian singsong proclaiming a raucous delight in life. Beside it, the other bird sounds, of which there were many, were reduced to simple background warbling.

As he lifted his head from the pillow the rest of his senses became active. Smell first, interpreting the thick, carnivorous odor of eggs and bacon frying in grease. Then hearing, bringing to him in addition to the bird noises McCracken's familiar mutter interrupted occasionally by Tai Tennison's higher but no less convincing tone.

"Good morning, Mr. Bohannon, sir." It was Alfred, a cup of steaming dark liquid held firmly in one hand, smiling encouragingly down at him.

Bohannon rolled over and sat up, rubbing at his eyes. Everyone else was awake, alert, and dressed. There was no sign of Stenhammer. He checked his watch: six o'clock.

"Am I the only one here who sleeps?"

"In this part of the country you might be right, mate." McCracken raised his own mug in a mock toast to his companion. Real toast was crisping on a camp grill.

Bohannon rose and slipped on his shoes and socks, remembering to first check the sneakers for uninvited guests. A small round beetle tumbled out of the left shoe. A shiny, innocuous spot the size of his thumbnail, its iridescent green carapace might have been cut from the hood of an East Los Angeles low-rider. As Bohannon looked on, it scuttled across the floor in search of concealment.

In addition to the bacon and eggs there was coffee, and marmalade to go with the toast, and salt and pepper for the eggs. He accepted a plate from Tai but had difficulty meeting her eyes.

"Look," he murmured so the others would not hear, "I'm sorry about last night. I've been carrying a lot of shit around with me and not all of it is your fault."

"But a large chunk of it is, is that right?" When he did not reply, she smiled resignedly. "Forget it, Steve. I've heard worse and been called worse."

For a long moment he did not touch his meal, content merely to inhale the wondrous steamy aroma rising from his plate. "All this—the utensils, the food, the condiments, everything—you and Stenhammer carried in on your backs?"

She nodded as she attended to the tiny grill. "Rags did most of it. All the way from Yogonda and Porgera and points southeast. He tries to avoid going back and forth to the same store. Too conspicuous, he says. So he'll walk another thirty or forty kilometers to preserve his anonymity."

Bohannon dug into the eggs and looked around the tree house. "Where is he?"

"Getting things ready. I've tried to get up before him. Never been able to manage it. He doesn't sleep much."

Or well, Bohannon thought, remembering the cries in the middle of the night. The distinctive avian chortling came again, ricocheting around the room and distracting him.

"What's that?"

Raising a spatula, she pointed toward the far window. The protective night screens had been removed to reveal the lush rainforest vista outside.

Strolling over, he tried to peer through the trees, to penetrate the mysterious tangle of foliage. Then something fluttered toward him and landed on a branch not ten feet away, in full view. While he stared, it opened its beak and brayed anew. Colored the most intense orange he had ever seen, it had two tail feathers which looped down, up and around, and looked exactly like a pair of ten-gauge wires snipped from a coil of blue steel.

"That," he declared breathlessly, "is the most beautiful bird I've ever seen in my life."

Lips glistening with bacon grease, McCracken glanced idly out the window. "Magnificent bird-of-paradise. Personally, I prefer the King, but then I'm partial to red." As if the avian spectacle outside was an everyday occurrence unworthy of further comment, he returned to his meal.

Like a vision from Coleridge, the subject of the discussion spread implausible wings and took flight, vanishing back into the canopy. Only feathers, Bohannon reminded himself. They were only feathers.

A considerably larger figure filled the door frame. Showing no aftereffects from his uneasy sleep, Stenhammer stood there studying his guests. Bohannon found himself wondering if Tai ever mentioned the nightmares to their progenitor. Or did she keep the knowledge of them to herself, leaving the big man to believe that night after equatorial night, he slept the sleep of the just?

Nothing for him to concern himself with, he decided. Before long they would start back to Yogonda, and he would be done with Stenhammer and all his peculiarities.

"Still eating?" Their host's initial contempt gave way to grudging sympathy. "Perhaps it is just as well. You are going to need your strength."

McCracken waved a fork in his direction. "See here now, mate, I like gold as much as the next bloke, but don't expect us to do any heavy digging."

More than anything this seemed to amuse Stenhammer. "No digging, Mr. McCracken. At least, not as you are thinking of it. I promise you. If all goes as planned, I will only need your help to do some lifting."

The wary expat grunted and returned his attention to his plate. When they were ready, Stenhammer led them down out of the tree and off to the south. An bulging oversize duffel rode on his back while Tai labored beneath a much smaller pack. Since the guests were not asked to bring their own gear, they left it behind. Bohannon, for one, was relieved at the chance to be free of the irritating burden.

A semblance of a trail led through the rainforest, making walking easy. Where the occasional difficult place or drop-off intervened, stone or log steps had been rammed into the earth. There were even handrails, fashioned from the boles of small trees. Testimony to the boundless fecundity of the forest, many of the cut poles sported green sprouts, mosses, and infant epiphytes.

The path paralleled the river that cut through the bottom of the narrow valley. Vegetation along its banks consisted primarily of bushes and small, fast-growing plants: proof that like every other watercourse in the ancient mountains it flooded seasonally. The open space above the fast-flowing stream allowed them to see the green-carpeted mountains that towered above them on all sides. Their crests were hidden beneath a solid blanket of heavy, white cloud.

"Wait, wait!" The others halted while McCracken dropped to his knees, his legs creasing the muddy grasses. When he finally rose, he held out his open palm for all to see.

It blazed with flakes of gold and flattened, fingernail-size nuggets. The expat's face was alight. "It's all over the place, here in the grass! This is just like the first days at Kare." Shoving his find into a pocket, he encompassed the visible river with a sweep of one hand. "I don't see any giant nuggets like the one you showed us last night," he told Stenhammer, "but a man could pick up five thousand a week here without even using a pan."

Their host considered the grass, the bank, and the fast-flowing current. "Very probably."

"Then why go any farther? Why not just camp here and work these diggings?"

Stenhammer's gaze fastened on the other man. "Because I have something to prove, Mr. McCracken, and you are going to help me prove it. If I am wrong, I promise you can come back here and reap to your heart's content."

McCracken hesitated only briefly, then nodded. "That's bonny fair enough. Let's get on with this proof, then, and get it over with."

"That's the spirit." Bohannon could not tell if the big man was being sarcastic or not. "Tell me, Mr. McCracken, how well do you know the Kare Puga?"

The guide reflected on the question. "Been there a few times, walked around, talked to a lot of people. Why?"

"Are you familiar with the geology of the area? Specifically, with Papesa Creek?" Balancing the enormous pack on his shoulders, he stepped effortlessly over a fallen log.

McCracken brightened. "Ain't that the one that disappears down a sinkhole?"

Stenhammer was quietly pleased. "Very good, Mr. McCracken."

Bohannon edged closer to Tai. "What's a sinkhole?"

"It forms in limestone, especially in karst country like this." She strode along easily under her load, not even breathing hard, and he was forced once again into admiring her fortitude. "This terrain we're walking through, and over, is all karst. There are a lot of caves. When the roof of a cave collapses because of erosion, you get a sinkhole. Sometimes a stream or river will flow right into one—and not out again." She smiled. "Then you have a vanishing river."

He'd been hearing a distant roaring for some time. As they

continued to descend, it grew progressively louder. It reminded him of his last visit to Manhattan. Walking over subway ventilation gratings set in the sidewalks, you both heard and felt the deep-throated rumble of passing trains down in the depths. That was the kind of sound he was hearing now.

It moderated slightly as they crossed a deep ravine using a suspension bridge Stenhammer had laboriously woven from strong vines in the native style. They then climbed a broken limestone pinnacle. On the far side the roaring resumed afresh, louder than ever. It also revealed its source.

The river they had been paralleling almost since they had left the tree house camp vanished into a hole in the ground. Surrounded by twenty-foot-wide mud flats, it stormed down an unseen cavity in a froth of giant bubbles, heaving swells, and transitory whirlpools.

Bohannon had to raise his voice to a near shout to make himself heard above the aqueous thunder. "Okay, I'm impressed!" Nearby, Stenhammer was staring at the freshwater maelstrom with all the intensity of a man possessed, if not by something real, then by an idea, a notion. A dream. "Where does it come out?"

Drawing himself back with a visible effort from contemplation of the gargantuan drain, the big man turned slowly. "I do not know, Mr. Bohannon. I have searched much but by no means all of the country downstream of here. In a very short while it becomes unbelievably rugged and all but impassable. That the water emerges somewhere below, either in the form of another cataract or a succession of springs, there is no doubt. But because of the difficulty of the terrain I have not been able to find it." He nodded once at the boiling, frothing cauldron. "Anyway, it does not matter. The question is of academic interest only. My real interest is in what lies here, at the bottom of this sinkhole."

Bohannon hesitated, not sure that he had heard right. "At the bottom, you said?"

"That is correct."

"I see," Bohannon replied, not knowing what else to say. "How deep is it?"

"I do not know. I tried a sounding line, but the turbulence of the water makes an accurate reading impossible. Needless to say, I do not have access to portable sonar equipment."

While he had been studying the phenomenon, McCracken had also been listening to the conversation. "So you built that tree house, carved a place out for yourself here in the middle of nowhere, and have been living and working in this canyon all along—just so you could get a look at what's at the bottom of this pit?"

"That is correct." Stenhammer was watching the other man closely.

McCracken pushed his battered Akubra back on his head and scratched at his receding hairline. "Well, I don't quite know how to tell you this, mate, but there's a respectable-sized river pouring into your hole, and it happens to be keeping it full of water."

"You are disingenuous, Mr. McCracken. Despite what you may think of my mental condition, I can tell you that I am fully aware of these facts. It has been my intent all along to get rid of the water."

"Um-hum." The guide eyed him questioningly. "And how, if you don't mind a dumb cobber like meself asking, do you plan to do that?"

"By moving the river."

A broad smile creased the other man's face. "Now why didn't I think of that? We'll just ring up the local river movers and set 'em to work."

Sarcasm slid off Stenhammer as readily as rain. Pushing past both men, he stepped up on a rock that raised him even higher above the surrounding brush, and pointed, his voice rising resonantly above the roar of the river.

"Remember the ravine we just crossed on my bridge? It lies on the other side of this eroded pinnacle." Turning to his right, he pointed at the cliff-face upstream on the opposite side of the river. "If that mass of rock up there can be brought down, the volume of material should be sufficient to block the channel. The water will rise slightly behind the resultant dam and then flow into the ravine and behind this pinnacle. Instead of in front of it, as it does now." He hopped down off his temporary podium.

"This section of river will immediately dry up and the sinkhole will drain out through its underground channel, leaving the borehole dry and open to examination."

"I ain't partial to fantasy meself." McCracken suppressed a laugh.

Perhaps because he was entirely innocent of matters geologic, Bohannon was more taken with the scenario. "Assuming it works, what do you expect to find at the bottom of the hole?"

Stenhammer put a comradely arm around the other man's shoulders, and the American felt enveloped. "Mr. Bohannon, have you ever swam beneath a waterfall?"

"There's a hotel in Paradise Valley, in Arizona, that has a pretty good size waterfall in its swimming pool. I've backstroked under that."

Knowing full well what it was like to be laughed at, the big man did not smirk at this admission. "No, I mean beneath a real waterfall of significant volume."

"I'm afraid not."

The arm withdrew. "There is a formula for calculating the amount of force falling water generates. It is a function of volume, velocity, and height. I will not bore you with it. Suffice to say that at the base of many large waterfalls there is a hole or depression that has been gouged out by the constant pressure." He nodded in the direction of the sinkhole. "Limestone is not only water-soluble, it is soft. I expect there to be a hole at the bottom of this pit that is deeper than the underground channel that drains away the river.

"Alluvial and colluvial miners always look for holes and eroded eddies in the banks and bottoms of gold-bearing streams. This is because the heavier gold will fall to the lowest point in the water and remain there."

"So you expect to find some gold concentrated in a depression at the bottom of the sinkhole?"

A hint of a smile emerged from the normally stony visage. "Yes, Mr. Bohannon. I expect to find some gold at the bottom of the sinkhole."

"Nobody's ever tried anything like this." McCracken was studying the rush of water and shaking his head. "At least not in this country. Even if you could bring down enough rock to divert the river, it will seek to return to its original channel. Rivers are like that."

"I agree with you, Mr. McCracken. That is why I need your help. My most optimistic calculations tell me that there will be a safe window of only a few days for exploration and recovery before the temporary dam created by the landslide is breached. With five people working instead of two, a great deal more can be accomplished."

"And if there's no cavity at the bottom of the sinkhole?" McCracken asked him straight out. "If its surface is flush with the drainage channel and all the gold has washed right on through to Hades itself?"

Stenhammer's reply showed that, despite his obsession, he had not blinded himself to the possibility of failure. "Then in that event,

Mr. McCracken, you may set up camp anywhere you wish along this unnamed stream and harvest colluvial material until you drop from exhaustion."

The guide nodded appreciatively. "Since you've thought of everything else, I suppose you've worked out a way to get down this hole, assuming you can pull the plug on it?"

"I have." Glancing down at his wrist, the big man checked his watch, then shielded his eyes as he scanned the terrain upstream. "The charges I planted this morning while the rest of you slept should detonate very shortly. Each one has been carefully set, but there could be some flying detritus. I suggest we take cover." He turned and pointed. "Over there, behind the large tree the strangler fig has killed." Spinning on his heel, he strode off in the indicated direction, Tai matching him stride for stride.

In their wake, his three guests exchanged stunned looks.

"What the bloody hell do you mean, 'detonate shortly,' mate?" McCracken whirled, his gaze focusing on the cliff-face upstream. "The bastard's already set explosives!"

"If you will excuse me please, sirs." His reactions uncomplicated by second-guessing, Alfred took off after their hosts.

"Come on, Sorley." Bohannon had his fingers wrapped around the other man's arm and was tugging anxiously. "If Stenhammer thinks it advisable to go hide behind a tree, then I want to hide behind him."

"But the son of a bitch didn't say anything!" McCracken allowed himself to be pulled along. "The crazy fucker never said a word about what he was doing."

Ahead of them, Stenhammer looked back over a shoulder. "We have Mr. Bohannon to thank for this."

"Me?" Baffled, the American gaped at their host.

"Yes. In all the years I have spent in this place, Mr. Bohannon, I have never had a guest. Not even nomadic hunters have visited this canyon. The reason Tai was in Lae was to pick up the dynamite timers I had ordered. As I have already explained, to allay any suspicions these had to be paid for with paper money, with kina. Your money, Mr. Bohannon." Halting, he waited for the others to catch up.

"So when I detected your presence outside the cave, I was understandably suspicious, wondering if the purchase of the timers had aroused unwanted interest in spite of the care with which it had been arranged. I thought you might have followed her from Lae for that reason." Again the ghostly, infrequent smile showed itself. "Hence my inhospitable greeting at our first meeting." He gestured upstream, at the silent wall of the mountain on the other side of the river.

"That was what I was doing this morning, while you slept. Checking and setting the timers. They all appear to be functioning properly. Microprocessors are, in their own way, as marvelous a creation as an orchid or bird-of-paradise.

"I have spent some time working out where the charges should be placed and preparing receptacles for them. It involved some difficult rock climbing and a lot of excavating by hand, but I think I have done my job well. We will know soon enough." He beckoned. "Hurry, please. At this point it would distress me greatly to see anyone hurt."

"Why?" McCracken growled under his breath. "Because it'd be one less convert to bow down before your glorious triumph?"

"Quiet," Bohannon told him. "Maybe nothing will happen."

When he was little, he and his two sisters had a favorite game they used to play in their parents' bedroom. The big king-size bed snugged up against a walnut and oak headboard, an elaborate construct of cabinets and mirrors, lights and drawers. While two of them sat cross-legged on the bed near the headboard, the third would climb to the top of the highest cabinet and leap off, landing feet first as close as possible to the others. The resultant deep depression of the mattress springs would send the two seated siblings flying. They would play this game over and over until they grew tired of climbing the headboard, or until the next half-hour of good cartoons came on.

Eventually they grew too big for the game and their parents put a stop to it. But it remained a favorite family memory of carefree weekend mornings.

That childhood sensation of effortless lift, of temporary bedroom weightlessness as one was catapulted high above a benign mattress, was briefly and energetically repeated as the earth ballooned upward beneath him. Tai would have fallen had Stenhammer not steadied her. Alfred grabbed a convenient branch, and McCracken, who had legs of tempered rubber, merely swayed slightly without losing his balance. It was left to Bohannon to fall ignominiously on his ass.

Bruised only in dignity, he rolled over and sat up in time to see an immense cloud of dust and pulverized rock avalanche from the side of the mountain upstream. The echo of the simultaneous charges bounced around inside his head, rattling his perception. For an instant the cliff seemed to pause, to hover suspended between earth and mountain peak. Then, with a roar of complaint much louder and more violent than the detonation that had preceded it, the vast mass of earth, soil, and stone plunged into the valley below.

Stenhammer was on the move before the reverberations started to fade or the dust to settle. Slipping free of his heavy duffel and setting it on the ground, he took off like a big blond greyhound, racing away in long, loping strides. As the others followed at a much more leisurely, cautious pace, he scrambled agilely up the side of the limestone pinnacle. There he stood, like a statue of a biblical prophet rendered by Michelangelo, immutable and unmoving, until the cloud of dust at last began to dissipate. Then he turned and called down to them.

"Come up and see!"

Utilizing the route by which they had originally crossed over, the others trudged to the top. Particulates still hovered in the windless, humid air, as if the displaced fragments of distraught earth were uncertain which way to fall.

The collapsed cliff completely blocked the river. As they watched, first a trickle, then a rush, and finally a flood began to spill from the pool that had risen behind the immense mass of debris. Finding its usual channel blocked, it began to flow northeast instead of due north. With each passing moment the flow increased, as if the molecules of water trapped behind the still settling earthen dam were increasingly intent upon resuming their seaward journey. Above the diverted torrent, the suspension bridge swayed but held.

"Bugger me," McCracken murmured as he took in the sight. "The crazy bastard did it."

Another man would have leaped for joy at the vindication of so much effort, or at the very least let out a whoop of triumph. For all the expression that appeared on Stenhammer's weathered face he might just as well have failed completely.

"Let us have a look at the sinkhole."

Returning to the base of the pinnacle, they made their way back downstream. As they did so a new sound reached their ears. It was the deepest, most resonant gurgle Bohannon had ever heard. Somewhere not far ahead of them, a tiny portion of the island's plumbing was experiencing a profound transformation.

The noise faded as they approached, sluicing away underground along with the last of the river itself. Trailing Stenhammer, Bohannon soon found himself slowing. They had left the moist, glistening riverbank and were walking across a pebbly surface that until moments ago had been the bed of the river, thirteen feet underwater. Of that formerly impassable watercourse, a tiny trickle was all that remained.

Ahead, like some Promethean socket from which the tooth of a god had been removed, gaped a hole black and unnerving as the Pit itself.

While he halted at a safe distance, Stenhammer and Tai walked to the very edge of the chasm and peered in. Both of them, Bohannon decided, must have ice water in their veins. McCracken approached as close as he dared before pausing. Remaining well behind, Bohannon felt a hand nudge him in the ribs. Alfred's bushy beard rose and fell as he nodded in the big man's direction.

"Maybe Mr. Stenhammer, he is only part crazy. If so, I think he is now showing one of those parts."

"You and me both, Alfred." The American shuddered slightly. "I don't handle heights well."

It was not long before the quintet reassembled near the now-exposed riverbank. It was rapidly drying out, leaving bewildered fish and small crustaceans stranded. There was a glow to Stenhammer's features that in any other man would have passed for excitement barely held in check. But where their host was concerned, one could never be sure.

"I was right. The sinkhole is clear. All the water has drained out." He glanced upstream. "The riverbed here is all but dry and it appears that my dam is holding as predicted. Now we must measure the depth of the chasm and see if we have enough rope."

"Assuming you do, and that you're going down into that thing, what are the rest of us supposed to do?" Bohannon inquired. "Wait up here and unload any gold you find?"

Stenhammer's gaze transfixed him like a beetle on a mounting board. "Only one person stays on the surface, Mr. Bohannon. One person is enough to transport whatever we may find and send up, from the edge of the pit to the safety of high ground. Where many hands are needed is down below, to search and gather and fill collecting sacks."

"Makes sense to me," he readily agreed. "I hereby nominate myself as the one to stay behind."

"You are not used to the humidity and the altitude, Mr. Bohannon. Nor from the look of you, and I assure you I mean no disrespect, are you someone who is used to hard physical labor. Whoever remains here must not only be physically able to carry any gold from the pit rim to the top of the riverbank, but also be able to haul it up from the bottom of the sinkhole, in addition to returning to the tree house from time to time to bring back food and other necessities."

"I can do that." Despite his insistence, Bohannon did not sound very convincing even to himself.

Stenhammer would brook no argument. Looking past the American, he directed his attention to the tracker. "Alfred, I would like for you to stay here and pull up anything we might find."

The Highlander nodded obediently. "I will do that, Mr. Stenhammer, sir. You can count on me."

"Good. That's settled." He turned away.

"Now wait a second . . . !" A displeased Bohannon started after the big man, only to find Tai blocking his path.

"It's no use arguing with him, Steve. Not once he's made up his mind."

"Then I'm staying up here, too." He set his feet as firmly as his intentions. More softly, he added, "There isn't a lot I'm really afraid of, Tai, but heights is one of them."

She smiled winningly. "You'll be all right, Steve. I'll watch out for you. Rags has bought the best equipment available. It's perfectly safe. Besides, aren't you curious to see what's down there, if anything?"

He eyed her uncertainly. " 'If anything'? You mean, you're not a true believer?"

She looked away. "I believe in Ragnarok. In his drive, in his abilities, in his knowledge. That doesn't mean I believe he's omnipotent."

"Well, that's a relief. All this time I thought you were a devotee, and now I find out you're only deluded. Of course, that doesn't change your status as a self-confessed thief."

"Thank you so much for the concession," she replied dryly.

Stenhammer rejoined them, both big, callused hands working to recoil a wire-thin line. A simple lead weight hung from one end. Brightly colored plastic tags attached to the wire at precalibrated distances allowed for easy visual estimation of length.

"Forty-five meters. Deeper than I hoped, shallower than I feared." He held up the weighted end of the sounding cable. "As predicted, there is a pool at the bottom. While it is difficult to say for absolute certain, I estimate it to average no more than three meters in depth." He regarded them confidently. "I anticipate no trouble. Mr. McCracken?"

The lanky guide met his gaze without blinking. "I still think this is crazy, but I admit you've got me curious to see whatever's down there. Besides mud and fish shit, I mean."

Stenhammer turned to the most reluctant member of the group. "Mr. Bohannon?"

Visions of a bad childhood fall from a roof of slippery asphalt shingles, of teetering atop a lifetime of rickety ladders, of flying between sheer mountain walls in a small plane—all came flooding into his mind, overwhelming his thoughts and washing away logic with waves of irrational emotion. Despite this, he heard himself say (though his throat was dry):

"Fuck it. You can only die once."

It should have been enough to bring forth a smile from any man, but Stenhammer simply stared back at him out of those pale, ethereal, unreadable blue eyes, and nodded.

XVII

In Stenhammer and Tennison's efficient hands, the contents of the duffel and backpack they had hauled from the tree house gradually revealed themselves. First to appear were long, perfect coils of strong nylon climbing rope—the same ropes Tiny Hong had told him about that day in the little general store at Mt. Yogonda. Their purpose was no longer a cause for speculation. One was bright red with alternating white, the other dark blue with black markings. Each looked strong enough to hold more than one person at a time.

Less easy to identify were two nylon waistband-harnesses from which dangled an assortment of straps, belts, hooks, and loops. Brightly colored rounded metal rectangles and other mountaineering gear jangled from integrated loops. There were also large flashlights in heavy plastic cases, a pair of folding plastic shovels, cans and packages of food, and perhaps most prominently, half a dozen industrial-strength backpacks, no-nonsense containers devoid of fancy rain flaps and snaps. A pair of adjustable leather shoulder straps dangled from each.

"Wait here," Stenhammer ordered them. Bohannon needed no urging.

They watched while the big man and Tai stretched the blue coil from the edge of the chasm to a huge cedar growing out of the opposite riverbank. Stenhammer tested the knots by throwing a loop of the rope over a branch and hanging from it, pulling and jerking hard on the end both to test the rope's strength and further tighten its grip on the trunk. Satisfied, he and his helper rejoined the others.

"These are for bringing up anything we find." He picked up one of the oversize backpacks. "No internal aluminum frames to hold shape, no multiple pockets, no denier ripstop nylon flaps, no lubricated zippers: just a big pocket with shoulder straps and plastic buckles. But they're European, virtually indestructible, and they'll hold a lot of gear. Or weight."

Tossing the pack onto the pile, he removed the belt from his pants and set it carefully aside, checking to make sure the enormous pistol would be readily accessible in the event he had to make a dive for it. In its place he picked up and donned the larger of the two climbing harnesses. Stepping into first one, then the other loop that hung down from the waistband, he pulled the arrangement up to his waist as if he was putting on a pair of pants. The contraption buckled securely around his waist.

While he readied himself for the descent, Tai used the other harness as a visual aid, explaining its various functions and accoutrements. "This is a climbing harness. You step into these loops, tighten them around your legs and up against your crotch and backside, and secure the belt portion around your waist. These rectangular metal rings are carabiners." She jiggled a couple of the bright red and blue metal loops. "Usually they're made of steel. These are titanium."

"Where the hell do you get titanium carabiners?" McCracken fingered one of the loops. It was virtually weightless.

"Rags says that the Russians are making them. They've got a lot of the stuff and since they're not making nuclear submarines anymore, they need to develop markets. Lucky for us." She held up a foot-long steel loop with what looked like small weights attached.

"This is a rack. The swinging weights are your brakes. See the grooves that have been worn into them? That's where the rope goes. Under the upper arc, over the first brake, which snaps onto the opposite bar. Then under the next brake, over the third, and so on, over and under, depending on how many brakes you think you'll need." Stepping into the harness, she demonstrated how the rope ran through the rack, which snapped onto a carabiner attached to a loop at the front of the waistband.

"You hold the part of the rope that's behind you like this." She demonstrated, putting her right hand behind her and holding onto the rack with her left. "Raising up on the rope brakes you. Letting it down allows it to slide through the rack and lets you descend. You're in complete control of your movements at all times. Just remember not to bring the part of the rope that's behind you around in front."

Bohannon eyed the arrangement dubiously. Titanium or no, he thought it decidedly flimsy. "That's it? That's all that's holding you?

Just the one rope running through that metal guide-thing? What about backups, safety lines?"

"No need for them, Steve. You'd just get tangled up. It's perfectly safe. As long as you hold onto the rope there's no way the rack will let you fall."

"Unless I faint and let go of everything." He was still not convinced.

Stenhammer had reloaded his duffel. Clipped to a carabiner at his waist, it hung down below him as he stepped out over the edge of the pit. Swinging himself around, he braced his feet against the wall and began to descend. The rope slid smoothly and silently through the rack as he lowered himself into darkness. While the others moved to the edge of the hole to follow his progress, Bohannon hung back. Standing too close to the drop-off made him dizzy.

Like a wind rising from the center of the earth, Stenhammer's voice reached them loud and clear. "I am about halfway down. As your eyes adjust to the diminished illumination you can see the bottom. There's enough sunlight filtering in."

"Do you see anything, Rags?" Tai balanced fearlessly on the precarious rim.

"As I mentioned earlier, there is water at the bottom, but it is too silty to see through. That is hardly surprising. There is still a small trickle flowing from the river. Some seepage at the base of the dam was to be expected." Several moments of silence followed this announcement.

"I am nearly down. The river channel, or in this case, tunnel, is pretty dry. I am going to swing around and unhook where the tunnel abuts the bottom of the hole. Except for scattered rocks, it is fairly smooth. Easy footing." More silence, then, "All right, I am off line. Send the next one down. I will belay from here."

Tennison straightened. "Who's next?"

McCracken stepped forward. "I've hung out the open door of a Beechcraft at ten thousand feet to clean a dirty windshield. I think I can handle this."

While Bohannon paid close attention to the procedure, Tai helped the guide into the harness. For a second time she explained the workings of rope and rack. McCracken nodded and walked to the edge of the pit, leaning out and over the sheer drop.

"Always thought I'd end up going this direction, but not of me own accord." Turning to face them, he waved once and stepped out and over, bracing his boots against the bare rock as Stenhammer had done.

As his confidence rose he eased off on the rope, increasing the speed of his descent. Before long the big man's voice boomed from below.

"McCracken is off line. I am sending up the harnesses and racks!"

With three of them hauling on the rope they quickly retrieved the climbing gear from the depths. Tai slipped into the smaller harness and helped a nervous Bohannon into the other.

"How does the rope go? I forget." He studied the complex arrangement helplessly.

"Here, I'll do it for you. See—rope through the top of the rack like so, then over the first brake. Flip the second brake closed, bring the rope down, and so on."

"Aren't you going to set all the brakes for me?"

"Four is more than enough. Any more than that and it'll take you an hour to get down." Her gaze met his. "Is that what you want?"

"No, but I don't want to hit bottom in four seconds, either."

"Just hang onto the rope behind you." She positioned his right hand for him.

"Let us get moving up there, shall we?" Though muffled by distance, Stenhammer's voice rang accusingly in his ears.

"Oy, c'mon, mate!" That was McCracken, chiding him. "Don't worry if you fall. I'll catch you!"

"The hell with it." Walking to the rim, he turned to face Tai, who smiled encouragingly. Then he stepped off into emptiness.

Holding the rope behind him in a death grip, he found that he had to ease off on the pressure or he would not move. A little at a time, in fits and starts, he began to descend. The view as he lowered himself was uninspiring, perhaps because he had his eyes closed the whole time. Only when Stenhammer sounded close by did he finally open them again.

The walls of the sinkhole were smooth as bathroom porcelain, slick gray stone worn to a fine polish by the downward spiraling and cutting action of billions of gallons of water. Swirled grooves twenty feet high had been cut into the rock, as if the circular abyss had been threaded to take a gigantic screw. Just as he was beginning to enjoy himself, he felt his feet touch something yielding.

Looking down, he saw that he hung suspended over a sheet of

motionless, dirty water. Off to his right, Stenhammer was beckoning to him.

"Swing this way, Mr. Bohannon. Put your feet against the wall and kick."

It took several tries to build up enough momentum to describe a sufficient arc, but on the third try he swung out over the dry rim of the pit bottom. Stenhammer and McCracken grabbed him and held him until he could be released from the harness. As a greatly relieved Bohannon steadied himself on the dry, sleek surface, the big man set himself once more in belaying position and shouted upward.

"Off line, Tai! You can come down now!"

Still not quite able to believe that he had actually done it, Bohannon took a moment to study his surroundings. Stenhammer's duffel lay near the far wall atop a large, water-polished stone outcropping. The flashlights it contained were not needed, as enough light poured down the shaft to illuminate the pool at the bottom as well as the entrance to the tunnel behind them. Sloping gently downward and off to the north, the twenty-foot-high natural conduit in the rock disappeared into a blackness deeper than he had ever seen. For the first time in millennia, it was empty of water except for a few lingering puddles.

Tai joined them in a tenth of the time it had taken Bohannon to make the descent. As she unclipped herself from the rope, Stenhammer confronted them all.

"Right. Anyone besides me feel like a swim?"

A surge of adrenaline boosted Bohannon's spirits. He might be terrified of heights, and not much of a long-distance hiker, but from childhood he had been half fish. Here at last was something he could do.

"I'll come."

Stenhammer turned to him. For an awkward moment, Bohannon thought the older man was going to deny him the opportunity. What puzzled him was why that should matter. Stenhammer was nothing to him, an obsessed enigma who might very well be mentally overstressed. Why should he care what the bearded, ragged-haired man thought, least of all of him? Why should his opinion matter?

But it did matter, and it tied Bohannon's thoughts in knots as he tried to figure out why.

"There are certain moments in every man's life when he has the opportunity to confront destiny, Mr. Bohannon. Such occasions are infrequent, and not always recognized for what they are. This is one of them. I welcome your company." With that, he began to strip.

Naked, he was even more impressive than when clothed in shirt and pants and boots. He did not have the physique of a bodybuilder. Instead, his muscularity was lean and taut, like that of a much-experienced long-distance swimmer. His flesh seemed composed entirely of ropes and strands, a body that was all range and ridges with nary a bulge or depression. If there was any fat on him, Bohannon could not find it. When the big man turned to the water and waded in, nothing shifted beneath his skin except the muscles required to carry out the immediate movement.

As for his nudity, it caused no comment. Standing in waist-deep water, he waited for Bohannon. Carefully removing his clothes and placing them on a dry surface, the American joined him. He did not grin or leer or offer any off-color comments when Tai handed each of them one of the bright red plastic flashlights. The dank, dimly-lit pit was about as unerotic a venue as could be imagined.

The water was cold, but swimming would warm him. The beam from the flashlight was focused and intense.

"Underwater lights," Stenhammer explained, "made for scuba diving. Do not worry about leaks."

Bohannon nodded. Standing naked next to the other man, he played his beam over the surface of the broad pool. The thin trickle of water falling from above rang like holiday chimes as it struck the surface opposite.

"What now?"

"We survey, Mr. Bohannon. By sight if possible, by feel if not." A gnarled hand pointed. "You take that half and I will scrutinize this one. Check the bottom, come up, move on a few feet, and check again. Let us see what, if anything, we can find."

Bohannon nodded. Turning, he swam out until he could no longer feel the bottom of the sinkhole with his toes. Aiming the light downward, he found it would only penetrate the silt-laden liquid as far as his waist. A diving mask would have been a great help, but they did not have any diving masks. Perversely, he was pleased. Stenhammer had not thought of everything. The man was not infallible.

Taking a deep breath, he plunged beneath the surface, the cold water pricking his face like needles as he dove. There was no need to arch his back in a dolphin dive since Stenhammer had assured him the pool was no more than ten feet deep.

Eyes closed to keep out suspended particles of dirt and grime, he held onto the light with one hand and felt the bottom with the other. It was composed of irregular but waterworn pebbles, tumbled smooth as polished marble by the action of tons of falling water. Clutching a handful, he let the air in his lungs lift him gently back to the surface. A couple of kicks carried him back into the shallows.

Exhaling and breathing in, he turned the flashlight's beam on his other hand, hoping to spot some color among the reclaimed gravel. A few grains or, if they were lucky, flakes; anything promising would catch the light.

The reflection, unexpected and brilliant, made him blink. Slipping the rubber loop that was attached to the end of the flashlight over his wrist, he used his free hand to wipe frantically at the dirty water that was dripping into his eyes. Dangling from the loop, the flashlight banged against his face. He didn't care.

Instead of golden flakes among the gravel, there were bits of limestone and granite among the gold. He gawked at his open palm and the handful of smooth, gleaming nuggets that lay there. A few spilled through his fingers back into the water. He ignored them.

Most of the pebbles were the diameter of a quarter or a nickel. A couple were the size of golf balls. None were spherical, having been pounded and eroded by the whirlpool that had filled the sinkhole. There were depressions and bumps, swollen edges and even a few specimens with holes worn clean through them. Using his free fingers, he picked out the granite and limestone bits and tossed them onto the floor of the tunnel. Except for a few impurities, every one of the nuggets was solid gold.

McCracken's excited whoop brought him out of his reverie. That, and a presence close by. He turned to see Stenhammer standing behind him, looking over his shoulder. The long, weathered face betrayed no hint of excitement, or pleasure, or even the vindication he claimed to be seeking. The man's lack of any visible reaction was unnatural, but Bohannon was too elated and stunned to dwell on the evident emotional shortcomings of their host.

"I'd say you have about a pound there, Mr. Bohannon. After meltdown and refining, that is. Something over six thousand U.S. dollars." He raised a closed fist. "I too have been playing in the sand."

His fingers opened to reveal a single nugget the size of a grapefruit. It glistened wetly in the beam of his flashlight, a yellow star resurrected from a watery grave. Turning, he tossed it shoreward.

"Here you go, Mr. McCracken! Another plaything to help you fall asleep."

This time the expat did not try to play catch. Instead, he hopped backward and let the mass of golden metal fall to earth. It hit the bare rock with a dull *thunk* and rolled to a stop. McCracken bent and picked it up, holding it high so that it caught the light from above. Looking over at Stenhammer, he grinned hugely.

"I can tell you this, mate: it beats cuddling a teddy bear. Find me a few more like this one and I'll make meself up a right fine pillow." Setting it lovingly aside, he started to remove his shirt.

"Restrain yourself, Mr. McCracken. For now, Mr. Bohannon and I will handle the recovery while you and Tai fill the rucksacks. When all are full, Alfred will use the red rope to take them up. While he is doing that the rest of us can break for lunch. Afterwards, if you like, you may go for a swim."

Seeing the look on McCracken's face, Bohannon tensed. The expat was not the sort to take orders from others, not even from a man like Stenhammer. But gold can be a wonderful tranquilizer. Slowly the tall, slim guide lowered the hem of his shirt back down to his waist.

"As you like it, mate. Scoop it up or toss it out, it's all the same to me. So long as you're bowling gold, I'll be happy to play the wickets." Recovering the huge nugget, he shoved it into the bottom of one of the heavy-duty backpacks. Bohannon did not recognize the tune he began to whistle.

Stenhammer worked the right side of the pool while Bohannon scavenged the other. They soon discovered it did not matter. No matter where they dove; in the shallows, on the far side of the watery expanse, in the center, the bottom was coated with gold. All the gold that had washed down from the three mountains, all the gold drained by innumerable small tributary streams, had come to rest here, in the hollow excavated at the bottom of the sinkhole by the raging river. Both men dove and dove. The cold and damp had long since ceased to be a factor. The promise of unimaginable riches was enough to insulate them.

One time Bohannon shoved his hand as far into the gravel as it would go, digging and forcing his fingers downward until his arm was buried up to the elbow. It did not matter. As deeply as he could dig, as far as he could reach, his hand still emerged clutching a fistful of gold. They did not have the means to accurately take the full measure of the pool's hidden treasure, but for a diameter of thirty yards and a depth of at least two feet, it was one solid mass of broken, tumbled, pounded gold interspersed with fragments of shattered limestone.

To pass the time (as if any kind of diversion was needed!) an unspoken contest developed between Stenhammer and Bohannon to see who could recover the biggest nugget. Not unexpectedly, Stenhammer triumphed in this as well.

A struggling Bohannon managed to wrestle a single mass of gold the size of a man's skull out onto the stony beach, only to see Tai sitting on a throne of solid yellow metal. The waterworn lump was two feet long by a foot wide by eight inches high. There was a slight concavity in the top that neatly accommodated her backside. Shaking droplets from his hair, he emerged from the water, drew up his knees, and sat down beside her, both of them oblivious to his lack of clothing. Out in the center of the pool Stenhammer breached like a hirsute salamander, silently took in air, and dove again.

"He's just checking the depth." Tai ignored the nakedness of the man sitting next to her. As for Bohannon, he had long since ceased to be conscious of it. "There's no point in bringing up anymore for awhile. The backpacks are all full."

"No reason to hang onto these, then." With studied casualness he let the nuggets he had gathered on his last dive tumble from his left hand. A few rolled back into the water. He ignored them. "I'm ready for lunch."

She looked at him and smiled. "I'm not surprised. Between the cold and all that swimming you must be starving." She threw back her head to reveal the exquisite curve of her neck. Tied back in a single ponytail, her red hair was almost black in the muted light. Behind them, McCracken struggled to force still one more nugget into an already swollen backpack.

Bohannon glanced over at the expat. "Look at him. He'll rip the packs."

She shook her head. "Not those. They're heavy-duty nylon." Her attention returned to the pool. "As soon as Rags is finished we'll have Alfred drop the other line and haul them up. In between loads he can lower down something to eat." In the filtered glow from above, her sun-browned face took on the aspect of some mischievous earth sprite recently released from a period of long dormancy. The tiny nose seemed to twitch, once.

Reaching across his middle, her arm brushed his crotch. Chilled and wrinkled, he did not respond. It was not her intention to have him do so. Picking up a couple of the larger nuggets he had just dropped, she offered them to him.

"Here." Her smile widened slightly, fey and expectant.

"What's this?"

"Repayment out of my share for the money I borrowed from you."

Tired and hungry, it took him a moment to react. When he did it was to lunge for her. "You sarcastic little bitch!"

Laughing, she skipped out of his reach and continued to do so as he chased her around the pile of packs. When he finally was forced to halt, winded and footsore, she taunted him.

"You don't catch me, Steve. I might catch you, but you don't catch me!"

"Fine." He sat down heavily. "I think I've had about enough exercise for one morning."

"If it's justice you want, mate, why not hit her with a rock?" McCracken threw him a fist-sized nugget that landed at Bohannon's feet. "Go on; beat her to death with ten grand. Not a bad way to go." He chuckled at his crude joke.

Bent over, hands on knees, breathing hard, and with a cool breeze from the depths of the earth exploring his naked backside, Bohannon turned his head sideways to regard the expat. "Thanks, but I think I'll wait for lunch." He indicated the overstuffed backpacks. "Don't tear any of those. Tai says you can't, but if it was me I wouldn't count on that."

"Don't worry, mate. We'll be wanting to use them again, right?" He tugged on the straps of the nearest pack, dragging it close to another. "My guess is there's about thirty kilos in each of these. Me math ain't the greatest, but I figure that's near about U.S. four hundred thousand per bag, with all six packs filled. Not bad payback for a cold morning's dip." His gaze inclined upward.

"I figure a week's slumming down here and we can all retire like kings. Even on half of what we can carry out. That was the deal, if you remember."

"I remember." Bohannon was starting to shiver. It would not do to catch cold. Not here, not now. Nearly dry, he straightened and walked over to where he had laid out his clothes prior to entering the pool. Taking his time, he began to dress. From behind, Tai chided him.

"*Now* what am I supposed to do for recreation?"

Looking back over a shoulder, he had to grin. The presence nearby of two and a half million in gold with the promise of tens of millions more to come had a tendency to mitigate any lingering animosity he might have felt toward her.

"You'll have to settle for ogling Stenhammer for awhile. I'm cold." Carefully, he stepped into his shorts.

Using both hands to smooth his long hair back off his face and forehead, the big man emerged from the pool, water pouring from every inch of his exposed flesh.

"There are a couple of deeper spots. Maybe twelve or thirteen feet. But nothing we cannot easily reach." With his gnarled hands he brushed droplets from his skin. "Food down first, I think. While you are eating I will send the packs up."

Bohannon stared at the big man. Bathed in the dilute, pale light, standing naked before the dark pool of unimaginable riches, he looked like a Greek frieze come to life.

"What about you, Ragnarok? Aren't you going to eat?"

"Food means little to me, Mr. Bohannon. But yes, I will need the fuel, the energy. Calories are heat. So I will have to waste some time eating. Some day someone will devise a better system for powering the human body. But until then, it is crackers and cheese and bully beef." Walking over to where he had piled his clothes, he picked up his pants and shook them out.

You have your triumph, Bohannon thought, watching the other man. At last, the enigma has his vindication. One would never know it to look at him. Bohannon hoped the breathtaking discovery had brought the other man some satisfaction. It certainly had not brought happiness. Some terrible tragedy had etched the lines in that young-old face. In what ought to have been a moment of glorious epiphany, a profound emptiness continued to haunt him. Bohannon would have asked about it if he could have figured out how to do so.

He turned away. If he did not pay attention to tying the laces of his sneakers he was liable to fall flat on his face, providing further amusement for his companions at his own expense. Having done that on several occasions already he had no particular desire to repeat himself.

Rising and cupping her hands to her mouth, Tai shouted at the circle of light that delineated the rim of the sinkhole. "*Alfred!*" In response to her call a bearded face, its features rendered indistinct by distance, peered cautiously over the lip of the chasm. "Send down some food from the supplies! Use the red rope!"

"Coming, Miss Tennison!" The face disappeared. Moments later, a weighted plastic sack commenced its descent at the end of the second line.

As Bohannon positioned himself to retrieve it, Tai ventured a caution. "You might want to give it some room, Steve. In case it tips or breaks. Be a shame to have come all this way and found all this wealth only to be killed by a falling tin of canned tuna."

It was hard not to snap at someone who was always right, but he managed. He retreated several steps, until the bag was within arm's reach.

It contained tinned fish, corned beef, and crackers, which Tai passed out among them. To the famished Bohannon, the fatty beef might as well have been a porterhouse from Smith and Wollensky, the cold tuna a Creole masterpiece from Brennan's, and the salt-laden crackers baguettes fresh from the Papeete bakery. Sitting on a wide, smooth rock, he devoured his share ravenously.

From Stenhammer's duffel Tai removed a small, portable purifier. With this she filtered water from the gold pool for them to drink, one cup at a time.

"They've improved these a lot," she commented. "This one removes all the minerals and nearly all the microorganisms, including giardia." Having served everyone else, she prepared a cup for herself.

"There's a liquor that comes from Germany called Goldwasser." Bohannon lingered over his last cracker, taking smaller and smaller bites to make it last as long as possible. "It's clear and has gold flakes in it. The gold settles to the bottom of the bottle, just like it settles to the bottom of the pool here. The distillers claim that the gold is good for the digestion."

Nearby, McCracken was slowly masticating a piece of beef. "I'll keep me gold in me pocket, thanks. A bit harder to carry, but easier to get at." Once more, he laughed uproariously at his own crudity.

Bohannon popped the last bit of cracker into his mouth. As he did so he grew aware of a faint trembling. At first he thought it was just him and that he was shivering again from some kind of secondary reaction to the time spent in dank surroundings. Or maybe it was due to lingering aftereffects from his long morning swim.

Then he saw that Stenhammer had risen to his feet and was staring upward. An instant later Tai was doing likewise, turning a slow circle, her eyes focused on the opening overhead. Only McCracken, lost in his lunch and the fortune at his feet, seemed heedless.

But when the trembling increased and was joined by a rising thunder from above, he too stood and stared.

"What is it?" Anxiously, Bohannon sought the source of the sound and the gathering vibration. Overhead, the circlet of sky and cloud was unchanged.

The ground was shaking slightly, the floor of the cave succumbing to whatever unknown force was intensifying outside. Having spent his whole life in Southern California, Bohannon had lived through many earthquakes, and this neither felt nor sounded like one. There was an eerie inevitability about it, a rising progression from simple disturbance to something unidentifiable but unmistakably sinister.

Stenhammer's shout shattered his contemplation, reverberating off the tunnel and sinkhole walls like a clarion call from a lookout stationed atop a clipper ship's tallest mast. Simultaneously, Bohannon felt a dread chill of anticipation.

"Earthslip!"

XVIII

A hundred questions raced through him, not one of which he was given the chance to ask. Grabbing not one but two of the heavily-laden backpacks, Stenhammer slung one over each shoulder while booming orders.

"Everybody, grab something! Back into the tunnel, quickly!"

"But . . ." Bohannon started to object. No one was listening to him, no one was paying him the least attention. McCracken and Tai were each wrestling with backpacks of their own. Figuring there would be time enough for questions and explanations later, Bohannon hastened to do likewise.

Snatching up the sack containing the remaining food in one hand and flicking on a flashlight with the other, Stenhammer started off down the tunnel. Despite his weighty burden he managed a good pace. Tai was right behind him.

McCracken looked longingly at the remaining sackful of nuggets. Then he muttered a curse in indecipherable strine and hurried off after the others.

Slowed by indecision, Bohannon brought up the rear. The vibration had increased only a little, but the awesome rumble overhead had risen to the point where conversation, even shouted conversation, had become impossible. The seventy or so pounds of gold on his back made it hard for him to run, but at least he didn't have to carry a flashlight. Everyone else had grabbed one, and their multiple beams illuminated the tunnel floor from one side to the other.

A powerful gust of dense, moldy air struck him unexpectedly from behind, overtaking him with a roar and nearly knocking him off his feet. His lungs labored to strain the effluvia. It stank of decomposition and growing things, as if ten tons of humus and potting soil had suddenly been blown sky-high. It was followed by a second, stronger blast that knocked him off balance. He went down, hands reaching out to break his fall, skinning both knees on the slick, scoured stone floor.

Something clutched at his feet, burying his sneakers and ankles, crawling inexorably up his legs. It held him fast and kept him from rising. Looking back over his shoulder, he let out an inarticulate, choking cry of pure terror.

The sinkhole was gone, vanished, completely filled by a compressed mass of earth, rocks, and pulverized vegetation. Slowed but still advancing, this compacted detritus was now spreading into the tunnel, trying to fill it up as well. It was up to his hips already; a toothless, lugubrious antagonist that in another few seconds would cover him completely, smothering him in its damp embrace, rendering him immobile and crushing his bones. He envisioned himself trying to scream for help, the warm, moist earth rushing in to fill his open mouth, choking off his air, his lungs bursting. . . .

Strong hands were on his wrists, pulling hard. He thrust and kicked as violently as he could. Reluctantly, the clinging earth loosened its grip. Scrambling to his knees, balancing the heavy backpack against his shoulders and spine, he staggered to his feet. Lifting his eyes, he expected to see Stenhammer.

It was Tai.

"Thanks." It was a wholly inadequate response and all he could think of to say. Crud filled his lungs and he hacked up dirt and pleghm.

"Keep moving! I think it may have stopped, but more weight above could push it further in." Her light turned away from the fallen hillside behind him and back down the tunnel.

The earth did slip a little deeper inward before finally halting. Only then did Stenhammer call a rest. Unused to running, much less with seventy pounds of gold on his back, McCracken was doubled over from the exertion, head down, his hands resting on his knees. Tai was breathing hard and Bohannon—he was thankful simply to be breathing.

Despite carrying a double load in addition to food and flashlight, Stenhammer appeared relaxed and ready to go on. While the others stood around and tried to catch their breath, he walked up to the slanting wall of dirt that now filled the tunnel and examined the broken, torn vegetation buried within. Turning back to his companions, he switched off his beam.

"We burn one torch at a time. Tai's, for now." Without comment, McCracken switched off his own flashlight, cognizant of the need to conserve their batteries.

"What . . ." Bohannon was still fighting for air, "what happened?"

The big man studied the subterranean earthen slope. "PNG suffers hundreds of major earthslips—or landslides as I believe you Americans call them—every year, Mr. Bohannon. Villages are wiped out, bridges destroyed, and major roads blocked. The entire island is tectonically active. There are volcanoes, earthquakes—and landslides. Earthquakes registering six and seven on the Richter scale are a commonplace occurrence. The soil is water-saturated and unstable and as you know, the mountains are very steep. This land of New Guinea, this island, exists in a continuous state of collapse and upheaval."

"Helped along from time to time by the ill-conceived use of too many explosives, you brainless arsehole!" Putting down his head and charging, McCracken screamed, "You've killed us all!"

He slammed into Stenhammer before the other man could get out of his way, knocking him backward and sending both of them tumbling to the ground. Their movements constrained by the sacks of gold on their backs, they nonetheless managed to roll over and over several times, locked in unaffectionate embrace.

"Stop it, both of you!" Avoiding thrusting legs and flailing arms, Tai danced around the two men, shouting at the top of her lungs. "Steve, do something!"

"I am." As the dust from the earthfall that had filled the sinkhole continued to settle behind them, he found a suitable rock and sat down, cupping his face in his hands and staring moodily at the floor.

McCracken rolled over with Stenhammer seated on top of him. Bohannon marveled at the big man's control—or was it a complete absence of feeling? Whatever the reason, his expression still had not changed, though the line of his mouth had tightened perceptibly.

His left hand was locked around the expat's throat, the arm stiff and unbending as a steel rod, pinning the other man's head and neck against the ground. Trying to free himself from that unyielding grip, the sputtering McCracken might as well have tried to move one of the dock pilings in Port Moresby harbor. Stenhammer drew his right hand back behind his shoulder, the fingers balled into a huge fist.

Tai grabbed his arm. "That's enough, Ragnarok! That's enough!"

The big man hesitated, for a moment motionless as a Borglum tableau. Bohannon knew that despite her deceptive strength, Tai could not have prevented that closed fist from descending. Were he so inclined, Stenhammer could still bring his hand down and smash McCracken's face. Tai would simply travel with it, yanked off the ground and forward with the blow.

Instead, Stenhammer spoke softly as he rose and stepped away from the prone figure. His voice was that of imminent doom. "Do not touch me again, Mr. McCracken."

Rubbing at his throat, the expat sat up slowly. "I meant what I said." The anger was still present, but his tone was subdued.

Stenhammer rearranged the packs on his back. They had shifted during the fight. "If you will stop a moment to think, Mr. McCracken, you will note that, contrary to the feelings you just expressed, you are not dead. None of us is. A few moments ago you were so happy you could hardly stand it, nor could you stop singing my praise. Now I am a 'brainless arsehole.' "

"All right then; you're not a brainless arsehole. You're just a bloody fool." McCracken climbed to his feet, the golden load making it difficult for him. "You used too fucking much dynamite."

"So now you are an explosives expert, Mr. McCracken? Maybe you can tell me: how much is too much? How much would have been just enough? I did the best I could." The big man's voice carried not a scintilla of apology as he turned to scrutinize the slanting wall of earth behind them. "The earthslip could have been the result of natural forces. Probably the hillside, or sides, involved have been unstable for some time, like so many of the steep slopes in these mountains. But I do not doubt that the explosive charges exacerbated an already untenable condition."

Bohannon asked the inevitable question, to which he was afraid he already knew the inevitable answer. "Can we get out of here?"

Sadly, Stenhammer did not surprise him. "Not the way we came in. The sinkhole is plugged tight. Even if we had the tools with which to dig and the food to support the activity, excavating at the bottom would only cause more debris to fall in from above. From the sound and duration of the slip I would estimate that several million tons of material was involved. It is entirely possible that this whole end of the valley was buried, from above my tree house to well below the site of the sinkhole."

Bohannon's eyes widened and he rose as if he had been shot. "Alfred!"

Stenhammer regarded him unblinkingly. "Unless he was a very

fast and alert runner indeed, he is probably dead. Another body claimed by these mountains, never to be found."

Bohannon slumped. "So what do we do now?"

The big man turned and snapped on his flashlight just long enough to point it down the dark, conduit-like tunnel. "Since we cannot go back, we must go forward. This channel, like the river it once carried, must emerge somewhere. If as a river, we may be able to walk out. If as springs, we will have to dig."

"Too right," mumbled the distraught McCracken. "And while we're walking, what do we do for food?"

Stenhammer looked at him as if their fight had never taken place. "The tunnel floor is not smooth, so there should be depressions full of water. The portable purifier is here." He held up the food sack. "As for something to eat, we have one small box of crackers and two tins of sardines. When they are gone, Mr. McCracken, I suggest you think nourishing thoughts." Without another word he started off down the tunnel. The others followed.

It soon became apparent that a single flashlight was insufficient to show the way and that two were necessary: one to pick out the easiest path, the other to illuminate the floor underfoot. The tunnel was no place to step in a hole and sprain an ankle—or worse. Fortunately, the water-scoured surface offered easy hiking. Though still damp, the rock underfoot was smooth and the downward slope gentle. A few places required that they pay careful attention to their footing, and in others the heavy backpacks had to be removed and passed hand to hand down the steepest drops, but they encountered nothing that severely inhibited their progress.

Time passed inexorably. Bohannon had long since given up looking at his watch. The numbers it displayed were meaningless, the time of day irrelevant. Within the tunnel it was impossible to tell direction. They could only be certain of one thing: that they were walking from the past into the future.

Stenhammer would have kept on without stopping, and McCracken was too mean to concede to anything, including exhaustion. But Tai and Bohannon at last were forced to call a halt, if only for a few hours.

The big man checked his own watch. "We'll spend the night here—or rather, we will sleep here, since night and day have no meaning in this place." Slipping off the backpacks, he removed the contents of the plastic food bag. While the others watched hungrily, he opened first one tin of sardines, then the other.

"Shouldn't we ration those?" Bohannon wondered.

McCracken had shut off his flashlight and in the near darkness Stenhammer's eyes could not be seen—but Bohannon knew they were focused on him. "Better to supplement what strength and energy you have left than let your body run down to the point where it is incapable of making proper use of the food." After distributing the crackers equally and instructing them on how to take their fair share of the canned fish, he rose to inspect their surroundings.

Tai ate slowly from the open tin, alternating bites of sardine with pieces of cracker. "Rags, aren't you going to eat?"

Along with the beam of his light, the big man's attention was focused on the surrounding walls. "You know I do not eat much, Tai. Thank you for your concern, but I will be all right."

McCracken attacked his share of the fish with gusto. "That's right admirable of you, mate. If I didn't hate your guts so much I'd thank you." Olive oil dripped unctuously down his chin.

"I can live without your gratitude as well as without your food, Mr. McCracken."

When they had finished, everyone did their best to find a soft rock. Cold and fatigued beyond measure, Bohannon curled himself up against a waterworn boulder. Utilizing his backpack for a headrest, he wondered how many ancient potentates and modern Croesuses could boast of having gone to sleep on a pillow of solid gold. Thinking that it would be nice to have a few feathers to lay atop the gold, he closed his eyes.

When he opened them what seemed moments later it was to a darkness so absolute that it intruded on his optic nerves and seemed to seep into his brain. McCracken and Stenhammer had switched off their flashlights, leaving them all in total blackness.

Pushing a button on his watch, he was rewarded with several seconds of blue-green luminescence. The numbers did not interest him: only the light, which provided proof that his eyesight still functioned.

A hand touched his side, feeling its way, and then withdrew. "Don't take this the wrong way," Tai whispered. "All I want to share is your body heat. It's cold in here."

"Suit yourself," he replied. "Stenhammer's a lot bigger than me. I'd have thought you'd snuggle up next to him."

"I would." He felt her soft warmth pressing up against him as she tried to find a comfortable position on the hard ground. "But Ragnarok has a tendency to toss and turn a lot in his sleep, and sometimes he strikes out with an arm or leg."

"At what? Imaginary demons?"

"Internal ones, anyway. Don't judge him too harshly, Steve. You don't know him. You don't know him at all."

"I'm willing to be enlightened." Her body heat was more soothing, more appreciated than he could say. He hoped he was reimbursing her with as many calories as she was sharing with him.

He felt her turning over back to face him. "Maybe sometime I'll do that. But not now. I'm too tired."

She said nothing more, which was just as well, because within minutes he was past hearing anything anyway.

XIX

When he awoke it felt as if he had only just laid down and closed his eyes, but a check of his watch revealed that he had been asleep for nearly ten hours. Tai's warm weight pressed against his back. As he stirred, she mumbled something in her sleep. He was unaccountably pleased that he was not the last of the group to awaken.

"Good morning, Mr. Bohannon." That was Stenhammer, close at hand and if his brisk elocution was anything to go by, fully awake. "I trust you slept well?"

"I'll let you know as soon as I see if I can move." Sitting up, he stretched. Though he was stiff all over, nothing snapped or flew apart. "How did you know I was awake?"

"I could hear you moving about."

Reaching down in the darkness, Bohannon nudged the still recumbent form alongside him. Tai muttered something unflattering.

"How'd you know it was me and not Tai?"

As always, the big man's voice was innocent of humor. "You and Tai move differently."

"I'd drink to that." That was McCracken's voice, feisty as ever. Sleep had, however temporarily, rejuvenated him. "That is, I would if I had anything worthwhile to drink."

"I'll filter some water." Yawning, Tai switched on her light and fumbled with the plastic bag. The purifier was all it contained now, since they had finished off the food. Bohannon's stomach pleaded for breakfast. A round of greasy bacon and eggs would have been fine with him. Or pancakes, for a change, or waffles with butter and hot maple syrup, or . . .

Struggling erect, he forced himself through a few simple knee-bends and arm swings. They took his mind off food, if only temporarily.

Everyone downed at least two cups of water, dipped from a

nearby pool on the cave floor and run through the compact purifier. When they had finished, Tai took charge of the precious device, securing the plastic bag to her belt.

"We've got to get out of here," she declared. "Another day in total darkness and I might start to lose my tan!"

Bohannon chuckled appreciatively. It took an effort.

Less than an hour after they resumed walking, the downward slope of the tunnel increased. While still negotiable without climbing gear, it demanded more concentration than ever. The damp rock underfoot remained slick and treacherous.

Everyone slipped and fell at least once, Bohannon several times. No one made fun of him. Their heavy loads made it difficult to maintain balance on the increasingly steep grade.

It was early afternoon, or the equivalent in the outside world, when McCracken's flashlight failed. Stenhammer would have continued on using only one, but the slippery footing made it imperative they be able to see where they were stepping as well as where they were going. It was decided to continue with both remaining lights for as long as they lasted, then with one, and finally in darkness, using a wall to guide them as they felt their way along.

Tired and hungry, Bohannon was convinced he would give out before the batteries did. Nonetheless, he refused to abandon his heavy backpack. It held his share of the gold, won through difficulty and retained with determination. He forced himself to straighten beneath the load and lengthen his stride. So he was a little hungry, so what? There was four hundred thousand dollars in the bag on his back, and their retreat was still all downhill, wasn't it? The tunnel had to open up before it reached the sea, didn't it?

The feminine outline just ahead of him stumbled slightly, righted itself, and fell out of the single-file line. "I—I'm sorry. I have to rest, Ragnarok. Just for a moment."

Stenhammer's light turned to illuminate her as she dropped into a sitting position. Nearby, McCracken slipped free of his golden burden and joined her.

"Oy, it's time for a rest, it is. Just for a few moments, mate." Though he would never admit to it, the underpinnings of false resilience in the guide's voice suggested that he, too, was close to the breaking point.

Bohannon did not have to be persuaded to join them. Only Stenhammer, phlegmatic and stolid as ever, remained standing. His light played over each of them in turn, revealing the slumping forms, the lowered heads, the legs and backs that had been pushed to the verge of collapse.

"Catch your breath. I will scout out a little ways ahead." Removing the two heavy backpacks he had continued to carry, he lowered them to the rocky floor. Then he pivoted on his heel and strode off down the tunnel.

Bohannon followed the bobbing glow of the big man's flashlight. It reminded him of a runaway jack-o'-lantern as it disappeared into the distance. It was easy to track the fading light because as soon as the big man left, Tai had switched hers off to conserve battery strength. So long as they did no more than sit and talk, they had no need of the light.

Remembering where she had sat down, he spoke in her direction. "Think we'll ever get out of here?"

In the darkness her voice was clear as church chimes. "You're the cheery one, aren't you?"

"Sorry." He resisted the urge to activate his watch light just to have something to look at. "I was thinking that this is a lousy place to die."

"Any place is a lousy place to die, mate." Determination had replaced McCracken's momentary despondency. "I don't know about you two, but I ain't dying in here. Not with a sackful of gold to call my own."

"Half a sack." Tai could not keep herself from reminding him.

He chuckled nastily and Bohannon imagined he could see the other man leering in the darkness. "Cheeky bitch, aren't we?" There was a pause, then the sound of a hand striking flesh.

"There's no gold there, Sorley, you bastard."

"Now, that might be open to discussion, lass. Depends how you define 'gold.'"

"Discuss it with yourself. While you're playing with yourself. But keep your hands off me."

"She'll be right, luv. Plenty of time to thrash things out when we get out of this rat burrow." McCracken did not sound in the least abashed or intimidated.

They waited there, in the darkness, for Stenhammer to return. While they waited they hungered, and thought, and imagined sunlight, and green trees, and running water, and hungered some more.

Bohannon stood it as long as he could before giving voice to the unpleasant thought that refused to go away. "I wonder if he's coming back."

"Don't be an idiot, Steve." Tennison's tone was accusing. "Of course he's coming back."

"Then where is he? He's had more than enough time to 'scout' the terrain ahead."

"Oy, the lad's right. Maybe it's struck our dear demented leader that he can move a lot faster without the gold and without us slowing him down. Maybe he figures he can leave us to die here and come back for all the gold later." Fumbling in the darkness, McCracken switched on Tai's light.

She hastily shielded her eyes from the unexpected brightness. "Turn that off, Sorley. You're wasting batteries."

"Am I?" In the faint, suggestive glow Bohannon could just make out the sharp highlights of the other man's anxious face. "I ain't sitting here no longer. You can stay if you want. Me, I'm moving on. I'm getting out of here." He bent to pick up his pack and sling it onto his back.

Bohannon rose quickly to block the expat's path. "Stenhammer said we were to wait for him here."

"Now, what's this?" His expression set, McCracken gazed evenly back at the other man. "You're the one who was just mouthing off about whether or not he were coming back."

"I'm frustrated and tired, just like you, Sorley. I was just making noise."

"Sounded like mighty sensible noise to me. Get out of me way, Steve. I don't want to hurt you." He started to step around the man blocking his path.

Bohannon moved to intercept him. "I can't let you do that, Sorley. We need that light."

Retreating a step, McCracken sized up his opponent. If the look that came over his face was anything to go by, he was less than intimidated. "Last chance, mate. Like it or not, I'm coming through."

"Coming through where?" The question boomed off the sculpted walls and echoed down the tunnel.

Forgetting about McCracken, Bohannon whirled. "Stenhammer!" He squinted into the blackness. "Where's your flashlight?"

"Here." A second beam cut through the darkness. "I only needed it going the other way. I memorized the location of any difficult places so I would not have to use the light on my way back." Looking past the speaker, his gaze settled on the tense form of McCracken. "What's going on here?"

"Nothing, mate. Not a bloody thing. We were just getting a bit worried about you, that's all." The lanky expat smiled sheepishly as Tai yanked her flashlight from his grasp. "We were just wondering where you'd got off to."

The big man pondered this response for a long moment, his eyes piercing the darkness. Then, without a word, he bent to pick up the two overstuffed backpacks he had left behind.

"Let's move. It gets a little easier up ahead."

Groaning and complaining, they took up their burdens and staggered off in his wake. Bohannon kept his eyes fastened on the illuminated oval Tai's flashlight cast on the tunnel floor, determined not to slip and fall again. Only occasionally did he glance up to see where Stenhammer was leading them.

It was on the third such look that he became convinced his eyes were playing tricks on him.

"Tai, turn off your light."

"What?" Looking back at him, she slowed to move a little closer. "What are you talking about?"

"Just turn it off!"

"Okay," she responded dubiously, "but don't blame me if you trip and break your leg."

The light went out. Straining, he rubbed at his eyes with both hands. Either he was going blind, or losing his mind, or . . .

"There's light up ahead!"

The weighty pack jouncing against her back, she moved next to him. "You're crazy, Steve. You . . ." she broke off. "You're right, you're right! I can see it, too!"

From his position at the front of the line, Stenhammer looked back. "I told you it got easier up ahead." The corners of his mouth did not curve upward, his deeply lined cheeks did not bunch into jolly apple shapes, but for the first time in a long while there was a glimmer of a smile in those pale, pale blue eyes.

So overpowering was the light of late afternoon after their long sojourn underground that they had to approach it slowly and with care. Even so, eyes watered painfully as they struggled to adjust to the intense sunshine.

There had been a waterfall of some stature where the underground river had burst forth from the mountainside. The exhausted refugees stood on the lip of the now dry drop-off confronting a vista utterly different from the one they had left behind.

Ahead stretched a succession of low, jungle-clad hills flanked on either side by higher mountains that were themselves considerably less imposing than those they had recently crossed. Stenhammer and McCracken agreed that in the course of traversing the tunnel they had also descended several thousand feet.

With the two backpacks riding high on his back, the big man pointed to a line of puddles and ponds far below them. "That is where the river ran. Its demise is a blessing for us. Instead of having to hack our way through the forest, we can follow the dry riverbed until its tributaries begin to fill it once again. Then we can make a raft and float our way out."

Bohannon was not sure he had heard correctly. "Aren't we going back up the canyon to the tree house and then on to Mt. Yogonda?"

Stenhammer turned to him. "As I stated earlier, Mr. Bohannon, given the suspected size of the earthslip I do not think my tree house any longer exists. If you will come out here and stand next to me, you will see why it is impossible in any case."

A cautious Bohannon advanced to the edge of the drop. Following the other man's lead, he leaned out and looked up. The absent waterfall had emerged from a precipitous cliff-face. Where broken rock and ledges had formed, bushes and even entire trees had taken root and sprouted. Below their present position the slope was difficult but passable. Higher up—he found himself nodding in agreement.

"I see what you mean."

"I think I could make the ascent," Stenhammer told him, "but without the gold. I am not sure the rest of you could manage with or without it. In any case, we have struggled too long and too hard to abandon our gains now, especially in exchange for a climb that might well prove impossible. Logic and our burdens dictate that we go down and not up." Moving to his left and facing the rock wall, he headed off along a narrow ledge.

"Follow me, Mr. Bohannon."

I'm getting tired of following you, Stenhammer. But he had no choice, none at all. *Just don't look down*, he told himself. *Don't look down, and hug the rock, and concentrate on where you're putting your feet.*

"What happens when we find enough water to float a raft?" He suspected that he knew, but anything was better than thinking about where he was presently walking and what he was doing.

Stenhammer replied without looking back at him, as casually as if they had embarked on a Sunday stroll in the park. The broken limestone underfoot, the treacherous ledge, seemed not to concern him at all. Indefatigable and fearless, the man must also be part mountain goat, Bohannon decided. Despite carrying a double load he paused and reached back frequently to help the anxious American across one difficult spot after another.

"Every stream, every river in the northeast part of this country flows into the Sepik, which flows on to the Solomon Sea. There are villages all along the middle and lower Sepik itself, and on many of the major tributaries. The people who live there have access to motorized dugouts. We will hire a couple to take us to Timbunke. There is a road there, and if we are really lucky we may be able to hire a plane."

Bohannon nodded but chose not to pursue the conversation. It required all his concentration to put one foot in front of the other without letting his eyes and his thoughts stray to the potentially fatal plunge that beckoned only inches from his feet.

Only the first couple of hundred yards beyond the end of the tunnel were really bad. After that they found themselves scrambling over talus and rubble, where a man could take a bad tumble but a slip of the foot was unlikely to lead to his death. Seeking the sun, young trees forced their way through the crumbling sedimentary detritus. They offered an increasing number of secure handholds and places to rest.

It was good that they did, because the lower the three men and one woman descended, the more the humidity increased. By the time they reached the base of the dried-up waterfall and stood, panting but relieved, in the barren riverbed, it approached one hundred percent.

Perspiration did not drip from Bohannon. It flowed, in salty streams that threatened to erode channels in his own skin. It stained his shirt and jeans dark and plastered his hair down on his head.

"Have to be careful with the backpack," McCracken warned him. "If it feels like it's rubbing against your spine, adjust the straps. Pull it higher or lower, but don't let it take the skin off under your shirt. You don't want to rub open any sores in this country." He showed dirty teeth. "For a lot of the little critters that hang out here, an open cut is prime real estate. The last thing a man wants in this place is to become a condo for a bunch of unidentified microbes."

"I'll be sure and keep that in mind." The image McCracken had sketched was highly distasteful.

They found a shady spot by a deep pool, one of many left behind by the diverted river. While Stenhammer and Tennison went off to scrounge for food, McCracken and Bohannon divested themselves of their packs and laid down on the exposed river stones. Unseen creatures called between trees. Once, a flock of large brown birds brandishing outlandish beaks soared by overhead.

"*Kokomo.* Hornbills." McCracken lay on his back, his hands behind his head as he studied the sky. "Beautiful as they are grotesque. Me, I fancy 'em more than birds-of-paradise. Those blokes, they're gorgeous but too pretty for me. A hornbill now, I could see meself sharing a stubby with." He pointed as another flock of smaller, noisier fliers rippled through the sky on its way back to its evening roost.

"Rainbow lorikeets. And that there," he declared, singling out a flash of blue and white that darted from one side of the dry streambed to the other, "is a sacred kingfisher."

"You know your birds." Bohannon was impressed.

McCracken shrugged modestly. "A man that wants to spend much time in this country better learn all he can about it. Many's the time a life has been saved out here by a little knowledge." He winked at his companion. "Next time it might be yours."

Bohannon found his attention drawn to the dense jungle that crowded the riverbank and spilled over its edges. "Think they'll find anything?"

"What, to eat? I'd be surprised if they didn't. If they do come back empty-handed, I'll go have a looksee meself. There's plenty to eat in the forest, mate. The trick is not to look at it too closely while you're popping it down."

It was starting to get dark by the time the two scavengers returned. That they'd found something was indicated by the way the plastic bag swung heavily in Tai's hand. Bohannon's eagerness to see what they'd brought back was tempered by McCracken's earlier warning.

It was well founded.

A broad smile creased Tai's face as she negotiated the riverbank and scrambled down to the shady site they had chosen for a camp. "We'll eat well tonight. The forest provides, if you just know where to look." Behind her, Stenhammer bounded down the slope as gracefully as if he were schussing at Aspen.

She passed the plastic bag to Bohannon, who peered expectantly inside—and nearly flung it from him. It contained several dozen brown nuts the size and shape of quail eggs, and at least as many wriggling white larvae. Each of the latter was as big around as his thumb.

"God almighty." He swallowed hard. "You're not going to eat those?"

"You bet I am." The evident relish with which she responded nearly made him sick. "Rags found a fallen sago palm. His big knife is with his belt, buried back up in the mountains, but his Swiss army knife was still in his pocket. He used the blade to dig into the center of the log. Sago is very soft, but with a three-inch blade it still took awhile."

"That is why we were gone so long." Joining them, Stenhammer sat down and began to peel the foot-long lengths of purplish wood he was carrying beneath one arm. "It would be nice if we had some matches with which to start a fire. Unfortunately, neither Tai nor I smoke."

McCracken straightened, pleased for once to be the one to spring to the rescue. "Well mate, I'll take a puff off anything I can get me hands on. But since I don't expect we'll be stopping for a smoko any time soon, we might as well use this now." From a pocket of his pants he extracted a cheap butane lighter.

"It's not full," he declared, "but she should give us a few burns."

"Don't waste it," Tai told him, to forestall any unnecessary demonstrations.

The discussion left Bohannon feeling lost. "What the fuck do we need a fire for? This place is hotter than the hinges of Hell."

"You think she's hot here, mate, wait 'til we get down in the basin proper." McCracken grinned at him. "We need a fire to cook the grubs, of course. You can eat 'em raw, but me, I'd rather have mine toasted."

"You can have them any way you want." Bohannon fought to control his stomach, which was doing flip-flops. His very empty stomach, he reminded himself. "I don't eat bugs."

"Then in the jungle you often do not eat." Stenhammer passed him a length of the wood he had been stripping. "You will quickly find yourself growing tired of a very monotonous diet, Mr. Bohannon."

The American examined the length of pulpy material. "What's this?"

"*Pit-pit,*" Tai told him. "Wild sugarcane. It's a weed down here."

Experimentally, Bohannon bit into the pale yellowish pulp. Sweet sap filled his mouth. Delighted, he gnawed hungrily at the offering.

"Not too much too fast, Mr. Bohannon," Stenhammer warned him. "It will give you diarrhea." He gestured at their surroundings. "I cannot imagine more unpleasant circumstances in which to have the trots."

Bohannon immediately slowed down. But it was hard to take his time, what with his belly crying out for nourishment of any kind.

He nursed his way through the stick of cane while Stenhammer and McCracken carefully built a fire. As usual, the hardest part of the task was finding enough dry material to burn.

"If this was the Wet," Tai observed, "we'd be shit out of luck. In the Wet you'd be lucky to start a fire with a kilo of sawdust and a liter of lighter fluid."

Using his knife's blade, Stenhammer sliced thin lengths of palm frond and sharpened them at one end. This enabled each of them to suspend their larvae shish-kebabs over the small but precious fire without getting burned. The sago grubs hissed and crackled as they cooked, writhing for far too long on their individual spits. White they might be, but they did not much remind Bohannon of marshmallows.

He watched in silence as his companions chewed and swallowed. In place of nausea there was only contentment on their faces. The lining of his stomach felt raw and his insides throbbed complainingly.

"All right," he heard himself say finally, "I'll try one. But only one!"

"That's my boy." Removing her stick from the fire, Tai slid a well-browned grub off the end of the woody spike as delicately as if she were preparing a fine hors d'oeuvre. A reluctant Bohannon took it between thumb and forefinger.

"You're sure it's dead?"

"Me, I kind of like it when they wiggle going down." McCracken was grinning expectantly at him.

"Leave him alone!" Tai snapped. Turning back to Bohannon, she removed a second roasted grub, stuck its head in her mouth, and bit down. Her full, moist lips moved as she chewed. "Go on. Try it while it's still hot. Staring at it is not going to turn it into steak and mushroom pie, you know."

Closing his eyes, Bohannon thrust the grub into his mouth and forced his jaws to close. It took everything he had to begin chewing. When he did, he was more than a little surprised.

"Hey!" He opened startled eyes. "That's not half bad."

"Told you." Grinning mischievously, she popped the rear half of her own remaining larva into her mouth.

Maybe it was the muting effects of ravening hunger, or maybe his taste buds had been corrupted by weeks of eating strange food, but the roasted sago grub tasted like burnt butter with distinctly nutty overtones. Not a gourmet triumph, but far from the worst flavor in the world, either.

"Eat your share," Stenhammer advised him. "They are rich in fats, oils, and protein. We should be able to find them all the way along the river."

"Well," Bohannon swallowed, "I don't see them replacing hamburgers as the fast food of choice in the States. 'Have some grub' has an entirely different meaning there, and 'Over Ten Billion Grubs Sold' isn't a very catchy advertising slogan. But I have to admit, I've had lots worse. Flavorwise, it sure beats Vegemite."

"Ah," murmured McCracken longingly, "right now I'd give an ounce of gold for a jar of that!"

"And I'd sell it to you for a dime," Bohannon replied with feeling. Appeased, his belly sent out a polite call for more. "Throw another grub on the barbie for me, Tai."

"Good." A satisfied Stenhammer watched the other man eat. "Tomorrow, if we're lucky, we'll try you on snake."

XX

If he had not been sleeping so soundly on the bed of palm fronds Stenhammer had gathered for each of them, he might have awakened sooner. If it had rained, or if a wind had been blowing, or if his hunger had not been assuaged for the first time in days, he might have awakened more quickly. If they had posted a guard, that person might have sounded a warning.

But they were all exhausted, and rest-deprived, and in need of another long, deep sleep. It was purely by chance that Bohannon was the first to be attacked. Even so, he might have slept on had his inquisitive assailant not decided to crawl on top of him to begin eating.

Lying on his right side on the mat of green fronds, his arm beneath his head, Bohannon stirred uneasily in his sleep. He felt a pressure on his left arm just below the sleeve of his shirt, then a slight pain. Mindful of the multitude of warnings he had received about black mosquitoes and how they only bit at night, he swatted irritably at the site, hoping to kill the nocturnal intruder.

His hand made contact with something large, warm—and furry. Still more than half asleep, he felt something weighty shift against his ribs. What finally woke him completely from his lingering stupor was an angry squeal.

His attacker slid down his chest, retreated a yard or so, and turned to face him. Nearby, McCracken let out a startled oath as Tai exploded from her makeshift bed with a series of frantic, high-pitched shrieks. Behind them Bohannon could see the tall, silent figure of Stenhammer silhouetted in the dim light. The big man was swinging something massive in a long, looping arc. As it made contact, an unseen creature screamed shrilly in the darkness and went flying. Turning, Stenhammer brought the heavy backpack down a second time.

In the dark and chaos confusion reigned supreme. It became a running battle between the four humans and a horde of irate, ferocious, fast-moving invaders that swirled about their feet like a living tide, biting and nipping. Grabbing his left arm as he kicked frantically at the dimly glimpsed shapes, Bohannon felt blood trickling from the wound.

"I've been bit! Christ, something's bit me!" There was no response from his companions. They were too busy defending themselves to commiserate.

His bare foot smashed into something heavy and soft and sent it flying. Retreating, he nearly tripped and fell over McCracken's pile of palm fronds. Something hard and cold bruised the back of his foot—one of the flashlights! Bending, he picked it up and with shaking fingers had to fumble several times for the switch before he found it.

The bright beam parted the darkness, illuminating a pair of large four-legged shapes. Each was about three feet long, as heavy as a house cat, and covered in wiry gray fur. He saw small black ears, whiskers, a mottled pink nose, intelligent black eyes, and in the glare of the weaving light, sharp white teeth.

Some kind of possum, he thought wildly, not yet completely awake. Or one of those cuscus things everyone kept talking about. Or something not yet encountered. He blinked as the fast-moving shapes darted in and out of the light. Nipping at his leg, one of them bit clean through the tough denim of his jeans, but its teeth only grazed the skin. Kicking at it with his other foot, he sent it skittering away.

Behind him he could hear the others stomping and cursing. Occasionally there was a sickening *thwack* as Stenhammer's pack smashed one of the invading horde between gold and ground. Unable to wield his with similar skill, McCracken held his backpack in both hands and used it like a sledge, pile-driving one assailant after another into the damp soil.

Then, abruptly, it was over. Chittering and squealing, the survivors scattered, melting back into the trees. The stink of human sweat and animal blood and feces hung over the riverbank. It took a while for the battle's repugnant aftermath to dissipate.

"Everyone okay?" Coolly solicitous, Stenhammer's voice was immediately reassuring.

"I got bit." Holding his left arm and covering the bloody gash with his right hand, Bohannon handed the flashlight to Tai. She moved his fingers aside to examine the wound.

"It's not deep. Damn, but I wish we had some soap, or something."

"Let me see." Stenhammer was at her side in an instant. "There are gilip palms here. If I can find some green nuts I can make a paste. When it hardens it will seal the opening against flies and give it a chance to heal." He pushed past them into the darkness.

"Wait." Returning to her own makeshift bed, she returned moments later with the cup from the water purifier. "Move your hand." When he did so, she bathed the injury in clean fresh water, using the hem of her blouse to wipe it dry. "There." In the glow from the flashlight her expression was apologetic. "I'm afraid that's the best we can do until we can get hold of some antibiotics. If the saliva was clean it won't get infected."

"Thanks." He studied the noxious injury. "What the fuck were they?"

"You didn't see?"

"Everything happened so fast and they kept avoiding the light. Some kind of possum?"

She regarded him silently for a moment, then turned, hunting with the flashlight. "Have a closer look."

It did not take long to pick out one of the many corpses. The one she settled on had its side crushed by Stenhammer's flailing pack. It was easier to focus on the details of a motionless body. Bohannon recognized the same ears, eyes, whiskers, and snout he had seen earlier. They were highlights in a white-patched face that was almost familiar. As she played the light down the body, past the pinkish, clawed feet and high pelvis, he got his first good look at the long, gray, naked tail. It looked exactly like a rat.

A three-foot long rat.

He swallowed hard. Recognition made the bite on his arm throb even worse. "That isn't what I think it is—is it?"

Still breathing a bit raggedly, McCracken joined them in examining the corpse. "Black-eared giant rat. *Mallomys rothschildi*." He grinned. "I remember that one because I always wondered how the Rothschilds would feel if they knew they'd had a giant rat named after them." Seeing the look on the other man's face, he continued.

"Oh, it's a fair dinkum rat, all right. One of the largest in the world, though I shouldn't have to point that out to you by now, mate. Not your average, run-o'-the-mill roof rabbits, these." Picking the dead rodent up by its tail, he started up the bank.

"Where are you going with that?" Having never had occasion to make use of a dead rat, giant or otherwise, Bohannon could not imagine a purpose for one.

"Going to tie it by its tail to a branch, mate. That Swiss army gadget of Stenhammer's ain't no proper skinning knife, but it'll have to do."

"Skin it?" A flurry of unpleasant possibilities sprang immediately to mind. "Why would you want to skin it?"

The guide's voice called back to him from the darkness. McCracken sounded positively chipper. "Well now, mate, you can have your meat with the fur on if you like, but that's not for me. See, when fur is cooked, it gets brittle and stringy. Sticks in the teeth."

Bohannon turned back to Tai. "Is he serious?"

"Of course." She eyed him questioningly. "You've never had rodent before?"

Bile churned in his belly. Queasiness, he tried to tell himself, was only a state of mind. Trouble was, his stomach insisted on arguing the point. "You don't usually see it on the menus of the restaurants I frequent."

"It's not bad at all. Make a nice change from sago grubs." She nudged another corpse with her foot. This one had its skull crushed. "There's a lot of meat on one of these. I wish we had some salt and pepper, though."

"Why not wish for a nice béarnaise while you're at it?" All around the field of battle, lifeless eyes glistening like black mabe pearls seemed to stare back up at him. Try as he might he could not envision himself eating anything that had whiskers.

Hunger, however, is the ultimate arbiter of taste. Skinned, butchered, and dismembered, the bodies smelled far better broiling over an open fire the following morning than they had looked in the middle of the night. When Tai handed him a lightly charred, dark brown haunch it was difficult to distinguish it from any other piece of cooked flesh. What was it McCracken had said when they had confronted the pair of cannibal travelers at Mopingo? "Meat is meat."

"Sorry there's no white meat." As he watched, she bit down on the hunk of flank she had been chewing. Exposed by her busy teeth, small bones protruded from her meal. Ribs. Rat ribs.

With his stomach locked down and out of the mental portion of his personal food loop, Bohannon brought the haunch up to his face and sniffed hesitantly. It did not smell bad. It smelled, in fact, like any other piece of cooked meat. How could it be worse than barbecued bugs? Closing his eyes, he took a bite. The seared flesh was sticky, with a light, neutral taste not unlike chicken. Tai was right: salt and pepper would have helped.

But it went down, stayed down, and when he finished the haunch he found himself asking for more.

"Too bad we can't jerk some of it." Shouldering his backpack with renewed energy, McCracken looked longingly at the numerous bodies they were forced to leave behind. In the high heat and overpowering humidity, unrefrigerated meat would spoil quickly.

"The river people preserve fish by rolling the meat in rock salt." Stenhammer led the way downstream. "Unfortunately, we do not have any of that, either. How is that gilip patch holding up?"

Bohannon looked down at his arm. The white goo Stenhammer had smeared there had set up like plaster. "Looks good so far."

The big man nodded once. "Let me know if it peels and we will make up a fresh application."

The substantial feed, the first they had enjoyed since leaving the tree house, had rejuvenated Bohannon. Despite the humidity there was a gleam in his expression and a bounce in his step that had not been there for some time. Having already handled sago grubs and black-eared giant rats, he was almost eager to try snake.

By mid-afternoon his enthusiasm had largely waned. The pools they regularly encountered provided ample water not only for drinking but for washing, but no amount of water splashed on the face could counteract the effects of the overpowering heat and mugginess. They were in true lowland jungle now, where the temperature hovered all day in the nineties and sometimes topped one hundred, while the water content of the steamy, saturated air was oft-times indistinguishable from that of the streams they crossed.

These small tributaries emerged from crevices in the high banks, joining forces in an attempt to reestablish the river that had once flowed down the now largely dry arroyo. By the morning of the next day the streambed was half full, though in the absence of the high volume of the original flow a clear, easy walking path still existed between forest and the much reduced watercourse.

As evening approached a familiar rushing sound could be heard: water spilling over rocks. The riverbed bent to the west. As they rounded this curve the jungle dropped away, revealing a panorama worthy of a Church or Bierstadt.

Tributary water tumbled in a series of shallow rapids down a steep but easily negotiable slope. Beyond lay no more forest-covered mounds, no distant peaks. They were out of the mountains and about to emerge from the last foothills into the heart of the Sepik River basin.

As far as the eye could see stretched an unbroken carpet of green, utterly flat and interrupted only by the silvery glare of sunset reflecting off multiple sheets of stagnant water. Shape and light diffused by a thick haze, a Turneresque sun was setting in the distance, nestling into a bower of dark fog like a red-hot stone swallowed by a pile of ash. As it descended, it decorated the dozens of shallow lakes with streamers of pink and gold foil.

At the limits of his vision Bohannon saw one feathery white shape after another take wing and glide in silence like distant angels off to the southwest. Egrets, he decided, of several sizes and species. That was one bird he was familiar with. He was promptly reminded of his ignorance as several unidentified somethings cawed demandingly in the trees below.

"Palm cockatoos." Next to him, Tai drank in the view. The setting sun turned her skin the color of burnished copper. "Noisy fellows, aren't they?" Slightly inclining her head to one side, she smiled. "Hear that other noise?"

He strained to listen. The clownish cockatoos made it difficult to hear anything else. It took him a moment to pick out the rising choir of croaking underneath, an unmistakable *grik* chorus.

"Frogs?"

She nodded approvingly. "More good eating—if we can catch some. *Roc-rocs*, the river people call them. You'll find that many of the creatures here are named after the sounds they make."

"That would make me a whine-whine." Feeling his inadequacies more than usual, he looked away from her. "I know I've done a lot of complaining."

He felt her hand on his bare arm. "This isn't your world, Steve. You were never raised to survive in a place like this. Very few outsiders are. A lot of what you've gone through has not been by choice, and yet you're still alive. I'd have to say that you've done well."

Looking down at her, he found that her face was very close. But so were Stenhammer and McCracken. He had to settle for looking at those full lips, at the deep blue eyes, and smiling. Now that the matter of the money she had taken from him had been more than adequately resolved, he found that he was able to think of her in terms that more nearly approximated those he had applied to her during their initial encounter.

"You're sure we can find a village?" Gazing out across the vast savanna and swampland he saw no buildings, no power or telephone lines, no roads. No jet contrails streaked the purpling sky, no smoke from factories mossed the air. Here there was only water, and birds, and bugs, and an endless sea of green.

This, he thought silently, is what the Florida everglades must have looked like ten thousand years ago, only magnified a hundredfold.

They spent the night at the top of the rapids because, as Stenhammer explained, it would be cooler than down below. Bohannon had a difficult time envisioning any kind of increase in heat or humidity, but the following morning's descent enlightened him. What had been merely brutal at the top of the scanty cataract became hellish at the bottom of the hill. Pausing at the pool that had formed at the base of the rapids and splashing water on his face, he was convinced that it might be less humid beneath the water's surface.

McCracken covered his head with a colorful bandanna drawn from a pocket, but his companions were not so well equipped. Bohannon was surprised how much he missed the battered old Akubra. In its place, Stenhammer fashioned crude hats from palm fronds, twisting and knotting them in such a way that they did not fall apart. The makeshift headgear was incongruous, awkward, and kept falling off, but as they trudged along beneath the brutal sun it proved invaluable. Like the others, Bohannon's interest lay in staving off sunstroke, not in making a fashion statement. They were not going to perish of thirst, and apparently not of hunger, but as Tai pointed out, in this kind of country heat prostration could kill even a healthy man in less than a day.

It was the following morning when Stenhammer found what he had been looking for. The stand of wild bamboo growing along the riverbank was impenetrable, but that did not matter. He had no intention of trying to force a path through it.

"A bush knife would be a great help here." He studied the solid wall of yellow-brown poles while his companions rested in the shade, leaning up against the exposed riverbank. Tai had removed her boots and was dangling her feet in the water. Recharged by numerous small tributaries, the reconstituted river was now flowing northward at about two-thirds of its original volume. It was more than enough for their purposes—if they could manage the bamboo.

"An ax would be better." From where he sat cross-legged next to Tai, McCracken scrutinized the grove. Some of the grasses were twenty feet high. "Or a bloody chainsaw."

"We will just have to make do." Taking the Swiss army knife from a pocket, the big man started to work.

McCracken made a disparaging sound. "If you're going to try and cut enough to make a raft with that little pinsticker, we'll be here 'til typhoon season."

Attending to his work, Stenhammer replied without looking up. "I agree, which is why I am just making one cut on each stem. Even if we had the time and could go faster, the blade would not last."

Having made deep cuts on several trunks, the big man gripped one in both hands, reaching as high up on the bole as he could. Placing first one booted foot and then the other on the bamboo below the cut, he leaned backwards and pulled, pushing hard with both feet. The tall strand bent toward him. Normally it would have bent all the way to the ground before springing back, but the cut weakened it at a critical juncture.

There was a loud, sharp crack as the bole snapped at the cut. Catching himself as lithely as a cat when the bamboo broke beneath his weight, Stenhammer twisted in time to land on hands and feet. Straightening, he walked around the fallen trunk to examine his work. Bohannon joined him.

Since the strand was alive, it was too green to make a clean break possible. The felled stem was still attached to the stump by a number of yellow strips. Stenhammer handed Bohannon the small knife, but not before closing the blade and pulling out a two-inch long wood saw to take its place.

"Take your time and cut each piece loose as I break them down. This will work better and we can save the main blade."

Bohannon cast a dubious eye on the miniature saw. "I don't think I'll have much choice about taking my time."

The big man gave him an encouraging slap on the back. It made a wet sound against the sweat-soaked shirt. "Have courage, Mr. Bohannon. In a week you will be sitting in Wewak, dining in air-conditioned comfort on the biggest steak PNG can provide. I will sell your share of the gold for you and have the proceeds converted into dollars for you to take home. Unlike your usual garden-variety braggart and liar, you will have money to support your tale of adventure."

"Right now I'd trade all the adventure and a lot of the gold for a seat on the next Qantas flight out of Mosby." Bohannon kept up a steady stream of complaint as he sawed at the bamboo. Grumbling helped him to pass the time and forget about the rising sun, which brought with it higher temperatures and rapidly increasing irritability.

When the American's fingers threatened to blister, McCracken took over. Then it was Tai's turn. Only by working the tiny saw in shifts did they manage to keep up with Stenhammer.

But even that herculean form was forced to halt for several hours at midday. No one, not even the river people themselves, Tai explained, could do any significant work when the sun was at its highest. If the relentless humidity didn't drain a man of energy, the sun overhead would fry the brains within his skull.

After a lunch of water, pandanus, and sago nuts, and some edible flowers that were almost too beautiful to eat, they resumed work. By nightfall they had harvested sufficient bamboo to make a raft big enough to carry all of them in addition to the gold.

Having nothing to cook, they needed no fire. While a dancing blaze would have been a welcome evening's companion, it was more important to conserve the remaining fuel in McCracken's lighter. *Roc-rocs* resumed their nightly Baching, and in the trees that fronted the riverbank small owls commenced their querulous *whoo-whoo, whoo-oo.*

"Tomorrow we will assemble the raft." Stenhammer lay on his back, hands behind his head as he stared up at the cloud cover that concealed the stars. "I have cut some smaller bamboo for arrows, and several lengths of black palm for a bow. Your fingers are dexterous, Mr. Bohannon."

He smiled thinly. "It's all the typing I do."

"Good training for this. I'll give you the knife so that you may sharpen the points."

"Going hunting?"

In the waning light the big man turned to look at him. "No, fishing." Rolling over, he picked up a yard-long length of bamboo no more than half an inch thick. "You make a cut across the top, then another perpendicular to the first. Saw them both down until you have four separate strands each about six inches long. Whittle back the tip of each strand, file it to a point, and you have a four-pronged fishing arrow."

Bohannon tried to picture the result. "What about a bowstring?"

"There is a certain vine that is easy to peel into strips. Several will bind the lengths of black palm together to form the bow. Another, soaked until it is flexible, will attach to both ends of the bow through notches at either end that I will cut with the knife. Make the arrows well, Mr. Bohannon. I know you will prefer fish to what you have been eating these past days."

"Hey, it's not that I'm not growing fond of sago grubs and pandanus nuts. I'd even go for another helping of roast rat. But yeah, a change would be nice."

Betraying not a flicker of humor, Stenhammer said, "We will see what we can do." He raised his head slightly. "Tai, come here, please. I will need your help putting the raft together and we need to discuss options." Rising from her resting place, she moved to join him, her supple shape a tempting succession of curves against the night.

A short distance upstream, a small flame flicked on and off several times. Rolling over, Bohannon raised his voice. "What's the idea, Sorley? You know we're supposed to conserve lighter fuel."

"Got something to show you, mate! Get off your lazy arse and come have a look."

A glance showed Stenhammer and Tennison deep in conversation as they discussed construction procedures for the proposed raft. With a sigh, Bohannon raised himself from his bed of fresh palm fronds and carefully picked his way through the gathering darkness to where the expat waited.

"Well, what is it?" He was tired, his hands were sore from sawing bamboo all day, and he wanted sleep.

"Beautiful, ain't it?" In the light of the half moon hidden behind the clouds, the partially filled riverbed took on the color of molten lead, glowing gray against the darker banks. Vine-draped trees crowded one another for access to the sunlit sky while lesser flora competed for those open spaces that remained. Unseen owls continued to ask questions to which there were no answers.

Bohannon found himself searching the dark gaps between the trees for giant rats. Where he and McCracken stood on the still dry upper bank of the river, the forest loomed very near against their backs.

"Okay, so it's beautiful. So what? Is that what you called me over here for?"

"Not entirely, mate." Peering past him, McCracken nodded in the direction of the temporary camp. "I ain't never been one to dance around things, so I'll just come out and ask. How much do you trust our Mr. Stenhammer?"

Completely unexpected, the question caught Bohannon off-guard. Following the expat's line of sight if not his thoughts, he turned back toward the sleeping site. Neither Tai nor the subject of McCracken's inquiry could be discerned among the shadows.

"I don't follow you, Sorley. Even though he'd be better off without us to slow him down, ever since the landslide he's done everything to keep us alive." He tried to see deeper into the other man's eyes, but the lack of light made it difficult. "What the hell are you getting at?"

At least he could see the expat shrug, the slight upward heave of McCracken's shoulders silhouetted against the dream-like vista of the river. "Nothing specific, mate. I just don't trust the bloke, that's all. Haven't from the start. And another thing—ain't you sick of taking orders from him? We're all in this together, right? So how does he come off telling you to make arrows and me to help with the heavy work and Tai to come running when he calls her? Who crowned him king, boss, leader, and great high-muck-a-muck?"

Bohannon blinked as the other man's rapid-fire words washed over him. Come to think of it, Stenhammer *had* issued any number of orders that had not been phrased as requests or suggestions. Bohannon had followed and obeyed as readily as everyone else, without thinking.

"His suggestions make sense," he finally heard himself replying. "So why not follow them?"

"Because maybe somebody else might have an idea, you know?"

"Like yourself?"

McCracken drew himself up in the darkness. "Sure, why not me, mate? I know as much about this bloody country as he does!" He stabbed a finger in the camp's direction.

"Granting that, Sorley, someone still has to make decisions."

"And you're siding with him, is that it?"

Bohannon could feel the expat staring hard at him in the darkness. "For now, at least, yes. I'm alive, I'm not starving, and even my arm is feeling a little better. That's all his doing. So if he asks me to whittle him a few arrows, I'm damn well going to do it."

"Orders you to make a few arrows, you mean." McCracken's tone was faintly contemptuous.

Bohannon refused to be baited. "Call it what you will."

He thought the other man was through, but he was wrong. "One more thing, mate, before we call it a night."

Bohannon inhaled resignedly. "What now?"

The expat brought his face close to that of his companion. Close enough so that moonlight kissed his eyes. Bohannon could see reflections there, but no pupils. Even though there was little chance of them being overheard, the other man's voice fell to a cautious whisper.

"There's more than two million U.S. dollars in gold in those backpacks, mate. By Stenhammer's reckoning, my share and yours is half of what we can carry out. Two hundred thousand apiece. Gold's real pretty, you can sell it anywhere, and it don't go bad, but there's one drawback to the stuff. It's heavy. Goddamned heavy. Takes more than one man to carry it all. Even that big son of a bitch can't manage it by himself. He needs help. Our help."

Bohannon's jaw dropped slightly and he did his best in the weak light to search the other man's face. Anything there stayed hidden, masked by the night shadows and concealed from view.

"I don't think I like what you're getting at, Sorley."

"I ain't asking you to like it, mate. Just to consider it. Think, man! He's lying over there supposedly talking to Tai about putting a raft together. For that we've got his word only. For that matter, so does she. Now, once he gets this raft built he doesn't need anybody to carry the gold. We're out of the mountains, there's no rapids between here and the Sepik, and he can float the stuff out slick as you please until he reaches a village where he can hire a powerboat."

Bohannon turned away. "I'm not listening to any more of this. You got too much sun today, Sorley."

"Too much sun, is it, mate?" The guide grabbed his arm in an unbreakable grip. "I'm just asking you to think about it, that's all. You've got more than your share of the gold at stake here. There's the little matter of your life. Maybe it don't bother you to hand it over to a complete stranger for safekeeping, and maybe a daft one at that, but I ain't survived all these years in this country by accepting things without question and without watching me every step." Again he nodded in the direction of the temporary camp.

"Just try to step back a minute and consider things objective-like, mate. We're out here in the middle of noplace, where people die and are forgotten all the time. He's in control because we let him be in control. He says do and we jump, whether it has to do with the gold, Tai, or our lives. I'm not saying that's wrong, mind, or even bad. Just that it behooves a sensible man to hold off and take a second look at things from time to time." He released his companion's arm.

"We've been through a lot together, mate. A lot. In all that time, have I ever once done you false?"

"No," Bohannon conceded.

"Probably saved your life up in Tari, in that marketplace."

"I won't argue that. I can't." A sudden remembrance leaped to the forefront of his thoughts. "Stenhammer told me that when we reached Wewak he'd sell my share for me and convert it into dollars."

In the enfolding night McCracken nodded as if confirmation had been found for all his suspicions. He was close enough for Bohannon to smell his breath. "Now that's thoughtful of him, ain't it? We're not halfway to the coast and already *he's* decided what to do with *your* gold. What if he plans to do just that—sell it for you? Only maybe you won't be around to pocket the proceeds. Or me, or even Tai." Stepping back, he walked around the stunned Bohannon and started back toward camp.

"Pleasant dreams, mate."

Bohannon turned to follow the tall, limber figure as it shrank into the shadows. His mind, focused firmly if not comfortably on surviving the heat and on getting enough to eat and drink, was now awash in thoughts and notions previously uncontemplated. Like tropical bacteria, McCracken's sly, insidious insinuations took hold and began to fester.

The expat had finally lost it, Bohannon decided. The piercing heat, the soul-sucking humidity, had driven him over the edge. He was the sick one, not Stenhammer. If the big man wanted them out of the way he'd had a dozen opportunities to take care of it by now.

Except—he needed help to move the gold. Needed it, until the raft was ready. Or perhaps until they reached a village where he could hire help. Bohannon did not doubt the big man could hire a dozen strong-backed locals for considerably less than two hundred thousand per man. Control them, too, with his voice and his presence.

Unable to decide anything, drained by the day's heat and exertions, he damned both men equally as he trudged weary and worried back toward his waiting bed of palm fronds and leaves.

XXI

"I need another pole here, Mr. Bohannon!"

Nodding slowly and envying McCracken his lightweight bandanna instead of the itchy, uncomfortable makeshift chapeau of leaves, Bohannon wiped sweat from his face and forehead as he lifted the end of yet another of the trimmed bamboo shafts. Soon they would have to break for lunch. It could not be soon enough for him. Unused as he was to extended physical exertion, lifting and ferrying the poles down to the water's edge was almost more than he could manage. Several times he felt ready to pass out, only to have Tai notice his condition and revive him with a cupful of water to the face.

Such periodic shock treatments were losing their efficacy as the day wore on and the sun rose higher into the hazy, cloud-filled sky. It was not that the bamboo was especially heavy. For its length it was comparatively light. It was the repetitive act of carrying and descending, only to have to climb the bank again and again. Like Sisyphus, he thought, only in his case there was no rock: only endless lengths of bamboo.

When they'd begun early that morning it was McCracken who had done the fetching and carrying while Bohannon had been assigned the task of shaping and sharpening the fishing arrows. Only after several failed attempts during which he had not only over-split and therefore wasted the bamboo shafts but managed to pierce himself with several painful long splinters had Stenhammer directed the two men to switch tasks.

Pausing at the bank's edge he gazed enviously at the more nimble-fingered expat, whose deft fingers were rapidly turning out one arrow after another. McCracken's work allowed him to sit in the shade while he, Bohannon, could only do so in between loads. Given the speed at which Stenhammer and Tennison made progress, his breaks were short and infrequent.

The long arc of the pole dug into his shoulder, threatening to rub the skin raw. He would have switched to the other shoulder if it were not in worse shape than the one he was currently using. Unbidden, McCracken's words of the night before drifted in and out of his thoughts, accumulating bitterness and anger.

Dropping his arm listlessly, he let the pole fall to the ground. Everyone looked up.

At least Tai had the courtesy to be momentarily alarmed. "Steve, are you all right? I told you to keep drinking. I don't mind refilling the purifier."

Swaying a little, he stared across at her. "I'm not thirsty."

"Thirst has nothing to do with it." Stenhammer looked up from where he was tying off a strip of palm around two lengths of bamboo. "You have to continually replace the fluids your body is sweating out."

Bohannon turned to face the big man. He was feeling no pain. He was also slightly dizzy. "Whatever you say, massa."

Tai's expression switched from concern to one of sudden bafflement. "Steve?" Off to the right, he could see McCracken slaving attentively over an arrow. The tinniest suggestion of a smile wrinkled the expat's face.

Bohannon glared in the direction of the raft. "I'm not carrying any more fucking poles!"

Sitting back from his work, Stenhammer pursed his lips as he considered the other man's ultimatum. "Very well. From now on I will carry the bamboo. You make the raft." Rising, he ascended the bank in two long strides and picked up the length of bamboo Bohannon had dropped.

"Well? I am waiting." Sliding easily down the slope, he placed the log alongside the raft. "Let me know when you need the next one." Whereupon he strolled off into the shade, sat down, and closed his eyes. Tai stared. Beneath his tree, a smirking McCracken whittled on.

Feeling like a complete idiot standing there in the sun, Bohannon stumbled down the riverbank. A glancing plea for understanding in Tai's direction caused her to turn away from him and back to her own work, disgust and disappointment plain on her face. Feeling lost as well as stupid, he looked to the stone-faced Stenhammer. The big man had opened his eyes and was studying him, not unkindly.

"It is all right, Mr. Bohannon. We are all frustrated. But we will be done with this soon, I promise." Rising, he resumed stripping rope-like lengths from a long vine. "We could use one of the smaller logs I trimmed down here. When you feel up to it."

"Yeah. Sure." While not exactly naked sympathy, Stenhammer's response came as close to qualifying as understanding as the big man could manage. Bohannon sensed that it would have to suffice.

Behind him, the dry riverbank loomed, a stand-in for every dune in the Sahara, every unclimbed face in the Himalayas. Girding himself, he started upward, putting one foot in front of the other. His expensive sneakers, cream white and royal blue when new, were now so thoroughly impregnated with dust, dirt, mud, and his own sweat that recovery of the original tint would not be possible even with the aid of an acid bath—one of which their owner would have gladly subjected himself to had it been available at that moment.

They finished the raft several hours before sundown. Roughly twenty feet long, with extra reinforcing in the middle to help support the gold, it had been put together without a single nail or screw.

Stenhammer saw the look on his face. "Do not worry, Mr. Bohannon. The wetter the strips of vine become, the tighter they will bind. Not enough to split the bamboo, though I would not want my leg similarly bound."

"What about a rudder? Couldn't we split some bamboo and tie the flat sections together?"

Stenhammer eyed him approvingly. "A good thought, but unnecessary for this country. From where it re-enters PNG at the border with West Papua, the Sepik drops less than seventy meters by the time it reaches the Solomon Sea. There is very little perceptible current even on the main river. Here in these remote backwaters there is literally none. Depending on rainfall the rivers here may flow backward and upstream as readily as down. A rudder *would* be useful if we had an engine, which we do not, or if there was a usable current, which there is not. We will steer as well as propel ourselves with the long poles."

These were ten-foot-long lengths of bamboo that were larger in diameter than the shafts chosen to become arrows but narrower than those that formed the body of the raft. In order to progress downriver they would have to pole themselves along, pushing against the bottom where possible and fending themselves off the banks if they drifted too close inshore. The alternative, Tai pointed out, was to get in the water behind the raft and kick. Refreshing, but ultimately exhausting. And there was also the matter of certain unfriendly creatures who lived in the depths.

"Not way up here," she told him, "but further downstream in the larger channels."

"Like what?" With a grunt he passed one of the bulging backpacks to Stenhammer, who placed it carefully in the middle of the raft. A small platform constructed of extra bamboo set crosswise had been added there and tied down securely to provide additional support for the consolidated weight.

Shading her eyes, she gazed downriver. "Snakes. Catfish with poisonous spines. Leeches larger than any you've seen before. But mostly it's the crocs. There's been a lot of hunting on the Sepik itself, but in the less visited tributaries they say you can still find some big ones, living quietly and unnoticed." She squinted up at him. "Five, six meters long." She held thumb and forefinger six inches apart. "With teeth this big."

"Okay, you've convinced me. No water polo." Lowering his voice, he nodded in Stenhammer's direction. "Tai, has he said anything to you about his plans when we reach a village with a powerboat?"

She looked at him as if he had suddenly taken odd. "Rags has already told you. We hire it and head for Timbunke."

"All of us, in one dugout?"

Her frown deepened. "Not necessarily. Don't you remember him saying that if necessary we'd hire two? Or more, if we need them? What's your point?"

"No point." He turned away from her. "Just rambling."

"That's dangerous in this heat. You could overload your circuits." Leaving him, she began loading the push poles onto the raft.

When everything had been stowed as efficiently as was possible, they boarded. Despite its knocked-together, unwieldy appearance, the raft proved surprisingly stable. Intentionally overbuilt, it floated high in the water, demonstrating a reassuring buoyancy. Bohannon was moved to compliments.

"Thank you." Stenhammer accepted the encomium as his due. "We could have made it smaller and finished sooner, but it would not be as comfortable. This way there is room to sit, and move around." He indicated the large pile of elephant-ear sized leaves Tai had gathered from the forest. "Not a floating gazebo, exactly, but any shade is better than none. On the other hand, you will find that it is cooler in the middle of the river, and as we make progress, we will generate our own breeze."

Later, after they had pushed off from the bank and begun poling their way downstream, Bohannon reflected that Stenhammer was right—after a fashion. It was not cooler in the center of the stream—but it was less hot. As for generating a breeze, any movement of air that facilitated evaporation was a welcome relief. The difference was far from polar, but it was apparent.

Immense trees crowded the water's edge, tiered with vines and lianas. Periodically, an explosion of carmine would mark the presence of a tree in bloom. Around such locales great iridescent butterflies swarmed, though none were as large as those Bohannon had seen in the eastern Highlands. Like splinters of rainbow or oversize confetti they flitted about the six-inch-long blooms that hung in clusters like crimson bananas, inhaling nectar through their coiling mouthparts.

While the others took turns poling, Stenhammer stood at the prow of the raft with bow and arrow in hand, a great wild blond figurehead eyeing the tepid water with preternatural patience. From time to time Bohannon looked up as he heard an arrow strike the surface. Most of the time that was all the sharpened bamboo shafts pierced. Stenhammer would wordlessly reel them back in by the thin strands of vine attached to each one, position himself anew, and resume the wait.

Only occasionally would the brief snick of arrow striking water be followed by a longer, louder splashing. Then the big man would pull in not only his arrow but, transfixed on one or more of its quartet of sharpened spikes, a silvery fish with fine bright scales and bulging, vacant eyes. By evening, a small mound of these had grown near the backpacks. Flopping and gasping for air, they died by inches. Bohannon was too hungry to sympathize.

Pulling into shore, they made camp. By now the river, swollen from the input of hundreds of individual tributaries, had risen nearly to its banks. Tying up beneath an overhanging branch, Bohannon was securing the line when he began hopping about like a madman and threatening to topple everyone into the drink.

Tai got a hold of him and helped him to force his right arm into the water all the way up to the shoulder.

"They're still on me!" he yelled. "*Ow*—the little fuckers!"

"Oh, quit bawling! They aren't that bad. Easy now." Calmly

searching his shirt and exposed skin, she pulled several tiny creatures off him and flicked them into the river one by one. "We can't tie up here, Ragnarok."

"I can see that." Stepping past them, the big man reached up and unfastened the line as quickly as possible. While he brushed something off his hands, McCracken used a pole to push the raft back out into the river.

Tai was examining Bohannon's right arm. Tiny red blisters were already starting to rise.

"We need some vinegar to take away the sting." She smiled sympathetically. "We're fresh out of vinegar, I'm sorry to say."

"Never mind." He gritted his teeth against the pain. "I seem to be fair game for anything in this country that bites."

"You just have to be careful where you put your hands. Always look first."

"I know, I know. I just forget. My body may be acclimated to this place but my mind is still trailing way behind."

"You'll learn." Dipping water from the river with her hands, she gently washed his exposed, inflamed skin. It helped—a little.

"What were they, anyway?" Contact with the lukewarm liquid made him grimace, but he let her continue her ministrations.

"Yellow ants. They have an evil sting. Be glad you only tied the line to the branch and didn't try climbing out on it."

Even fatigue had its uses. By the time they turned in, after a fine meal of fresh fish, wild mango, and unnamed greens, Bohannon was so tired he was able to fall asleep despite the pain.

Morning brought with it a renewed sense of purpose, aided by the fact that the pain in his arm had almost disappeared. He still looked like a man afflicted with a highly localized case of the measles, but that, he could stand. There were no hypochondriacs around to flee from him anyway.

The vast forest gave way to smaller but still impressive trees rising from dense, woody undergrowth. Stands of wild *pit-pit* formed an impenetrable wall along each bank. So formidable were these lush ramparts that for the next two days they were forced to sleep in the middle of the river, tied by a single line to one of the many dead trees that had been washed downstream during the Wet, only to end their seaward journey prematurely by embedding themselves in the river bottom.

On the following day, even the *pit-pit* surrendered to the grass. Isolated trees growing from clusters of dense brush were all that remained of the eternal forest, the bushes clinging to the one or two tall trunks in their midst as if seeking surcease from the surrounding savanna.

Great white egrets glided past overhead, gazing imperiously down at the trespassers on their fishing grounds. Startled herons rocketed from roosts hidden in the grass while kingfishers of a dozen different descriptions darted back and forth among patches of reed, lightning-fast bullet-shapes flashing metallic blue wings.

The hornbills were there as well, comical everywhere but in flight, and the lorikeets, and the cockatoos, shrieking like refugees from a bad cartoon. Brown falcons and lesser hawks proclaimed their mastery of the air. A comb-crested jacana patrolled a patch of water lilies on splayed feet larger than its body.

McCracken spotted a lumbering brown mass among the grass. Maneuvering itself like a trash can on wheels, it slipped silently into the water.

"Soft-shelled river tortoise." Before the expat could say anything else, Bohannon made a silent bet with himself. Conveniently, he won. "Largest freshwater tortoise in the world."

Before the morning was done his companions had, between the three of them, identified forty or fifty additional species of bird, several each of turtle and fish, and one unprepossessing crocodile no more than four feet long.

"That's a freshwater croc," Tai explained. "They don't get very large and they're generally considered to be harmless. It's the big salties who are dangerous."

"Salties?" Bohannon commented. "As in, saltwater crocodiles?" She nodded. "I didn't think we were anywhere near the ocean."

"We're not. 'Saltwater crocodile' is something of a misnomer. It doesn't mean they live mostly in saltwater, or even that they're especially fond of it. Just that they tolerate the stuff, and can often be found surprisingly far out at sea. Actually, their preferences are no different from any of the other crocodilians. They all prefer deep rivers and streams."

He looked over the side of the raft. "Doesn't look very deep here."

"It's probably not. Unlike up in the Highlands, where everything is channeled downhill and there are few natural large bodies of water, here it spreads out over the whole basin. In the Wet it would back up all the way to the base of the rapids where we came out."

"So this would all be underwater?"

"Not a bit of it." She grinned. "Have a look."

Picking up one of the poles, she walked to the edge of the raft. Selecting part of the nearest grassy bank, she stuck the pole into it and pushed hard. As Bohannon stared, the section of bank bent beneath the force of her push. When the pole was removed, it sprang back, rocking gently back and forth.

"Looks like solid ground, doesn't it?"

Duly impressed, he commented, "Obviously it's something else."

With a sweep of her arm she encompassed the surrounding savanna. "Except where you see real trees or bushes, most of the 'land' here is composed of floating islands. Everything's held together by the grass, but sections and pieces are always breaking loose to meander slowly down to the Sepik. Sometimes they crash together, although crash is probably too strong a word, and form larger islands. Other times they break into smaller and smaller pieces and eventually disintegrate. On the bigger rivers you can see whole ecologies floating lazily downstream, complete with flowering bushes and even trees, none of it growing on solid land." She laid her pole aside.

"You can walk on it, if you take care and watch your step. One place will support you just fine, and the next your foot will go right through." She indicated the grassy sward they were drifting past. "Tomorrow that island will be thirty meters to the east and three smaller ones will have taken its place. Or this whole channel will be filled up and blocked. Even local people get lost in here."

He looked up and around, searching for signs of human habitation. As usual, there was nothing to see. "People live in here?"

"Not this far up, but lower down, where we're headed. They pole themselves around just like we're doing, only they use dugout canoes, not rafts. A man poling or paddling a heavy canoe can slip through narrower channels and push the smaller islets out of the way." She spread her hands in a gesture of helplessness. "Without axes there was no way we could cut down and hollow out a tree for a dugout. So we have to make do with a raft."

He nodded as he took in the endless sweep of swamp and savanna. "This would be a bad place to be stuck."

Her expression turned somber. "Even a powerboat wouldn't save you in here. There are no landmarks except the distant mountains, and from out here in the middle of this they all look the same. You'd go around and around until your petrol ran out, looking for the channel you came off the river on, never knowing that floating islands had closed it off behind you. If you didn't know how to catch fish, and have with you the means to do so, you'd starve. Starve in the midst of plenty, but plenty that isn't so easy to come by." Again she moved to the edge of the raft and pointed, this time straight downward.

"Have you looked at the water since we left the river?"

He smiled, knowing the response she was after. "It's black. Black as strong tea."

"Tannin, from all this plant life. The water here is an organic soup, full of nutrients. But it makes it impossible to tell which islands are solid and which are adrift. The only way to tell for sure is to get out and walk. And you don't want to get out here and walk."

"Snakes," he commented. "And crocs."

"That's right. But there's one good thing." She turned toward the front of the raft, where McCracken and Stenhammer were poling and picking their way through the sea of grass. "So long as we head toward the setting sun, we've got to eventually strike a navigable tributary of the Sepik."

Her declaration of renewed confidence allowed him to temporarily forget the oppressive heat and unrelenting humidity. His optimism lasted until the following morning.

XXII

It was as if God, bored and with nothing to do, had decided to rerun the book of Noah in a place where no one would notice the consequences. It started raining just before dawn, a steady drizzle that within the hour had turned into a deluge of truly Old Testament proportions. Preceded by a rolling barrage of thunder, a line of immense black clouds had come barreling down off the distant surrounding mountains to spread out and completely bury the great river basin.

There was nothing they could do and nowhere to hide. In the eerie absence of wind, the rain came straight down in pile-driver-sized drops. Visibility dropped to the length of the raft. It became impossible even for Stenhammer to use the push-poles, but that did not matter because they could not see where they were going anyway.

They huddled together beneath the inadequate elephant-ear leaves Tai had brought aboard. Soaked to the skin, every square inch of themselves and their clothing all but underwater, they passed the interminable hours daydreaming of dryness. To pass the time and occupy his mind, Bohannon made a game of imagining drier places. The center of the Sahara, southern Arizona, the Namib and the Kalahari, Alice Springs—all qualified. Unfortunately, none of the images the exotic names conjured up made him feel any less miserable. The humor of it, like his tolerance, quickly wore thin.

Even though they could not use the poles, Stenhammer's choice of transportation proved its worth. A dugout would have required constant bailing, but the interminable rain simply ran off between the bamboo logs. These did become dangerously slippery, but that threat was more hypothetical than real since no one was standing up, much less walking around.

More serious even than their inability to move about or find their way was the absence of game. It did not matter that Stenhammer could not see to use his bow and arrows, because there was nothing to shoot at. Every bird and amphibian and reptile had gone to ground, or wherever it was they waited out such downpours in the sodden savanna. At that moment, Bohannon would readily have shared a dry burrow with the biggest python in Papua New Guinea.

It was equally impossible to tell if there were fish about. The rain drove them down, away from the surface, where Stenhammer could not take aim at them even if he had been able to utilize the bow. The building of any kind of warming, drying fire was of course out of the question.

"There's probably a hundred fish, fat and slow and tasty, right here, taking shelter under this raft." A morose McCracken peered out from beneath a leaf, water dripping down his nose and chin. "And frogs, with big tender legs."

"I'm hungry." Tai blinked away water as she tilted her head back slightly to scrutinize the sky. Or rather, the place where the sky used to be.

"We're all hungry, luv." McCracken edged a little closer to her and she did not back away. "Don't worry. This'll rain itself out and clear off by nightfall."

She looked over at him. "You really believe that?"

He shrugged, but his usual joie de vivre was absent. Washed away, like so much else. "I have to believe that, lassie. I have to."

Too waterlogged to participate in the byplay, Bohannon looked over at the massive, hunched form seated nearby. "What about it, Stenhammer? What do you think?"

One thing the rain could not affect was the voice, indomitable as ever, that rumbled out from beneath the leaf. "I do not know what to think, Mr. Bohannon. I am no meteorologist. Mr. McCracken could be right: this may stop, or at least let up, by evening."

"Or?" Bohannon prompted him.

"Or it could continue like this for days, or even weeks."

"But I thought this wasn't the time of year for the Wet?"

"That is correct. The real wet season is not for another month yet. You should know by now that nothing is predictable in this part of the world, least of all the climate."

Bohannon had more to say, but somehow it did not matter. Nothing mattered as long as the rain continued. Only after it ceased could life resume.

Perhaps an unseen deity chose, on a whim, to grant McCracken's wish and make him seem the prophet. Perhaps the saturated atmosphere could hold only so much moisture. Whatever the reason, it did stop raining that evening, but only after the unseen sun had set. Tired and hungry, no one suggested trying to pick their way through the savanna in the dark.

"It will be sunny in the morning, you'll see." Fortified by the success of his prediction, McCracken readily ventured another. "Stenhammer can hunt, and we'll have something to eat—even if it's sashimi."

Bohannon's stomach ached at the thought. "I'll eat a perch, scales and all. On a bed of river grass."

Close by, Tai turned wistful. "It would be better broiled, with butter and a little lemon."

"You're a sadistic little meri, Tai." McCracken swallowed painfully.

"Sorry." She turned to Bohannon, who was shaking visibly. "You cold, Steve?"

"No." The downpour had been warm. Seated in a hotel pool, with room service readily available, it would have been a pleasant experience. "Just hungry. It's my stomach. I didn't know you could get cramps from being empty."

"We will get some food tomorrow." Stenhammer did his best to sound reassuring. "The problem is that we have not been eating properly for days. In a situation like this, our bodies have little in the way of reserves on which to draw." Bohannon saw the big man raise his head to stare out into the darkness. "I could try hunting by flashlight, but the water visibility is still very bad. And there are other considerations."

"What considerations?" Bohannon started. "If there's a chance of catching anything . . . !"

McCracken cut him off. "Crocs like light, too, mate. You want a big croc crawling up onto the raft to check out the source?"

"Oh." A crestfallen Bohannon subsided. "I didn't know that. I guess it would be better to wait 'til morning."

No one commented.

No one slept much, either, even after they spread themselves out flat on the raft. It was not the hollows between the logs that made sleep difficult so much as the constant dampness that refused to release them from its unrelenting, soggy grasp. True, the rain had stopped, but in its wake normal heat and humidity returned. Nothing had a chance to dry out, which presented another problem. Untreated, their clothing and eventually their skin would start to play host to invasive, voracious fungi and molds. PNG, McCracken helpfully pointed out, was home to diseases that had yet to be given names.

Morning brought with it not desperately needed sunshine but a ground-hugging, impenetrable fog. Not a San Francisco fog, chill and clammy, but given their sodden state the absence of sunlight alone was enough to make them start to shiver despite the ambient warmth. If the thick blanket did not lift by afternoon they would have more than hunger to deal with. Only the absence of contractible germs kept them from falling ill immediately.

With nothing else to do, Stenhammer tried bow and arrow, but the fog made it difficult to see any distance away from the side of the raft. The few arrows he did get off struck nothing but grass.

Reaching over the side, Bohannon grabbed a handful and wrenched it out by the roots. He inspected the sample of green mat closely. "You'd think you'd find mushrooms in a place this damp, but there's only the damned grass." He ran a couple of stalks through his fingers. "Is it edible?"

Stenhammer stood foursquare near the front of the raft, bow in hand. He looked solid enough to support rigging and sail. *Might as well wish for food as for that,* Bohannon thought. Hunger was making it difficult to think straight. *How about a hundred horsepower Evenrude while you're at it, God?*

"You can eat the grass, Mr. Bohannon, but you will gain no nourishment from it. You will only fool your stomach into thinking you have eaten."

"Right now I'd settle for that."

"Also, the grass is likely to be alive with microorganisms, any one of which will probably not kill you, but will make your insides feel even worse than they do now."

Hesitatingly only momentarily, Bohannon put the handful of grass aside. Not yet, he told himself. Wait and see if the fog lifts and the big man can catch something. The grass would always be there.

"If we could find a patch of water lilies," Stenhammer murmured, "we could try eating the bulbs. They are mostly fiber, but it would be good to have something in the belly." It was the nearest the big man had come to confessing having his own craving.

The morning passed without any sign of the fog lifting. If anything, it seemed to grow thicker. Around noon the air brightened as the unseen sun filtered down from above, but they still could not see to move. Their surroundings now consisted of light fog instead of dark fog. As a change of scenery it was welcome if not helpful.

Stenhammer could see a little better to fish, but the underwater inhabitants of the savanna refused to cooperate. It was as if they too were waiting for the return of full, unadulterated sunshine.

This must be what it is like to lose one's mind, Bohannon thought wearily. Without food you start to hallucinate, then the hallucinations displace reality, and finally you surrender control of your body as well as your mind to a fevered imagination. For example, he thought he could see shapes moving in the fog. Overheated and undernourished, his mind was turning from realistic perception to wish-fulfillment. But at least he was still aware enough to realize that he was starting to lose it.

"Somebody talk to me, keep me engaged," he mumbled.

Alarmed at the quaver in his voice, Tai turned to him. "What's wrong?"

"I'm starting to see things. Right now I think I see people walking on the water." Raising an unsteady hand, he pointed.

Following his shaky finger, she squinted into the mist, frowning. On hands and knees she crawled past to him, to the very edge of the raft. Then she began waving—and shouting.

"Hey—hey, over here! Over this way! *Yupela kam hia!*"

Oh God, Bohannon thought: not Tai, too. One delerious crazy on the raft was enough, and he had already put in for the label. But then McCracken was rising behind him, waving and shouting, and even Stenhammer's resonant tones thundered out through the fog.

What was worse, his hallucination seemed to be turning toward them.

Walking not on water but standing in a low gray dugout and propelling themselves by means of long wooden poles that spread out to form paddles at the bottom, the two men pulled silently alongside the raft. As they did so McCracken, despite his weakness and hunger, fumbled with the backpacks to make certain not a single glint of gold was exposed to the newcomers.

It was immediately apparent even to Bohannon that their visitors were different in every way from the people of the Highlands. Their facial features were not as broad or flattened, they wore their hair cropped very short, and they were slimmer and less muscular. Also taller. Both men could look Tai in the eye. One wore the last shreds of a cotton vest and a pair of tattered shorts while his companion was clad in a short sarong-like strip of cloth and nothing else.

Disdaining any formalities and casting aside any pretense at dignity, McCracken pushed forward. Eyes wide, he thrust his fingers toward his mouth and made elaborate chewing motions. Ignoring his pantomime, first Stenhammer and then Tai tried to communicate with the boatmen. They showed interest but did not otherwise respond.

"There are seven hundred languages in this country," Tai pointed out to Bohannon. "These two don't speak any English. That's to be expected. But neither of them seems to know Pidgin, and that means they have little or no contact with the world outside."

"Not true," argued Bohannon. "Look at their clothes."

"Doesn't mean anything." Every time she spoke, the men looked in her direction. "Those shorts probably passed through a dozen different hands before making it this far up the basin. The people at the end of the trade line get the worst goods. Judging by the condition of their attire, we are way, way up the line, quite possibly at its very end."

"Look, have you got any food? Anything at all?" McCracken was nothing if not persistent.

His exaggerated gestures if not his words finally produced results. The man in the front of the canoe suddenly began nodding vigorously and aping the guide's eating motions. Then he turned and pointed behind him, into the mist. Dropping his long pole-paddle back into the water, his companion made an unmistakable gesture for them to follow.

"They must come from a village nearby." Hope lent strength to Tennison's movements as she picked up one of the poles. "It can't be too far. The river people will travel long distances and spend weeks fishing a favorite site, but not in this kind of weather. They can become lost, too."

"Even if it's only a fisherman's camp," McCracken declared, "they'll have supplies. Dried fish, if nothing else, and salt to preserve it. Probably some fruits and vegetables as well." He smacked his lips, barely visible in the center of his whisker-clad face. "One thing's for damn sure. We can pay!"

At first their saviors tended to disappear into the fog, but they soon realized that unlike their dugout, the awkward raft they were guiding did not skim gracefully over the surface of the water. After that they stayed near, for which Bohannon was grateful. No one expected them to abandon the strangers, but it was reassuring to see those two strong backs paddling along in front, a smiling face occasionally glancing over a shoulder to see how the visitors were doing. Once when their canoe turned slightly, Bohannon saw that the prow had been carved to resemble the head of a crocodile.

"Wherever we're going has to be close." McCracken was digging at the water like a madman. "There's no food in their boat, and they wouldn't go any distance without taking along at least a few sago pancakes for a quick lunch."

Despite Bohannon's throbbing hunger, he found the image conjured by the expat's words unappealing. Noticing his expression, Tai managed a hoarse laugh.

"Silly, the pancakes aren't made from the grubs."

"Oh." Her companion was visibly relieved. "What then?"

"After a sago palm is felled, men with axes take turns cutting into the heart. The middle of the tree is soft and pulpy. They chop it up until they've reduced it to chips and splinters. Then the women grind it into a powder. Mix in a little water, throw on a flat rock above a fire, and you've got sago pancakes. They're pretty bland."

"Christ, right now I'd eat one raw." The thought of anything cooked set dormant juices in his mouth flowing uncontrollably.

In the absence of any current they made steady if slow progress. It soon became apparent that they were traveling down a channel that had been deliberately cleared of drifting organic matter. Not having to push miniature floating islands or chunks of bobbing soil and grass out of the way made poling the raft easier. Bohannon could not be sure of his companions, but as for himself, he felt he had about one day's poling left in him. After that the locals would have to find a way to put him in tow.

Stenhammer raised a hand and pointed. "There! Just ahead and to the right."

Leaning on his pole for support, Bohannon strained to penetrate the clinging fog. Then shapes began to appear. Materializing out of the mist, high wooden buildings more substantial than any of the traditional architecture he had encountered in the Highlands slowly floated into view.

Resting atop stout pilings that thrust down through water and muck to find footing in the unseen, solid earth, these structures were rectangular in shape. Sturdy walls of woven reed and palm frond boasted multiple windows. Sharply raked thatched roofs overhung front and back porches made of palm frond laid over logs taken from the isolated islands that dotted the savanna.

Drawing nearer, the man in the bow of the dugout raised an arm and shouted. Multiple cries greeted his hailing. As the raft floated into the village between flanking lines of houses, women and children crowded the unbarred doors and windows, gawking in silent speculation at the strange visitors.

The dugout dropped back slightly to parallel the raft. As it did so, both paddlers gestured for its occupants to keep poling forward. Noticing that the dugout drew only a few inches of water, Bohannon marveled at how its owners, standing erect in the shallow, foot-wide interior, kept from falling out or tipping over.

There was a slight jar, and the raft came to a stop. They were, for the first time in days, blissfully, safely, wonderfully aground.

As Stenhammer started to step off, McCracken grabbed his arm and thrust his face close to the other man's ear. "The gold, mate, what about the gold?"

Stenhammer looked down at him. "What about it?" he replied calmly.

The expat's eyes were flicking about like agitated beetles; from houses to occupants, from the men of the village who were coming to greet them, to the two smiling fishermen in the dugout. Scanning the endless vista of savanna behind the raft, McCracken's gaze came to rest on the pile of heavily-laden backpacks that dominated the center of the raft.

"We can't just bloody leave it here! If not the women, then the kids will start poking at it. If we take it with us they'll think it's only our own personal gear."

Bohannon groaned at the thought of hauling the heavy load. In his present condition he was afraid he would be unable to haul himself. But McCracken was adamant, and even Stenhammer had to concede that the expat's point was well taken. They had gone through much for the gleaming cargo. The inhabitants of this village might dwell far outside civilization's loop, but not so far that they would fail to recognize gold when they saw it.

One by one the backpacks were parceled out, everyone straining as best they could to make the loads seem lighter than they actually were. The big man handled both of his as if they were stuffed with feathers.

"Careful." Stenhammer looked back at his companions. "There is solid ground here, but there are also water-filled holes and plenty of mud."

Bohannon, for one, did not care. It felt great to be back on any kind of land, to be walking again. Even the seventy or so pounds of gold pressing remorsely against his back and shoulders seemed lighter than before, though he knew the feeling was a consequence of temporary euphoria and would soon wear off.

The men of the village crowded around them, some talking rapidly and with animation to the pair who had encountered the raft, others simply staring at the tall strangers. Occasionally one would reach out to touch or feel this new phenomenon, fingering shirts, shorts, and backpacks. Either they did not recognize the straps and buckles that held the packs shut or else they were, fortunately, too polite to go digging into them without permission.

Many wore the uniform of the two paddlers: fraying shorts and tattered shirts or vests. Others were clad in traditional bunches of strategically placed leaves or palm frond. More than a few had bird-of-paradise feathers and flowers woven into their short hair. In matters of personal adornment, at least, these men were one in spirit with their Highland cousins. Necklaces of pale gray palm seeds and rich, brown, highly polished pandanus nuts hung in strands from many throats. Several faces flashed streaks of yellow face paint, though Bohannon saw nothing in color or design to rival the personal decorations of the Huli.

A number of older men soon joined the crowd. These must be the village leaders, Bohannon immediately inferred. Or big men, as such were called in PNG. Their face paint and headgear were more elaborate than that of their comrades, who confirmed his suspicions by falling silent at the elders' approach. The three old men studied the strangers intently, their heads moving slowly from side to side as they carried out the inspection.

Instead of multiple necklaces of bead and nut and bone, the youngest of the trio wore around his neck a single carved crocodile tooth suspended from a knotted cord. It hung down to the center of his bare chest. Only when he turned did Bohannon get a look at the man's back.

Running in neat lines from his waist up to his shoulders and curving inward to meet at the back of his neck, a series of raised bumps marred the coffee-hued skin. Each fleshy nodule was about an inch long and half again as wide. Looking around, Bohannon noticed that many of the other men were similarly marked. It took him a moment to realize what they reminded him of. The raised lumps looked exactly like the scales of a crocodile.

"What is that all about?" Leaning close to Tai, he pointed out the deformations.

"Ritual scarification. Still practiced, obviously, among the more primitive, isolated river tribes. They believe that by taking on the skin of the crocodile they also gain its strength and stealth. The ceremony is carried out when the male villagers are young men."

Bohannon could not take his eyes off the astonishing, barbaric marks. "But how—they're so numerous. And big."

"I've never seen the ceremony in person, but I've seen pictures. Ethnographic film. It's not pretty to watch. The young man is placed on his stomach with his arms stretched out above his head. Strong men hold him down while another does the work. For each scar, the skin is sliced open with a bone knife. Dry, cold ash is rubbed into the wound. That's what makes the bumps rise. There is an amazing amount of blood." Lengthening her stride, she stepped from one soggy patch of ground to another, clearing a deep puddle. "Apparently, the boys never cry out."

"Shit," Bohannon muttered. Feeling a hand fumbling at the straps of his backpack, he turned sharply but was careful to smile as he did so. The man whose fingers had been busy responded with a friendly nod and the attempted intrusion was not repeated. For now.

"Hey!"

Whirling sharply, he saw a grinning warrior remove his hand from the hem of Tai's shorts. Acutely aware of their helplessness in the face of numerous throwing sticks, bows and arrows, spears and axes, he gritted his teeth and did nothing. There was no place in this country, he remembered, where women were not looked upon as property, to be bought and sold for so many pigs or to be treated with suspicion. Tai had only her considerable individual presence and that of her three companions to protect her. In an environment as primitive and isolated as the village, that could quickly wear thin.

Ahead loomed a structure so unexpectedly imposing that it momentarily took what was left of Bohannon's breath away. Mounted on wooden pilings fashioned from the largest tree trunks, its peaked roof thrust out and forward like the prow of a sailing ship, some four stories above the ground. At its apex, leaning out over the ground below at a forty-five degree angle, was the sculpted figure of a naked man.

The gray pilings were similarly carved; a plethora of bulging eyes, protruding tongues, enormous ears, and grinning teeth alternated with naturalistic and highly-skilled representations of crocodiles and birds. Many had been highlighted with red ocher and white paint. Hands of cedar clutched spears and axes while log-like penises hung nearly to the ground. Bohannon sought but could not find among the treasury of primitive art a single representation of a woman. Once again overwhelmed by his ignorance, he requested an explanation from Tai.

"That's a Haus Tamburan," she explained. "The men's spirit house. Women aren't allowed in there. They're not even allowed in the cooking and living area underneath. Anyone caught inside or on the grounds would be severely punished, or in the most serious instances, put to death."

A series of wooden steps eight feet across and two wide supported by finely carved posts led from the marshy ground to the second-level floor. Covered in finely woven mats, the walls flanking the open portal at the top of the stairs shouted the buildings' importance. Wild renderings in brown and white of abstract lines and staring eyes that seemed to float free of the walls and out into the swirling fog gazed down at the visitors.

Above the second-story entrance was a mask three feet in diameter. Built up from strips of cured palm, dark clay, and dried mud laid over a shield-like wooden backing, it was decorated with embedded cowrie shells, thin black cassowary feathers, knotted cords that dangled from nose and ears, and spiked teeth. Two enormous pig tusks pierced the nose. With its empty, glaring eyes, it was a nightmare wild and primeval enough to put all the other carvings to shame.

Off to the left, a line of a dozen gray stone slabs varying in height from one to four feet had been planted in the mushy earth. Each was heavily streaked with black stains. They looked like the broken, jagged teeth of a buried giant. "What are those?" Bohannon asked Tai as they walked past. "Some kind of fence?"

She looked in the indicated direction. Her expression was solemn. "Bloodstones. Carried down from the mountains, since there is no rock here. They're probably quite old. Until very recently these people were headhunters and cannibals. In the old days they used to ritually slay their enemies on special stones sanctified to that purpose." She nodded in the direction of the now-ominous gray line. "Stones like those."

A fine mist began to fall, as if the sky could not decide whether it was tired of raining or not. Helpful hands urged them forward, away from the stairway and toward a gap in the hanging strips of beige-colored palm and thatch that formed a curtain around the underside of the spirit house. From within, Bohannon detected the almost overpowering scent of meat cooking. Lazy smoke drifted out through the gaps in the curtain.

Several of the men drew it aside and beckoned for them to enter. Apparently, as an outsider, an exception to the males-only rule was being made for Tai, since no one moved to stop her from entering. Once through the gap, more warriors waited to greet them. The dry understory of the Haus Tamburan was furnished with tables, crude benches, worksites marked by the presence of primitive tools, and a pair of cooking pits lined with stones. After an exchange of excited words among the elders and warriors, the visitors were offered food. Bohannon did not even bother to try and identify the hunk of broiled meat that was handed to him. The taste of his first bite as it spread through his mouth was so intense that he almost fainted.

Roast pork.

There was chicken, and broiled small green bananas, and mangoes and papaya and yes, even the ubiquitous pandanus nuts. Bohannon quickly discovered that a bland sago pancake about a foot across made an excellent substitute for a corn tortilla. Into one of these he rolled dried fish, salt, and pulped sweet potato. He would not have traded the result for a meal a month hence in a Michelin three-star Paris bistro.

When their hunger had been partially sated, Tai filtered water dipped from a clay jug one cup at a time. Standing close to the open cooking fire while cramming food into their mouths allowed their clothing, for the first time since the rain had afflicted them, to start to dry out.

Half an hour later they heard people moving about in the spirit room overhead, followed by footsteps on the ceremonial stairs. "Probably the headman coming to check on us," McCracken surmised. "For a feed like this, I'll get down on the ground and kiss his ugly, old, bare toes, foot fungus and all."

The thatch curtain parted to admit the three elders, just as the guide had surmised. There were three more in the party: two particularly tall and well-built warriors, and one other.

Bohannon dropped the leg of chicken he had been stripping and even Stenhammer looked startled. McCracken's mouth opened but no sound emerged from between his parted lips. Among them all, only Tai found herself able to give voice to the shock all of them felt.

"Alfred!"

XXIII

"Yes, it is I." Grinning, the tracker stepped fully into the room. His pants' legs were fraying badly at the hems and his shirt was a succession of rips and tears, but otherwise he seemed unharmed. He still had his sandals and much more importantly, he was wearing the belt Stenhammer had left behind when they had rappelled into the sinkhole. Knife, tools, flashlight, even the oversize handgun in its holster, all were still firmly attached to the band of black leather.

"How the hell did you survive?" Like everyone else, Bohannon could not stop staring at the man who by rights ought to be a ghost.

The Highlander moved further inside, stepping past the silent, watching elders. "When I felt the earth start to move I looked up and saw that the whole upper valley was caving in and rushing toward me. I shouted a warning down to you. Then I picked up the first thing I saw, which was Mr. Stenhammer's belt, and turned and ran for my life. Never before have I run so hard for so long. Once, the wind that the earthslip was pushing ahead of it nearly knocked me down. If I had fallen I would have been buried alive for sure. It was like a dozen storms all thrown together as one." He straightened proudly. "But I kept my feet, and my wits.

"Several times I stumbled but did not fall, because I knew that if I fell, I would die. All the time I could hear nothing except the earth chasing me. When I could run no more, I climbed the tallest tree I could find and covered my face. More wind whipped around me, and rocks flew like bullets, but I was behind the trunk of the tree and it protected me. Then I saw the earth swallowing up the bottom of the tree, as it had swallowed up everything else in the valley. It rose higher and higher, like the sea, and then began to push the tree over." He paused, looking past them as he remembered.

"But the slip was losing its strength, and I was not buried. After it had stopped, I waited for the dust and dirt to settle. Then I climbed down and tried to find the sinkhole. There was no sign of the place where it had been. The whole riverbed was completely buried."

"Why didn't you try to make it back to Mt. Yogonda?" Bohannon asked him.

Alfred's attention shifted to him. "I did, but the earth was so soft I was afraid it might swallow me up. Also, many smaller slips followed close upon the first. Clearly, it was too dangerous to try and walk back up the valley. The river Mr. Stenhammer had diverted was already trying to break through, and that made the ground even more unstable. The mountains on either side where the earth had not given way were too steep to climb.

"Not knowing what else to do, I decided the best thing was to get as far as possible away from the unstable valley. So I followed a ridgeline north." With a wave of one hand he indicated the assembled villagers.

"I speak several of the Sepik tongues. Some fishermen from this village found me and brought me here. I did not know if you had been killed. It seemed likely, but I kept hoping. I knew that if you survived the earthslip you would have to follow the river channel underground until it emerged from the mountains. But if you made it that far I thought sure you would try to return to Mt. Yogonda." He indicated the backpack at Bohannon's feet. "Now I see why you did not. It would be almost impossible to climb back over the mountains carrying what you recovered from the bottom of the sinkhole."

Stenhammer spoke quietly, evenly. "How do you know that is what we brought with us?"

"What else could it be?" The tracker's high spirits were infectious. Only the presence of so many armed men, silently attentive and watching, mitigated against an out-and-out celebration. "You took very little in the way of supplies down with you, yet here you are with five very full and apparently very heavy packs." His gaze shifted to the man standing next to Tai.

"I know for certain that Mr. McCracken, surely, would not give up his part of the treasure or leave it behind. He would die first."

The expat stiffened slightly, then forced a smile. "Yeah, too right, Alfred me mate!" His gaze narrowed as he surreptitiously scanned the crowd of warriors. Though they could not understand what was being said, they continued to follow the proceedings with unmistakable interest. "So we managed to bring out a few nuggets. No point in denying it." He indicated their hosts. "Looks like you got this lot eating out of your hand."

"We quickly came to an arrangement," the Highlander admitted easily. "They will do whatever I ask of them."

"That's great!" Tai exclaimed. "That means we can hire boats to take all of us out of this savanna and downriver." She smiled conspiratorially. "Along with our salvaged 'supplies,' of course."

"I am curious about one thing." Stenhammer did not appear to share his companions' relief. His eyes remained fixed on the tracker. "These people owe you nothing. Just because you can speak a little of their language does not entitle you to the prerogatives due a long-lost relative. Why are they being so accommodating?"

"Oh, that's easy to explain." Reaching down, the Highlander unsnapped the big man's holster and exhumed the enormous pistol. As he gripped it in his right fist and waved it casually in front of him, the trio of elders retreated a step while several of the assembled warriors flinched back. Others murmured something approving—or placating.

"Oy, be careful with that cannon, mate!" McCracken retreated behind the crude wooden table against which he had been leaning.

"Relax, Mr. McCracken. I know how to use a handgun." Turning the weapon sideways to face him, he admired the heavy steel barrel. "Though I have never seen a pistol like this before, I know it must be very expensive. In a place like PNG it is really priceless." Once again he turned a broad grin on Stenhammer. "You could never get a permit to carry one."

"You do not want that going off by accident." Hand outstretched, the big man took a step forward. "Thank you for saving it. You can give it back to me now."

Calm, completely composed, and still smiling, the tracker turned the gun so that the muzzle was pointing directly at the other man's midsection. He held it firmly, his forefinger resting lightly on the trigger.

"No, Mr. Stenhammer, *sir*, I do not think I will do that."

Except for the spit and crackle of burning charcoal in the stone-lined cooking pit, it was dead silent in the under-room of the Haus Tamburan. The expressions on Tennison and McCracken's faces reflected their complete confusion and utter dismay, while Bohannon wore the look of a thirty-year company employee who had abruptly and unexpectedly been fired from his position for no apparent reason.

Only Stenhammer was not visibly shaken. "The gun will do you no good, Alfred, so you might as well give it back. That is a seventy-two ounce Desert Eagle magnum. It fires a fifty-caliber round. You cannot get bullets for it."

"Ah, but there you are wrong, Mr. Stenhammer." The open, innocent smile they were familiar with vanished, to be replaced by something different, more sophisticated, and considerably less pleasant. "That is a military caliber, and poorly-paid soldiers are always willing to sell a little of their equipment here, a little there." With his free hand he gestured in the direction of the two backpacks lying at Stenhammer's feet. "I believe I will be able to afford a bullet or two, don't you think? Meanwhile, I will have to be content with the ten rounds in the clip." With his free hand he patted the butt of the heavy pistol.

Furious, McCracken started forward, only to find his way blocked by a dozen raised spears and knives. "Look here, mate, I don't know what you're thinking, but you can't get away with it."

Alfred's eyes widened and his reply was colored with mock naiveté. "I can't? Why, goodness me, Mr. McCracken, I guess you must be right. After all, I am only a poor, ignorant Highlander, one step removed from the Stone Age. What right have I to any of that gold, just because it was taken from my land?"

Nervously licking his lips, McCracken took a step back from the assembled spearpoints. "Well now, mate, there's no need to get all upset about it. We were going to cut you a share, you know that."

"Yes, as a matter of fact, I do. I do believe that you were going to share your diggings with me."

The expat was visibly relieved. "Well then, no harm done, is there?" With a foot he nudged the backpack he had carried all the way out of the mountains. "I'll give you some of mine, and so will the others." He looked around, eyeing his companions anxiously. "Ain't that right, mates?"

"Sure," agreed Bohannon readily. "You can have a part of mine, Alfred. We'll all share equally."

"Share equally." The tracker set the fingers of his free hand to tapping against the side of his head. "The gold from the land of my people. Yes, that would be fair, I suppose. But you know, I have another idea." He paused, feigning thoughtfulness. "What if—what if I just keep all the gold for myself?"

"You fucking Huli bastard!" Again McCracken started forward, and again he was restrained by a forest of spears.

Alfred's lips tightened and at the same time, a hint of smile returned. Bad combination, Bohannon thought. "Pressure is an interesting phenomenon, don't you think, Mr. McCracken? It is only under pressure that our true feelings sometimes emerge."

"He's not speaking for the rest of us," Bohannon heard himself saying. "Why would you want to do something like this, Alfred? I liked you. That's why I hired you, when I could have hired someone else. I treated you as an equal member of the party right from the start. Don't do this."

"Why would you do this?" Tai was shaking her head slowly, staring at the Highlander in disbelief.

"Because I can. That is the way life is in the Highlands, remember? You are experienced enough to know that."

"All right." A sullen McCracken glowered at the tracker. "You can have the bloody gold. Take all of it. Hold it tight to you at night, so that it crushes you in your sleep."

"Mr. McCracken, why would I want to sleep with it? That is a perversion peculiar to yourself, I should imagine. But you are right. I *will* have all the bloody gold. I will have anything I want, because I understand western culture better than you think." The humorless smile widened. "He who has the gun delineates the culture. It makes me civilized, does it not?"

"Not a bit of it, mate." McCracken rambled on oblivious to the possible consequences of intemperate words. "The gun don't mean shit, and your *gutpela* English don't mean shit. No matter how hard you try you'll never be anything more than a dumb, yam-chewing, pig-sucking, betelnut-juice spitting, bamboo-through-the-nose jigaboo."

"Actually, I prefer a cassowary quill," Alfred ventured into the ensuing silence. Smiling thinly, he squeezed the sides of his wide nostrils. "No chance of splinters. But perhaps you are right. Perhaps that is what I am. In that case my actions will not surprise you." He stared penetratingly at each of them in turn.

"From you, Mr. Stenhammer, I want this belt, with its wonderful gun and knife and other toys. And your gold, of course." He turned to confront the enraged but helpless expat. "From you, Mr. McCracken, I want also the gold—and perhaps later, a few teeth and other body parts, so that you may learn humility." Taking a step forward, he looked Bohannon up and down. Thankfully, the subject of his inspection was still too stunned by the turn of events to be really frightened.

"From you, Mr. Bohannon, I will take only the gold, since that is all you have to give. You were polite to me, but you were not kind. You used me, as every white person who I have ever had contact with has used me."

"Maybe that has something to do with your engaging personality, as opposed to your ethnic background." Stenhammer spoke as if nothing untoward had happened, as if events were continuing down a familiar and comforting path. "I have lived all my life in PNG. My parents were born here, I was born here, and I have far more friends among nationals than I do among expats. I do not know one of them who would want to have anything to do with you or who would wish to bring you into their family." He added something in Pidgin that completely escaped Bohannon.

Whatever it was, it was strong enough to finally crack the tracker's reserve. "Shut up, you! Just you keep your mouth shut!" Raising the barrel of the pistol and holding the heavy weapon in both hands, he took aim at Stenhammer's chest. Those warriors who happened to be standing in the big man's vicinity scattered.

Everyone held their breath. Even the smoke from the cook fires seemed to stand still. Slowly, the tracker lowered the gun. "But why should I waste a valuable bullet on a crazy man? You are crazy, you know, even if you did find some gold. Everyone says so. What you just said to me proves it. Only a crazy fellow would speak words like that to a man holding a gun on him." With a last dismissive glance at Bohannon, he turned finally to Tai.

"And from you, *nais meri*, I want also, of course, the gold, and," he added in a voice so glacial it might have issued from the constricted throat of a Death Adder, "your ass."

Tai stared back, unable to believe what she was hearing. When she finally managed to whisper a response, her words were barely audible fragments of contempt. "I thought you were educated, Alfred. I thought you were a civilized man."

Head and beard snapped in McCracken's direction. "Your friend thinks otherwise."

Up until now Tai had been an exemplar of self control. Now her voice started to break. She could not escape from the hundred male eyes that were focused on her, none of them friendly, none of them sharing her view of what constituted civilized behavior. Their standards had been formed by ten thousand years of isolation, and theirs were not hers.

"That's his opinion. I don't share it." She took a step backward, but there was nowhere to go. "Don't do this, Alfred. Please don't do this."

Her words slid off him as easily as had the veneer of civilization. "But I will."

"But why—why?" Her voice quivered as she began to lose control. Bohannon had never seen her scared before, or even frightened. Now there was a new look in her eyes—the terrified glazed stare of a rabbit being pursued by foxes.

The tracker almost, but not quite, smiled. "Because I can," he replied pleasantly. "And because I want to." He barked something at one of the elders, who nodded and addressed the taut, expectant assembly in brusque, clipped tones.

Then all hell broke loose.

Bohannon felt himself seized by a dozen hands that looped like cables around his arms and shoulders. His arms were wrenched back behind him. Strips of vine bound his wrists together so tightly that they started to bleed. Other warriors swarmed over Stenhammer and McCracken. Fewer were needed to restrain Tai, who unlike her companions was not bound.

It took only a few moments. Holstering the huge pistol, Alfred approached the big man first. "If you will permit me, Mr. Stenhammer? Or if you will not." Starting at the shoulders, he ran his hands over the other man's clothes, patting him down carefully and paying particular attention to the area under the arms as well as all pockets.

From one of the latter he removed the compact device that had proven so vital to their survival in the course of the flight from the tunnel. "Good Swiss army knife." He promptly pocketed it. "Thank you. I could of course now buy several hundred of my own, but I take additional pleasure in possessing yours."

Moving to confront McCracken, the tracker studied the weathered, angry face. "There is no point in looking at me like that. If you keep grinding your teeth together you will soon be in need of some serious dental attention. You have been in this country long enough, I suspect, not to be surprised by what is happening." Leaning forward, he repeated the careful pat-down.

When he reached McCracken's front pockets, having to kneel slightly to do so, the expat spat out a terse suggestion. "Keep going a little to your right, mate, and you can suck my dick."

Alfred rose slowly, shaking his head. "What an unrepentant man you are, McCracken. I suppose there is something admirable, or at least curious, in one who lets his anger take control of him so completely." Bringing his right arm back sharply, he smashed his closed fist into the expat's face. McCracken's head snapped sideways. When he again met the tracker's gaze, a thin trickle of blood was dribbling from his nose. Since his hands were bound behind him he could only sniff at it.

The grim-faced Highlander appeared satisfied. "That's better. As to your suggestion, I will mention it to some of my new friends. They might find it interesting, only in reverse." He moved on to the last bound prisoner.

"You I do not understand, Mr. Bohannon. This is not your country and you clearly are out of place here. Unlike these other two I know it was not gold that brought you to the Highlands. You said it was her." He indicated the silently staring Tennison. "But I am not sure I believe that either." He moved forward, to stand so close that his beard brushed the other man's chin. "Why, then?"

Bohannon felt not only the tracker's eyes but those of his companions. I ought to say something clever, he thought, or at least be defiant like McCracken. But spur-of-the-moment wit had never been one of his attributes. Like most people, he needed time to rehearse his comebacks.

"There's no point in telling you, Alfred. You wouldn't understand."

The tracker stared a moment longer, searching the other man's face. Then he stepped back. "Perhaps. Our worlds are very different, Mr. Bohannon. Too bad for you that you had to intrude into mine."

"A murderer is a murderer in any culture."

Alfred shrugged. "I will risk payback from your clan." Turning away, he walked over to Tai. She struggled helplessly in the hands of the warriors who were restraining her.

"And you, *nais meri*. Do you know how you looked at me? Not as another man, like your companions, but as an instrument, a tool for furthering your ends and attending to your needs. Never as a man. I was just another indentured native, something to make the rough parts of your life a little easier." Gripping her chin in one hand, he pulled her roughly forward and hissed softly into her face. "Now I am going to make your life a little harder."

Stepping back, he spoke to one of the elders. The old man approached and let his gaze travel the length of the prisoner's body, from head to foot and back again. Then he reached out, grabbed her left breast hard, and squeezed. His eyes never left her face. Bohannon saw her inhale sharply, but she would not give any of them the satisfaction of hearing her plead.

Letting go, the elder broke out into a wide smile and announced something to the assembly. The warriors promptly erupted in a chorus of high-pitched, bestial hoots and bone-chilling yells. Bohannon felt rough hands on him again as he was pushed and dragged outside and forced up the wide stairway leading to the second floor. Somewhere nearby McCracken was spewing obscenities while Tai alternated curses with entreaties. Stolid as ever, Stenhammer uttered not a word.

Bohannon was not being brave; he simply had no more idea what to say than what to do. He was caught in a predicament for which he had no reference, trapped in a situation which his life experience had not prepared him for. He was not cursing or shouting or accusing because he was trying to think of the next thing to do, or say. But without precedent, he was lost. Eventually, a feeling of utter hopelessness would move in to occupy the vacancy in his mind.

The upper floor of the Haus Tamburan consisted of a single spacious room. A complex crisscrossing of poles and logs supported the steeply-peaked roof of heavy thatch, the apex of which rose two stories over their heads. Like the external pilings, the interior support poles were magnificently carved. Crocodiles, birds, possums, and ancestor spirits peered back at them in a riot of bulging eyes, gnashing teeth, hooked claws, and exaggerated genitalia.

The walls were lined with bark paintings executed by young men transiting puberty. In shades of white, ocher red, and dark brown, they formed a sea of sweeping abstract lines and curves interspersed with grotesque faces and free-floating eyes. The Haus Tamburan was a shrine to an ancient tradition of barbaric art that was far more sophisticated and elegant than those who had raised it.

There were no windows and only the one door. Lest women spy on men's doings, Stenhammer explained. Near the far end of the room, smoke rose from a stone firepit and found its way out through a ventilation hole in the roof. The floor consisted of heavy woven mats laid over small logs spaced a foot apart.

A couple of massive orator's chairs, eight-foot tall sculptures of naked ancestor spirits whose backsides protruded to form seats, glared menacingly from the center of the room. Off to the right, a pair of ceremonial garamut drums rested lengthwise on wooden blocks. Each drum was six feet long, four feet thick, and had been fashioned from the trunk of a single tree whose interior had been laboriously hollowed out. Both were elaborately inscribed with scenes of village life that covered the exposed yellow-gold surfaces from one end to the other. Cut lengthwise through the top of each drum was a slot three feet long and six inches wide that supplied air to the resonating chamber. Save for the orator's chairs there was nothing in the way of furniture elsewhere in the room.

On Alfred's command the three male prisoners were forced to sit next to each other, their backs against one wall. Warriors came forward to bind the prisoners' extended legs together at the knees.

"I want you to watch." The tracker spoke between clenched teeth. "I want you to listen. When I am done, the men who found me and took me in will have their turn, and when they are done the elders will come, and then the rest of the village. And when the last of them has finished it will start again." The maddening smile returned.

"But I do not want you to be bored. Some of these river people will fuck anything. You want to contribute to the conservation of local culture, don't you? I do not know what they will do to you except that you will not like it. I am particularly sorry for you, Mr. Bohannon. You look soft."

Turning, he spoke rapidly to the elders. One nodded and the three of them turned to address the warriors who were crowding into the single entrance. Murmuring among themselves, they turned and departed. Bohannon could hear them filing back into the understory directly beneath where he was sitting. He also heard a few fading laughs.

The two warriors who had accompanied the entrance of the elders remained, each holding one of Tai's arms. Strong as she was, in struggling against them she might as well have been trying to break free of wire coils.

The tracker approached, grabbed the hem of her shorts, and tugged. She kicked and fought, but the grip of the two villagers was unyielding. Alfred simply pulled until her legs were off the ground, kept pulling until her booted feet slid through the leg holes of the culottes and fell back to the woven mats.

Tossing the shorts aside, he walked back up to her, put a hand in the waistband of her panties, and yanked them from her body. Bohannon winced as the elastic ripped. The shirt went next, buttons popping as he wrenched it open. The jogging bra gave him some trouble. Frustrated by the tough material, he drew Stenhammer's oversize blade. While everyone momentarily held their breath, he cut the tough fabric from top to bottom and pulled the shreds from her shoulders.

Too alert to drift within range of her knees, he directed the warriors to turn her around. Then he approached, grabbed a handful of hair, and pulled her head back, back, until he could see her face.

"I am afraid the next hours will not be so pleasant, *nais meri*. For you, that is."

Breathing hard, her chest heaving, she met his gaze unswervingly. "Fuck you."

He shrugged ever so slightly. "You people fuck my country, I fuck you. Not very poetic, as justice goes, but it will serve."

That was when, with nothing else to lose, she spat directly into his eye. "You go straight to Hell!"

"Sorry. Not my theology." Releasing her hair, he wiped at his face. "That was very cinematic. You have seen too many movies, *nais meri*. No one is going to ride to your rescue here. The Phantom is not going to come crashing through the roof to save you. In a few hours you will be hurting too much to scream. By nightfall you will wish you were dead. It is what I would like to see happen to everyone who has ever exploited this country. But I can only do it to you, and to your friends."

"Who do you think you are fooling?" They all looked to Stenhammer, who had been silent for some time. "Yourself, maybe, but no one else. You are no righter of wrongs, no arbiter of the social order, Alfred. You are a plain, ordinary, garden-variety thief, rapist, and murderer. In Mosby they would not even give you a cell to yourself. You are not that important."

"Not in Mosby, perhaps." This time the big man's words failed to rattle the tracker. "But here, in the northwest, I will be legend. Thanks to the gold." Turning away from them, he barked orders.

The two warriors bent the still struggling Tai over the nearer of the two drums, her naked backside thrust high in the air. Pulled out to the sides, her wrists were fastened with strips of vine to the blocks that supported the heavy instrument. Her legs were similarly spread and the ankles tied down. Bohannon could hear her breathing hard, in her present position unable to see what was happening behind her. She did not plead, did not cry. The former had already proven futile, and she would not give her tormentors the satisfaction of the latter.

Alfred moved up behind her until he was resting one hand on her left buttock. With his other he undid his pants. As the tracker liberated his erection, Stenhammer addressed him in a voice that could have frozen fire. Though they shared the same fate and were on the same side, it chilled Bohannon's blood. Even the two warriors, not understanding a word, looked up uncertainly.

"Touch her and I will kill you. If not in this life then in another."

If the Highlander was shaken by that tone or disturbed by the words that had been spoken, he concealed it well. He glanced only briefly back over his shoulder. "You are right about one thing, Mr. Stenhammer. There will be killing here, but you will not be the one to do it." Turning away, he rammed himself between Tai's splayed thighs. She uttered a gasp but did not scream.

Bohannon looked down, trying to concentrate on the pattern woven into the floor mat, looking anywhere but at the atrocity that was being perpetrated on the other side of the room. When he glanced to his left he saw McCracken twisting and contorting against his bonds while Stenhammer strained silently at his own.

Teeth clenched, sweat beading his forehead and cheeks, the large vein pulsing in his neck, Alfred slammed repeatedly and viciously forward with his hips. From time to time he glanced over at them. "Go ahead and fight, gentlemen. Break your restraints." He snickered loudly, lost in the delirium of his obsession. "Crawl over here and nip at my heels like dogs! I will flee in terror." Throwing himself forward yet again, he finally succeeded in coaxing a moan from his victim.

But that was all. Her stolid indifference to what was happening behind her became transformed, in the possessed Highlander's mind, into an intolerable insult.

"Does this feel good, *nais meri*? Are you liking this?" When she did not respond, in any way, his anger exploded. She was cheating him of his conquest, and he would not stand for it.

He snapped an order at the two attentive warriors. One walked to a corner and from the impenetrable shadows retrieved a fistful of something indistinct. When he returned, he knelt down close to Tai's dangling head and smiled at her. Bohannon could just make out what he passed to his companion, who had set himself cross-legged on the other side of the helpless woman.

Bohannon couldn't see what they were doing—any more than he could shut out the full-throated ringing of her screams. The perspiration beading his forehead began to drip down into his eyes, stinging and burning. The more she screamed, the harder he struggled against his bonds. His efforts served only to intensify his feeling of utter helplessness.

Expending a supreme effort, McCracken wrenched violently. The vines restraining his wrists parted and his arms flew free. He had been working at his wrist bindings ever since they had been applied, slowly and patiently, and now his hands were loose. Alfred immediately saw what had happened and reported it to his attentive assistants. One of them climbed to his feet.

"Those lengths of vine are unbreakable, but they can slip. Wave madly while you can, McCracken. It will not last long."

The expat did not wave. He did not try to pull himself, hand over hand, to the doorway. There was no point in that anyway, not with dozens of impatient, waiting warriors taking their ease just beneath the floor. He did not even give the tracker the finger. What he did do was lean forward and reach for his right ankle. Sudden remembrance enlightened Bohannon. Alfred had searched each of them for weapons, had emptied their pockets and patted them down thoroughly.

But he had stopped at McCracken's knee.

XXIV

From its contoured ankle holster McCracken drew the compact little pistol Bohannon had last seen used just outside the Tari market. The most surprised look he had ever seen on a human face contorted Alfred's features as he recognized the lethal shape in McCracken's fist. Then the gun went off with a sharp, firecracker *pop* and a neat hole appeared in the exact center of the tracker's forehead. His expression never changed as he sank slowly to the floor, his legs folding beneath him like warm putty, his flaccid organ flopping loosely between his legs.

As the approaching warrior dropped the fresh lengths of vine he was carrying and turned to flee, McCracken put two bullets into his back. Scrambling erect from his seated position, the man's horrified companion made a mad dash for the doorway. McCracken's last shot just grazed his back. The tiny pistol only held four rounds.

Querulous, unsettled shouts rose from the confused villagers assembled beneath the Haus Tamburan. Struggling with his own bindings, Bohannon caught a glimpse of Stenhammer. The big man's chest had expanded massively and his cheeks were puffed out and turning blue. There was a muffled woody *snap* as he burst the unbreakable vines restraining his wrists.

Rising to his bound feet, he hopped toward the fallen tracker. Alfred had collapsed facedown, a pool of blood spreading slowly from the hole in his skull to form a crimson aureole around his head. Footsteps and agitated voices could be heard on the bottom of the stairway.

Stenhammer threw himself forward and fumbled frantically with the snap of the holster. As the first warriors appeared at the top of the stairs, spears raised and arrows notched, the big man drew the enormous handgun, took aim, and fired.

Hailing as he did from Southern California, Bohannon had heard guns before. Most made little cracking sounds, especially the compact, illegal automatic pistols so favored by organized gangs. Others snapped, or went bang like McCracken's gun. The big Desert Eagle spoke with a somewhat different voice.

A tremendous *bahhh-whooommm* reverberated through the spirit room, shaking the bark paintings on the walls and stunning Bohannon's ears. Even McCracken jumped. The bullet blew an astonishingly large hole in the chest of the elder who had just appeared in the doorway, literally lifting him off the floor and hurling him violently backward. Already dead, he slammed into the men behind him and sent half of them careening and tumbling down the stairs. The rest vanished, running or leaping from where they had been standing.

While Stenhammer kept the muzzle of the pistol aimed at the only entrance to the spirit room, McCracken struggled to his feet and hopped past him. Dropping to his knees and dividing his attention between the dead man's waist and the doorway, he proceeded to draw the big steel knife from Stenhammer's belt and saw away at the vines binding his ankles.

"Nice shot." He was breathing hard and fast as he worked the blade back and forth. Beneath it, the constricting vines parted like pasta.

"Not as nice as yours." Lying prone in firing position and resting his hands and the pistol on the tracker's lifeless back, the big man glanced over at McCracken. "I did not know you had a weapon."

"You didn't ask me, mate." As soon as his ankles were freed, he went to work on Stenhammer's leg restraints. "He did." The guide nodded in Bohannon's direction.

"I'd forgotten all about it." He struggled with his own bindings. Would the villagers decide to rush them? They had the advantage of numbers, and he did not doubt their courage. But they did not know that McCracken's pistol was empty, and it would take a brave man indeed to charge the barrel of Stenhammer's weapon. If they had any knowledge of firearms at all, it probably revolved around an occasional isolated encounter with one of the notorious homemade shotguns. For all the villagers knew, both Stenhammer and McCracken had access to a hundred rounds for each pistol.

Unless they were reckless to the point of suicide, these were matters that cautious warriors would want to discuss before having another go at the stairs. As Bohannon was mentally racing through the possibilities, McCracken came over and started sawing at his ankles.

"Hey, watch it!" he admonished the energized expat. "Just the vines!"

"Oy now, mate, you wouldn't notice a little nick, would you?" In seconds Bohannon's feet were free and the expat had moved behind him to work on his wrists. The relief when those restraints fell away bordered on the sensuous. As Bohannon sat rubbing the circulation back into his hands, McCracken hurried past the prone Stenhammer and over to Tai, keeping low as he ran in case some enterprising warrior thought to send a few arrows flying through the entrance.

"Sorry, luv," he murmured tightly. "Really sorry."

She turned her head to watch him as he worked with the knife to liberate her left wrist. Her hair spilled down over her face and droplets of cold sweat dripped from her chin. Wincing, she somehow managed, unbelievably, to smile.

"You did fine, Sorley."

Stenhammer looked away from the pistol's sights only long enough to urge McCracken to hurry his work.

"What d'you think I'm doing here, mate? Making espresso?" The knife slashed through the last of the vines binding Tai's ankles.

Gently, she was helped off the drum. One arm around her naked, sweat-soaked back, Bohannon leaned over to peer into her face. "Can you walk, Tai? We have to get out of here."

She looked up at him, unconsciously brushing loose strands of hair from her face. "You think I want to hang around? I was trying to shut myself down, to prepare myself for another thirty or forty like that asshole." For a second time, she spat at the body of the dead tracker. This time he did not react. "Yeah, I think I can—walk." With every passing second her spirit, so badly damaged, rose a little more. Alfred had violated it, but thanks to McCracken's well-placed bullet, he had not had time to break it.

"My—my clothes." Shrugging off both men, she painfully struggled back into what was left of her clothing. The brassiere was ruined, cut to shreds, and every button had been ripped from the shirt. Slipping it over her shoulders and putting her arms through, she twisted the hem and knotted it beneath her breasts. Then she turned, wincing, to McCracken.

"Why didn't you shoot the bastard sooner?"

"Couldn't get my hands free, luv. Believe me, it weren't for lack of trying."

Rising from his prone position while keeping the pistol trained on the doorway at all times, Stenhammer unbuckled his absent belt from the dead Highlander's waist and strapped it around his own. Shoving the body over onto its side, he recovered his Swiss army knife from an open pocket.

"Any other surprises you are keeping from us, Mr. McCracken?"

"Well now, mate, I wish I could say I had a hand grenade or two tucked between the cheeks of me backside, but unfortunately I don't." He took a last look around at the impressive but frightening interior of the spirit house. "If I did, I'd blow this fucking hellhole halfway to Wuvulu." He passed the big knife back to the other man. "Yours."

Stenhammer took it and slid it into its black leather sheath. "Thank you. Now I think it is time for us to continue on our way." Peering over at Tennison, his voice softened. "Are you sure you are up to this, Tai?"

Her smile was defiant and she was no longer trembling as badly. Bohannon had seen stronger women—but only in the movies. Easy to be tough on film, he thought. Things were a bit different when real life was improvising the script instead of some uninvolved overpaid hack slumped over a keyboard in his bathrobe. Their idea of savagery revolved around battles over position on screen credits or being cut off in front of a yellow light on Santa Monica Boulevard. Confronted by any real violence, most of them would crap in their pants.

"Let's go," Stenhammer said curtly. "Mr. McCracken, keep your gun up and act as if it is still loaded."

The expat glared at him. "You don't have to tell me what to do—mate."

The big man looked as if he wanted to add something, but decided it could wait. Gripping the Eagle in one massive fist, he crept cat-like toward the portal. Holding her shirt together, Tai staggered along next to McCracken. Bohannon brought up the rear, having thoughtfully picked up the barb-tipped spears abandoned by the two warriors. In similar circumstances back home he would have been too stunned, too paralyzed to do anything. Here, he was learning, the stunned and the paralyzed died quick, unlamented deaths. Notions of civilized behavior had to be bent, local culture and mores adapted to. Here violence was not the exception but the rule, not an isolated outrage but a traditional way of life. Children were raised to accept it as normal, even laudable. To stay alive in a place like PNG you had to learn the local customs, and learn them fast. For the first time since his university days, he was being forced to play the alert student. The reward for a passing grade was survival.

Most of his adult life had been spent sitting behind a computer, or escorting clients around blissful, bustling, wonderfully-civilized San Diego. Violence was something you read about in the morning paper or tut-tutted over when it flashed by on the evening news: sound bites garnished with television-flat, impersonal, sanitized images of death whose impact was instantly diluted by bright, cheery follow-up commercials for new cars or fast food. Usually it got no more personal than a half-overheard story at the office of a co-worker who had been mugged or so-and-so's cousin whose car radio had been stolen. It did not intrude on one's personal reality.

In contrast, the essence of *violence* took on a different meaning when one was treading lightly across woven mats soaked with human blood, following a woman who had just been brutally raped, and knowing that only a few yards away several dozen total strangers with whom you could not even communicate waited in hopes of taking your life at the first opportunity. Even the notion of friendship had to be looked at in a different light when your supposedly civilized companions were men who had killed before and were ready at a moment's notice to do so again.

The message conveyed by the mountains and picked up by the rivers and sung by the birds and the bugs and the people was clear to anyone with sense enough to hear it: adapt, or die. Ignore it at your peril. Bohannon had changed a little when he had decided to come looking for Tai Tennison. He had changed some more when he had engaged Sorley McCracken to assist him in that search, and again when he had insisted on continuing on through the high mountains against the expat's explicit wishes. Picking up the two spears marked another small step in his transformation. He stared down at them in amazement. Six years of university, years of negotiating commerce and contracts, and here he was, carrying—spears.

It was a long way from the air-conditioned confines of the Pacific Stock Exchange.

If he survived, he found himself wondering, would any of his friends and acquaintances still be able to recognize Steven Bohannon? Would he? And would he want to?

Outside the Haus Tamburan lay a village whose inhabitants were not far removed from the Stone Age. Among them were a number of old men and women who could, if queried, describe from experience the taste of human flesh. Beyond lay the boundless flood basin of the great Sepik River, populated by species of birds and insects and fish and reptiles many of which had yet to be described and named by science.

What had happened to him since he had landed in Papua New Guinea was not what he had been seeking, but it was more than he had hoped to find.

"Watch out for arrows!" McCracken warned his companions. As if, Bohannon thought wryly, he could dodge them like bean bags or water balloons.

The villagers were still too disorganized and confused by the unexpected turn of events to mount a concerted counterattack. As their former prisoners descended the steps, the warriors huddled within the understory and argued among themselves, trying to decide what to do next. Understandably, the manner of the elder's sudden death as well as that of the Highlander they had befriended made them hesitant.

It was one thing to chance catching a bullet. That was simply a concession to more modern methods of warfare and little different from taking an arrow. It was quite another to have one's chest blown apart. Though unfamiliar with sophisticated firearms, it was obvious that anyone who drew the attention of the big gun stood little chance of surviving.

Why should they risk their lives, several of the more prominent among them argued? One honored village elder was dead already. Was it worth dying for a couple of guns and a few bullets? The woman was special, but she was only a woman. As for the peculiar heavy sacks on the strangers' raft, what of real value could they contain? Food, a few boxes of medicine, some clothing? No, no, it was not worth it.

A number of the younger warriors protested the decision not to contest the strangers' departure. Were they men, or *roc-rocs,* to hide beneath the lily pads? Ultimately, wiser heads prevailed. There is courage in the face of the enemy, they argued, and then there is blind stupidity. Did they not see what the tall stranger's gun had done to old Ruapi? There were women to care for and children to raise. It made no sense to sacrifice themselves blindly for so little potential gain.

As the debate raged, the subjects of the controversy were making their way across the muddy grass toward the raft. Wide-eyed faces peered at them from houses on either side as the terrified women and children of the village huddled together behind matted walls.

Once they were clear of the Haus Tamburan, Stenhammer let Bohannon take his place in the lead. The big man fell behind, the muzzle of his gun tracking slow and steady as a tank cannon from left to right and back again as he watched for any sign of pursuit. There was none. Though the fleeing prisoners could hear them yelling and arguing, the men of the village stayed out of sight beneath the spirit house.

Only when they reached the water did he rejoin them. "Forget the raft." Standing in the shallows, he beckoned with his free hand. "Pass me the backpacks." With a nod, he indicated the largest of the moored dugouts. "We are taking this canoe."

"What?" Bohannon eyed the native craft dubiously. Like the others, it had been hollowed from the trunk of a single tree. The carved crocodile prow was especially ornate. More than twenty feet long, it had a three-foot beam. "Will that hold us *and* the gold?"

The big man kept his attention on the village as he replied. "Us, and the gold, and another six people if it was required. These dugouts are unsinkable, and more stable than they look. This one is rosewood, not cedar. It will be much faster. Quickly, now!"

McCracken looked as if he might want to argue, but whatever unspoken objections he held, he chose not to voice them. As Tai settled herself slowly and carefully into the big dugout, Bohannon and the expat formed a line to pass the heavy backpacks one at a time to Stenhammer, who placed them end to end in the middle of the craft.

When the last one had been transferred from the raft, he holstered the pistol, climbed into the back of the canoe, picked up one of the long pole-paddles, and pushed off, straining against the saturated earth. McCracken and Bohannon grabbed the three-inch wide gunwale and pushed, putting their weight into it, their feet straining at the muck under their shoes as together they bulled the heavily-laden dugout out into deeper water.

Once the boat's bottom was clear of the clinging mud, they climbed in. Unused to so narrow a craft, Bohannon nearly went over the other side but did just manage to steady himself. In front of him, McCracken was standing up and paddling madly.

"Come on, mate! This ain't no place to sit down on the job. There's one more pole. Grab it and paddle."

Gripping the sides of the boat, Bohannon struggled to stand up. The dugout shifted beneath him, rocking from side to side. He looked helplessly at the expat.

"I can't, Sorley. I'll fall out, I know it."

"Well then, do what you can." Refraining from his usual sarcasm, McCracken used his foot to nudge the remaining paddle in his companion's direction.

Bohannon picked it up. Nearly as tall as he was, it was awkward to use from a sitting position. Gripping it tightly just above the flat blade of the paddle, he forced himself to dig at the black water. His shoulders protested violently at the unnatural motion, but he refused to acknowledge the signals of distress shouting from his muscles. If he could not even manage to stand up, the least he could do was help with the paddling.

He found that by scooting his butt back in the damp bottom of the boat until it was pressed up against the first backpack, he could gain a little support from the first sack of gold. The pain in his shoulders did not go away, but it eased. Looking back, he could see Tai trying to do something with her shirt. As she worked with the hem, her breasts hung free.

Behind her, Stenhammer stood straight as one of the limestone pinnacles they had left far behind, high up in the central mountains. His arms rose and fell, rose and fell, as he dug tirelessly and methodically at the flat water. Every couple of minutes he would change his grip and paddle on the opposite side.

The village was receding into the distance. Into the mist, into the past, into memories Bohannon hoped he would one day be able to forget. At any moment he expected to see a fleet of canoes launch from the shallows to chase them down. But there was nothing; no sign of pursuit, no flying arrows, no trailing war cries. He did not blame the warriors. Even without the lethal threat posed by the oversize handgun, he would not have been eager to confront an angry Stenhammer.

He could not stand, and the narrow interior of the dugout was cramped compared to the spacious expanse of the raft, but it was many times faster. In addition, it glided effortlessly between masses of floating island that would have stopped the raft dead. From time to time Stenhammer would bend to check the water for signs of current. Bohannon tried to do the same, but could detect no movement at all.

The big man saw the water differently. Arms throbbing, McCracken had finally been forced to sit and rest, and from his uncomfortable seated position Bohannon could muster no more than a minute or two of paddling at a time before his shoulders began to give out. But Stenhammer pushed them on, resolute and untiring as a machine, driven by an inner strength that seemed more than human.

"We are in luck," he informed them, straightening after checking the water once more. With a hand he pointed slightly to the right of the crocodile prow. "There is flow that way."

Bohannon looked over the side at the dark, flat surface. To his eyes it was as motionless as a pane of smoked glass.

In front of him, up near the bow, McCracken was nodding appreciatively. "Damn lucky." He turned to grin at the American. "With all the rain we had, this here channel could just as easily be flowing upstream, back toward that rotten village." He dipped a hand into the water, pulled it out and shook it dry. "The farther north we go, the stronger the current ought to get, but even big rivers can flow backward here." Tilting his head, he squinted at the hazy sky.

"Just pray it doesn't rain heavy again and raise the water table until we're out of this."

Had Bohannon seen the exhibition dugout in the national museum in Waigani he would have flatly declared one impossible to sleep in. But he was not in Waigani, not spending a day casually touring the capital district's sights in the company of some knowledgeable chauffeur. No soft hotel bed awaited him at day's end, no gourmet supper, no broadcast news on channel six (the only national channel) reassuring him that the rest of the world still existed. Exhaustion is a wonderful soporific, total fatigue the most effective sleeping pill. So completely worn out was he that even his hunger was insufficient to keep him awake.

The sun did not so much set as dissipate within the mist, dissolving like a lemon drop in hot water. Dawdling shards of pink and yellow light abandoned by the vanished sun danced and flew free on the western horizon; carbonated sunshine. From time to time the great white skeletal shape of an egret would pass between the disintegrating sunset and the dugout, interrupting his line of sight and imprinting itself on his retinas like some visiting heavenly specter. It was not a real bird he was seeing, he decided, but a graceful arrangement of dreams dressed in ivory froth and held aloft by the elegiae stanzas of some forgotten Arabian poet.

The last of the sun evaporated, taking with it the last of the light. A slight afterglow lingered, kicked around within the tiny airborne droplets of water that constituted the mist. Eventually they too disappeared, allowing everything—light, mist, savanna and ghost bird—to merge silently with the night.

XXV

Unaware of when or how he had fallen asleep, Bohannon awoke with a start. There was pressure on his lower legs: pressure, and movement. Slowly raising his head from where it had been resting on the nearest mound of gold, he looked down at himself.

The snake's body was less than an inch thick, but it was very long. As he stared, hardly daring to breathe, it slithered wetly across his legs just above the ankles, traveling from the left side of the boat to the right. The head paused, moving ever so slightly back and forth, the wire-like tongue flicking rapidly in and out. For a brief moment of stark terror it looked directly at him, cold blood confronting warm.

Finding nothing to satisfy its curiosity or its hunger, it resumed its exploration. The elegant, flattened skull vanished over the right side of the boat. Like a rope feeding through a pipe, endless feet of snake slid from the water on the left side of the canoe up over and in, and out the other side. Only when the tapering tail crossed his legs and disappeared over the gunwale did Bohannon find he was able to breathe freely again.

It struck him then that despite the darkness he had been able to follow the intruding reptile's movements easily. That was, he realized, because while it was still night out, the darkness was no longer complete. The air was sharp and clear and fresh, and for the first time in days he was able to see more than a few yards in front of him. Tilting back his head, he immediately discovered the reason.

The moon was out, waxing toward fullness. Familiar, friendly, all but beaming down on him personally. He could see the moon.

Utilizing the lumpy backpack for support, he pushed himself up on one elbow, not wanting to disturb his companions. The mist and fog that had plagued them for so long had vanished as if it had never been. In the pale, still twilight he could make out floating islands, individual spears of high grass, isolated outcroppings of solid land knit together by trees and bushes. A few isolated, heavy clouds hung separate and distinct in the torpid sky, adrift like becalmed galleons waiting for a breeze to fill their sails and coax them out of the doldrums. The black shadow of a ghost bird pealed *pee-eep, pee-eep* as it winged its solitary way along a hidden avian sky path toward an unseen nocturnal rendezvous.

McCracken lay on his back in front of him, his hands folded over his chest as if rehearsing his own demise. Intermittent snores belied any hint of death. Turning, Bohannon saw the supple form of Tai. Her head lay on another of the gold-filled backpacks, her face turned away from him, the only color in her hair that which the moon bestowed upon it. Utterly calm and at ease, she lay stretched out full-length in the rough-hewn bottom of the canoe, its high narrow sides cradling the sinuous curves of her body much as the banks of a river constrained its liquid meanderings.

Behind her, beyond her feet and the stained hiking boots that seemed so incongruous a termination to so feminine a form, a ramrod figure stood straight and solid as a mainmast near the stern of the boat. His gaze fixated on the surface ahead, Stenhammer propelled the canoe through the water silently and without apparent effort. With each dip of the pole-oar the paddle blade seemed to melt into the licorice-colored fluid, generating no ripples and producing no sound.

The man was a machine, Bohannon concluded in silent awe. As quickly as he had reached it, he changed his decision. No, not a machine. Machine-like in many ways, but not a machine.

"I guess it wasn't poisonous." He kept his voice to a whisper, not wanting to wake Tai.

Perhaps too much of a whisper. Shadowed eyes lowered to meet his own. "What?"

"The snake." Bohannon glanced meaningfully down at his legs, then back up at the big man.

As always, Stenhammer's expression did not change. The paddle rose and dipped noiselessly. "I think it was an elapid. They are all quite poisonous."

In the moonlight Bohannon's expression crashed. "Then why the hell didn't you do something?"

The big man's shoulders twitched with the most insignificant of shrugs. "What could I have done? If I had tried to reach you with my knife I could have upset the boat. If I had warned you of the danger you probably would have panicked, frightening the snake and provoking an attack. This way neither you nor the snake was harmed."

" 'Nor the snake'? Fuck the goddamn snake!" Bohannon hissed tightly.

Stenhammer's lecturing tone did nothing to improve his companion's disposition. "This is the snake's country, this is the snake's water."

"Yeah, yeah." Bohannon shifted his position. The sackful of nuggets made for an awkward cushion. "I know all that. I just don't much care for snakes."

Down and back, forward and down, the paddle dipped. "They are much misunderstood creatures who have suffered from ten thousand years of bad press. Have some sympathy, Mr. Bohannon. Try to think of them as quadriplegic lizards."

"God, but you're a weird one, Stenhammer. You keep saving my life, for which I'm grateful, but I still think you're weird. In my book anyone who shows more sympathy for snakes than for people is deranged. How'd you get like this? What made you this way?"

The big man took no umbrage at the other's imputation. That voice that never changed, those eyes always focused on something distant and unseen, the mind forever distracted by contemplations unshared: praise the man or damn him, Bohannon mused, it was all the same to him.

"What made me which way, Mr. Bohannon?"

"All right, so don't tell me. Probably wouldn't make any sense anyway." Across the water, a night heron implored from its nest of sticks in a lone tree.

"That would depend on the vantage point from which you viewed any explanation. Yours would be shallow."

"Is that so? Let me tell you some . . ."

"Shush!" Stenhammer nodded at Tai's sleeping form. "You will wake the others. A good sleep is a precious commodity not to be wasted." He paused a moment before adding, "I know, because I enjoy it so rarely."

Bohannon had another retort ready on his lips. Then he remembered the night in the tree house: remembered the other man's agonized moans and turbulent tossing and turning. That had been only days ago—or was it weeks? In the endless landscape of tree and savanna, mountain and swampland, time became an imprecise thing, days and nights merging seamlessly and without definition into one another, like honey into tea. Memory wilted in the heat, while the mind simmered with a perceived reality that was often composed only of reflections of what really was.

He had accused Stenhammer of a lack of sympathy, yet here was a man whose own sleep was tormented by unknown demons. Just when Bohannon thought he had the big man half figured out, Stenhammer went and said something that kept him off balance. Bohannon felt it could not be deliberate, but the timing was uncanny.

Lying there against the backpack, he stared at the emotionless, relentless paddler and tried to penetrate the wall the man had erected around himself. Stenhammer ignored him—or rather, did not react to the scrutiny. After awhile, Bohannon gave up. Easier to penetrate the lead shielding around the core of a nuclear reactor than to puzzle out another man's character, he decided. Stenhammer's motivations must remain forever his own. The big man was keeping them alive, and Bohannon knew that should be enough to satisfy him. But somehow it was not.

Why did he care? Why did he give a damn? With luck they would make it to the Sepik and hire transportation back to civilization, after which they would go their separate ways and he would never see the morose, lumbering enigma ever again. Why was it suddenly so important to know Stenhammer, as opposed to simply knowing of him? Lying there, surrounded by gold and wood and water and moonlight, he came to a conclusion that was really no mystery. It had only a little to do with the big man, and much more to do with himself.

Fuck it, he told himself angrily. That's why you've been traveling. You came here to put that sort of thing behind you, not find more of it in someone else. Whatever had happened to make Ragnarok Stenhammer the way he was was Ragnarok Stenhammer's business and no one else's. Certainly not Steven Bohannon's.

Turning onto his back, he found that he was able to descry the distant stars more sharply and clearly than his much nearer self. In the vicinity of the mirror-bright moon they were overwhelmed, but elsewhere they sparkled in hitherto unseen profusion. Cleansed of mist and fog, the night air was utterly still and transparent. Outlines shouted with definition, sounds echoed with unaccustomed lucidity, and every smell was richer and more pungent than usual: the perfume that was Tai, the rankness of McCracken's boots, the thick, penetrating damp of the rosewood canoe, the all-pervasive effulgence of damp vegetation—each odor was distinct and in its own way, rejuvenating.

Half asleep, he felt wholly awake. Suspended between the ever-present possibility of death and an uncertain future, he saw himself frozen in a moment of primeval, ethereal beauty. Moon, stars, black glass water and sorrowfully serenading birds, the occasional rickety outburst of frogs telegraphing to one another, the rich bouquet of smells: all combined to put him at ease. He was floating through one of Nature's forgotten masterpieces, the savanna a low-lying verdant Venice, with Stenhammer his own personal gondolier.

Putting his hands behind his head, he closed his eyes, opened his ears, and inhaled deeply. Tomorrow death and discomfort and disease might again come calling, but for the rest of the night, at least, he had the opportunity to be more a part of the real world than any of his citified, suburbanized, career-obsessed friends had ever dreamed of being.

Paradise is full of thorns, but for those who do not panic and run blindly it is possible to find the interstices between.

Morning returned heat and humidity with a vengeance, but the occupants of the dugout did not mind. It was not raining, they could see where they were going, there was still no sign of pursuit, and the canoe was making much better time than the awkward, abandoned raft.

Tai's invaluable little purifier continued to provide them with a steady supply of clear drinking water, but the presence of so much rotting foliage and other large organic particles in the water necessitated an intermediate step between scooping it out of the swamp and final purification. This was accomplished by first filtering the water through McCracken's hat and then gathering what came through into the purifier.

Food was, as always, their biggest concern, but now it was more one of palatability than abundance. Utilizing one of the two weapons Bohannon had taken from the Haus Tamburan, Stenhammer speared one fish after another, but in the absence of dry kindling they could not build a fire. The cured and hardened bottom of the dugout would have supported one without burning through, but the endless fields of grasses and sedges offered nothing in the way of combustible material.

So they ate their fish raw, expertly skinned and filleted by McCracken. None of them got sick, which did not surprise Bohannon. By this time he felt that his own stomach was lined with so much ingested wood, fish bone, and insect chitin that it must be impervious to all but the most ferocious gastrointestinal invaders.

By the morning of the next day they found themselves traveling between flanking ramparts of impenetrable *pit-pit.* Strips of the wild sugarcane made a welcome addition to their diet.

Sitting in the bow and taking his turn with the paddle, Bohannon looked toward the back of the canoe. Tai and McCracken were facing each other over the backpacks, chatting and laughing softly. Refusing to rest, Stenhammer continued to man the stern.

"When are we likely to find our way out of the savanna?" Bohannon called back to their helmsman.

Stenhammer's pole rose and fell. "Look around you, Mr. Bohannon. We have been out of it all morning. The *pit-pit* is proof. We are back on a river."

Bohannon twisted around. He could see no bank on either side and the water beneath the crocodile prow seemed as motionless as ever. "How can you be sure? We've seen *pit-pit* in the savanna."

"Yes, but not in high, parallel rows like this. Notice the presence of larger trees where the *pit-pit* has not killed them off. Also, the current here is stronger and the aquatic life different."

Frustrated by his inability to detect any difference in their surroundings, Bohannon studied the water. He could see nothing beneath the dark surface, nor could he detect movement of any kind. But he was not about to dispute Stenhammer.

"All right, so we're on a river again. Which river?"

The big man inspected the walls of wild sugar cane. "Impossible to tell. I am sure we are too far west to be on the Karawari. It could be the Salumei, or the Korosameri, but I think it more likely to be one of the tributaries of the Blackwater. If so, then we should hit the lower Korosameri soon. There is a village, Mameri, where we might be able to hire a power canoe to take us down to Timbunke. That is, if we have not passed downstream of it already."

"What if we have?"

"Then we will just keep going. Mindimbit is a larger village on a tributary of the Sepik. The people there are visited regularly by outsiders and will be able to provide us with food and shelter until transportation becomes available."

"Sounds good to me." The inside of his mouth throbbed at the remembrance of meals past. "Right now I'd give five bucks for a sago pancake. And another five for a teaspoon of maple syrup to dribble on top—even the fake kind."

Having overheard, Tai looked up at him and smiled. "With a fried grub in the middle?"

He grinned back. "No can handle the extra calories. I have to watch my girlish figure." How much weight *had* he lost these past days, he wondered? Keeping his pants from falling down had become a daily chore. As he prepared to resume paddling, a dragonfly landed on the tip of his pole. It had three-inch wings of stained glass—iridescent purple highlights alternating with perfectly transparent membrane. Slowly, he extended a finger in its direction. It rose from the wood, helicoptered for a few seconds, and then settled obligingly on his finger. Its tiny, clawed feet tickled.

"See if he can bring over some of his friends," Stenhammer called from the back of the boat. "They eat the mossies."

In truth, mosquitoes had bothered but not plagued them since they had left the savanna behind and entered the river. "You don't know how lucky you are, mate," McCracken had told him when he had commented on the dearth of blood-sucking insects. "In the Wet, they'll cover you like a blanket and drain you dry."

"Sorley's right." Twisting around to look over at him, Tai revealed more of herself than she might have intended. He stared, and she stayed. On a small wet boat there is little room for modesty. "Myself, I worry more about the biting flies."

"Because they bite harder?"

"No. Because some of them carry a variety of diseases that haven't been studied yet. You can get malaria from a mosquito, or dengue fever, but some of these flies are full of bugs the scientists haven't even named. That's scary."

"Yeah, it is." Seemingly innocuous flying black specks suddenly took on new meaning. Not that there was much any of them could do about it. They had no repellent with them and precious little covering.

Large forest trees began to appear, the spaces between them soon filling in with smaller, light-loving growth. Green packed tight against green as tree warred with bush, vine with epiphyte, and the omnipresent *pit-pit* finally surrendered its domination of the riverbanks to the jungle. The land on both sides of the river soon came to resemble the terrain they had crossed at the base of the foothills, only with bigger trees and even denser vegetation. Forest voices called boldly to one another in the verdant depths.

Stenhammer squinted at the sky, then pointed ahead and to the left. "I see a place where the bank has been broken down. Probably by crocs using it to sun themselves. A good place to pull in." Using his paddle like a rudder, he started to turn the boat.

Bohannon blinked. The sun was high and bright in a clear sky. "What for? It's still early." He gestured at the river. "We can still cover some ground."

"Not on empty stomachs. I thought it might be nice to have something to eat besides raw fish and lily bulbs."

The dugout turned and Bohannon continued to paddle as he spoke. "Like what, for instance?"

The big man studied the tree line. "Possum is quite good. A tree kangaroo would be better. If I can catch one asleep, we will have real meat again."

Bohannon gestured at the other man's waist. "Think you can hit one with that cannon?"

Stenhammer replied dryly. "I am sure I could, but it would be counterproductive. One of these rounds would scatter fragments of possum all over the forest. I will use the spears you took from the spirit house."

Bohannon didn't see how anyone could hit a possum in a tree with one of the tapered, barbed shafts, but after making the stupid remark about using the pistol he wasn't about to comment further. If Stenhammer said he could kill a possum with a spear, who was Bohannon to dispute him?

The heavy dugout made an earthy crunching sound as it grounded on the muddy bank. Once everyone had disembarked, splashing through the dark water and onto dry land, Stenhammer pulled the boat up onto a stranded log so it would not drift away. Then he picked up the two spears in one sun-browned fist and turned to examine the solid wall of dense rainforest that backed up against the small slice of exposed shore where they had landed.

"How are you going to get through that?" Studying the luxuriant barrier, Bohannon could not see a place where an energetic dog might fashion an entrance.

"Once you get a little ways off the river it opens up quite a bit. Under the canopy where the big trees block out much of the sunlight the growth is less chaotic." Stenhammer started forward. "The rest of you try and get some rest. Mr. McCracken, you might consider laying the foundation for a fire."

"Aye, sir, aye Captain. Whatever you say, sir. Your order is me command."

Looking back at the expat, Stenhammer frowned. "Is there something troubling you, Mr. McCracken?"

"What, me? Why, nothing troubles me, mate. Good old jolly Sorley, the soul of good humor, that's me. Just having a bit of a giggle at your expense."

The big man held the speculative stare a moment longer, then nodded once. "Right. Of course, if you would rather have your kangaroo tail raw . . ."

"Oy, I'll build the damn fire." Unsure exactly what was happening in front of him but not wanting it to escalate, Bohannon stepped between them. "Just make sure I'm not wasting my time," the expat told Stenhammer, looking past the American. "Go kill something."

Stenhammer nodded again, then pivoted on his heel and started toward the outer wall of bushes. Darting forward, Tai cut him off and put a hand on one arm to draw his face down to her level. She whispered something in his ear, then stood on tiptoes to kiss him soundly on the cheek. Straightening, he smiled slightly, murmured a reply, and turned away. In seconds, he had vanished from sight.

There was sufficient canopy to shade fallen branches and broken twigs not only from the unrelenting sun but from rain as well. Such places were not common, but there were enough of them to supply Bohannon with an armful of comparatively dry wood. Cradling this bounty of kindling against his chest with both arms, he started back toward the landing.

He was nearly there when the sound of agitated voices reached him through the brush. Tai and McCracken were arguing loudly. Or as the expats would have put it, having a row, he thought with a smile. The smile faded as he drew nearer. Whatever they were fighting about was clearly no source of amusement. He quickened his pace.

So absorbed were they in their acrimonious exchange that neither of them noticed him emerge from the forest. Watching and listening absorbedly without drawing attention to himself, he knelt and quietly set his armful of firewood on the ground. McCracken's voice was the louder of the two, grating and uneven, at once accusatory and despairing.

". . . and why him? Why is it always him? Why is *he* the one who gets the bloody kisses and affectionate pats on the arm and dewy-eyed smiles, and me who gets the formal, polite, tea-cozy thank-yous?" The expat was raging back and forth in front of her, arms waving and thrusting to emphasize his points, his face a mask lifted whole from a last-act tragedy by Aeschylus.

Throughout his anguished frenzy, Tai's expression remained one of stunned disbelief. "Sorley, I never imagined—you never said anything."

He halted abruptly in front of her and his voice fell slightly. "What the Devil was I supposed to say? Tai Tennison, I want you? Tai Tennison, I worship the ground beneath your feet? Tai, I love you, I will always love you, and I've been bloody well in love with you ever since the first moment I clapped eyes on you?"

Clearly taken aback, she had no idea how to respond. "I—I don't know, Sorely. But you should have said *something*."

" 'Said something'? Something, what?" Whirling, he cast a stricken gaze on the silently watching Bohannon. "You tell me then, mate. What the hell was I supposed to say?"

"Sorley, I . . ." The agitated expat did not really want to hear his response, did not want another intruding on the discussion. Turning back to Tai, he rambled on without waiting for the other man's reply.

"Couldn't you tell that I wanted you? These past couple of years that we've known each other, the times that our paths have crossed, couldn't you *see*?"

"See what?" she replied coolly. "Every man wants me."

"*No!* No, no, no, goddamn it, that's not what I mean, and you know it!" Unbelievably, tears began to run down the expat's cheeks. Real tears, something so out of keeping with and so alien to McCracken's personality that Bohannon had to look several times to make sure that what he was seeing was not just an excess of sweat.

"All those times I 'accidentally' bumped into you—not only in Lae, but in Madang, in Goroka, in Mosby, didn't you ever think to count up the number of 'coincidences'? The number of times I was there to offer you help, even if you didn't need it? How I always managed to show up with money or transportation when you were a little short? What about the number of times I turned up at your place, what about that?"

"I thought—I thought it was Rose you were serious about," she stammered. "Rose thought so, too."

"Rose—Rose is a sweet darling. Sure I like her. Who wouldn't? Sure I sweet-spoke to her. But it was to get closer to you, Tai. It was always you." His anger had given way to abject pleading. "Come with me."

"Come with you?" Bohannon was not sure he had heard correctly. "Come with you where?" What part of the conversation had he missed?

They ignored him. "I won't do this, Sorley. Even if I felt about you the way you say you feel about me, I wouldn't do it. Never mind that it isn't right. It wouldn't be fair to Rags."

McCracken exploded. "*Fuck him!* Fuck that snotty stone-faced know-it-all Viking arsehole! How can you think of staying with him? The bastard never smiles, never laughs, never has a joke to share with his mates."

"Maybe he has reason to be that way," she replied softly.

"He's a walking dead man, a freaking zombie! I'll bet he wears the same expression when he screws. *If* he knows how to screw," he snorted derisively.

Tai looked him straight in the eye. "He does."

For a long, terrible moment McCracken just stared. Just stood there without moving looking back at her, eyes unblinking, thin sunburnt lips slightly parted. Then he unleashed a torrent of the wildest, harshest laughter anyone was likely to overhear anywhere outside the confines of a madhouse. It was pure distilled pain, well leavened with irony.

"*I saved your fucking aimless, wonderful life!*" McCracken held both hands out in front of him, the fingers curling like claws toward his chest. "*I'm* the one who saved your ass from that homicidal highland prick. Not him, *me*. Me, me, me! Why do you want to stay with him? Just tell me. Explain it to me. Is that too much to ask? Is it?" Feral-eyed, he looked back at Bohannon, who remained frozen to the spot where he had put down the firewood. "You tell me, mate—is that too much to ask?"

Tai spared the other man the necessity of having to formulate a reply. "I don't know for sure why I stay with him, Sorley. I don't even know for sure why I'm attracted to him. Maybe it's the independence. I've never met a man so indifferent to the rest of the world or its opinion of him. Or maybe it's because he's in pain, and in need."

"In pain?" The extent of McCracken's disbelief was something to behold. "In need? What the fuck do you think I'm going through?"

"I see that now, Sorley, and I'm sorry. For any misunderstanding between us, and for anything you may have felt, now or in the past. But it's a choice I've made, and it's one I'm sticking with."

"Are you in love with him?" It was clearly all the expat could do to choke out the words.

"No. It's not love. Not the kind of love you're thinking about, anyway. It's something that's hard to explain. He needs me, and I need someone like him to need me. It may not be love, but it's a bond. A bond I can't break. A bond I don't think I want to break." Raising a conciliatory hand, she took a step toward him. "I'm sorry."

He swatted sharply at her extended fingers and she flinched. "I don't want your goddamn pity! I'd give you anything, Tai. My plane, my share of the gold, the blood in my veins. What can he give you?"

She shook her head sorrowfully, regretful but resolute. "He gives me what I need. Whatever that is. However you want to define it."

"Well then, may you both be happy as a pair of baconers in clover waiting for the killing knife, and the Devil take you both!" Bohannon jumped slightly as the other man turned on him. "Get the boat, mate, and let's high it out of here."

"I don't follow you, Sorley." Bohannon indicated the wall of jungle. "We can't leave yet. Stenhammer's not back."

"That's exactly why we're going. Think about it, man! We leave now and it's a million and a quarter apiece instead of the stinking two hundred thousand he's so graciously allowing us." Smirking sarcastically, he turned back to Tai. "I'll hold onto a meri's share for you, in case you change your mind when you get out of here. Don't worry about trying to find me. I'll contact you when I'm sure he isn't around."

"He'll always be around. If you do this he'll find you, Sorley. He'll find you no matter where you go."

"You think so, you think so?" The expat was teetering on the edge of, if not sanity, then rationality. "Horseshit! You'll never get him out of those freaking mountains. He may not love you, but he sure as shit loves them! I've seen it in his face, in his eyes. You can't win him away from that, Tai. Not even you. I've seen that look before, in other blokes too far gone to know what's bloody happened to them." This time it was he who extended a hand. "Don't throw your life away on some stupid great sod who's too lunatic to appreciate you. Come with us. Come with *me*."

Deliberately, she took a step backward. "No, Sorley. Like I said, even if I felt differently about him, I wouldn't do something like this. If not for him there wouldn't be any gold. It belongs to him before it belongs to any of us."

"Is that a fact?" A sinister giggle crawled up from the depths of the expat's throat to emerge from his mouth, as if he'd swallowed a particularly nasty species of nematode he was only now regurgitating. "Possession bein' the proverbial nine-tenths, right now I'd say it's mine." Licking nervous lips as he watched the forest wall, he shot an anxious glance at his other companion.

"Get the canoe off the log, mate. A million and a quarter. Think about it!"

"I have." Striding purposefully toward the water, Bohannon put both hands under the crocodile-head prow of the dugout. Using his legs and back in tandem, he lifted and pushed simultaneously. The muddy ground offered little in the way of purchase for his filthy sneakers, but despite the treacherous footing he succeeded in getting the heavily laden craft off the log and back out into the water.

Shocked but not surprised, Tai started toward him. "Steve, no! This isn't right!"

"Right?" McCracken blocked her path to keep her from interfering. "What's 'right,' luv? Maybe this is one time right gets left." He chuckled humorlessly at his own vapid witticism. "Change your mind?"

She stopped trying to go around him. "No. Especially not now."

"Go ahead and glare! You think you can hurt me any more than you have already? I'd rather you hated me. It's better this way. At least hate acknowledges my existence. Anything's better than your goddamned fucking indifference."

It was then that he became aware that Bohannon, having raised the bow of the dugout off the log, was continuing to push it stern first out into the river long after the hull had been freed.

"Mate, what the bloody fuck are you doing?" Abandoning the woman he wanted more than the gold, but who had spurned him, he sprinted for the water.

The river bottom fell away beneath Bohannon's feet. Giving the dugout one last powerful shove, he turned back toward shore. Behind him, the canoe began to pick up speed as the swifter current out in the middle of the waterway took hold of the buoyant, unoccupied shape.

Lifting his legs high, McCracken plowed into the water. Bohannon tried to dodge but the expat was too fast for him. He tried to block the punch and partially succeeded, but the glancing blow still left him dizzied and stunned. A spidery, powerful hand closed around his throat, forcing his head below the surface. In the distance he could hear Tai screaming. She seemed to be drifting further and further away, her voice receding along with the daylight. Water and darkness closed in above him.

Then he was breaking the surface, flailing weakly with both arms, making Halloweenish gasping noises as his starving lungs sought to breathe in twice their normal volume. When he tried to stand, he lost control in the slick mud and fell backward with a violent splash.

Strong hands grabbed him beneath the arms. With Tai's help he managed to stagger out of the water and collapse on the bank, choking and spitting up water and bits of organic debris.

She helped him roll onto his back, but he refused to lie still. "Sorley . . . he . . ."

"It doesn't matter," she told him. "We'll find him, and the gold. Or Ragnarok will. But it doesn't matter. The gold was never worth anyone's life to me—including mine." Her smile was a shaky blessing. "Looks like I owe you all over again."

"Where is he—where is the tricky, scheming bastard?" He fought to sit up.

She turned and pointed.

McCracken was swimming like a madman for the dugout, which continued to pick up speed. Bereft of its human cargo, it slid across the water like a leaf. But the expat's determination was fueled by the anger and madness that burned within him. Overtaking the canoe, they saw him reach for the stern with one hand. His first grab missed, but the second latched securely onto the low stern. He hung there for several minutes, catching his breath, before starting to pull himself up and in.

The attack came suddenly, in dead silence, and without any warning. All the expat's frantic kicking and splashing as he'd chased down the dugout had scared away any fish and turtles and salamanders in the vicinity, but that which frightened the majority of the tributary's inhabitants only served to pique the interest of its largest denizen.

The jaws alone were four feet long, the yellow-stained teeth five inches and more. Jaws and teeth were all they saw of the croc. Doubtless McCracken had a better view, because he screamed like a trapped hare as they snapped shut on his midsection. No industrial vise locked so tightly or with such an unyielding grip. Dragged downward by more than a ton of relentless reptiles, he disappeared in a flash. The last they saw of him were his hands, flailing desperately above the surface, calling for the help that would never come.

Heavy with gold, the dugout continued on its way downstream. It went around a bend and, less violently but just as absolutely as McCracken, vanished from sight.

XXVI

"I was convinced from the first that he was reckless. It showed in the way he carried himself, in his manner of speaking, in how his eyes moved. Small, sharp, and hunted they were. But I did not believe he would try anything like this. And he thought I was the crazy one."

Having rejoined them, the furry brown mass of a dead tree-kangaroo slung across his broad shoulders, Stenhammer stood at the water's edge and stared downstream as he listened to the tale being told by those he had left behind. When Tai had finished, he dumped his wooly burden on the ground.

"This will not be good raw. We will do better to stick with fish, nuts, and fruit."

In the eternal heat Bohannon was nearly dry. Or rather, less wet, as perspiration replaced the river water his clothing had absorbed. "Sorley had the lighter and I, for one, ain't going after it."

"I don't think any of us are." Tai looked to the big man. "What now, Rags? Rubbing sticks together, if we can find a couple that are dry enough?"

He was studying the flat, tepid surface of the silent stream. "There is not a river in the Sepik basin that flows in a straight line for more than a hundred meters. Soon this one will bend. Then it will twist. It may even turn back on itself. There will be rocks on the bottom, swept down from the mountains and carried seaward by the Wet, that will divert the main current toward shore. Snags that will catch anything floating downstream. Drifting logs that push and trap one another against both banks." He eyed his companions.

"We had better get moving while there is still enough daylight to show the way. With any luck, the dugout will fetch up on shore somewhere not far from here."

"With any luck," Bohannon groused as they started off into the trees.

Stenhammer was right: it was easier going inland than along the river. But "easier" was a relative term, in the sense that the torments of the First Circle of Hell were less hellish than the Second. It was possible to make progress without the use of a bush knife. This was fortunate, since they did not have one and Stenhammer could only do so much with the big belt knife he carried.

From time to time he would leave them to plunge into the seemingly impenetrable tangle of vegetation off to their right. Having checked the river, he would return, shaking his head, and they would push on.

It was Bohannon who spotted the snake, lying stretched out at the base of a log. Both of his companions identified it as a Death Adder.

"It's sleeping," Tai told him as they gave the log a wide berth. "Nocturnal. Second most dangerous snake in PNG."

"What's the worst? No, don't tell me. Whatever it is it's probably the most dangerous in the world, right?"

Though exhausted and filthy, she responded with a gentle smile. He must look at least as bad, he knew, but by now he hardly noticed the omnipresent film of perspiration that coated his skin like sodden cellophane. After days and days of nonstop sweating he'd grown used to the condition, if not comfortable with it. It was as if he was wearing an extremely thin, continuously-wet set of long underwear that he was unable to take off.

"The one you don't want to meet is the taipan." She pushed through a curtain of green vines. "Seven or eight milligrams of its neurotoxin is enough to kill in a couple of hours, and a mature one can deliver ten times that amount with one bite. The poison interferes with the body's nerve endings. Taipans are monocolored, usually a pale lavender, with red-orange eyes. A big one can reach five meters. But don't worry—they're shy. On the other hand, if you corner one, you'd better get clear. When confronted, they're aggressive as hell."

During such conversations, Bohannon found that fallen branches and sinuous tree roots tended to take on deeper meaning. In his strained, overstressed brain, the inanimate acquired movement, and that which was normally motionless tended to quiver and tremble, if only in the recesses of his overheated mind.

"I'll keep an eye out."

"No need. Not for the taipan, anyway. They're pretty much grassland residents It would be unusual to find one in the mountains, or down here in the Sepik."

"Why didn't you tell me that in the first place?"

She looked back over a shoulder and grinned. "You didn't ask me that in the first place."

Maybe he spent too much time staring at the ground, especially after spotting the Death Adder. Or maybe he was just tired, or was wiping sweat from his eyes when it happened. The sharp pain in his shoulder and arm brought him up short.

Looking down at himself, he saw where the vine clung to his arm. Instead of being smooth and cord-like like the majority of vines they had encountered, this one was flat, brown, and slightly concave. Both edges were serrated like a knife. When he tried to move away, the barbs dug deeper into his clothing and skin.

"Hey!" At his urgent call, his companions halted and looked back.

"What is the trouble, Mr. Bohannon?" Out in front, Stenhammer had to lean to one side to peer back through the brush.

The American pointed at his entrapped arm. "This damn tree grabbed me."

Retracing her steps, Tai had a look at him. "Lawyer's cane. Latches hold and doesn't let go." She threw Stenhammer a glance. "I'll get him out."

The big man nodded. "While you are helping him I will make another check of the river." Lowering his head, he pushed off to the right.

Tai evaluated her companion's situation, taking care not to make contact with the vines that dangled threateningly all around him. Picking her path, she advanced toward him and very gently took hold of the vine that was fastened to his arm.

"I'm going to hold onto this. If I try to pull it loose it will only wrap tighter around you. There are two more hanging just behind you and to your right, so be careful where you step. You have to back out of this stuff. You can't go forward. Try doing so and you'll cut yourself to ribbons."

He nodded. Keeping her instructions in mind, he commenced a slow, measured retreat. The serrated edges of the vine tore at his skin and he gritted his teeth against the pain, but in a couple of moments he was clear. Once he was safe, she let go of the vine and stepped back.

"Nasty stuff." Together, they examined his right arm. The wounds were painful, but not deep. "Wish we had some peroxide, or even rubbing alcohol. Dettol would be best." She smiled reassuringly. "Purified water will have to do until we get out of here. I know it sounds impossible, but do your best to keep the cuts covered. Otherwise they'll start to turn septic."

Salty sweat stung the multiple tiny gashes. He was almost too tired to feel the pain. It had been hot in the canoe, but at least when they had been floating downstream there had been some semblance of a breeze. The heat on shore was brutal. Here, in the depths of the jungle itself, it was like hiking through a gigantic sauna, where the temperature never dropped and the humidity was always set on maximum. No wonder most of the forest's inhabitants slept during the day and moved about only after dark, leaving the sweltering daylight to those birds and insects that could tolerate it.

When the big man finally rejoined them his expression was unchanged, but there was a new spring in his step. Anyone else would have whooped with joy, or at least smiled. Not Stenhammer. Triumph or tragedy, it seemed all the same to him.

His companions were not so restrained. They shouted and hugged each other when he announced that he had found the boat.

"Sorry." Seeing the look on Bohannon's face, Tai pulled back. In the exhilaration of the moment she had forgotten about the cane cuts and had wrapped both arms around him.

"Never mind." Using the back of one forearm, he wiped sweat from his mouth so he could smile without drinking in the salty fluid. "At least we'll get out of this muck. No more lawyer's cane."

"And no more snakes," she added gaily. He decided against telling her about the one back in the savanna that had crawled into the canoe and across his legs.

Stenhammer led the way through the wall of snarled vegetation that lined the river. When they finally emerged into the sunlight they found themselves standing on the edge not of a gentle slope but a high, steep bank a good four feet above the water.

Bohannon's gaze flicked upstream, then down. There was no sign of the dugout. It would be just like the big man to announce impassively that he had found the canoe, then neglect to add that it was ten feet underwater. But that couldn't be right, Bohannon told himself. The native dugouts were solid wood. They could roll, but not sink.

"Where is it?"

Stenhammer raised an arm and pointed. "Over there."

Following the line of his arm, his companions finally located the perambulating watercraft. It had fetched up near the dry mouth of a tiny tributary stream, caught between the notch the feeder creek had cut in the opposite bank and a pair of small trees growing out of the shallows. Flowing water generated glassy ripples that surged against the side of the craft that faced the current. Fat and full of promised riches, all five backpacks were clearly visible in the middle of the canoe. Elegantly ignorant of the cash value of its perch, a pied kingfisher sat atop the biggest pack, watching for minnows.

Wordlessly, Stenhammer unbuckled his belt and placed it on the ground, taking care to keep holster and the gun clear of the damp soil. Straightening, he began to remove his boots and socks. There was no need to question his intent: it was defined by his actions. As far as Bohannon was concerned, however, the other man's sanity had once more been thrown open to discussion.

"You're not going to do what I think you're going to do—are you? Have you forgotten what happened to McCracken?"

"No, I have not forgotten."

"Then what the hell do you think you're doing?"

The big man carefully draped a sock over each boot. The original color of the cotton had long since vanished beneath an impenetrably opaque coating of grime. "I am going to get the canoe." His eyes met those of the disbeliever. "McCracken did a lot of thrashing about when he was in the water, made a lot of noise. I will be quiet."

"You really think that will make a difference?"

"What would you suggest, Mr. Bohannon? That the three of us stand here and shout 'Here, boat, here boat!' until we get a reaction?" Turning, he walked barefoot to the edge of the high bank.

Equally stunned by the big man's intentions and the fact that he might actually have made a joke, Bohannon found himself unable to reply. He could only stare as Stenhammer turned his back to the river and stepped over the edge of the embankment, trying to lower himself as slowly and as quietly as possible. His feet dislodged chunks of dirt, but when he finally entered the water it was with nary a ripple.

Settling on a slow breast stroke as the quietest means of propelling himself, he started across, his head and neck never dipping below the surface. He looked neither to right nor left, but kept his attention focused always on the dugout that waited so temptingly on the far side.

"Why doesn't he look around?" Bohannon found himself whispering without being conscious of it.

Tai was similarly subdued and equally tense. "If—if he's hit, it will be from below. As dark as the water is here, he wouldn't see anything until it was directly under him, anyway. So he's not wasting time looking for what he can't see."

Bohannon slowly shook his head as he expressed his admiration. "I couldn't do that. Even if I couldn't see a damn thing I'd still be looking around all the time."

"So would I. But Rags has the ability to focus, to concentrate on one thing and shut out the rest of the world completely. I've seen him do it before." She spoke without turning, without taking her eyes off the slowly swimming figure.

"Christ, he's taking his time!" Bohannon found himself searching the flat water for any sign of movement. His eyes widened and he pointed. "What's that?"

Tai's gaze jerked upstream, but only for a second. Her tone did not change. "Log. Look for ripples at the back, where a tail would be moving from side to side."

Bohannon nodded apprehensively, continuing to divide his attention between the shrinking shape of the swimming man and the vast expanse of threatening water. It must demand incredible self control, he knew, for Stenhammer to swim at half speed instead of kicking all out for the canoe. But the big man knew it was more important to minimize disturbance than to make speed. If he did not draw the crocs' attention, he would not have to try and outswim them.

Impossible as it seemed, Bohannon found himself sweating even more than usual. Something touched his left hand. Glancing down, he saw Tai's fingers fumbling for his own. He let them slide together, and squeezed. She squeezed back.

Stenhammer was ten yards from the dugout. Then he was five, then one. Tai waved as the big man finally boosted himself up and into the hollowed-out rosewood log, water cascading from his broad shoulders, his long hair trailing like yellow seaweed down the back of his head. Disturbed, the kingfisher delivered itself of an opinion before transferring its attention from the top of the backpack to a nearby low-hanging branch. The burst of iridescent blue sat there, watching.

Standing erect, Stenhammer picked up one of the pole-paddles and used it to push the rear of the canoe away from the notch in the bank. As it floated out into the river, the current caught it and turned it around, freeing the prow from the grasp of the two small trees. The current was not strong enough to prohibit him from paddling across to where his relieved companions waited.

The carved crocodile head rammed into the soft earth of the riverbank, helping to hold the canoe in place. Tai boarded first, mimicking Stenhammer's earlier descent, sliding down the wall of red earth until her feet contacted the boat. Dropping to hands and knees, she crawled backwards until she reached its center.

Lying flat on his chest and belly on the edge of the riverbank, Bohannon handed down the big man's footgear and then the heavy leather belt, with pistol and knife attached. He waited while Stenhammer slipped back into his socks and boots and Tai settled herself against the packs. Then he turned and started down, facing the embankment as he descended.

Dirt stung his eyes and spilled into his mouth as he tried to dig fingers and toes into the soft bank. His efforts slowed his descent so he did not fall, but he was relieved when he finally felt solid wood beneath his questing right foot. While the big man held the dugout steady, his paddle jammed into the river bottom, Bohannon backed cautiously into the craft. He started to sit down, then abruptly changed his mind. If Stenhammer could paddle standing up, then by God, so could he.

Shaky and unsteady, but determined, he straightened, holding his hands out to his sides for balance. The primitive dugout was remarkably stable. Either that, or else he was becoming used to its eccentricities. Bending, he picked up one of the poles and proceeded to push off against the bank. He nearly fell as the prow broke free of the dirt and they drifted backwards. Nearly, but not quite. As pleased with himself as if he had just mastered the flight controls of an F-22, he dipped the paddle into the water and began pushing river.

Emotionally exhausted, Tai had stretched out in the bottom of the boat, her head propped against a convenient sack of gold. Stenhammer did not compliment Bohannon's efforts, but the American thought he could detect a hint of approval in the other man's expression. Why the opinion of a madman should matter to him Bohannon did not know. He knew only that it did.

"We ought to have reached Mameri by now." Stenhammer peered

past him, studying the river ahead. "That means we've probably passed it. We will have to try for Mindimbit. No matter. That is the place where we are most likely to find transportation anyway."

Paying attention to his paddling, and on maintaining his balance, Bohannon replied without turning. "Hey, I'm just glad to be back on the river. Not to put too fine a point on it, but jungle sucks. When the moon is up, the snakes are on the prowl, and when the snakes sleep, the trees go after you. Give me crocs anytime."

"I wish I *could* give you one." There was a touch of yearning in the big man's voice. "I wish I could give one to all of us. Of all the creatures in these forests, croc is the best eating. I would take grilled crocodile tail over the biggest steak in Mosby."

"Well then, why don't you hop in and splash around until one comes over to investigate? Then you could shoot it."

"It is not that simple, Mr. Bohannon. If we could catch one asleep on the bank, that would be a possibility. But they have been hunted here for thousands of years, and are wary. The closer we get to civilization, the more cautious they become. As for shooting one while it is in the water, that would only draw every croc in the vicinity to the feast."

Bohannon considered. "You could kill it with your knife."

"It would have to be a very small croc. Once they grow longer than four feet they become difficult to handle. Especially in their element, which is the water." Blue eyes met his. "I don't know what you think of me, Mr. Bohannon, but I am only human. I have my limits."

Could've fooled me so far, Bohannon decided. He knew that back in the States, in the South, people ate alligator tail all the time, and raved about it. But it seemed he would have to wait a while longer yet for the opportunity to sample that particular gourmet treat.

"How much farther?" Ahead, the river twisted to the right. Once around that bend, he surmised, it would curve back to the left. As he now knew, none of the streams in the basin of the Sepik ever ran straight. It was a hydrological condition that layered frustration atop their exhaustion.

They had endured landslide, snakes, bugs, disease, suspect water and bad food, a crazed companion and hostile locals. He decided that he could handle a little boredom. In his newly callused hands the paddle rose and dipped methodically. He was tired, hungry, sweat-soaked, and sore. The cane cuts on his arm stung like lemon juice on an open wound. He felt more alive than he ever had in his life.

They camped for the night on the bank of a small tributary, a stagnant brook that was wide and deep enough to allow them to paddle inland several yards from the main river. Not only did this remove the dugout from the grip of the current, but unlike the steep banks of the river, the tributary afforded easy access to the land. The branches of trees growing on opposite sides of the lazy stream met overhead, blocking out much of the direct sunlight and giving the creek the look of a shady cloister in an emerald cathedral.

Using their paddles, they swept an area ten feet square clear of fallen leaves, twigs, and other forest litter. In so doing, they also cleansed it, however imperfectly, of the irritating ants that utilized the litter for cover and forage. While Bohannon continued sweeping and Tai secured the dugout, Stenhammer took the two spears and went off in search of something for them to eat.

Finishing up his housekeeping, Bohannon put the paddle aside and took a seat by the water's edge to watch the antics of the aquatic insects that darted back and forth on the sun-dappled surface. Held aloft by surface tension, water striders skated in fits and starts between broken twigs and sagging leaves. Submersible hunters and tireless browsers bobbed to the surface for air, lingering only momentarily in the dangerous world above before vanishing once more into tea-colored depths. Minnows and tadpoles wriggled energetically in the shallows. Once, a flower came drifting downstream, the blossom twice the size of his palm and red as the lipstick on a high-paid hooker. He imagined how pretty it would look in Tai's hair.

He sensed motion behind him. A moment later she was sitting down, stretching her legs out on the humid earth. "What are you doing?"

"Losing myself." He gestured at the water. "In there."

"Be careful." Her expression was serious. "I've seen too many men do that in this heat. They sink too deeply into their dreaming and sometimes they never come back."

He looked up at her and smiled. "Don't worry. I've got too much on my mind to lose it." He picked up a fragment of wood and tossed it into the creek. It sank a little before bobbing back to the surface. Not exactly casting bread upon the waters, he reflected, but it would have to do.

They sat quietly for a while, side by side, observing the small gymnastics of the stream, the church light shafting down between the leaves overhead, and the pure untrammeled peace of the place.

"You really think we'll make it out of here?" he asked finally.

"Of course." Her reply was full of the indomitable cheerfulness he had come to associate with her. "All we have to worry about is disease, black mossies, snakes, uncooperative villagers, crocs, drowning, going mad from the heat, and getting lost and wandering around and around on some of these looping, intersecting rivers for the next six months."

He had to smile. "Glad I asked."

She gave him a reassuring pat in the vicinity of his right thigh. "She'll be right—mate. So long as it doesn't rain to excess. As long as we have a current running downstream to follow we have to hit the Sepik eventually."

"And if it starts raining like it did back in the savanna?"

She turned away, her gaze lost in the trees on the opposite side of the creek. "Then we have to hope that the water doesn't rise to the point where the current reverses and all the rivers in this area flow upstream."

They shared the silence, interrupted only by the calls of hornbills and lorikeets, the buzz-crackle of Brobdingnagian insects and bloodthirsty mosquitoes. She studied him uncertainly.

"You know, Steve, you never told me what you were doing here. In Papua New Guinea."

He looked up, shrugged slightly, and gave her an odd little lopsided grin. "No point in hiding it. I'm running, I guess. I started by heading east. I ran through Europe, then I ran through Africa, then India and Asia and Australia. I was running through the South Pacific when I got tripped up here." He smiled. "By a beautiful but mercenary woman."

She flipped a pebble into the water and watched it scatter bugs as it sank out of sight. "And what will you do when you leave PNG? Continue your running?"

"I don't know." He looked away from her, up into the trees where columns of yellow-green light fell like pillars of citrine between canvases splashed olive and emerald and umber. "I was about out of money." He indicated the dugout and its cargo. "Now it looks like that's not going to be a problem. The problem is me." Pulling his knees up toward his chest, he rested his arms on them and his chin on his arms.

Leaning forward slightly, she tried to see into his face. "Tell me, Steve: were you running away from something, or toward it?"

"Both, I guess." *How still the water was, Darjeeling red-brown and full of life.* "The more people I met in my travels, the more convinced I became that everyone is running, all the time. Most people just don't realize it. Admittedly, I was doing it to excess, even before I started on my journey." Looking up at her, seeing the sincere concern in her face, he felt ashamed.

"Everybody has it all backwards, you know. It's not, you have to learn to walk before you can run. It's the other way around. Those who have realized the truth are the ones who've learned how to stop running, and to walk."

He would have told her more, would perhaps finally have unburdened himself and explained to someone, but Stenhammer chose that moment to return. Later, he promised himself. She had offered herself as a willing receptacle for his misery and despair, a place where he could rinse out his soul without fear of judgment or condemnation. He needed that outlet badly, but it would wait. It had waited for some time now.

The dead tree kangaroo Stenhammer carried was at once smaller and larger than he had expected. Smaller, because most of the roos he had seen in Australia had been bigger. Larger, because it was hard to imagine anything so massive and, well, roo-like, actually living up a tree.

Using the big knife, Stenhammer skinned and dressed it in less than an hour. He then set about the task of making a fire without the aid of the lighter, which had gone down with McCracken, or matches, or any other flammable appurtenance of modern civilization. Sharpening a hardwood twig a little larger than a number two pencil, he placed the point in the crack of a dry, flat piece of branch collected from the base of the tree from which it had fallen.

Placing his palms on either side of the sharpened twig, he began spinning it rapidly back and forth, at the same time pushing down to grind the point into the crack. An attentive Tai periodically added tiny, dry slivers of wood to the growing hole. Calluses were absolutely essential to the job, as the constant rubbing would have worn bloody the skin of softer hands.

After what seemed like an eternity, a thin wisp of smoke began to rise from the cleft, like a tiny genie emerging from a perfume bottle made of wood. Stenhammer redoubled his efforts. The smoke thickened and Tai added another pinch of slivered wood to the site. Bohannon saw sparks as the fire sprang to life. While the big man continued twirling the twig, Tai bent over and blew carefully on the birthing blaze.

They had fire, much as man had had it tens of thousands of years ago.

The roo was tough and gamey, but palatable. In the dark shadow of hunger, everything tasted good. As Tai promised, Bohannon found the tail especially succulent.

It had been a while since any of them had gone to sleep on a full stomach. Shrunken as that organ was, it did not take a great deal to satiate him. After first checking for ants, scorpions, and other unwanted visitors, they made beds of leaves and pillows of twigs. The invasive moonlight was much reduced by the canopy, and they fell instantly and gratefully asleep. In the nearby creek the canoe sat motionless, swollen with golden promise.

XXVII

Bohannon was not sure what woke him: movement he did not see, a sound he did not hear. The jungle was petrified stillness around him; absent of wind or the beat of insect wings to disturb the air. Faint echoes of distant snaps and rustlings were all that hinted at the presence of night-loving life-forms.

He rolled over and blinked, staring. He was not the only one awake. Stenhammer was sitting up, a motionless granitic outline silhouetted against the moon-kissed darkness. The big man's arms rested on his knees as he peered into the surrounding forest.

Bohannon watched him for what seemed like a long time. In the trees a branch snapped; not loud, but distinct. Reaching for the belt he had placed next to his bed, Stenhammer noiselessly removed the big knife from its sheath. Noticing his watchful companion, he put one finger to his lips, requesting silence as he rose. Bohannon followed the big man's movements as he slipped wraith-like into the trees.

Trying to keep his breathing to a minimum, he lay on his mat of accumulated vegetation and waited. And waited. It was nothing, he thought. A possum, or a patrolling quoll, or an owl wrestling with some tiny life already lost. He was drifting back to sleep when the scream split the night air. It degenerated into a choking gurgle as Bohannon fought to get to his feet.

The scream was echoed by shouts, vibrant and bloodcurdling. Man-shapes materialized from among the brush, eyes white and alive in the pale light. Faces and bodies were painted in bold patterns and clenched hands waved long, lethal shapes. The bumps and ridges on their bare torsos stood out in sharp relief: crocodile skin.

Many of them clustered around a much taller figure, the heaving mass of skirmishing humanity surging back and forth on the far side of the little clearing. Above the chaos, moonlight flashed on metal. It was Stenhammer's knife, and every time it caught the light another man died. The shouting and screaming, the war-cries and the gasps of mortally wounded men, were terrible to hear.

To his right, Tai was on her feet and fending off one of the attackers with a spear. Thus far Bohannon had been overlooked. The intruders' strategy was clear: bring down Stenhammer first and then finish off his less redoubtable companions. His thoughts still fogged with sleep and shock, he climbed to his feet. Through the mental mist and enveloping madness, above the yells and howls, he could hear Stenhammer's penetrating voice.

"*The gun, man—get the gun!*" It was all he said. It was all he had time to say.

One of the attackers came lurching toward Bohannon. Balling his hands into fists, he tried to remember what he could of the two months of boxing instruction he had taken five years ago at a local gym. Two months only, because he had been unable to spare the time for anything more. As he had so often been unable to spare the time for anything more.

The onrushing assailant fell at his feet, both hands clutching his throat in a death grip in a futile attempt to stem the flow of blood that gushed from severed arteries. Flashing him a quick look, Stenhammer was quickly drawn back into the thick of the fight. Leaping over the dying man, Bohannon made a dive for the motionless snake shape of the big man's belt where it lay on the ground.

As death raged around him, he fumbled frantically with the snap and strap that secured the pistol in its holster. The gun, when he finally pulled it free, was impossibly massive, unreasonably heavy. Rolling over and sitting up, he took aim in the darkness at a short, spear-carrying figure. He had never fired a pistol in his life, much less contemplated ever handling anything the size of the Eagle. But the past weeks had seen him following through on any number of things he had never contemplated doing.

Holding the weapon firmly with both hands, as he had seen Stenhammer doing on the floor of the Haus Tamburan, he squeezed the trigger. Nothing happened. The silhouette with the spear saw him and turned.

Safety—don't these things have a safety? Trembling, sweaty fingers fumbled around the circumference of the trigger guard, the grip, the back of the barrel. He saw the spear outlined against trees and night sky as its wielder raised it high.

With a tiny *click*, something small and metallic gave beneath his frantically pushing thumb. For a second time, his finger contracted on the trigger. The world seemed to detonate in his hands. Unprepared as he was for the resultant recoil, the gun's kick knocked him flat on his back. But he was soon sitting up and searching for another target. The first had vanished, and he had no way of knowing if he had hit the man or missed him completely.

The thunder of the gun going off was enough to shatter the circle of assailants who had surrounded Stenhammer. Rising to take aim at a group of them, Bohannon fired again. This time he was ready for the reaction. While the muzzle of the pistol kicked up and back in his hands, this time it did not knock him down.

Dark shapes fled into the trees. As they did so he felt a sharp, stinging pain in his left leg. Something bumped up against his right side and he started to sweep the pistol around to bring the muzzle to bear on it. A powerful hand grabbed his wrist, restraining him.

"It's me, Steve. Let me have it!"

Bohannon did his best to comply, but Stenhammer still had to half-wrench the weapon from the other man's cramped, clenched fingers. As he stumbled backward, Bohannon saw the big man take aim and fire; once, twice, three times. Roaring thrice in rapid succession, with the echoes of each concussion piling up and building upon one another, the pistol sounded like an avenging typhoon.

After the third shot Stenhammer turned and loped off to his right. Bohannon tried to follow—and nearly fell. Looking down, he saw a three-foot-long hunting arrow protruding from his left calf. The sharpened, barb-tipped bamboo shaft passed completely through the muscle. It felt exactly as if someone had stuck a piece of kindling into his flesh and set it alight.

Had someone described such an injury to him in the safety of his San Diego residence, he might well have become ill. The actuality of it, in his present surroundings, was actually less debilitating. There was an arrow sticking through his leg. Fine. In good time, he would do something about it. The ability of the human mind to selectively shut down certain receptors and thoughts at such moments could not really be described. It had to be experienced.

Despite the pain, Bohannon was cognizant enough to wish he could have avoided the experience.

Fighting to ignore the feeling that someone had doused his leg with gasoline and set it alight, he limped after his companion, dragging his left leg behind him like a dead thing. He arrived at the embankment in time to see a dugout pulling out into the river. Another remained tied to the shore. Its occupants would not be fleeing.

Putting down the bloody knife, Stenhammer raised the pistol with both hands, his arms parallel to the ground, and took aim. His arms did not tremble, his hands did not shake. How many rounds did the huge gun hold? Bohannon tried to remember. Eight, wasn't it? No, ten.

The Eagle roared. Part of the retreating dugout exploded, sending splinters and chunks of wood flying in all directions. One man toppled into the slow river. It embraced him silently and he did not re-emerge. His companions paddled as if caught in a race with Charon's boat.

Stenhammer tracked the canoe, the muzzle of the pistol following its progress as precisely as if it was being directed by radar. But he did not fire again. Only when the dugout disappeared out of sight upstream did he finally lower the weapon. He was breathing hard and his clothing had been torn or cut in several places, but in the moonlight, at least, none of the wounds appeared serious.

"Why didn't you shoot the rest of them?" Outraged, angry, and hurt, Bohannon eyed the big man accusingly.

Stenhammer turned to him, his eyes leaving the river. Dangling from his fist, the pistol pressed against his right leg. "If there are any others camped upstream, they need to know what happened here. They need to know that they have to leave us alone. If there is no camp, there is no need to kill anymore. Also, there are only a few rounds left. Who knows but that we may need them downriver."

Bohannon digested this, then nodded. "I never heard them. I never heard a fucking thing until they jumped us."

"I knew somebody was out there. I just could not tell how many."

The strangest sensation came over Bohannon. It washed over him like a straight shot of strong Scotch, leaving him light-headed but electrified, stunned yet more alert than he would have believed possible. It was a feeling that went back a hundred thousand years and more and was nothing to be proud of. He did not pound his chest with both hands and howl at the stars, but neither did he, as some would have, fall to the ground and vomit. He was not proud, neither was he contrite. His thoughts were confused, and mildly appalled, but his body reacted with a rush of hormones that ten thousand years of supposed civilization had done nothing to mitigate.

I have killed. I should be rending my garments in sorrow, a part of him cried out. *I should be delivering myself of tearful apologia*. But he did not.

No matter how he knew he ought to have felt, the truth of it was that he felt otherwise. Men had stolen into the camp in the middle of the night with the avowed purpose of seeking his death, and he had responded by slaying. The only thing that saddened him, he discovered to his rising chagrin, was that Stenhammer had not killed them all.

The big man's gaze fell. He spoke quietly. "You have an arrow in your leg." With the reminder, the pain returned redoubled. Bohannon sat down awkwardly, gripping the injured limb just behind the knee.

Stenhammer knelt in front of him and set the pistol aside. Using the knife, he cut through the shaft of the arrow as close to the flesh as possible and flung the bloody piece aside. The front stub with its barbed tip continued to protrude from the other side of Bohannon's calf.

Intense, penetrating eyes met those of his injured companion. "The rest of this has to come out. You know that, don't you?"

"I figured as much." The fire in Bohannon's leg was unrelenting. "I don't know if I can keep from screaming. I really don't."

"Go ahead and scream, if you want." Leaning forward, Stenhammer curled the fingers of his right hand around the shaft just where it emerged from the other man's flesh. He placed his left palm against the leg above the arrow, bracing himself.

"I will count to three and then pull. Are you ready?"

"No. Go ahead." Clenching his teeth, Bohannon closed his eyes and dug his fingers into the meat of his thigh until it hurt.

"Ready. One . . ."

Bohannon nearly rose from the ground as the bamboo shaft was yanked free of his calf. It felt as if someone had poured naphtha on the fire.

"You fucking bastard," he mumbled. "You didn't count to three."

"I will apologize later." Using the knife, the big man was cutting a sleeve from his shirt. The other hung in shreds. Wrapping the makeshift bandage around the leg of his injured companion so that it covered both the entry and exit wounds, he knotted it securely enough to slow the flow of blood but not so tight that it cut off the circulation.

Slipping an arm around Bohannon's back, he helped him to his feet. "Can you walk?"

"Let's see what happens when I put one foot in front of the other." The pain made Bohannon wince. But that was different from making him surrender. There was a time when he would have done so. To do so now, here, in this place, would mean his death.

Also, perversely, and for reasons he still could not explain, he did not want to disappoint Stenhammer. "If I fall on my face you'll have your answer." He did not fall. His calf complained violently, and the complaint shot all the way up his leg to his pelvis, but he found that after a couple of tries with the big man's help, he was able to limp forward on his own.

"Hey Tai!" he called out as he preceded his companion into the clearing. "We got one more of the bastards! Tai?"

"Here, Steve."

She was lying on her back alongside the creek, the bloodied spear she had been using to fend off her attackers close by her right hand. Her face stared at the night sky, unmoving in the moonlight. She did not turn to look at him as he limped over to her side. When he tried to kneel down next to her, his leg conceded to reality and he collapsed. Gritting his teeth so hard he feared they would crack, he stopped himself from screaming.

As he started to raise himself up he became aware that his hands had landed in the creek. They were soaking wet. It was only when he wiped one against his cheek and some of the liquid dripped onto his lower lip that he tasted the warm, thick, salty essence of blood and realized that his hands had struck the ground short of the water.

"Tai?" In what pale light the trees permitted to reach the ground the blood on his hands might as well have been water. Water dark as that which had carried them down from the mountains and into the savannas and swamps and jungle of the Sepik.

The moonlit shadows of her face shifted slowly as she turned to face him. It was untouched, the skin perfect and smooth. Nothing had been damaged, nothing was wrong.

"Steve. I'm cold."

Around them the forest simmered in the humid night, a pungent stew of moist humus and pithy decay, of resplendent unrestrained growth and recent death. "Here . . ." His own pain forgotten, he started to remove what was left of his shirt, to place it over her in lieu of the blanket he did not have.

A big hand dropped onto his shoulder and he jerked around sharply. Stenhammer was staring down at him. Stenhammer, his voice subdued but the tone unchanged. Always unchanged.

"Do not bother."

Twisting away from the lightly gripping fingers, Bohannon struggled out of his shirt. Gently, he laid it across her torso, tucking the collar up around her neck. She smiled at him.

"Thanks, Steve. I'm afraid I've made a mess of things, too right."

"Not at all." He tried to return the smile, only to find that his mouth would not work even as well as his leg. "What's wrong? Where are you hurt?"

"I'm not sure, but I can't feel anything below my waist. I don't remember being cut, but I guess I was. I—I think it might be bad."

"Whatever it is, we'll patch it up. Ragnarok fixed my leg and . . ." His voice trailed away. He stared.

Below her hips, below the hem of her dirty, torn shorts, was a lake of blood. Glimmering darkly in the diminished light, shaded by her body, it flowed into the creek in a steady, wide stream. Much too wide a stream, that merged with the torpid water like two brooks coming together. Slowly the rainforest creek carried the mixing of jungle waters and Tai's essence down toward the larger stream they had descended in the dugout. From there it would flow into the Sepik and eventually, into the sea.

The gash on her right thigh had been inflicted by a machete. It was long and very, very deep. In the moonlight, exposed bone glistened like wet ivory. Jamming his fist into his mouth, he bit down until he could taste his own blood, his eyes wide and staring. Life continued to pump from the half-severed limb, though the flow had slowed considerably. How long she had been lying there bleeding like that it was impossible to know.

"The femoral artery has been cut." Behind him, Stenhammer spoke not from the grave, but to it. For the first time his voice might possibly, just possibly, have been a little shaky. Spellbound with horror, the other man did not notice. "There is nothing we can do."

Bohannon jerked the fist from his mouth and looked up. "Build up the fire. Cauterize the wound. . . ."

Against the night sky the big man's head moved slowly from side to side, as regular and methodical as the pendulum of a great clock. "The wound is too deep and she has already lost too much blood." He gestured helplessly. "You can see for yourself."

Bohannon could but did not want to. Leaning forward on hands and knees, he brought his own face close to hers. Even in the absence of daylight he could see that she was beginning to grow wan beneath the dark tan. Somehow he choked out a few words.

"How—are you doing?" he murmured inanely. "Does it—are you in pain?"

She spoke without looking at him, her gaze fixed on the patch of tropical sky that was visible through the trees—a cutout in a mirror. Somewhere, a small brown owl hooted as if unsatisfied with the silence.

"No. No, it doesn't hurt at all, Steve." Again the faint flicker of a smile. "Isn't that funny? You'd think it would." She turned her head to him. "I always wanted to die rich."

In his mind he told her, "*You're not going to die.*" In reality, the reality of the heat and the jungle and the night-sounds, he found he could not lie. It was extraordinary. Prevarication had been so much a part of his profession, of his entire life, and now he could not do it, not even a little. So he said nothing at all, simply forced himself, somehow, to return her smile.

"Really cold." A hand, small yet strong, reached up with sudden strength to grab him by the shirt.

The silence was worse than anything he could say. "Is there anything you want, Tai? Is there anything I can bring you?"

Enough life remained for contemplation, and understanding. She was so quiet that for an instant he believed she was gone. But consciousness, still toying with existence, had not quite bled away.

"A butterfly. Bring me a butterfly, Steve. A birdwing, from the mountains."

She smiled again. Then the fingers unclenched, and like a sigh, slowly fell away.

He took her cold, cold arm in his fingers and laid it across her chest. Then he turned away and let the tears come. Mixing with her blood, they too would find their way to the distant ocean.

Stenhammer was no longer behind him, but he did not care.

XXVIII

They buried her in the soft, fresh light of morning, there between the river and the sky, making a place in the damp earth with knife and spear. Stenhammer carried her on his shoulders as they pushed through the undergrowth until they located the highest point of land around. No mountain, not even a hill, the big man assured him it was high enough to remain above all but the most exceptional flood. It was the best they could do.

Birds-of-paradise attended, albeit from a safe distance, their cries and those of the other forest birds sufficing for a choir. Bohannon muttered a few words, found himself unable to continue, and looked expectantly at Stenhammer. There was neither quaver nor hesitation in the other man's voice.

"I did not love her—but I should have. It would have been better for me if I had, but in my life I have made more than one wrong decision. I do not think she loved me. There was something there—something very strong that was not love, but that I felt. I respected her more than any woman I have ever known, including the one I loved."

That last was a revelation, for Bohannon had come to doubt that Stenhammer had ever loved anyone, much less himself. He wanted to ask him about it, to probe a little deeper, but this was not the time or place. Somewhere else, someplace away from here, where the memory of Tai would be less immediate—there he might ask. He turned to go—and nearly fell.

Stenhammer was at his side in an instant, supporting him. Bohannon wanted to shake him off, but he did not want to fall down. In the ensuing argument he had with himself, pride sensibly lost. He let the other man help him back the way they had come, back through the forest.

While they rested near the creek, Stenhammer used strips of vine and short pieces of wood to fashion a crude but serviceable crutch from the two spears. With this makeshift support, Bohannon found he was able to get around reasonably well. He still needed help climbing back into the dugout, however. The place where Tai's life had run out was already dry, the earth having soaked her up as rapidly and efficiently as it did every other living thing that lingered too long in the valley of the Sepik.

Stenhammer pushed the heavy canoe out into mid-creek and climbed into the stern. Using the long paddle, he propelled them out of the trees and back into the middle of the river. Lying in the front of the dugout with his back propped up against the packs, Bohannon watched until the creek mouth and its arch of framing vegetation faded from view. He did not have to struggle to memorize the place, did not have to mark certain trees or lines of light. It would automatically remain forever fixed in his mind, a place he could go to without effort whenever he so desired.

The river widened and merged with a larger river that was still, according to Stenhammer, nothing more than another tributary of the great Sepik itself. Fish jumped on both sides of the boat and once, a great crocodile crawled out onto a sandbar to sun itself. Bohannon let it all drift in and out of his vision, closing his eyes to the sights as well as the sun. Behind him, Stenhammer paddled on, tireless and mute. Exhausted, emotionally as well as physically drained, Bohannon fell asleep.

When he opened his eyes it was to the sight of afternoon waning and vultures circling. With a start he tried to sit up, to wave his arms at them and proclaim his aliveness. "I'm not dead yet, you ugly sons of bitches!" He gasped as agonizing pain raced up his injured leg.

"Calm down, Mr. Bohannon!" Clear and alert, the voice of assured indifference assailed him from the back of the boat.

The excruciating pain made it almost impossible to focus on anything else. "The vultures, they . . . !"

"They are not vultures." Tilting his head back slightly, Stenhammer studied the sky. "Those are brown eagles. Though they would not leave your carcass untouched, they much prefer fish. Now settle yourself, or you will upset the boat."

"Can't have that." In the heat Bohannon panted like a dog. "Might lose me. Then there'd be only you, Stenhammer. Just you, and all that gold."

"Shut up," the big man responded tersely. "If I wanted you out of the way, Bohannon, I would have dumped you hours ago."

Borderline delirious, the American ignored the pain so he could turn to face his companion. "Oh, so you're going to save my fucking life, are you? McCracken's dead, Tai's dead, but me you're going to save?"

"Yes, that's right." Stenhammer spoke quietly as always, but there was a hint of unaccustomed tightness in his voice. "I am going to save your fucking life. Now shut the hell up before you make me regret my decision."

"Don't you tell me to shut up, you soulless asshole!" Bohannon strained against the backpacks as if he wanted to crawl over them and attack the paddler. "I don't need a goddamn fucking robot to tell me to shut up! Oh, Christ!" Wrenching around, he grabbed at his tortured leg.

Expressionless, Stenhammer leaned forward. "All that flopping about has started your calf bleeding again. Stupid." Dipping the long paddle into the water on the left side of the boat, he angled for shore. "It will be getting dark soon and the dressing needs to be replaced anyway."

Bohannon would have cursed him afresh if his leg had not been hurting so badly, but the pain overrode and made impossible any clever, insouciant response. By the time they reached shore and Stenhammer found a place where they could land, his injured companion was too tired to say much of anything.

Bohannon lay in the shade, the spear-crutch by his side, while Stenhammer went in search of the makings of a fire. Neither man spoke for some time, Bohannon glaring silently at the big man while Stenhammer laboriously coaxed to life still another blaze, this time without any assistance. Bohannon fully expected him to disappear into the forest in search of warm-blooded meat, but he was surprised. Borrowing the crutch, the big man went fishing instead. Was it possible that even he was growing tired?

As he stared at his sole surviving companion, much of Bohannon's anger seeped away, as if an unseen physician of the spirit had silently slipped a tube into his soul to drain away the bile that had accumulated there. It struck him forcefully that Stenhammer was not responsible for Tai's death. He could not even remotely be considered the cause. Tai Tennison had chosen her own road, no one had forced her down it, and if it had ended prematurely and unexpectedly, well, that was part of making a choice, too.

On sharpened bamboo skewers hacked from a nearby grove, Stenhammer spitted the scaled and gutted fish he had caught. Bohannon watched him turn them over the fire, letting the firm white meat brown slowly.

"I'm going to die out here, aren't I? Just like the others. And there isn't a damn thing you can do about it."

The big man looked over at him, peering across the crackling flames. "You are not going to die, Steve. You are not going to die because I am going to keep you alive."

Bohannon laughed as much as the pain in his leg would permit. "You spin beguiling truths, Stenhammer, but you're a lousy liar. I know. I'm an expert on lying. It was a big part of my business." He looked away. "Too big a part."

As ever, the other man was utterly unperturbed. "Really? What business are you in, Steve?"

"Was in. Real estate. I sold real estate. Or sometimes, unreal estate." He grimaced through the agony that threatened to consume him. Shards of white-hot pain tangoed on the inside of his retinas. "Oversize lots, overpriced homes, overvalued businesses. In Southern California, San Diego County. I was good at it, too. Knew my stuff. Could close faster than a virgin's thighs at a Tailhook reunion."

Fish sizzled over the sputtering fire, the drippings exploded softly in the flames. Overhead, a flock of hornbills hooted their way nestward, soaring effortlessly toward distant roosts and waiting chicks.

"What happened?" Stenhammer continued to turn the fish.

"Nothing happened. At least, not as far as business was concerned. Life happened." Rolling onto his back, Bohannon blinked up at the sky. The canopy was thin here and he could see the drifting clouds clearly. Last night Tai had lain on her back and stared at the same sky, and died.

"For six years I didn't take a vacation. Was never away from my desk for longer than three or four days. I just kept selling, and making money, and opening one bank account after another. I counted CD's and mutual funds and stocks and muni bonds the way other men tallied their golf scores, or the number of women they slept with."

"So you were rich." There was a peculiar undertone to the way Stenhammer said it but, lost in reminiscence, his injured companion took no notice. Now that he was finally talking about what had driven him from his home, from his life, the details of his history spilled out of him like wine from a broken bottle; sweet, sticky, and impossible to hold onto.

"No. I had money. There's a difference. I didn't know that at the time, but I do now. I had a wife, Stenhammer." Swallowing hard, making himself ignore the pain in his leg, he forced himself to go on. "Her name was—Dana. Dana Diana Bohannon. Her parents couldn't make up their minds on a first name, so they gave her two. She wasn't beautiful, like Tai, but she was pretty. I thought she was more than that, she always thought she was less. Typical woman, if I can generalize for a moment."

"Go ahead and generalize." Lifting a stick off of the fire, the big man studied the fish it skewered, decided it needed to cook a while longer, and placed it back over the welcoming flames.

"She loved me, you know? It had nothing to do with the money. We'd married long before I developed the knack of selling and reselling the same big chunks of San Diego every other month. She loved me for me. We had two little girls. Tracy and Katherine.

" 'Why don't we take a real vacation?', she'd always ask me. 'You never take any time off, we never have a chance to do anything together. The girls are growing up and you're missing it. Someday soon they'll be off to college, and then they'll be married, and you'll wonder why you missed their childhood.' "

"What did you do?" Stenhammer offered the one fully cooked fish to his companion, who impatiently waved it off. Bohannon wanted to talk, not eat. With a shrug, the big man started in on the meal himself.

"I was busy, you know? I was always so goddamn busy. But I saw how badly Dana wanted to get away. So I set it up for the summer, when the kids would be out of school and they'd have some time. As you might guess, I'd made a lot of friends in the business community. One of them had a condo in Dominica. Three bedrooms, two baths, cook, maid, everything. You ever been to Dominica, Stenhammer?"

"No. I have been all through Asia and the Pacific, but nowhere else."

Bohannon turned wistful. "The pictures were wonderful. It's a high, green island in the Caribbean. Real mountains, clear warm water, not overrun with tourists. A great place to get away. I made a deal with the guy who owned the condo to lease it for a month. I arranged for the airline tickets. First class, all the way." Pausing for a moment to get a firmer grip on his emotions, he continued.

"The tickets were a package deal. I would never pay a dollar for something I could get for a quarter. Restricted travel times and dates. Change them and you have to pay a penalty, you know? It was the last week in June. We were all set to go. Then I got a call. Somebody had made an offer on an apartment building in La Jolla that was listed with my company. A cash offer." Invisible gnomes had mistaken his left leg for a suckling pig and were roasting it whole, but he ignored them.

"I kissed my family good-bye and sent them off to the airport. Dana wanted to wait until I consummated the deal so we could all travel together, but that would've meant taking a big penalty on the airfare because I'd have to change all the travel dates. So I told them no, to go ahead, and that I'd meet them there in a couple of days. I figured my ticket wouldn't be docked." His expression contorted into a tormented parody of a smile. "Business emergency, see?

"They made it as far as San Juan, Puerto Rico. From there it's a hop in a twin-engine prop job to Dominica. Because of the mountains the runways there are short and can't take jets. The weather wasn't too good. Stormy. The pilot was new. The FAA inspectors said he misread his approach. 'Misread his approach.' He misread it, all right. It was the last anything he ever misread." Overhead, the clouds looked down in silence. The first stars were beginning to appear, heralding the onset of evening's translucent sky.

"Ran right into the side of the biggest mountain on Dominica. You can't miss it—it's in all the tourist brochures. He died instantly, along with his co-pilot and all seventeen passengers. If I had listened to Dana, if I'd forgotten about the stupid fucking fare penalty, we'd have left a week later. Together. She'd still be alive. My daughters would still be alive. Growing up." Using the spear-crutch as a prop, he forced himself into a sitting position. "I'll take that fish now."

"And you have been running from that decision ever since." Stenhammer picked small white bones from between his teeth. Twilight was settling over the forest and it was starting to grow dark.

Bohannon shrugged, looked elsewhere. "I don't particularly want to die out here, Stenhammer, but I don't particularly want to live, either. I've been running my way around the world, chasing something I'm never going to catch, and I'm about out of places to run to."

"I understand."

Bohannon shot him an angry look. "The hell you do!"

For awhile the big man did not reply. He just sat and ate his fish. Bohannon did likewise. Two men, alone in one of the last unexplored jungles on earth, sharing fish. Two men utterly different, and yet . . .

Throwing an ivory backbone and its attached ribs aside, Stenhammer wiped his hands on his pants. The fish grease could not penetrate the hardened layer of dirt. His companion was still eating, but the big man did not wait for him to finish. Legs crossed, he leaned forward slightly and stirred the fire with a stick. The flickering yellow-red glow that sprang up cast his chiseled, weathered features in an unholy light.

"Tell me, Bohannon: have you ever heard of Rabaul?"

The other man looked up and spat out a bone. "Rabaul? I don't think so. Who is he?"

"It is not a 'he.' Rabaul is a place. A state of mind some might say, except that it would be too much of a cliché. The country of Papua New Guinea is composed of many islands, of which New Guinea itself is only the largest. There are thousands of others. Most are small. Several are quite sizable. After New Guinea, the island of New Britain is the biggest. Its capital has always been Rabaul."

Bohannon looked up, interested in spite of himself. For Stenhammer, the explanation constituted an extended speech. And it seemed that the big man was not through. "Okay. Why would somebody call it a state of mind?"

Stenhammer peered at him across the fire. "Because it used to be the most beautiful port in the whole South Pacific."

"Used to be." Bohannon's reiteration was flat.

"A foolish place to put a town, really. The Germans did it first. Made it the capital of their colony of New Guinea. When the Australians took over the mandate for the whole area, they moved the administration to Port Moresby. Not the best choice, perhaps, but certainly a more sensible one than Rabaul."

"Why? What's wrong with Rabaul?"

"The harbor is a volcanic caldera surrounded by active volcanoes. Every fifty years or so, one or more of these blow up, sometimes modestly, sometimes not. During World War Two the Japanese made it the center for their fleet operations in the South Pacific. So you see, it is a place that is attractive to many different kinds of people, for many different reasons. As it was to my grandparents."

That did surprise Bohannon. He looked up sharply. "Your grandparents?"

"They ran one of the first general goods stores in the town. Since they were not German, when the colony was surrendered, they stayed. My parents were born in Rabaul. So was I. Skin color notwithstanding, I am as much a native of this country as any national."

"That's very interesting," Bohannon admitted. But it fell far short of explaining the man seated across the fire from him.

Stenhammer was far from finished. "I too had a wife, Bohannon. She was much younger than I, and famously beautiful, from a well-known island family. We had a son. To support them I worked at many jobs; cane cutter, schoolteacher, construction worker, and more. There is not a lot of well-paying work on New Britain, and my family only did well enough to leave me enough money to build a small home in the town.

"To support them I sometimes had to take jobs off-island. One of the best was on an oceangoing tuna boat. An American tuna boat. Every tuna boat in the world wants a license to fish PNG's territorial waters. The government issues far too many licenses and soon it will not matter because the tuna and mackerel will all be gone, but at the time of which I am speaking there were big fish everywhere, and men like myself could make thousands and thousands of dollars from working a single trip."

"What time are you talking about?" The last of Bohannon's anger had gone now, and he found himself wholly absorbed in his companion's tale.

"It was not so very long ago, but such things do not always make big news beyond the Pacific. It was September of 1994. I was on the *Princess Tiata* when the volcanoes blew. All of them. Simultaneously. It was the worst eruption on New Britain since 1937, when Vulcan erupted and killed over five hundred people. Parts of Rabaul were buried under ten meters of ash. The entire town was destroyed." He stopped, not unable to continue; just barely able to remember.

Bohannon had to prompt him to go on. "Your wife and son?"

Stenhammer took a deep breath, and it seemed that he inhaled all that was the Sepik and the surrounding mountains with it. "They had no car. No one needs a car on New Britain. Our friends had no cars. Our house was on the side of town nearest the volcanoes. What happened was told to me—after.

"There was man with a flatbed truck. A local man, but one who was no longer like most Islanders. He had been changed by the same kind of change that angered and destroyed Alfred. He had been to Mosby and learned money. While everyone was running around crazy trying to get away from the eruption, he was charging them for transport. Someone who had paid their way onto his truck saw my wife and son begging this man for a ride. They had no money with them. He refused them and drove on before anyone could offer to pay their way." The big man's voice had fallen to a barely audible whisper, a ghost of the ghosts that lived inside him.

"They died. Matupit and Vulcan swallowed them as they swallowed many others. I do not even know where they are. They are entombed in that part of Rabaul that has yet to be excavated, as surely as the Romans were at Pompeii and Herculaneum." Rising to his feet, he turned his back to the fire and gazed out across the river, past the trees, to an island in the shape of a great crescent that lay on the far side of the Solomon Sea.

"They died because they did not have any money." The barren, weathered face turned slowly until Bohannon could see the powerful profile outlined against the sky. Firelight illuminated the monolithic form as far up as the waist, but could reach no higher. "Your wife and children died because you had too much."

Bohannon said nothing. What was there to say? What could be said? In the midst of mountains they had found gold. In the middle of the jungle they had stumbled across irony, that most debased of all individual currencies. He, lost and adrift on his own private pain, could not comfort the other man. Stenhammer, wracked with self-accusation, could not accept a confession from a fellow traveler.

Unable to think of anything else to say into the stony silence, Bohannon finally murmured, "I have pictures." It sounded so incredibly empty. But it was all he had, at that moment, to offer.

The big man peered down at him out of eyes that no longer saw as other men did, out of a face torn and twisted by anguish so deep it no longer could find its way to the surface. And there, in the fevered air of jungle night surrounded by the decaying dross of downpour and flood, a truly amazing thing happened.

Stenhammer smiled.

"It would be very kind of you to show them to me."

"Yeah, sure, I'd be glad to. I'd be honored to."

Fumbling in the right-hand pocket of his filthy, blood-stained, sweat-soaked jeans, he pulled out a brown eel-skin wallet in the last stages of decrepitude. The same wallet Tai had taken from him that night in Port Moresby. Within lay a California driver's license, a library card from which the oft-submerged ink had all but been washed, and a handful of other cards proclaiming membership in assorted meaningless societies, from health facilities to golfing clubs to professional organizations of no real worth.

There were also four water-damaged photographs with curling, torn edges. Their subjects were still clearly visible, smiling out from the past with the bright, untarnished innocence of youth. Family portraits of people with freshly pressed clothes, perfectly coifed hair, recently scrubbed faces. Father, mother, children. Suburban Americana idealized: only the surface showing, only the veneer, everything else neatly compartmentalized and hidden away. They were his history, and they lived again as he shared them, lovingly and one at a time, there in the middle of the ancient forest and the primeval night with a man who had reason to hurt as much or more than himself.

Morning brought mutual compassion if not understanding. Morning also brought sunshine, mirror-bright and razor-sharp, and renewed pain in his lower left extremity. Unfastening the makeshift bandage, Stenhammer examined the wound. Unable to see it himself, Bohannon settled instead for watching his companion's face. It was not an especially useful face to study in such circumstances because, as usual, it revealed little and gave nothing away.

"How does it look?" he finally had to ask.

Stenhammer spoke while retying the strip of fabric. A dark stain ran around its middle, a black equator pregnant with foreboding. "You need medical attention."

"I know that." Bohannon growled like a big dog tied too long on a short run. "It reminds me every time I stand up. What's it look like?"

"It is starting to ulcerate. Without medication it will spread rapidly." The eyes that looked up at him seemed a little less pale, but that was just the effect of morning sunshine. "If you do not receive proper treatment within a week, there is a good chance you will lose the leg."

Lose the leg. In the supposedly cutthroat world of business or in the highly competitive golf matches he had played in, that was a phrase he had not had occasion to overhear. It was not even a street term, an unreadable warning scrawled in graffiti on the walls of third-rate buildings in fourth-rate parts of town. It belonged to places like this, to the remote and hostile, where Nature was a far more unforgiving and unfeeling opponent than any underprivileged youth flashing transitory gang colors and childish hand signals.

"How can I lose it?" he replied lamely. "I know right where it is."

"You still have your sense of humor. That's good. In the coming days you are going to need it." Bending, he slipped an arm beneath his companion and helped him to his feet. Then he handed him the spear-crutch. "Time to go."

Bohannon nodded. Every time he put any weight on his left leg it was like stepping on a land mine—or at least, was what he imagined stepping on a land mine must feel like. Stubbornly, he refused to let Stenhammer carry him. But when they reached the boat he had no choice. He could not make the awkward step into the narrow dugout on his own without collapsing.

Days later it no longer mattered. How many days he could not have said. Light and dark, day and night swirled together in his delirium, from which comprehension emerged only fitfully. Perceiving the world around him and finding it unchanged and unsatisfactory, he would slip rapidly back into the raging fever that threatened to consume far more than just his leg. Meanwhile, the infection in his left leg blossomed and deepened.

I have turned septic on the Sepik, he thought, and laughed far too loudly and too often.

It must have been a sight, one crazy man escorting another soon to surpass him in madness. He was sorry he could not step back and watch it develop objectively, but out-of-body viewing held no appeal for him. Forsake your sanity but one time in a place like this, he suspected, and you might not be able to find it again.

The spirited hallucinations, however, he enjoyed. It gave him the opportunity to see his wife and children once more, and he cried. He revisited happier places and climes, and he laughed.

Perhaps the best of the visions, though, was the cabin cruiser. Though quite small, no more than a two-bunk job, it looked just like the ones that raced back and forth across Mission Bay and the main harbor back home. Its white fiberglass hull was scarred and stained, indicating it was used for more than just weekend barbecues while tied up snug and secure in a yacht-basin slip.

It was really amusing to watch Stenhammer hail the hallucination. When it actually pulled alongside the dugout, Bohannon could not keep from chuckling softly to himself. Even the boat's passengers were a hoot: small brown men with close-cropped black hair and concerned faces.

He felt hands beneath him, lifting him aboard. In the long litany of delirious visions the powerboat certainly held its own. The bunk he hallucinated belowdecks was particularly realistic. It had a green mattress. Naturally it would. These past weeks, he had come to see the whole world in varying shades of green.

Two things combined to winch him up out of the mental pit into which he had fallen. The first was a calendar hanging on the wall by the foot of the bunk. Its greatest virtue was its un-greenness. The picture reproduced above the lines of neat squares with their black numbers showed a dainty, sloe-eyed young woman posing demurely in a scrap of a swimsuit. She was smiling at date-watchers-to-be while holding a silvery can in one hand. He did not recognize the name of the beer, nor the language in which the attendant commercial come-on was written. Even the script was unfamiliar to him.

The second realization hit him in the face like the hand of Gabriel. Cool air. The hallucination was air-conditioned. He had forgotten there was such a thing.

Three men crowded into the cabin, filling it to capacity. A fourth stood framed in the hatchway. A national, he wore rubber sandals, clean shorts, and a knit shirt. I once owned a knit shirt, Bohannon dreamed. It was white, with embroidered golf clubs that crossed my heart.

Two of the others in attendance were the men he had hallucinated on the side of the boat, staring down at him. Their expressions were anxious. One held a long white box on which was emblazoned a red crescent moon. Opening it, he began removing bottles and a coiled roll of clean, white surgical bandaging. His friend took one of the bottles and poured something all over Bohannon's lower leg. At first it was soothing, then it burned, and then the burning started, for the first time in forever, to go away.

While they worked, they chattered incessantly. Stenhammer, who had to bend nearly double to avoid banging his head on the roof of the cabin, added what observations he thought appropriate. Bohannon wanted to ask about the men, about their language, about what they were doing to his leg, but the relief was so intense that he could not bear to interrupt it with speech.

It was left to Stenhammer to explain. "I will be right back," was all he said, leaving Bohannon to the care of strange small men speaking a language that did not sound like anything he had ever heard before. They smiled reassuringly as they talked, and he found that as long as his leg raised no objections to their actions, there was no need for him to interrupt their activities with inane comment.

Stenhammer returned carrying one of the five backpacks. This he tucked carefully in the far corner of the bunk, against the wall and close to his companion's head.

"Your personal effects. I have already explained everything to Tuan and Chukai." Behind him, the two men smiled at the mention of their names. "They are on their way downriver and have promised to look after you." In a singsong tongue, he murmured something to the two men. They nodded their understanding and left the cabin.

Bohannon fought for coherence as he struggled to comprehend. "What do you mean, 'they' have promised to look after me?"

"I told these men that we have been out collecting rare insects and that we became lost, and that you fell on a broken snag and injured your leg. Trying to get back in the canoe, you overturned it and we lost our medical kit.

"They have agreed to change their own plans and proceed straight to Angoram. There is a main road there, or what passes for a main road in this part of the world, that connects with Wewak. In Wewak there is a hospital. They will personally escort you to the hospital and see to it that you are properly taken care of." He glanced toward the open hatch.

Weighed down by thoughts that were still not clear, Bohannon did his best to digest all this. "Not that I'm complaining, but why would a couple of complete strangers go so far out of their way to help another couple of strangers?" His left leg felt almost normal, which was to say that he could not feel it at all. As far as that particular limb was concerned, ignorance was truly bliss.

Reaching down, the big man turned a pants' pocket inside out. Bohannon could see where the lining had been slit open. "I always travel with ten thousand in cash. I gave them half to take you to the hospital, and promised to send the rest to whatever address they stipulate as soon as a letter from you stating that you are all right arrives at a certain postal box in Mosby." He shoved a piece of paper into an outside pocket of the tightly sealed pack. "There is the box number. Don't lose it. As for the money I gave them, some of it came straight from Tai. So it is probably yours anyway."

Turning his head slightly to the right, Bohannon stared at the bulging backpack. "You're going to leave me in this condition, with four hundred thousand in gold, on a boat with a bunch of total strangers? What makes you think they won't take the five thousand you've already given them, feed me to the crocs, and continue their cruise downriver laughing to themselves all the way?"

"Because they do not know what is in your backpack and have no reason to suspect it contains anything other than peculiar insect specimens of great scientific interest but no special monetary worth. There is no gold in the Sepik basin, and no one comes into the Sepik via the mountains. They will do what they have promised because I have paid them, and in accepting payment they have assumed an obligation. They will do what they have promised because I told them," he concluded icily, "that if a letter from you did not appear in the postal box the number of which I just gave you within two weeks, that I would find them."

It was not necessary for Stenhammer to go into detail about what would happen if he was required to embark on that particular course of action. Bohannon doubted that he had to explain it to the boat's owners, either.

The big man continued. "They believe that the backpacks in the dugout contain clothing, camping supplies, collecting equipment, and insect specimens. There is no reason for them to believe otherwise, just as there should be no reason for them to want to see what is in the pack I have left with you. Even if they do, I think they have taken my words to heart."

"I expect you're right." Even for a few hundred thousand in gold, it would be a foolish or deluded man who would risk an avenging visit from the likes of Stenhammer. While such a prospective theft could easily be consummated, the thief would spend the rest of his life looking nervously over his shoulder.

"I still don't understand. You're not coming along?"

"No." The big man straightened as much as the low ceiling allowed. "I cannot travel with these people. These two seem honorable. They gave me their business cards to prove their good intentions toward you. Unfortunately, the business they are in is one I happen to have open disagreements with."

"I thought they were tourists, seeing the river."

Stenhammer shook his head. "They are Malaysians, from Kuala Lumpur, here seeking forestry concessions."

Bohannon raised himself up on his elbow. Through the single port he could see the dugout, tied up alongside the powerboat. The back-packs piled in the middle were undisturbed.

"There are good lumber companies and bad lumber companies," he told the big man. "Not all of them are out to rape the forest."

"Maybe that is true in North America, but in this part of the world it does not matter what company you are dealing with. They are all controlled by Rimbutan Hujal. If one company is fined for clear-cutting, it simply goes out of business and another, more 'eco-friendly,' materializes to take its place. Rimbutan Hujal is one of the world's great shadow combines, controlling most of the logging that goes on in Southeast Asia. The people who run it are very clever. They hide their puppet strings well. There are companies within companies, but all the orders and all the money eventually lead back to Rimbutan Hujal." Turning, he glanced up the hatchway.

"Though some good people work for them, I will have nothing to do with any of their enterprises." He turned back toward the bunk. "You have no such choice. You need help and cannot be particular about who provides it."

Bohannon started to get up. "Fuck you, Stenhammer. I'm not leaving like this."

An irresistible hand pressed gently against his chest, pushing him back down onto the mattress. "Yes you are, Steve. You do not belong here. You need to go home. If you stay, this country will kill you. Do not feel singled out. It has killed better men than you or me, and will kill plenty more. Dealing daily with death is an attraction best left to obdurate madmen. Like myself." For only the second time since Bohannon had known him, he smiled.

"Go home now. Go back to your well-policed streets and two hundred channels of television and supermarket cornucopias. Go back to your shiny new cars and tranquilizing politicians and safe, warm houses that are only occasionally broken into by people who want your television set and not your life." Taking the prone American's hand in his, he squeezed gently. "Good-bye, Steve Bohannon. I am sorry for all the bad things that have happened to you, and take no credit for the good." Pivoting on one foot, he lowered his head and ducked as he climbed out through the hatchway.

"Hey, hey wait a minute! You can't just go like this!" There was no reply from above.

Substituting anger for energy, Bohannon levered his feet off the bunk and stood on his right leg. Using the walls for support, he struggled up the open hatch in Stenhammer's wake.

The boat's owners were standing on the back deck, gazing westward. Seeing Bohannon emerge from below, one of the them immediately rushed to his side, offering incomprehensible words of concern and a supportive arm. His associate tried by dint of gestures and exclamations to indicate that their guest should return belowdecks.

"In a minute, in a minute." Charged with anxiety, he hopped to the side of the boat and leaned against the heavily pitted chrome railing.

The dugout was already well away, moving silently and steadily upstream, propelled by the methodical strokes of the tall man standing in its stern. Why upstream, Bohannon could not imagine. Perhaps Stenhammer was trying to reach Mindimbit, the village on the Sepik he had mentioned earlier as their original goal. Possibly he sought a place whose location and identity he had chosen to keep secret from his companions. Maybe—maybe he was simply seeking. It might be he could no longer do anything else.

Unlike a very few other men, Bohannon understood. One thing he knew for certain: it wasn't about the gold. It wasn't about money—no matter what Stenhammer had told him.

"Hey!" Bohannon leaned out over the railing and waved madly, ignoring the sudden return of pain to his injured leg. "Hey, Stenhammer!"

The jungle had a way of swallowing noises that did not belong, of dispersing them in the heavy, humid air and muffling them beyond recognition. But Bohannon had been just quick enough, and his voice carried.

The tall, powerful figure looked back. An arm rose and waved once. It was a final farewell, a salute to life and death shared. Then he turned and resumed paddling, the long pole rising and falling as the dugout pushed on, until it disappeared around a bend in the river in the direction of far distant, unseen mountains.

"That was the last time I saw Ragnarok Stenhammer and his two million in gold. But I can see that you don't believe me. Not that I blame you. Hell, I was there and I don't believe a lot of it myself.

"He was right, you know. I don't belong here. Most of us don't, and need to get out while we can. You should, too. Me, I'm going, as soon as I deliver this package. This one here, that's been sitting on the bar while we've been talking. There are a thousand rivers out there, and a billion trees, but I think I can find that river and that tree and that little hillock again. I know I can!

"Want to see what's in the box? No harm, I suppose. We're the only ones down at this end and nearly everyone else has left. Just a second—the paper is strong—there, that's enough for you to see. Yeah, I knew you'd be surprised. It's not exactly what she asked for, but I think she'll be pleased. The cost came out of her share, anyway. Now, if you'll excuse me . . .

"What is it? Oh, I guess you can't see enough of it to tell. It's a butterfly, of course. What she wanted. Ten inches across, six wide, an inch thick. A birdwing butterfly, from the mountains. Had it made right here in Mosby, believe it or not. Solid gold.

"Kind of like she was. . . ."